The Great Lone Land

Sir William Francis Butler

Copyright © 2017 Okitoks Press

All rights reserved.

ISBN: 154719040X

ISBN-13: 978-1547190409

Table of Contents

PREFACE.

At York Factory on Hudson Bay there lived, not very long ago, a man who had stored away in his mind one fixed resolution it was to write a book.

"When I put down," he used to say, "all that I have seen, and all that I havn't seen, I will be able to write a good book."

It is probable that had this man carried his intention into effect the negative portion of his vision would have been more successfal than the positive. People are generally more ready to believe what a man hasn't seen'than what he has seen. So, at least, thought Karkakonias the Chippeway Chief at Pembina.

Karkakonias was taken to Washington during the great Southern War, in order that his native mind might be astonished by the grandeur of the United States, and by the strength and power of the army of the Potomac.

Upon his return to his tribe he remained silent and impassive; his days were spent in smoking, his evenings in quiet contemplation; he spoke not of his adventures in the land of the great white medicine-man. But at length the tribe grew discontented; they had expected to hear the recital of the wonders seen by their chief, and lo! he had come-back to them as silent as though his wanderings had ended on the Coteau of the Missouri, or by the borders of the Kitchi-Gami. Their discontent found vent in words.

"Our father, Karkakonias, has come back to us," they said; "why does he not tell his children of the medicine of the white man? Is our father dumb that he does not speak to us of these things?"

Then the old chief took his calumet from his lips, and replied, "'If Karkakonias told his children of the medicines of the white man--of his war-canoes moving by fire, and making thunder as they move, of his warriors more numerous than the buffalo in the days of our fathers, of all the wonderful things he has looked upon-his children would point and say, Behold! Karkakonias has become in his old age a maker of lies! No, my children, Karkakonias has seen many wonderful things, and his tongue is still able to speak; but, until your eyes have travelled as far as has his tongue, he will sit silent and smoke the calumet, thinking only of what he has looked upon."

Perhaps I too should have followed the example of the old Chippeway chief, not because of any wonders I have looked upon; but rather because of that well-known prejudice against travellers tales, and of that terribly terse adjuration-".O that mine enemy might write a book!" Be that as it may, the book has been written; and it only remains to say a few words about its title and its theories.

The "Great Lone Land" is no sensational name. The North-west fulfils, at the present time, every essential of that title. There is no other portion of the globe in which travel is possible where loneliness can be said to live so thoroughly. One may wander 500 miles in a direct line without seeing a human being, or an animal larger than a wolf. And if vastness of plain, and magnitude of lake, mountain, and river can mark a land as great, then no region possesses higher claims to that distinction.

A word upon more personal matters. Some two months since I sent to the firm from whose hands this work has emanated a portion of the unfinished manuscript. I received in reply a communication to the effect that their Reader thought highly of my descriptions of real occurrences, but less of my theories. As it is possible that the general reader may fully endorse at least the latter portion of this opinion, I have only one observation to make.

Almost every page of this book has been written amid the ever-present pressure of those feelings which spring from a sense of unrequited labour, of toil and service theoretically and officially recognized, but practically and professionally denied. However, a personal preface is not my object, nor should these things find allusion here, save to account in some manner, if account be necessary, for peculiarities of language or opinion which may hereafter make themselves apparent to the reader. Let it be.

In the solitudes of the Great Lone Land, whither I am once more about to turn my steps, the trifles that spring from such disappointments will cease to trouble.

April 14th 1872.

THE GREAT LONE LAND.

CHAPTER ONE.

Peace--Rumours of War-Retrenchment--A Cloud in the far West--A Distant Settlement-Personal--The Purchase System--A Cable-gram--Away to the West

IT was a period of universal peace over the wide world. There was not a shadow of war in the North, the South, the East, or the West. There was not even a Bashote in South Africa, a Beloochee in Scinde, a Bhoottea, a Burmese, or any other of the many "eses" or "eas" forming the great colonial empire of Britain who seemed capable of kicking up the semblance of a row. Newspapers had never been so dull; illustrated journals had to content themselves with pictorial representations of prize pigs, foundation stones, and provincial civic magnates. Some of the great powers were bent upon disarming; several influential persons of both sexes had decided, at a meeting held for the suppression of vice, to abolish standing armies. But, to be more precise as to the date of this epoch, it will be necessary to state that the time was the close of the year 1869, just twenty-two months ago. Looking back at this most-piping period of peace from the stand-point of today, it is not at all improbable that even at that tranquil moment a great power, now, very much greater, had a firm hold of certain wires carefully concealed; the dexterous pulling of which would cause 100,000,000 of men to rush at each other's throats: nor is this supposition rendered the more unlikely because of the utterance of the most religious sentiments on the part of the great power in question, and because of the well-known Christianity and orthodoxy of its ruler. But this was not the only power that possessed a deeper insight into the future than did its neighbours. It is hardly to be gainsaid that there was, about that period, another great power popularly supposed to dwell amidst darkness-a power which is said also to possess the faculty of making Scriptural quotations to his own advantage. It is not at all unlikely that amidst this scene of universal quietude he too was watching certain little snow-wrapt hamlets, scenes of straw-yard and deep thatched byre in which cattle munched their winter provender-watching them with the perspective scent of death and destruction in his nostrils; gloating over them with the knowledge of what was to be their fate before another snow time had come round. It could not be supposed that amidst such an era of tranquillity the army of England should have been allowed to remain in a very formidable position. When other powers were talking of disarming, was it not necessary that Great Britain should actually disarm? of course there was a slight difference existing between the respective cases, inasmuch as Great Britain had never armed; but that distinction was not taken into account, or was not deemed of sufficient importance to be noticed, except by a few of the opposition journals; and is not every one aware that when a country is governed on the principle of parties, the party which iscalled the opposition must be in the wrong? So it was decreed about this time that the fighting force of the British nation should be reduced. It was useless to speak of the chances of war, said the British tax-payer, speak-ing through the mouths of innumerable members of the British Legislature. Had not the late Prince Consort and the late Mr. Cobden come to the same conclusion from the widely different points of great exhibitions and free trade, that war could never be? And if; in the face of great exhibitions and universal free trade-even if war did become possible, had we not ambassadors, and legations, and consulates all over the world; had we not military attaches at every great court of Europe; and would we not know all about it long before it commenced? No, no, said the tax-payer, speaking through the same medium as before, reduce the army, put the ships of war out of commission, take your largest and most powerful transport steamships, fill them full with your best and most experienced skilled military and naval artisans and labourers, send them across the Atlantic to forge guns, anchors, and material of war in the navy-yards of Norfolk and the arsenals of Springfield and Rock Island; and let us hear no more of war or its alarms. It is true, there were some persons who thought otherwise upon this subject, but many of them were men whose views had become warped and deranged in such out-of-the-way places as Southern Russia, Eastern China, Central Hindoostan, Southern Africa, and Northern America military men, who, in fact, could not be expected to understand questions of grave political economy, astute matters of place.-and party, upon which the very existence of the parliamentary system depended; and who, from the ignorance of these nice distinctions of liberal-conservative and conservative-liberal, had imagined that the strength and power of the empire was not of secondary importance to the strength and power of a party. But the year 1869 did not pass altogether into the bygone without giving a faint echo of disturbance in one far-away region of the earth. It is true, that not the smallest breathing of that strife which was to make: the succeeding year crimson through the centuries had yet sounded on the continent of Europe. No; all was as quiet there as befits the mighty hush which precedes colossal conflicts. But far away in the very farthest West, so far that not one man in fifty could tell its whereabouts, up somewhere between the Rocky Mountains, Hudson Bay, and Lake Superior, along a river called the Red River of the North, a people, of whom nobody could tell who or what they were, had risen in insurrection. Well-informed persons said these insurgents were only Indians; others, who had relations in America, averreed that they were Scotchmen, and one journal, well-known for its clearness upon all subjects connected with the American Continent, asserted that they were Frenchmen. Amongst so much conflicting testimony, it was only natural that the average Englishman should possess no very decided opinions upon the matter; in fact, it came to pass that the average Englishman, having heard that somebody was rebelling against him somewhere or other, looked to his atlas and his journal for information on the subject, and having failed in obtaining any from either source, naturally concluded that the whole thing was something which no fellow could be expected to understand. As, however, they who follow the writer of these pages through such vicissitudes as he may encounter will have to live awhile amongst these people of the Red River of the North, it will be necessary to examine this little cloud of insurrection which the last days of 1869 pushed above the political horizon. Bookmark About the time when Napoleon was carrying half a million of men through the snows of Russia, a Scotch nobleman of somewhat eccentric habits conceived the idea of planting a colony of his countrymen in the very heart of the vast continent of North America. It was by no means an original idea that entered into the brain of Lord Selkirk; other British lords had tried in earlier centuries the same experiment; and they, in turn, were only the imitators of those great Spanish nobles who, in the sixteenth century, had planted on the coast of the Carolinas and along the Gulf of Mexico the first germs of colonization in the New World. But in one respect Lord Selkirk's experiment was wholly different from those that had preceded it. The earlier adventurers had sought the coast-line of the Atlantic upon which to fix their infant colonies. He boldly penetrated into the very centre of the continent and reached a fertile spot which to this day is most difficult of access. But at that time what an oasis in the vast wilderness of America was this Red River of the North! For 1400 miles between it and the Atlantic lay the solitudes that now teem with the cities of Minnesota, Wisconsin, Illinois, Indiana, and Michigan. Indeed, so distant appeared the nearest outpost of civilization towards the Atlantic that all means of communication in that direction was utterly unthought of. The settlers had entered into the new land by the ice-locked bay of Hudson, and all communication with the outside world should be maintained through the same outlet. No easy task! 300 miles of lake and 400 miles of river, wildly foaming over rocky ledges in its descent of 700 feet, lay between them and the ocean, and then only to reach the stormy waters of the great Bay of Hudson, whose ice-bound outlet to the Atlantic is fast locked save during two short months of latest summer. No wonder that the infant colony had hard times in store for it-hard times, if left to fight its way against winter rigour and summer: inundation, but doubly hard when the hand of a powerful enemy was raised to crush it in the first year of its existence. Of this more before we part. Enough for us now to know: that the little colony, in spite of opposition, increased and multiplied; people lived in it, were married in it, and died in it, undisturbed by the busy rush of the outside world, until, in the last months of 1869, just fifty-seven years after its formation, it rose in insurrection.

And now, my reader, gentle or cruel, whichsoever you may be, the positions we have hitherto occupied in these few preliminary pages must undergo some slight variation. You, if you be gentle, will I trust remain so until the end; if you be cruel, you will perhaps relent; but for me, it will be necessary to come forth in the full glory of the individual "I," and to retain it until we part.

It was about the end of the year 1869 that I became conscious of having experienced a decided check in life. One day I received from a distinguished military functionary an intimation to the effect that a company in Her Majesty's service would be at my disposal, provided I could produce the sum of 1100 pounds. Some dozen years previous to the date of this letter I entered the British army, and by the slow process of existence had reached-a position among the subalterns of the regiment technically known as first for purchase; but now, when the moment arrived to turn that position to account, I found that neither the 1100 pounds of regulation amount nor the 400 pounds of over-regulation items (terms very familiar now, but soon, I trust, to be for ever obsolete) were forthcoming, and so it came about that younger hands began to pass me in the race of life. What was to be done? What course lay open? Serve on; let the dull routine of barrack-life grow duller; go from Canada to the Cape, from the Cape to the Mauritius, from Mauritius to Madras, from Madras goodness knows where, and trust to delirium tremens, yellow fever, or: cholera morbus for promotion and advancement; or, on the other hand, cut the service, become in the lapse of time governor of a penitentiary, secretary to a London club, or adjutant of militia. And yet-here came the rub-when every fibre of one's existence beat in unison with the true spirit of military adventure, when the old feeling which in boyhood had made the study of history a delightful pastime, in late years had grown into a fixed unalterable longing for active service, when the whole current of thought ran in the direction of adventure-no matter in what climate, or under what circumstances-it was hard beyond the measure of words to sever in an instant the link that bound one to a life where such aspirations were still possible of fulfilment; to separate one's destiny for ever from that noble profession of arms; to become an outsider, to admit that the twelve best years of life had been a useless dream, and to bury oneself far away in some Western wilderness out of the reach or sight of red coat or sound of bugle-sights and sounds which old associations would have made unbearable. Surely it could not be done; and so, looking abroad into the future, it was difficult to trace a path Which could turn the flank of this formidable barrier flung thus suddenly into the highway of life.

Thus it was that one, at least, in Great Britain watched with anxious gaze this small speck of revolt rising so far away in the vast wilderness of the North-West; and when, about the beginning of the month of April, 1870, news came of the projected despatch of an armed force from Canada against the malcontents of Red River, there was one who beheld in the approaching expedition the chance of a solution to the difficulties which had beset him in his career. That one was myself.

There was little time to be lost, for already; the cable said, the arrangements were in a forward state; the staff of the little force had been organized, the rough outline of the expedition had been sketched, and with the opening of navigation on the northern lakes the first move would be commenced. Going one morning to the nearest telegraph station, I sent the following message under the Atlantic to America:--"To: Winnipeg Expedition. Please remember me." When words cost at the rate of four shillings each, conversation and correspondence become of necessity limited. In the present instance I was only allowed the use of ten words to convey address, signature, and substance, and the five words of my message were framed both with a view to economy and politeness, as well as in a manner which by calling for no direct answer still left undecided the great question of success. Having despatched my message under the ocean, I determined to seek the Horse Guards in a final effort to procure unattached promotion in the army. It is almost unnecessary to remark that this attempt failed; and as I issued from the audience in which I had been informed of the utter hopelessness of my request, I had at least the satisfaction of having reduced my chances of fortune to the narrow limits of a single throw. Pausing at the gate of the Horse Guards I reviewed in a moment the whole situation; whatever was to be the result there was no time for delay and so, hailing a hansom, I told the cabby to drive to the office of the Cunard Steamship Company, Old Broad Street, City.

"What steamer sails on Wednesday for America?"

"The 'Samaria for Boston, the 'Marathon for New York."

"The 'Samaria broke her shaft, didn't she, last voyage, and was a missing ship for a month?" I asked.

"Yes, sir," answered the clerk.

"Then book me a passage in her," I replied; "she's not likely to play that prank twice in two voyages."

CHAPTER TWO.

The "Samaria "--Across the Atlantic-Shipmates--The Despot of the Deck--"Keep her Nor'-West"--Democrat versus Republican--A First Glimpse--Boston

POLITICAL economists and newspaper editors for years have dwelt upon the unfortunate fact that Ireland is not a manufacturing nation, and does not export largely the products of her soil. But persons who have lived in the island, or who have visited the ports of its northern or southern shores, or crossed the Atlantic by any of the ocean steamers which sail daily from the United Kingdom, must have arrived at a conclusion totally at variance with these writers; for assuredly there is no nation under the sun which manufactures the material called man so readily as does that grass-covered island. Ireland is not a manufacturing nation, says the political economist. Indeed, my good sir, you are wholly mistaken. She is not only a manufacturing nation, but she manufactures nations. You do not see her broad-cloth, or her soft fabrics, or her steam-engines, but you see the broad shoulder of her sons and the soft cheeks of her daughters in vast states whose names you are utterly ignorant of; and as for the exportation of her products to foreign lands, just come with me on board this ocean steamship "Samaria", and look at them. The good ship has run down the channel during the night and now lies at anchor in Queenstown harbour, waiting for mails and passengers. The latter came, quickly and thickly enough. No poor, ill-fed, miserably dressed crowd, but fresh, and fair, and strong, and well clad, the bone and muscle and rustic beauty of the land; the little steam-tender that plies from the shore to the ship is crowded at every trip, and you can scan them as they come on board in batches of seventy or eighty. Some eyes among the girls are red with crying, but tears dry quickly on young cheeks, and they will be laughing before an hour is over. "Let them go," says the economist; "we have too many mouths to feed in these little islands of ours; their going will give us more room, more cattle, more chance to keep our acres for the few'; let them go." My friend, that is just half the picture, and no more; we may get a peep at the other half before you and I part.

It was about five o'clock in the afternoon of the 4th of May when the "Samaria" steamed slowly between the capes of Camden and Carlisle, and rounding out into Atlantic turned her head towards the western horizon. The ocean lay unruffled along the rocky headlands of Ireland's southmost shore. A long line of smoke hanging suspended between sky and sea marked the unseen course of another steamship farther away to the south. A hill-top, blue and lonely, rose above the rugged coast-line, the far-off summit of some inland mountain; and as evening came down over the still tranquil ocean and the vessel clove her outward way through phosphorescent water, the lights along the iron coast grew fainter in distance till there lay around only the unbroken circle of the sea.

ON BOARD.-A trip across the Atlantic is now-a-days a very ordinary business; in fact, it is no longer a voyage-it is a run, you may almost count its duration to within four hours; and as for fine weather, blue skies, and calm seas, if they come, you may be thankful for them, but don't expect them, and you won't add a sense of disappointment to one of discomfort. Some experience of the Atlantic enables me to affirm that north or south of 35 degrees north and south latitude there exists no such thing as pleasant sailing.

But the usual run of weather, time, and tide outside the ship is not more alike in its characteristics than the usual run of passenger one meets inside. There is the man who has never been sea-sick in his life, and there is the man who has never felt well upon board ship, but who, nevertheless, both manage to consume about fifty meals of solid food in ten days. There is the nautical landsman who tells you that he has been eighteen times across the Atlantic and four times round the Cape of Good Hope, and who is generally such a bore upon marine questions that it is a subject of infinite regret that he should not be performing a fifth voyage round that distant and interesting promontory. Early in the voyage, owing to his superior sailing qualities, he has been able to cultivate a close intimacy with the captain of the ship; but this intimacy has been on the decline for some days, and, as he has committed the unpardonable error of differing in opinion with the captain upon a subject connected with the general direction and termination of the Gulf Stream, he begins to fall quickly in the estimation of that potentate. Then there is the relict of the late Major Fusby, of the Fusiliers, going to or returning from England. Mrs. Fusby has a predilection for port negus and the first Burmese war, in which campaign her late husband received a wound of such a vital description (he died just twenty-two years later), that it has enabled her to provide, at the expense of a grateful nation, for three youthful Fusbies, who now serve their country in various parts of the world. She does not suffer from sea-sickness, but occasionally undergoes periods of nervous depression which require the administration of the stimulant already referred to. It is a singular fact that the present voyage is strangely illustrative of remarkable events in the life of the late Fusby; there has not been a sail or a porpoise in sight that has not called up some reminiscence of the early career of the major; indeed, even the somewhat unusual appearance of an iceberg, has been turned to account as suggestive of the intense suffering undergone by the major during the period of his wound, owing to the scarcity of the article ice in tropical countries. Then on deck we have the inevitable old sailor who is perpetually engaged in scraping the vestiges of paint from your favourite seat, and who, having arrived at the completion of his monotonous task after four days incessant labour, is found on the morning of the fifth engaged in smearing the paint-denuded place of rest with a vilely glutinous compound peculiar to ship-board. He never looks directly at you as you approach, with book and jug, the desired spot, but you can tell by the leer in his eye and the roll of the quid in his immense mouth that the old villain knows all about the discomfort he is causing you, and you fancy you can detect a chuckle, you turn away in a vain quest for a quiet cosy spot. Then there is the captain himself, that most mighty despot. What king ever wielded such power, what czar or kaiser had ever such obedience yielded to their decrees? This man, who on shore is nothing, is here on his deck a very pope; he is infallible. Canute could not stay the tide, but our sea-king regulates the sun. Charles the Fifth could not make half a dozen clocks go in unison, but Captain Smith can make it twelve o'clock any time he pleases; nay, more, when the sun has made it twelve o'clock no tongue of bell or sound of clock can proclaim time's decree until it has been ratified by the fiat of the captain; and even in his misfortunes what gran deur, what absence of excuse or crimination of others in the hour of his disaster! Who has not heard of that captain who sailed away from Liverpool one day bound for America? He had been hard worked on shore, and it was said that when he sought the seclusion of his own cabin he was not unmindful of that comfort which we are told the first navigator of the ocean did not disdain to use. For a little time things went well. The Isle of Man was passed; but unfortunately, on the second day out, the good ship struck the shore of the north-east coast of Ireland and became a total wreck. As the weather was extremely fine, and there appeared to be no reason for the disaster, the subject became matter for investigation by the authorities connected with the Board of Trade. During the inquiry it was deposed that the Calf of Man had been passed at such an hour on such a day, and the circumstance duly reported to the captain, who, it was said, was below. It was also stated that having received the report of the passage of the Calf of Man the captain had ordered the ship to be kept in a north-west course until further orders. About six hours later the vessel went ashore on the coast of Ireland. Such was the evidence of the first officer. The captain was shortly after called and examined.

"It appears, sir," said the president of the court, "that the passing of the Calf of Man was duly reported to you by the first officer. May I ask, sir, what course you ordered to be steered upon receipt of that information?"

"North-west, sir," answered the captain; "I said, 'Keep her north-west.'"

"North-west," repeated the president; "a very excellent general course for making the coast of America, but not until you had cleared the channel and were well into the Atlantic. Why, sir, the whole of Ireland lay between you and America on that course."

"Can't help that, sir; can't help that, sir," replied the sea-king in a tone of half-contemptuous pity, that the whole of Ireland should have been so very unreasonable as to intrude itself in such a position.

And yet, with all the despotism of the deck, what kindly spirits are these old sea-captains with the freckled hard knuckled hands and the grim storm-seamed faces! What honest genuine hearts are lying buttoned beneath those rough pea-jackets! If all despots had been of that kind perhaps we shouldn't have known quite as much about Parliamentary Institutions as we do.

And now, while we have been talking thus, the "Samaria" has been getting far out into mid Atlantic, and yet we know not one among our fellow-passengers, although they do not number much above a dozen: a merchant from Maryland, a sea-captain-from Maine, a young doctor from Pennsylvania, a Massachusetts man, a Rhode Islander, a German geologist going to inspect seams in Colorado, a priest's sister from Ireland going to look after some little property left her by her brother, a poor fellow who was always ill, who never appeared at table, and who alluded to the demon sea-sickness that preyed upon him as "it". "It comes on very bad at night. It prevents me touching food. It never leaves me," he would say; and in truth this terrible "it" never did leave him until the harbour of Boston was reached, and even then, I fancy, dwelt in his thoughts during many a day on shore.

The sea-captain from Maine was a violent democrat, the Massachusetts man a rabid republican; and many a fierce battle waged between them on the vexed questions of state rights, negro suffrage, and free trade in liquor. To many Englishmen the terms republican and democrat may seem synonymous; but not between radical and conservative, between outmost Whig and inmost Tory exist more opposite extremes than between these great rival political parties of the United States. As a drop of sea-water possesses the properties of the entire water of the ocean, so these units of American political controversy were microscopic representatives of their respective parties. It was curious to remark what a prominent part their religious convictions played in the war of words. The republican was a member of the Baptist congregation; the democrat held opinions not very easy of description, something of a universalist and semi-unitarian tendency; these opinions became frequently intermixed with their political jargon, forming that curious combination of ideas which to unaccustomed ears sounds slightly blasphemous. I recollect a very earnest American once saying that he considered all religious, political, social, and historical teaching should be reduced to three subjects: the Sermon on the Mount, the Declaration of American Independence, and the Chicago Republican Platform of 1860.

On the present occasion the Massachusetts man was a person whose nerves were as weak as his political convictions were strong, and the democrat being equally gifted with strong opinions, strong nerves, and a tendency towards strong waters, was enabled, particularly after dinner, to obtain an easy victory over his less powerfully gifted antagonist. In fact it was to the weakness of the latter's nervous system that we were indebted for the pleasure of his society on board. Eight weeks before he had been ordered by his medical adviser to leave his wife and office in the little village of Hyde Park to seek change and relaxation on the continent of Europe. He was now returning to his native land filled, he informed us, with the gloomiest forebodings. He had a very powerful presentiment that we were never to see the shores of America. By what agency our destruction was to be accomplished he did not enlighten us, but the ship had not well commenced her voyage before he commenced his evil prognostications. That these were not founded upon any prophetic knowledge of future events will be sufficiently apparent from the fact of this book being written. Indeed, when the mid Atlantic had been passed our Massachusetts acquaintance began to entertain more hopeful expectations of once more pressing his wife to his bosom, although he repeatedly reiterated that if that domestic event was really destined to take place no persuasion on earth, medical or other wise, would ever induce him to place the treacherous billows of the Atlantic between him and the person of that bosom's partner. It was drawing near the end of the voyage when an event occurred which, though in itself of a most trivial nature, had for some time a disturbing effect upon our party. The priest's sister, an elderly maiden lady of placidly weak intellect, announced one morning at breakfast that the sea-captain from Maine had on the previous day addressed her in terms of endearment, and had, in fact, called her his "little duck." This announcement, which was made generally to the table, and which was received in dead silence by every member of the community, had by no means a pleasurable effect upon the countenance of the person most closely concerned. Indeed, amidst the silence which succeeded the revelation, a half-smothered sentence, more forcible than polite, was audible from the lips of the democrat, in which those accustomed to the vernacular of America could plainly distinguish "darned old fool." Meantime, in spite of political discussions, or amorous revelations, or prophetic disaster, in spite of mid-ocean storm and misty-fog-bank, our gigantic screw, unceasing as the whirl of life itself, had wound its way into the waters which wash the rugged shores of New England. To those whose lives are spent in ceaseless movement over the world, who wander from continent to continent, from island to island, who dwell in many cities but are the citizens of no city, who sail away and come back again, whose home is the broad earth itself, to such as these the coming in sight of land is no unusual occurrence, and yet the man has grown old at his trade of wandering who can look utterly uninterested upon the first glimpse of land rising out of the waste of ocean:

small as that glimpse may be, only a rock, a cape, a mountain crest, it has the power of localizing an idea, the very vastness Of which prevents its realization on shore. From the deck of an outward-bound vessel one sees rising, faint and blue, a rocky headland or a mountain summit-one does not ask if the mountain be of Maine, or of Mexico, or the Cape be St. Ann's or Hatteras, one only sees America. Behind that strip of blue coast lies a world, and that world the new one. Far away inland lie scattered many landscapes glorious with mountain, lake, river, and forest, all unseen, all unknown to the wanderer who for the first time seeks the American shore; yet instinctively their presence is felt in that faint outline of sea-lapped coast which lifts itself above the ocean; and even if in after-time it becomes the lot of the wanderer, as it became my lot, to look again upon these mountain summits, these immense inland seas; these mighty rivers whose waters seek their mother ocean through 3000 miles of meadow, in none of these glorious parts, vast though they be, will the sense of the still vaster whole be realized as strongly as in that first glimpse of land showing dimly over the western horizon of the Atlantic.

The sunset of a very beautiful evening in May was making bright the shores of Massachusetts as the "Samaria," under her fullest head of steam, ran up the entrance to Plymouth Sound. To save daylight into port was an object of moment to the Captain, for the approach to Boston harbour is as intricate as shoal, sunken rock, and fort-crowned island can make it. If ever that much talked-of conflict between the two great branches of the Anglo-Saxon race is destined to quit the realms of fancy for those of fact, Boston, at least, will rest as safe from the destructive engines of British iron-clads as the city of Omaha on the Missouri River. It was only natural that the Massachusetts man should have been in a fever of excitement at finding himself once more within sight of home; and for once human nature exhibited the unusual spectacle of rejoicing over the falsity of its own predictions. As every revolution of the screw brought out some new feature into prominence, he skipped gleefully about; and, recognizing in my person the stranger element in the assembly, he took particular pains to point out the lions of the landscape. "There, serais Fort Warren, where we kept our rebel prisoners during the war. In a few minutes more, sir, we will be in sight of Bunker's Hill;" and then, in a frenzy of excitement, he skipped away to some post of vantage upon the forecastle.

Night had come down over the harbour, and Boston had lighted all her lamps, before the "Samaria," swinging round in the fast-running tide, lay, with quiet screw and smokeless funnel, alongside the wharf of New England's oldest city.

"Real mean of that darned Baptist pointing you out Bunker's Hill," said the sea-captain from Maine; "just like the ill-mannered republican cuss!" It was useless to tell him that I had felt really obliged for the information given me by his political opponent. "Never mind," he said, "to-morrow I'll show you how these moral Bostonians break their darned liquor law in every hotel in their city."

Boston has a clean, English look about it, peculiar to it alone of all the cities in the United States. Its streets, running in curious curves, as though they had not the least idea where they were going, are full of prettily dressed pretty girls, who look as though they had a very fair idea of where they were going to. Atlantic fogs and French fashions have combined to make Boston belles pink, pretty,-and piquante; while the western states, by drawing fully half their male population from New England, make the preponderance of the female element apparent at a glance. The ladies, thus left at home, have not been idle: their colleges, their clubs, their reading-classes are numerous; like the man in "Hudibras,"

"'Tis known they can speak Greek as naturally as pigs squeak;"

and it is probable that no city in the world can boast so high a standard of female education as Boston: nevertheless, it must be regretted that this standard of mental excellence attributable to the ladies of Boston should not have been found capable of association with the duties of domestic life. Without going deeper into topics which are better understood in America than in England, and which have undergone most eloquent elucidation at the hands of Mr. Hepworth Dixon, but which are nevertheless dlightly nauseating, it may safely be observed, that the inculcation at ladies colleges of that somewhat rude but forcible home truth, enunciated by the first Napoleon in reply to the most illustrious Frenchwoman of her day, when questioned Upon the subject of female excellence, should not be forgotten.

There exists a very generally received idea that strangers are more likely to notice and complain of the short-comings of a social habit or system than are residents who have grown old under that infliction; but I cannot help thinking that there exists a considerable amount of error in this opinion. A stranger will frequently submit to extortion, to insolence, or to inconvenience, because, being a stranger, he believes that extortion, insolence, and inconvenience are the habitual characteristics of the new place in which he finds himself: they do not strike him as things to be objected to, or even wondered at; they are simply to be submitted to and endured. If he were at home, he would die sooner than yield that extra half-dollar; he would leave the house at once in which he was told to get up at an unearthly hour in the morning; but, being in another country, he submits, without even a thought of resistance. In no other way can we account for the strange silence on the part of English writers upon the tyrannical disposition of American social life. A nation everlastingly boasting itself the freest on the earth

9

submits unhesitatingly to more social tyranny than any people in the world. In the United States one is marshalled to every event of the day. Whether you like it or not, you must get up, breakfast, dine, sup, and go to bed at fixed hours. Attached upon the inside of your bedroom-door is a printed document which informs you of all the things you are not to do in the hotel-a list in which, like Mr. J. S. Mill's definition of Christian doctrine, the shall-nots predominate over the shalls. In the event of your disobeying any of the numerous mandates set forth in this document-such as not getting up very early-you will not be sent to the penitentiary or put in the pillory, for that process of punishment would imply a necessity for trouble and exertion on the part of the richly-apparelled gentleman who does you the honour of receiving your petitions and grossly overcharging you at the office-no, you have simply to go without food until dinner-time, or to go to bed by the light of a jet of gas for which you will be charged an exorbitant price in your bill. As in the days of Roman despotism we know that the slaves were occasionally permitted to indulge in the grossest excesses, so, under the rigorous system of the hotel-keeper, the guest is allowed to expectorate profusely over every thing; over the marble with which the hall is paved, over the Brussels carpet which covers the drawing-room, over the bed-room, and over the lobby. Expectoration is apparently the one saving clause which American liberty demands as the price of its submission to the prevailing tyranny of the hotel. Do not imagine-you, who have never yet tasted the sweets of a transatlantic transaction-that this tyranny is confined to the hotel: every person to whom you pay money in the ordinary travelling transactions of life-your omnibus-man, your railway-conductor, your steamboat-clerk-takes your money, it is true, but takes it in a manner which tells you plainly enough that he is conferring a very great favour by so doing. He is in all probability realizing a profit of from three to four hundred-per cent. on whatever the transaction may be; but, all the same, although you are fully aware of this fact, you are nevertheless almost overwhelmed with the sense of the very deep obligation which you owe to the man who thus deigns to receive your money.

It was about ten o'clock at night when the steamer anchored at the wharf at Boston. Not until midday. On the following day were we (the passengers) allowed to leave the vessel. The cause of this delay arose from the fact that the collector of customs of the port of Boston was an individual of great social importance; and as it would have been inconvenient for him to attend at an earlier hour for the purpose of being present at the examination of our baggage, we were detained prisoners until the day was far enough advanced to suit his convenience. From a conversation which subsequently I had with this gentleman at our hotel, I discovered that he was more obliging in his general capacity of politician and prominent citizen than he was in his particular duties of customs collector. Like many other instances of the kind in the United States, his was a case of evident unfitness for the post he held. A. socially smaller man would have made a much better customs official. Unfortunately for the comfort of the public, the remuneration attached to appointments in the postal and customs departments is frequently very large, and these situations are eagerly sought as prizes in the lottery of political life-prizes, too, which can only be held for the short term of four years. As. A consequence, the official who holds his situation by right of political service rendered to the chief of the predominant clique or party in his state does not consider that he owes to the public the service of his office. In theory he is a public servant; in reality he becomes the master of the public. This is, however, the fault of the system and not of the individual.

CHAPTER THREE

Bunker--New York--Niagara-Toronto-Spring--time in Quebec--A Summons--A Start--In good Company--Stripping a Peg--An Expedition--Poor Canada--An Old Glimpse at a New Land--Rival Routes--Change of Masters--The Red River Revolt--The Halfbreeds--Early Settlers-Bungling--"Eaters of Pemmican-"-M. Louis Riel--The Murder of Scott

When a city or a nation has but one military memory, it clings to it with all the affectionate tenacity of an old maid for her solitary poodle or parrot. Boston-supreme over any city in the Republic-can boast of possessing one military memento: she has the Hill of Bunker. Bunker has long passed into the bygone; but his hill remains, and is likely to remain for many a long day. It is not improbable that the life, character and habits, sayings, even the writings of Bunker-perhaps he couldn't write!-are familiar to many persons in the United States; but it is in Boston and Massachusetts that Bunker holds highest carnival. They keep in the Senate-chamber of the Capitol, nailed over the entrance doorway in full sight of the Speaker's chair, a drum, a musket, and a mitre-shaped soldier's hat-trophies of the fight fought in front of the low earthwork on Bunker's Hill. Thus the senators of Massachusetts have ever before them visible reminders of the glory of their fathers: and I am not sure that these former belongings of some long-waistcoated redcoat are not as valuable incentives to correct legislation as that historic "bauble" of our own constitution.

Meantime we must away. Boston and New York have had their stories told frequently enough-and, in reality, there is not much to tell about them. The world does not contain a more uninteresting accumulation of men and houses than the great city of New York: it is a place wherein the stranger feels inexplicably lonely. The traveller has no mental property in this city whose enormous growth of life has struck scant roots into the great heart of the past.

Our course, however, lies west. We will trace the onward stream of empire in many portions of its way; we will reach its limits, and pass beyond it into the lone spaces which yet silently await its coming; and farther still, where the solitude knows not of its approach and the Indian still reigns in savage supremacy.

NIAGARA--They have all had their say about Niagara. From Hennipin to Dilke, travellers have written much about this famous cataract, and yet, put all together, they have not said much about it; description depends so much on comparison, and comparison necessitates a something like. If there existed another Niagara on the earth, travellers might compare this one to that one; but as there does not exist a second Niagara, they are generally hard up for a comparison. In the matter of roar, however, comparisons are still open. There is so much noise in the world that analysis of noise becomes easy. One man hears in it the sound of the Battle of the Nile-a statement not likely to be challenged, as the survivors of that celebrated naval action are not numerous, the only one we ever had the pleasure of meeting having been stone-deaf. Another writer compares the roar to the sound of a vast mill; and this similitude, more flowery than poetical, is perhaps as good as that of the one who was in Aboukir Bay. To leave out Niagara when you can possibly bring it in would be as much against the stock-book of travel as to omit the duel, the steeple-chase, or the escape from the mad bull in a thirty-one-and-sixpenny fashionable novel. What the pyramids are to Egypt--what Vesuvius is to Naples--what the field of Waterloo has been for fifty years to Brussels, so is Niagara to the entire continent of North America.

It was early in the month of September, three years prior to the time I now write of, when I first visited this famous spot. The Niagara season was at its height: the monster hotels were ringing with song, music, and dance; tourists were doing the falls, and touts were doing the tourists. Newly-married couples were conducting themselves in that demonstrative manner characteristic of such as responded freely to the invitation contained in their favourite nigger melody. Venders of Indian bead-work; itinerant philosophers; camera-obscura men; imitation squaws; free and enlightened negroes; guides to go under the cataract, who should have been sent over it; spiritualists, phrenologists, and nigger minstrels had made the place their own. Shoddy and petroleum were having "a high old time of it," spending the dollar as though that "almighty article had become the thin end of nothing whittled fine:" altogether, Niagara was a place to be instinctively shunned.

Just four months after this time the month of January was drawing to a close. King Frost, holding dominion over Niagara, had worked strange wonders with the scene. Folly and ruffianism had been frozen up, shoddy and petroleum had betaken themselves to other haunts, the bride strongly demonstrative or weakly reciprocal had vanished, the monster hotels were silent and deserted, the free and enlightened negro had gone back to Buffalo, and the girls of that thriving city no longer danced, as of yore, "under de light of de moon." Well, Niagara was worth seeing then-and the less we say about it, perhaps, the better. "Pat," said an American to a staring Irishman lately landed, "did you ever see such a fall as that in the old country?" "Begarra! I niver did; but look here now, why wouldn't it fall? what's to hinder it from falling?"

When I reached the city of Toronto, capital of the province of Ontario, I found that the Red River Expeditionary Force had already been mustered, previous to its start for the North-West. Making my way to the quarters of the commander of the Expedition, I was greeted every now and again with a "You should have been here last week; every soul wants to get on the Expedition, and you hav'n't a chance. The whole thing is complete; we start to-morrow." Thus I encountered those few friends who on such occasions are as certain to offer their pithy condolences as your neighbour at the dinner-table when you are late is sure to tell you that the soup and fish were delicious. At last I met the commander himself.

"My good fellow, there's not a vacant berth for you," he said; "I got your telegram, but the whole army in Canada wanted to get on the Expedition."

"I think, sir, there is one berth still vacant," I answered.

"What is it?"

"You will want to know what they are doing in Minnesota and along the flank of your march, and you have no one to tell you," I said.

"You are right; we do want a man out there. Look now, start for Montreal by first train to-morrow; by to night's mail I will write to the general, recommending your appointment. If you see him as soon as possible, it may yet be all right."

I thanked him, said "Good-bye," and in little more than twenty-four hours later found myself in Montreal, the commercial capital of Canada.

"Let me see," said the general next morning, when I presented myself before him, "you sent a cable message from the South of Ireland last month, didn't you? and you now want to get out to the West? Well, we will require a man there, but the thing doesn't rest with me; it will have to be referred to Ottawa; and meantime you can remain here, or with your regiment, pending the receipt of an answer."

So I went back to my regiment to wait.

Spring breaks late over the province of Quebec-that portion of America known to our fathers as Lower Canada, and of old to the subjects of the Grand Monarque as the kingdom of New France. But when the young trees begin to open their leafy lids after the long sleep of winter, they do it quickly. The snow is not all gone before the maple-trees are all green; the maple, that most beautiful of trees! Well has Canada made the symbol of her new nationality that tree whose green gives the spring its earliest freshness, whose autumn dying tints are richer than the clouds, sunset, whose life-stream is sweeter than honey, and whose branches are drowsy through the long summer with the scent and the hum of bee and flower! Still the long line of the Canadas admits of a varied spring. When the trees are green at Lake St. Clair, they are scarcely budding at Kingston, they are leafless at Montreal, and Quebec is white with snow. Even between Montreal and Quebec, a short night's steaming, there exists a difference of ten days in the opening of the summer. But late as comes the summer to Quebec, it comes in its loveliest and most enticing form, as though it wished to atone for its long delay in banishing from such a landscape the cold tyranny of winter. And with what loveliness does the whole face of plain, river, lake, and mountain turn from the iron clasp of icy winter to kiss the balmy lips of returning summer, and to welcome his bridal gifts of sun and shower! The trees open their leafy lids to look at the brooks and streamlets break forth into songs of gladness--"the birch-tree," as the old Saxon said, "becomes beautiful in its branches, and rustles sweetly in its leafy summit, moved to and fro by the breath of heaven "--the lakes uncover their sweet faces, and their mimic shores steal down in quiet evenings to bathe themselves in the transparent waters--far into the depths of the great forest speeds the glad message of returning glory, and graceful fern-and soft velvet moss, and-white wax-like lily peep forth to cover rock and fallen tree and wreck of last year's autumn in one great sea of foliage. There are many landscapes which can never be painted, photographed, or described, but which the mind carries away instinctively to look at again And again in after-time-these are the celebrated views of the world, and they are not easy to find. From the Queen's rampart, on the citadel of Quebec, the eye sweeps over a greater diversity of landscape than is probably to be found in any one spot in the universe. Blue mountain, far stretching river, foaming cascade, the white sails of ocean ships, the black trunks of many-sized guns, the pointed roofs, the white village nestling amidst its fields of green, the great isle in mid-channel, the many shades of colour from deep blue pine-wood to yellowing corn-field in what other spot on the earth's broad bosom lie grouped together in a single glance so many of these "things of beauty" which the eye loves to feast on and to place in memory as joys-for ever?

I had been domiciled in Quebec for about a week, when there appeared one morning in General Orders a paragraph commanding my presence in Montreal to receive instructions from the military authorities relative to my further destination. It was the long-looked-for order, and fortune, after many frowns, seemed at length about to smile upon me. It was on the evening of the 8th June, exactly two months after the despatch of my cable message from the South of Ireland, that I turned my face to the West and commenced a long journey towards the setting sun. When the broad curves of the majestic river had shut out the rugged outline of the citadel, and the east was growing coldly dim while the west still glowed with the fires of sunset, I could not help feeling a thrill of exultant thought at the prospect before me. I little knew then the limits of my wanderings-I little thought that for many and many a day my track would lie with almost undeviating precision towards the setting sun, that summer would merge itself into autumn, and autumn darken into winter, and that still the nightly bivouac would be made a little nearer to that west whose golden gleam was suffusing sky and water.

But though all this was of course unknown, enough was still visible in the foreground of the future to make even the swift-moving paddles seem laggards as they beat to foam the long reaches of the darkening Cataraqui. "We must leave matters to yourself, I think," said the General, when I saw him for the last time in Montreal, "you will be best judge of how to get on when you know and see the ground. I will not ask you to visit Fort Garry, but if you find it feasible, it would be well if you could drop down the Red River and join Wolseley before he gets to the place. You know what I want, but how to do it, I will leave altogether to yourself. For the rest, you can draw on us for any money you require. Take care of those northern fellows. Good-bye, and success."

This was on the 12th June, and on the morning of the 13th I started by the Grand Trunk Railway of Canada for the West. On that morning the Grand Trunk Railway of Canada was in a high state of excitement. It was about to attempt, for the first time, the despatch of a Lightning Express for Toronto; and it was to carry from Montreal, on his way to Quebec, one of the Royal Princes of England, whose sojourn in the Canadian capital was drawing to a close. The Lightning Express was not attended with the glowing success predicted for it by its originators. At some thirty or forty miles from Montreal it came heavily to grief, owing to some misfortune having attended the progress of a preceding train over the rough uneven track. A delay of two hours having supervened, the Lightning Express got into motion again, and jolted along with tolerable celerity to Kingston.

When darkness set in it worked itself up to a high pitch of fury, and rushed along the low shores of Lake Ontario with a velocity which promised disaster. The car in which I travelled was one belonging to the director of the Northern Railroad of Canada, Mr. Cumberland, and we had in it a minister of fisheries, one of education, a governor of a province, a speaker of a house of commons, and a colonel of a distinguished rifle regiment. Being the last car of the train, the vibration caused by the unusual rate of speed over the very rough rails was excessive; it was, however, consolatory to feel that any little unpleasantness which might occur through the fact of the car leaving the track would be attended with some sense of alleviation. The rook is said to have thought he was paying dear for good company when he was put into the pigeon pie, but it by no means follows that a leap from an embankment, or an upset into a river, would be as disastrous as is usually supposed, if taken in the society of such pillars of the state as those I have already mentioned. Whether a speaker of a house of commons and a governor of a large province, to say nothing of a minister of fisheries, would tend in reality to mitigate the unpleasantness of being "telescoped through colliding," I cannot decide, for we reached Toronto without accident, at midnight, and I saw no more of my distinguished fellow-travellers.

I remained long enough in the city of Toronto to provide myself with a wardrobe suitable to the countries I was about to seek. In one of the principal commercial streets of the flourishing capital of Ontario I found a small tailoring establishment, at the door of which stood an excellent representation of a colonial. The garments be longing to this figure appeared to have been originally designed from the world-famous pattern of the American flag, presenting above a combination of stars, and below having a tendency to stripes. The general groundwork of the whole rig appeared to be shoddy of an inferior-description, and a small card attached to the figure intimated that the entire fit-out was procurable at the very reasonable sum of ten dollars. It was impossible to resist the fascination of this attire. While the bargain was being transacted the tailor looked askance at the garments worn by his customer, which, having only a few months before emanated from the establishment of a well-known London cutter, presented a considerable contrast to the new investment; he even ventured upon some remarks which evidently had for their object the elucidation of the enigma, but a word that such clothes as those worn by me were utterly un suited to the bush repelled all further questioning-indeed, so pleased did the noor fellow appear in a pecuniary point of view, that he insisted upon presenting me gratis with a neck-tie of green and yellow, fully in keeping with the other articles composing the costume. And now, while I am thus arranging these little preliminary matters so essential to the work I was about to engage in, let us examine for a moment the objects and scope of that work, and settle the limits and extent of the first portion of my journey, and sketch the route of the Expedition. It will be recollected that the Expedition destined for the Red River of the North had started some time before for its true base of operations, namely Fort William, on the north-west shore of Lake Superior. The distance intervening between Toronto and Thunder Bay is about 600 miles, 100 being by railroad conveyance and 500 by water. The island-studded expanse of Lake Huron, known as Georgian Bay, receives at the northern extremity the waters of the great Lake Superior, but a difference of level amounting to upwards of thirty feet between the broad bosoms of these two vast expanses of fresh water has rendered necessary the construction of a canal of considerable magnitude. This canal is situated upon American territory-a fact which gives our friendly cousins the exclusive possession of the great northern basin, and which enabled them at the very outset of the Red River affair to cause annoyance and delay to the Canadian Expedition. Poor Canada! when one looks at you along the immense length of your noble river boundary, how vividly become apparent the evils under which your youth has grown to manhood! Looked at from home by every succeeding colonial minister through the particular whig, or tory spectacles of his party, subject to violent and radical alterations of policy because of some party vote in a Legislative Assembly 3000 miles from your nearest coast-line, your own politicians, for years, too timid to grasp the limits of your possible future, parties every where in your provinces, and of every kind, except a national party; no breadth, no depth, no earnest striving to make you great amongst the nations, each one for himself and no-one for the country; men fighting for a sect, for a province, for a nationality, but no one for the nation; and all this while, close alongside, your great rival grew with giant's growth, looking far into the future before him, cutting his cloth with perspective ideas of what his limbs would attain to in after-time,' digging his canals and grading, his railroads, with one eye on the Atlantic and the other on the Pacific, spreading himself, monopolizing, annexing, outmanoeuvring and flanking those colonial bodies who sat in solemn state in Downing Street and wrote windy proclamations and despatches anent boundary-lines, of which they knew next to nothing. Macaulay laughs at poor Newcastle for his childish delight in finding out that Cape Breton was an island, but I strongly suspect there were other and later Newcastles whose geographical knowledge of matters American were not a whit superior. Poor Canada! they muddled you out of Maine, and the open harbour of Portland, out of Rouse's Point, and the command of Lake Champlain, out of many a fair mile far away by the Rocky Mountains. It little matters whether it was the treaty of 1783, or 1818, or '21, or '48, or '71, the worst of every bargain, at all times, fell to you.

I have said that the possession of the canal at the Sault St. Marie enabled the Americans to delay the progress of the Red River Expedition. The embargo put upon the Canadian vessels originated, however, in the State, and not the Federal, authorities; that is to say, the State of Michigan issued the prohibition against the passage of the steam boat, and not the Cabinet of Washington. Finally, Washington overruled the decision of Michigan-a feat far more feasible now than it would have been prior to the Southern war-and the steamers were permitted to pass through into the waters of Lake Superior. From thence to Thunder Bay was only the steaming of four-and-twenty hours through a lake whose vast bosom is the favourite playmate of the wild storm-king of the North. But although full half the total distance from Toronto to the Red River had been traversed when the Expedition reached Thunder Bay, not a twentieth of the time nor one hundredth part of the labour and fatigue had been accomplished. For a distance of 600 miles there stretched away to the northwest a vast tract of rock-fringed lake, swamp, and forest; lying spread in primeval savagery, an untravelled wilderness; the home of the Ojibbeway, who here, entrenched amongst Nature's fastnesses, has long called this land his own. Long before Wolfe had scaled the heights of Abraham, before even Marlborough, and Eugene, and Villers, and V'endome, and Villeroy had commenced to fight their giants fights in divers portions of the low countries, some adventurous subjects of the Grand Monarque were forcing their way, for the first time, along the northern shores of Lake Superior, nor stopping there: away to the north-west there dwelt wild tribes to be sought out by two classes of men-by the black robe, who laboured for souls; by the trader, who sought for skins-and a hard race had these two widely different pioneers who sought at that early day these remote and friendless regions, so hard that it would almost seem as though the great powers of good and of evil had both despatched at this same moment, on rival errands, ambassadors to gain dominion over these distant savages. It was a curious contest: on the one hand, showy robes, shining beads, and maddening fire-water, on the other, the old, old story of peace and brotherhood, of Christ and Calvary--a contest so full of interest, so teeming with adventure, so pregnant with the discovery of mighty rivers and great inland seas, that one would fain ramble away into its depths; but it must not be, or else the journey I have to travel myself would never even begin.

Vast as is the accumulation of fresh water in Lake Superior, the area of the country which it drains is limited enough. Fifty miles from its northern shores the rugged hills which form the backbone or "divide" of the continent raise their barren heads, and the streams carry from thence the vast rainfall of this region into the Bay of Hudson. Thus, when the voyageur has paddled, tracked, poled, and carried his canoe up any of the many rivers which rush like mountain torrents into Lake Superior from the north, he reaches the height of land between the Atlantic Ocean and Hudson Bay. Here, at an elevation of 1500 feet above the sea level, and of 900 above Lake Superior, he launches his canoe upon water flowing north and west; then he has before him hundreds of miles of quiet-lying lake, of wildly rushing river, of rock-broken rapid, of foaming cataract, but through it all runs ever towards the north the ocean-seeking current. As later on we shall see many and many a mile of this wilderness--living in it, eating in it, sleeping in it-although reaching it from a different direction altogether from the one spoken of now, I anticipate, by alluding to it here, only as illustrating the track of the Expedition between Lake Superior and Red River. For myself, my route was to be altogether a different one. I was to follow the lines of railroad which ran-out into the frontier territories of the United States, then, leaving the iron horse, I was to make my way to the settlements on the west shore of Lake Superior, and from thence to work Round to the American boundary-line at Pembina on the Red River; so far through American territory, and with distinct and definite instructions; after that, altogether to my own resources, but with this summary of the general's wishes: "I will not ask you to visit Fort Garry, but however you manage it, try and reach Wolseley-before he gets through from Lake Superior, and let him know what these Red River men are going to do." Thus the military Expedition under Colonel Wolseley was to work its way Across from Lake Superior to Red River, through British territory; I was to pass round by the United States, and, after ascertaining the likelihood of Fenian intervention from the side of Minnesota and Dakota, endeavour to reach Colonel Wolseley beyond Red River, with all tidings as to state of parties and chances of fight. But as the reader has heard only a very brief mention of the state of affairs in Red River, and as he may very naturally be inclined to ask, What is this Expedition going to do--why are these men sent through swamp and wilderness at all? A few explanatory words may not be out of place, serving to make matters now and at a later period much more intelligible. I have said in the opening chapter of this book, that the little community, or rather a portion of the little community, of Red River Settlement had risen in insurrection, protesting vehemently against certain arrangements made between the Governor of Canada and the Hon. Hudson's Bay Company relative to the cession of territorial rights and governing powers. After forcibly expelling the Governor of the country appointed by Canada, from the frontier station at Pembina, the French malcontents had proceeded to other and still more questionable proceedings. Assembling in large numbers, they had fortified portions of the road between Pembina and Fort Garry, and had taken armed possession of the latter place, in which large stores of provisions, clothing, and merchandise of all descriptions had been stored by the Hudson Bay Company. The occupation of this fort, which stands close to the confluence of the Red and Assineboine Rivers, nearly midway between the American boundary-line and the southern shore of Lake Winnipeg, gave the French party the virtual command of the entire settlement. The abundant stores of clothing and provisions were not so important as the arms and ammunition which also fell into their hands--a battery of nine-pound bronze guns, complete in every respect, besides several smaller pieces of ordnance, together with large store of Enfield rifles and old brown-bess smooth bores. The place was, in fact, abundantly supplied with war material of every description. It is almost refreshing to notice the ability, the energy, the determination which up to this point had characterized all the movements of the originator and mainspring of the movement, M. Louis Riel. One hates so much to see a thing bungled, that even resistance, although it borders upon rebellion, becomes respectable when it is carried out with courage, energy, and decision.

And, in truth, up to this point in the little insurrection it is not easy to condemn the wild Metis of the North-west--wild as the bison which he hunted, unreclaimed as the prairies he loved so well, what knew he of State duty or of loyalty? He knew that this land was his, and that strong men were coming to square it into rectangular farms and to push him farther west by the mere pressure of civilization. He had heard of England and the English, but it was in a shadowy, vague, unsubstantial sort of way, unaccompanied by any fixed idea of government or law. The Company--not the Hudson Bay Company, but the Company-represented for him all law, all power, all government. Protection he did not need-his quick ear, his unerring eye, his untiring horse, his trading gun, gave him that; but a market for his taurreau, for his buffalo robe, for his lynx, fox, and wolf skins, for the produce of his summer hunt and winter trade, he did need, and in the forts of the Company he found it. His wants were few-a capôte of blue cloth, with shining brass buttons; a cap, with beads and tassel; a blanket; a gun, and ball and powder; a box: of matches, and a knife, these were all he wanted, and at every fort, from the mountain to the banks of his well-loved River Rouge, he found them, too. What were these new people coming to do with him? Who could tell? If they meant him fair, why did they not say so? why did they not come up and tell him what they wanted, and what they were going to do for him, and ask him what he wished for? But, no; they either meant to outwit him, or they held him of so small account that it mattered little what he thought about it; and, with all the pride of his mother's race, that idea of his being slighted hurt him even more than the idea of his being wronged. Did not every thing point to his disappearance under the new order of things? He had only to look round him to verify the fact; for years before this annexation to Canada had been carried into effect stragglers from the east had occasionally reached Red River. It is true that these new-comers found much to foster the worst passions of the Anglo-Saxon settler. They found a few thousand occupants, half-farmers, half-hunters, living under a vast commercial monopoly, which, though it practically rested upon a basis of the most paternal kindness towards its subjects, was theoretically hostile to all opposition. Had these men settled quietly to the usual avocations of farming, clearing the wooded ridges, fencing the rich expanses of prairie, covering the great swamps and plains with herds and flocks, it is probable that all would have gone well between the new-comers and the old proprietors. Over that great western thousand miles of prairie there was room for all. But, no; they came to trade and not to till, and trade on the Red River of the North was conducted upon the most peculiar principles. There was, in fact, but one trade, and that was the fur trade. Now, the fur trade is, for some reason or other, a very curious description of barter. Like some mysterious chemical agency, it pervades and permeates every thing it touches. If a man cuts off legs, cures diseases, draws teeth, sells whiskey, cotton, wool, or any other commodity of civilized or uncivilized life, he will be as sure to do it with a view to furs as any doctor, dentist, or general merchant will be sure to practise his particular calling with a view to the acquisition of gold and silver. Thus, then, in the first instance were the new-comers set in antagonism to the Company, and finally to the inhabitants themselves. Let us try and be just to all parties in this little oasis of the Western wilderness.

The early settlers in a Western country are not by any means persons much given to the study of abstract justice, still less to its practice; and it is as well, perhaps, that they should not be. They have rough work to do, and they generally do it roughly. The very fact of their coming out so far into the wilderness implies the other fact of their not being able to dwell quietly and peaceably at home. They are, as it were, the advanced pioneers of civilization who make smooth the way of the coming race. Obstacles of any kind are their peculiar detestation-if it is a tree, cut it down; if it is a savage, shoot it down; if it is a half-breed, force it down. That is about their creed, and it must be said they act up to their convictions.

'Now, had the country bordering on Red River been an unpeopled wilderness, the plan carried out in effecting the transfer of land in the North-west from the Hudson's Bay Company to the Crown, and from the Crown to the Dominion of Canada, would have been an eminently wise one; but, unfortunately for its wisdom, there were some 15,000 persons living in peaceful possession of the soil thus transferred, and these 15,000 persons very naturally objected to have themselves and possessions signed away without one word of consent or one note of approval. Nay, more than that, these straggling pioneers had on many an occasion taunted the vain half-breed with what would happen when the irresistible march of events had thrown the country into the arms of Canada: then civilization would dawn upon the benighted country, the half-breed would seek some western region, the Company would dis appear, and all the institutions of New World progress would shed-prosperity over the land; prosperity, not to the old dwellers and of the old type, but to the new-comers and of the new order of things. Small wonder, then, if the little community, resenting all this threatened improvement off the face of the earth, got their powder-horns ready, took the covers off their trading flint-guns, and with much gesticulation summarily interfered with several anticipatory surveys of their farms, doubling up the sextants, bundling the surveying parties out of their freeholds, and very peremptorily informing Mr. Governor M'Dougall, just arrived from Canada, that his presence was by no means of the least desirability to Red River or its inhabitants. The man who, with remarkable energy and perseverance, had worked up his fellow-citizens to this pitch of resistance, organizing and directing the whole movement, was a young French half-breed named Louis Riel--a man possessing many of the attributes suited to the leadership of parties, and quite certain to rise to the surface in any time of political disturbances. It has doubtless occurred to any body who has followed me through this brief sketch of the causes which led to the assumption of this attitude on the part of the French half-breeds-it has occurred to them, I say, to ask who then was to blame for the mismanagement of the transfer: was it the Hudson Bay Company who surrendered for 300,000 pounds their territorial rights? was it the Imperial Government who accepted that surrender? or was it the Dominion Government to whom the country was in turn retransferred by the Imperial authorities? I answer that the blame of having bungled the whole business belongs collectively to all the great and puissant bodies. Any ordinary matter-of-fact, sensible man would have managed the whole affair in a few hours; but so many high and potent powers had to consult together, to pen despatches, to speechify, and to lay down the law about it, that the whole affair became hopelessly muddled. Of course, ignorance and carelessness were, as they always are, at the bottom of it all. Nothing would have been easier than to have sent a commissioner from England to Red River, while the negotiations for transfer were pending, who would have ascertained the feelings and wishes of the people of the country relative to` the transfer, and would have guaranteed them the exercise of their rights and liberties under any and every new arrangement that might be entered into. Now, it is no excuse for any Government to plead ignorance upon any matter pertaining to the people it governs, or expects to govern, for a Government has no right to be ignorant on any such matter, and its ignorance must be its condemnation; yet this is the plea put forward by the Dominion Government of Canada, and yet the Dominion Government and the Imperial Government had ample opportunity of arriving at a-correct knowledge of the state of affairs in Red River, if they had only taken the trouble to do so. Nay, more, it is an undoubted fact that warning had been given to the Dominion Government of the state of feeling amongst the half-breeds, and the phrase, "they are only eaters of pemmican," so cutting to the Metis, was then first originated by a distinguished Canadian politician.

And now let us see what the "eaters of pemmican" proceeded to do after their forcible occupation of Fort Garry. Well, it must be admitted they behaved in a very indifferent manner, going steadily from bad to worse, and much befriended in their seditious proceedings by continued and oft repeated bungling on the part of their opponents. Early in the month of December, 1869, Mr. M'Dougall issued two proclamations from his post at Pembina, on the frontier: in one he declared himself Lieutenant-Governor of the territory which Her Majesty had transferred to Canada; and in the other he commissioned an officer of the Canadian militia, under the high-sounding title of "Conservator of the Peace," "to attack, arrest, -disarm, and disperse armed men disturbing the public peace, and to assault, fire upon, and break into houses in which these armed men were to be found." Now, of the first proclamation it will be only necessary to remark, that Her Majesty the Queen had not done any thing of the kind, imputed to her; and of the second it has probably already occurred to the reader that the title of "Conservator of the Peace" was singularly inappropriate to one vested with such sanguinary and destructive powers as was the holder of this commission, who was to "assault, fire upon, and break into houses, and to attack, arrest, disarm, and disperse people," and generally to conduct himself after the manner of Attila, Genshis Khan, the Emperor Theodore, or any other ferocious magnate of ancient or modern times. The officer holding this destructive commission thought he could do nothing better than imitate the tactics of his French adversary, accordingly we find him taking possession of the other rectangular building known as the Lower Fort Garry, situated some twenty miles north of the one in which the French had taken post, but unfortunately, or perhaps fortunately, not finding within its walls the same store of warlike material which had existed in the Fort Garry senior.

The Indians, ever ready to have a hand in any fighting which may be "knocking around," came forward in all the glory of paint, feathers, and pow-wow; and to the number of fifty were put as garrison into the place. Some hundreds of English and Scotch half-breeds were enlisted, told off to companies under captains improvised for the occasion, and every thing pointed to a very pretty quarrel before many days had run their course. But, in truth, the hearts of the English and Scotch settlers were not in this business. By nature peaceably disposed, inheriting from their Orkney and Shetland forefathers much of the frugal habits of the Scotchmen, these people only asked to be left in peace. So far the French party had been only fighting the battle of every half-breed, whether his father had hailed from the northern isles, the shires of England, or the snows of Lower Canada; so, after a little time, the Scotch and English volunteers began to melt away, and on the 9th of December the last warrior had disappeared. But the effects of their futile demonstration soon became apparent in the increasing violence and tyranny of Riel and his followers. The threatened attempt to upset his authority by arraying the Scotch and English half-breeds against him served only to add strength to his party. The number of armed malcontents in Fort Garry became very much increased, clergymen of both parties, neglecting their manifest functions, began to take sides in the conflict, and the worst form of religious animosity became apparent in the little community. Emboldened by the presence of some five or six hundred armed followers, Riel determined to strike a blow against the party most obnoxious to him. This was the English-Canadian party, the pioneers of the Western settlement already alluded to as having been previously in antagonism with the people of Red River. Some sixty or seventy of these men, believing in the certain advance of the English force upon Fort Garry, had taken up a position in the little village of Winnipeg, less than a mile distant from the fort, where they awaited the advance of their adherents previous to making a combined assault upon the French. But Riel proved himself more than a match for his antagonists; marching quickly out of his stronghold, he surrounded the buildings in which they were posted, and, planting a gun in a conspicuously commanding position, summoned them all to surrender in the shortest possible space of time. As is usual on such occasions, and in such circumstances, the whole party did as they were ordered, and marching out-with or without side-arms and military honours history does not relate-were forthwith conducted into close confinement within the walls of Fort Garry. Having by this bold coup got possession not only of the most energetic of his opponents, but also of many valuable American Remington Rifles, fourteen shooters and revolvers, Mr. Riel, with all the vanity of the Indian peeping out, began to imagine himself a very great personage, and as very great personages are sometimes supposed to be believers in the idea that to take a man's property is only to confiscate it, and to take his life is merely to execute him, he too commenced to violently sequestrate, annex, and requisition not only divers of his prisoners, but also a considerable share of the goods stored in warehouses of the Hudson Bay Company, having particular regard to some hogsheads of old port wine and very potent Jamaica rum. The proverb which has reference to a mendicant suddenly Placed in an equestrian position had notable exemplification in the case of the Provisional Government, and many of his colleagues; going steadily from bad to worse, from violence to pillage, from pillage to robbery of a very low type, much supplemented by rum-drunkenness and dictatorial debauchery, he and they finally, on the 4th of March, 1870, disregarding some touching appeals for mercy, and with many accessories of needless cruelty, shot to death a helpless Canadian prisoner named Thomas Scott. This act, committed in the coldest of cold blood, bears only one name: the red name of murder-a name which instantly and for ever drew between Riel and his followers, and the outside Canadian world, that impassable gulf which the murderer in all ages digs between himself and society, and which society attempts to bridge by the aid of the gallows. It is needless here to enter into details of this matter; of the second rising which preceded it; of the dead blank which followed it; of the heartless and disgusting cruelty which made the prisoners death a foregone conclusion at his mock trial; or of the deeds worse than butchery which characterized the last scene. Still, before quitting the revolting subject, there is one point that deserves remark, as it seems to illustrate the feeling entertained by the leaders themselves. On the night of the murder the body was interred in a very deep hole which had been dug within the walls of the fort. Two clergymen had asked permission to inter the remains in either of their churches, but this request had been denied. On the anniversary of the murder, namely, the 4th March, 1871, other powers being then predominant in Fort Garry, a large crowd gathered at the spot where the murdered man had been interred, for the purpose of exhuming the body. After digging for some time they came to an oblong box or coffin in which the remains had been placed, but it was empty, the interment within the walls had been a mock ceremony, and the final resting-place of the body lies hidden in mystery. Now there is one thing very evident from the fact, and that is that Riel and his immediate followers were themselves conscious of the enormity of the deed they had committed, for had they believed that the taking of this man's life was really an execution justified upon any grounds of military or political necessity, or a forfeit fairly paid as price for crimes committed, then the hole inside the gateway of Fort Garry would have held its skeleton, and the midnight interment would not have been a senseless lie. The murderer and the law both take life--it is only the murderer who hides under the midnight shadows the body of his victim.

CHAPTER FOUR.

Chicago--"Who is S. B. D.?"--Milwaukie--The Great Fusion-Wisconsin--The Sleeping-car--The Train Boy-Minnesota--St. Paul--I start for Lake Superior--The Future City--"Bust up" and "Gone on"--The End of the Track.

ALAS! I have to go a long way back to the city of Toronto, where I had just completed the purchase of a full costume of a Western borderer. On the 10th of June I crossed the Detroit River from Western Canada to the State of Michigan, and travelling by the central railway of that state reached the great city of Chicago on the following day. All Americans, but particularly all Western Americans, are very proud of this big city, which is not yet as old as many of its inhabitants, and they are justly proud of it. It is by very much the largest and the richest of the new cities of the New World. Maps made fifty years ago will be searched in vain for Chicago. Chicago was then a swamp where the skunks, after whom it is called, held undisputed revels. To-day Chicago numbers about 300,000 souls, and it is about "the livest city in our great Republic; sir."

Chicago lies almost 1000 miles due west of New York. A traveller leaving the latter city, let us say on Monday morning, finds himself on Tuesday at eight o'clock in the evening in Chicago-one thousand miles in thirty-four hours. In the meantime he will have eaten three meals and slept soundly "on board" his palace-car, if he is so minded. For many hundred miles during the latter portion of his journey he will have noticed great tracts of swamp and forest, with towns and cities and settlements interspersed between; and then, when these tracts of swamp and unreclaimed forest seem to be increasing instead of diminishing, he comes all of a sudden upon a vast, full-grown, bustling city, with tall chimneys sending out much smoke, with heavy horses dragging great: drays of bulky freight through thronged and busy streets, and with tall-masted ships and whole fleets of steamers lying packed against the crowded quays. He has begun to dream himself in the West, and lo! there rises up a great city. "But is not this the West?" will ask the new-comer from the Atlantic states. "Upon your own showing we are here 1000 miles from New York, by water 1500 miles to Quebec; surely this must be the West?" No; for in this New World the West is ever on the move. Twenty years ago Chicago was West; ten years ago it was Omaha; then it was Salt Lake City, and now it is San Francisco on the Pacific Ocean.

This big city, with its monster hotels and teeming traffic, was no new scene to me, for I had spent pleasant days in it three years before. An American in America is a very pleasant fellow. It is true that on many social points and habits his views may differ from ours in a manner very shocking to our prejudices, insular or insolent, as these prejudices of ours too frequently are; but meet him with fair allowance for the fact that there may be two sides to a question, and that a man may not tub every morning and yet be a good fellow, and in nine cases of ten you will find him most agreeable, a little inquisitive perhaps to know your peculiar belongings, but equally ready to impart to you the details of every item connected with his business--altogether a very jolly every-day companion when met on even basis. If you happen to be a military man, he will call you Colonel or General, and expect similar recognition: of rank by virtue of his volunteer services in the 44th: Illinois, or 55th Missourian. At present, and for many years to come, it is and will be a safe method of beginning any observation to a Western American with "I say, General," and on no account ever to get below the rank of field officer when addressing anybody holding a socially smaller position than that of bar-keeper. Indeed major-generals were as plentiful in the United States at the termination of the great rebellion as brevet-majors were in the British service at the close of the Crimean campaign. It was at Plymouth, I think, that a grievance was established by a youngster on the score that he really could not spit out of his own window without hitting a brevet major outside; and it was in a Western city that the man threw his stick at a dog across the road, "missed that dawg, sir, but hit five major-generals on t'other side, and 'twasn't a good day for major-generals either, sir." Not less necessary than knowledge of social position is knowledge of the political institutions and characters of the West. Not to know Rufus P. W. Smidge, or Ossian W. Dodge of Minnesota, is simply to argue yourself utterly unknown. My first experience of Chicago fully impressed me with this fact. I had made the acquaintance of an American gentleman "on board" the train, and as we approached the city along the sandy margin of Lake Michigan he kindly pointed out the buildings and public institutions of the neighbourhood.

"There, sir," he finally said, "there is our new monument to Stephen B. Douglas."

I looked in the direction indicated, and beheld some blocks of granite in course of erection into a pedestal. I confess to having been entirely ignorant at the time as to what claim Stephen B. Douglas may have had to this public recognition of his worth, but the tone of my informant's voice was sufficient to warn me that everybody knew Stephen B. Douglas, and that ignorance of his career might prove hurtful to the feelings of my new acquaintance, so I carefully refrained from showing by word or look the drawback under which I laboured. There was with me, however, a travelling companion who, to an ignorance of Stephen B. D. fully equal to mine own, added a truly British indignation that monumental honours should be bestowed upon one whose fame was still faint across the Atlantic. Looking partly at the monument, partly at our American informant, and partly at me, he hastily ejaculated, "Who the devil was Stephen B. Douglas?"

Alas! the murder was out, and out in its most aggravating form. I hastily attempted a rescue. "Not know who Stephen B. Douglas was?" I exclaimed, in a tone of mingled reproof and surprise. "Is it possible you don't know who Stephen B. Douglas was?"

Nothing cowed by the assumption of knowledge implied by my question, my fellow-traveller was not to be done. "All deuced fine," he went on, "I'll bet you a fiver you don't know who he was either!"

I kicked at him under the seat of the carriage, but it was of no use, he persisted in his reckless offers of "laying fivers," and our united ignorance stood fatally revealed.

Round the city of Chicago stretches upon three sides a vast level prairie, a meadow larger than the area of England and Wales, and as fertile as the luxuriant vegetation of thousands of years decaying under a semi-tropic sun could make it. Illinois is in round numbers 400 miles from north to south, its greatest breadth being about 200 miles. The Mississippi, running in vast curves along the entire length of its western frontier for 700 miles, bears away to southern ports the rich burden of wheat and Indian corn. The inland sea of Michigan carries on its waters the wealth of the northern portion of the state to the Atlantic seaboard. The Ohio, flowing south and west, unwaters the south-eastern counties, while 5500 miles of completed railroad traverse the interior of the state. This 5500 miles of iron road is a significant fact--5500 miles of railway in the compass of a single western state! More than all Hindostan can boast of, and nearly half the railway mileage of the United Kingdom. Of this immense system of interior connexion Chicago is the centre and heart. Other great centres of commerce have striven to rival the City of the Skunk, but all have failed; and to-day, thanks to the dauntless energy of the men of Chicago, the garden state of the Union possesses this immense extent of railroad, ships its own produce, north, east, and south, and boasts a population scarcely inferior to that of many older states; and yet it is only fifty years ago since William Cobbett laboured long and earnestly to prove that English emigrants who pushed on into the "wilderness of the Illinois went straight to misery and ruin."

Passing through Chicago, and going out by one of the lines running north along the shore of Lake Michigan, I reached the city of Milwaukie late in the evening. Now the city of Milwaukie stands above 100 miles north of Chicago and is to the State of Wisconsin what its southern neighbour (100 miles in the States is nothing) is to Illinois. Being, also some 100 miles nearer to the entrance to Lake Michigan, and consequently nearer by water to New York and the Atlantic, Milwaukie caries off no small share of the export wheat trade of the North-west. Behind it lie the rolling prairies of Wisconsin, Iowa, and Minnesota, the three wheat-growing states of the American Union. Scandinavia, Germany, and Ireland have made this portion of America their own, and in the streets of Milwaukie one hears the guttural sounds of the Teuton and the deep brogue of the Irish Celt mixed in curious combinations. This railway-station at Milwaukie is one of the great distributing points of the in-coming flood from Northern Europe. From here they scatter far and wide over the plains which lie between Lake Michigan and the head-waters of the Mississippi. No one stops to look at these people as they throng the wooden platform and fill the sheds at the depot, the sight is too common to cause interest now, and yet it is a curious sight this entry of the outcasts into the promised land. Tired, travel-stained, and worn come the fair-haired crowd of men and women and many children, eating all manner of strange food while they rest, and speaking all manner of strange tongues, carrying the most uncouth shapeless boxes that trunk-maker of Bergen or Upsal can devise--such queer oval red-and-green painted wooden cases, more like boxes to hold musical instruments than for the Sunday kit of Hans or Christian--clothing much soiled and worn by lower-deck lodgment and spray of mid-Atlantic roller, and dust of that 1100 miles of railroad since New York was left behind, but still with many traces, under dust and seediness, of Scandinavian rustic fashion; altogether a homely people, but destined ere long to lose every vestige of their old Norse habits under the grindstone of the great mill they are now entering. That vast human machine Which grinds Celt and Saxon, Teuton and Dane, Fin and Goth into the same image and likeness of the inevitable Yankee--grinds him too into that image in one short generation, and oftentimes in less; doing it without any apparent outward pressure or any tyrannical law of language or religion, but nevertheless beating out, welding, and amalgamating the various conflicting races of the Old World into the great American people. Assuredly the world has never witnessed any experiment of so gigantic a nature as this immense fusion of the Caucasian race now going on before our eyes in North America. One asks oneself, with feelings of dread, what is to be the result? Is it to eliminate from the human race the evil habits of each nationality, and to preserve in the new one the noble characteristics of all? I say one asks the question with a feeling of dread, for it is the question of the well-being, of the whole human family of the future, the question of the advance or retrogression of the human race. No man living can answer that question. Time alone can solve it; but one thing is certain-so far the experiment bodes ill for success. Too often the best and noblest attributes of the people wither and die out by the process of transplanting. The German preserves inviolate his love of lager, and leaves behind him his love of Fatherland. The Celt, Scotch or Irish, appears to eliminate from his nature many of those traits of humour of which their native lands are so pregnant. It may be that this is only the beginning, that a national decomposition of the old distinctions must occur before the new elements can arise, and that from it all will come in the fulness of time a regenerated society:--

"Sin itself be found, A cloudy porch oft opening on the sun."

But at present, looking abroad over the great seething mass of American society, there seems little reason to hope for required alteration. The dollar must cease to be the only God, and that old, old proverb that "honesty is the best policy" must once more come into fashion.

Four hundred and six miles intervene between Milwaukie, in the State of Wisconsin, and St. Paul, the capital and principal city of the State of Minnesota. About half that distance lies through the State of Wisconsin, and the remaining half is somewhat unequally divided between Iowa and Minnesota. Leaving Milwaukie at eleven o'clock a.m., one reaches the Mississippi at Prairie-du-Chien at ten o'clock same night; here a steamer ferries the broad swift-running stream, and at North Macgregor, on the Iowa shore, a train is in waiting to take on board the now sleepy passengers. The railway sleeping-car is essentially an American institution. Like every other institution, it has its critics, favourable and severe. On the one hand, it is said to be the acme of comfort; on the other, the essence of unrest. But it is just what might be expected under the circumstances, neither one thing nor the other. No one in his senses would prefer to sleep in a bed which was being borne violently along over rough and uneven iron when he could select a stationary resting-place. On the other hand, it is a very great saving of time and expense to travel for some eighty or one hundred consecutive hours, and this can only be effected by means of the sleeping-car. Take this distance, from New York to St. Paul, as an instance. It is about 1450 miles, and it can be accomplished in sixty-four hours. Of course one cannot expect to find oneself as comfortably located as in an hotel; but, all things considered, the balance of advantage is very much on the side of the sleeping-car. After a night or two one becomes accustomed to the noise and oscillation; the little peculiarities incidental to turning-in in rather a promiscuous manner with ladies old and young, children in arms and out of arms, vanish before the force of habit; the necessity of making an early rush to the lavatory appliances in the morning, and there securing a plentiful supply of water and clean towels, becomes quickly apparent, and altogether the sleeping-car ceases to be a thing of nuisance and is accepted as an accomplished fact. The interior arrangements of the car are conducted as follows. A passage runs down the centre from one door to the other; on either side are placed the berths or "sections" for sleeping; during the day-time these form seats, and are occupied by such as care to take them in the ordinary manner of railroad cars. At night, however, the whole car undergoes a complete transformation. A negro attendant commences to make down the beds. This operation is performed by drawing out, after the manner of telescopes, portions of the car heretofore looked upon as immoveable; from various receptacles thus rendered visible he extracts large store of blankets, mattresses, bolsters, pillows, sheets, all which he arranges after the usual method of such articles. His work is done speedily and without noise or bustle, and in a very short time the interior of the car presents the spectacle of a long, dimly lighted passage, having on either side the striped damask curtains which partly shroud the berths behind them. Into these berths the passengers soon withdraw themselves, and all goes quietly till morning-unless, indeed, some stray turning bridge has been left turned over one of the numerous creeks that underlie the track, or the loud whistle of "brakes down" is the short prelude to one of the many disasters of American railroad travel. There are many varieties of the sleeping-car, but the principle and mode of procedure are identical in each. Some of those constructed by Messrs. Pullman and Wagner are as gorgeously decorated as gilding, plating, velvet, and damask can make them. The former gentleman is likely to live long after his death in the title of his cars. One takes a Pullman (of course, only a share of a Pullman) as one takes a Hansom. Pullman and sleeping-car have become synonymous terms likely to last the wear of time. Travelling from sunrise to sunset through a country which offers but few changes to the eye, and at a rate which in the remoter districts seldom exceeds twenty miles an hour, is doubtless a very tiresome occupation; still it has much to relieve the tedium of what under the English system of railroad travel would be almost insupportable. The fact of easy communication being maintained between the different cars renders the passage from one car to another during motion a most feasible undertaking. One can visit the various cars and inspect their occupants, and to a man travelling to obtain information this is no small boon. Americans are always ready to enter into conversation, and though many queer fish will doubtless be met with in such interviews, still as one is certain to fall in with persons from all parts of the Union--easters, Southerners, Western men, and Californians--the experiment of "knocking around the cars" is well worth the trial of any person who is not above taking human nature, as we take the weather, just as it comes.

The individual known by the title of "train-boy" is also worth some study. He is oftentimes a grown-up man, but more frequently a most precocious boy; he is the agent for some enterprising house in Chicago, New York, or Philadelphia, or some other large town, and his aim is to dispose of a very miscellaneous collection of mental and bodily nourishment. He usually commences operations with the mental diet, which he serves round in several courses. The first course consists of works of a high moral character standard English novels in American reprints, and works of travel or biography. These he lays beside each passenger, stopping now and then to recommend one or the other for some particular excellence of morality or binding. Having distributed a portion through the car, he passes into the next car, and so through the train. After a few minutes delay he returns again to pick up the books and to settle with any one who may be disposed to retain possession of one. After the lapse of a very short time he reappears with the second course of literature. This usually consists of a much lower standard of excellence --Yankee fun, illustrated periodicals of a feeble nature, and cheap reprints of popular works. The third course, which soon follows, is, however, a very much lower one, and it is a subject for regret on the part of the moralist that the same powers of persuasion which but a little time ago were put forth to advocate the sale of some works of high moral excellence should now be exerted to push a vigorous circulation of the "Last Sensation," "The Dime Illustrated," "New York under Gas light," "The Bandits of the Rocky Mountains," and other similar productions. These pernicious periodicals having been shown around, the train-boy evidently becomes convinced that mental culture requires from him no further effort; he relinquishes that portion of his labour and devotes all his energies to the sale of the bodily nourishment, consisting of oranges and peaches, according to season, of a very sickly and uninviting description; these he follows with sugar in various preparations of stickiness, supplementing the whole with pea-nuts and crackers. In the end he becomes without any doubt a terrible nuisance; one conceives a mortal hatred for this precocious pedlar who with his vile compounds is ever bent upon forcing you to purchase his wares. He gets, he will tell you, a percentage on his sales of ten cents in the dollar; if you are going a long journey, he will calculate to sell you a dollar's worth of his stock. You are therefore worth to him ten cents. Now you cannot do better in his first round of high moral literature than present him at once with this ten cents, stipulating that on no account is he to invite your attention, press you to buy, or offer you any candy, condiment, or book during the remainder of the journey. If you do this you will get out of the train-boy at a reasonable rate.

Going to sleep as the train works its way slowly up the grades which lead to the higher level of the State of Iowa from the waters of Mississippi one sinks into a state of dim consciousness of all that is going on in the long carriage. The whistle of the locomotive--which, by the way, is very much more melodious than the one in use in England, being softer, deeper, and reaching to a greater distance-the roll of the train into stations, the stop and the start, all become, as it were, blended into uneasy sleep, until daylight sets the darkey at his work of making up the sections. When the sun rose we were well into Minnesota, the-most northern of the Union States. Around on every side stretched the great wheat lands of the North-west, that region whose farthest limits lie far within the territories where yet the red man holds his own. Here, in the south of Minnesota, one is only on the verge of that great wheat region. Far beyond the northern limit of the state it stretches away into latitudes unknown, save to the fur trader and the red man, latitudes which, if you tire not on the road, good reader, you and I may journey into together.

The City of St. Paul, capital and chief town of the State of Minnesota, gives promise of rising to a very high position among the great trade centres of America. It stands almost at the head of the navigation of the Mississippi River, about 2050 miles from New Orleans; not that the great river has its beginning here or in the vicinity, its cradle lies far to the north, 700 miles along the stream. But the Falls of St. Anthony, a few miles above St. Paul, interrupt all navigation, and the course of the river for a considerable distance above the fall is full of rapids and obstructions. Immediately above and below St. Paul the Mississippi River receives several large tributary streams from north-east and north west; the St. Peter's or Minnesota River coming from near the Coteau of the Missouri, and the St. Croix unwatering the great tract of pine land which lies West of Lake Superior; but it is not alone to water communication that St. Paul owes its commercial importance. With the same restless energy of the Northern American, its leading men have looked far into the future, and shaped their course for later times; railroads are stretching out in every direction to pierce the solitude of the yet uninhabited prairies and pine forests of the North. There is probably no part of the world in which the inhabitants are so unhealthy as in America; but the life is more trying than the climate, the constant use of spirit taken "straight," the incessant chewing of tobacco with its disgusting accompaniment, the want of healthier exercise, the habit of eating in a hurry, all tend to cut short the term of man's life in the New World.' Nowhere have I seen so many young wrecks. "Yes, sir, we live fast here," said a general officer to me one day on the Missouri; "And we die fast too," echoed a major from another part of the room. As a matter of course, places possessing salubrious climates are crowded with pallid seekers after health, and as St. Paul enjoys a dry and bracing atmosphere from its great elevation above the sea level, as well as from the purity of the surrounding prairies, its hotels--and they are many--are crowded with the broken wrecks of half the Eastern states; some find what they seek, but the majority come to Minnesota only to die.

Business connected with the supply of the troops during the coming winter in Red River, detained me for some weeks in Minnesota, and as the letters which I had despatched upon my arrival giving the necessary particulars regarding the proposed arrangements, required at least a week to obtain replies to, I determined to visit in the interim the shores of Lake Superior. Here I would glean what tidings I could of the progress of the Expedition, from whose base at Fort William, I would be only 100 miles distant, as well as examine the% chances of Fenian intervention, so much talked of in the American newspapers, as likely to place in peril the flank of the expeditionary force as it followed the devious track of swamp and forest which has on one side Minnesota, and on the other the Canadian Dominion.

Since my departure from Canada the weather had been intensely warm: pleasant in Detroit, warm in Chicago, hot in Milwaukie, and sweltering, blazing in St. Paul, would have aptly described the temperature, although the last named city is some hundred miles more to the north than the first. But latitude is no criterion of summer heat in America, and the short Arctic summer of the Mackenzie River knows often a fiercer heat than the swamp lands of the Carolinas. So, putting together a very light field-kit, I started early one morning from St. Paul for the new town of Duluth, on the extreme westerly end of Lake Superior.

Duluth, I was told, was the very newest of new towns, in fact it only had an existence of eighteen months; as may be inferred, it had no past, but any want in that respect was compensated for in its marvellous future. It was to be the great grain emporium of the North-west; it was to kill St. Paul, Milwaukie, Chicago, and half-a-dozen other thriving towns; its murderous propensities seemed to have no bounds; lots were already selling at fabulous prices, and everybody seemed to have Duluth in some shape or other on the brain. To reach this paradise of the future I had to travel 100 miles by the Superior and Mississippi railroad, to a halting-place known as the End of the Track-a name which gave a very accurate idea of its whereabouts and general capabilities. The line was, in fact, in course of formation, and was being rapidly pushed forward from both ends with a view to its being opened through by the 1st day of August. About forty miles north-east of St. Paul we entered the region of pine forest. At intervals of ten or twelve miles the train stopped at places bearing high-sounding titles, such as Rush City, Pine City; but upon examination one looked in vain for any realization of these names, pines and rushes certainly were plentiful enough, but the city part of the arrangement was nowhere visible. Upon asking a fellow-passenger for some explanation of the phenomena, he answered, "Guess there was a city hereaway last year, but it busted up or gone on." Travellers unacquainted with the vernacular of America might have conjured up visions of a catastrophe not less terrible than that of Pompeii or Herculaneum, but an earlier acquaintance of Western cities had years before taught me to comprehend such phrases. In the autumn of 1867 I had visited the prairies of Nebraska, along the banks of the Platte River. Buffalo were numerous on the sandy plains which form the hunting-grounds of the Shienne and Arapahoe Indians, and amongst the vast herds the bright October days passed quickly enough. One day, in company with an American officer, we were following, as usual, a herd of buffalo, when we came upon a town standing silent and deserted in the middle the Trairie. "That," said the American, "is Kearney City; it did a good trade in the old wagon times, but it busted up when the railroad went on farther west; the people moved on to North Platte and Julesburg--guess there's only one man left in it now, and he's got snakes in his boots the hull season." Marvelling what manner of man this might be who dwelt alone in the silent city, we rode on. One house showed some traces of occupation, and in this house dwelt the man. We had passed through the deserted grass-grown street, and were again on the prairie, when a shot rang out behind us, the bullet cutting up the dust away to the left. "By G---- he's on the shoot," cried our friend; "ride, boys!" and so we rode. Much has been written and said of cities old and new, of Aztec and Peruvian monuments, but I venture to offer to the attention of the future historian of America this sample of the busted up city of Kearney and its solitary indweller, who had snakes in his boots and was on the shoot.

After that explanation of a "busted-up" and "gone-on" city, I was of course sufficiently well "posted" not to require further explanation as to the fate of Pine and Rush Cities; but had I entertained any doubts upon the subject, the final stoppage of the train at Moose Lake, or City, would have effectually dispelled them. For there stood the portions of Rush and Pine Cities which had not "bust up," but had simply "gone on." Two shanties, with a few outlying sheds, stood on either side of the track, which here crossed a clear running forest stream. Passenger communication ended at this point; the rails were laid down for a distance of eight miles farther, but only the "construction train," with supplies, men, etc. proceeded to that point. Track-laying was going on at the rate of three miles a day, I was informed, and the line would soon be opened to the Dalles of the St. Louis River, near the hecad of Lake Superior. The heat all day had been very great, and it was refreshing to get out of the dusty car, even though the shanties, in which eating, drinking, and sleeping were supposed to be carried on, were of the very lowest description. I had made the acquaintance of the express agent, a gentleman connected with the baggage department of the train, and during the journey he had taken me somewhat into his confidence on the matter of the lodging and entertainment which were to be found in the shanties. "The food ain't bad," he said, "but that there shanty of Tom's licks creation for bugs." This terse and forcibly expressed opinion made me select the interior of a wagon, and some fresh hay, as a place of rest, where, in spite of vast numbers of mosquitoes, I slept the sleep of the weary.

The construction train started from Moose City at six o'clock a.m., and as the stage, which was supposed to connect with the passenger train and carry forward its human freight to Superior City was filled to overflowing, I determined to take advantage of the construction train, and travel on it as far as it would take me. A very motley group of lumberers, navvies, and speculators assembled for breakfast at five o'clock a.m. at Tom's table, and although I cannot quite confirm the favourable opinion of my friend the express agent as to the quality of the viands which graced it, I can at least testify to the vigour with which the "guests" disposed of the pork and beans, the molasses and dried apples which Tom, with foul fingers, had set before them. Seated on the floor of a waggon in the construction train, in the midst of navvies of all countries and ages, I reached the end of the track while the morning sun was yet low in the east. I had struck up a kind of partnership for the journey with a pedlar Jew and an Ohio man, both going to Duluth, and as we had a march of eighteen miles to get through between the end of the track and the town of Fond-du-Lac, it became necessary to push on before the sun had reached his midday level; so, shouldering our baggage, we left the busy scene of track-laying and struck out along the graded line for the Dalles of the St. Louis. Up to this point the line had been fully levelled, and the walking was easy enough, but when the much-talked of Dalles were reached a complete change took place, and the toil became excessive. The St. Louis River, which in reality forms the headwater of the great St. Lawrence, has its source in the dividing ridge between Minnesota and the British territory. From these rugged Laurentian ridges it foams down in an impetuous torrent through wild pine-clad steeps of rock and towering precipice, apparently to force an outlet into the valley of the Mississippi, but at the Dalles it seems to have suddenly preferred to seek the cold waters of the Atlantic, and, bending its course abruptly to the east, it pours its foaming torrent into the great Lake Superior below the old French trading-post of Fond-du-Lac. The load which I carried was not of itself a heavy one, but its weight became intolerable under the rapidly increasing heat of the sun and from the toilsome nature of the road. The deep narrow gorges over which the railway was to be carried were yet unbridged, and we had to let ourselves down the steep yielding embankment to a depth of over 100 feet, and then clamber up the other side almost upon hands and knees-this under a sun that beat down between the hills with terrible intensity on the yellow sand of the railway cuttings! The Ohio man carried no baggage, but the Jew was heavily laden, and soon fell behind. For a time I kept pace with my light companion; but soon I too was obliged to lag, and about midday found myself alone in the solitudes of the Dalles. At last there came a gorge deeper and steeper than any thing that had preceded it, and I was forced to rest long before attempting its almost perpendicular ascent. When I did reach the top, it was to find myself thoroughly done up--the sun came down on the side of the embankment as though it would burn the sandy soil into ashes, not a breath of air moved through the silent hills, not a leaf stirred in the forest. My load was more than I could bear, and again I had to lie down to avoid falling down. Only once before had I experienced a similar sensation of choking, and that was in toiling through a Burmese swamp, snipe-shooting under a midday sun. How near that was to sun-stroke, I can't say; but I don't think it could be very far. After a little time, I saw, some distance down below, smoke rising from a shanty. I made my way with no small difficulty to the door, and found the place full of some twenty or more rough-bearded looking men sitting down to dinner.

"About played out, I guess?" said one. "Wall, that sun is h--; any how, come in and have a bit. Have a drink of tea or some vinegar and water."

They filled me out a literal dish of tea, black and boiling; and I drained the tin with a feeling of relief such as one seldom knows. The place was lined round with bunks like the forecastle of a ship. After a time I rose to depart and asked the man who acted as cook how much there was to pay.

"Not a cent, stranger;" and so I left my rough hospitable friends, and, gaining the railroad, lay down to rest until the fiery sun had got lower in the west. The remainder of the road was thronged with gangs of men at work along it, bridging, blasting, building, and levelling--strong able-bodied fellows fit for any thing. Each gang was under the superintendence of a railroad "boss," and all seemed to be working well. But then two dollars a head per diem will make men work well even under such a sun.

CHAPTER FIVE.

Lake Superior--The Dalles of the St. Louis--The North Pacific Railroad--Fond-du-Lac-Duluth--Superior City--The Great Lake--A Plan to dry up Niagara--Stage Driving--Tom's Shanty again--St. Paul and its Neighbourhood.

ALMOST in the centre of the Dalles I passed the spot where the Northern Pacific Railroad had on that day turned its first sod, commencing its long course across the continent. This North Pacific Railroad is destined to play a great part in the future history of the United States; it is the second great link which is to bind together the Atlantic and Pacific States (before twenty years there will be many others). From Puget Sound on the Pacific to Duluth on Lake Superior is about 2200 miles, and across this distance the North Pacific Railroad is to run. The immense plains of Dakota, the grassy uplands of Montana and Washington, and the centre of the State of Minnesota will behold ere long this iron road of the North Pacific Company piercing their lonely wilds. "Red Cloud" and "Black Eagle" and "Standing Buffalo" may gather their braves beyond the Coteau to battle against this steam-horse which scares their bison from his favourite breeding grounds on the scant pastures of the great Missouri plateau; but all their efforts will be in vain, the dollar will beat them out. Poor Red Cloud! in spite of thy towering form and mighty strength, the dollar is mightier still, and the fiat has gone forth before which thou and thy braves must pass away from the land! Very tired and covered deep with the dust of railroad cuttings, I reached the collection of scattered houses which bears the name of Fond-du Lac. Upon inquiring at the first house which I came to as to the whereabouts of the hotel, I was informed by a sour-visaged old female, that if I wanted to drink and get drunk, I must go farther on; but that if I wished to behave in a quiet and respectable manner, and could live %without liquor, I could stay in her house, which was at once post office, Temperance Hotel, and very respectable. Being weary and footsore, I. did not feel disposed to seek farther, for the place looked clean, the river was close at hand, and the whole aspect of the scene was suggestive of rest. In the evening hours myriads of mosquitoes and flying things of minutest size came forth from the wooded hills and did their best towards making life a misery; so bad were they that I welcomed a passing navvy who dropped in as a real godsend.

"You're come up to look after work on this North Pacific Railroad, I guess?" he commenced-he was a Southern Irish man, but "guessed" all the same--"well, now, look here, the North Pacific Railroad will never be like the U.P. (Union Pacific) I worked there, and I know what it was; it was bully, I can tell you. A chap lay in his bunk all day and got two dollars and a half for doing it; ay, and bit the boss on the head with his shovel if the boss gave him any d---- chat. No, sirree, the North Pacific will never be like that."

I could not help thinking that it was perhaps quite as well for the North Pacific Railroad Company and the boss if they never were destined to rival the Union Pacific Company as pictured by my companion; but I did not attempt to say so, as it might have come under the heading of "d---- chat," worthy only of being replied to by that convincing argument, the shovel.

A good night's sleep and a swim in the St. Louis river banished all trace of toil. I left Fond-du-Lac early in the afternoon, and, descending by a small steamer the many-winding St. Louis River, soon came in sight of the town of Duluth. The heat had become excessive; the Bay of St. Louis, shut in on all sides by lofty hills, lay under a mingled mass of thunder-cloud and sunshine; far out in Lake Superior vivid lightnings flashed over the gloomy water and long rolls of thunder shook the hills around. On board our little steamboat the atmosphere was stifling, and could not have been short of 100 degrees in the coolest place (it was 93 at six o'clock same evening in the hotel at Duluth); there was nothing for it but to lie quietly on a wooden bench and listen to the loud talking of some fellow-passengers. Three of the hardest of hard cases were engaged in the mental recreation of "'swapping lies;" their respective exchanges consisting on this occasion of feats of stealing; the experiences of one I recollect in particular. He had stolen an axe from a man on the North Pacific Railroad and a few days later sold him the same article. This Piece of knavery was received as the acme of cuteness; and I well recollect the language in which the brute wound up his self-laudations: "If any chap can steal faster than me, let him."

As we emerged from the last bend of the river and stood across the Bay of St. Louis, Duluth, in all its barrenness, stood before us. The future capital of the Lakes, the great central port of the continent, the town whose wharves were to be laden with the teas of China and the silks of Japan stood out on the rocky north shore of Lake Superior, the sorriest spectacle of city that eye of man could look upon-wooden houses scattered at intervals along a steep ridge from which the forest had been only partially cleared, houses of the smallest possible limits growing out of a reedy marsh, which lay between lake and ridge, tree-stumps and lumber standing in street and landing-place, the swamps croaking with bull-frogs and passable only by crazy looking planks of tilting proclivities--over all, a sun fit for a Carnatic coolie, and around, a forest vegetation in whose heart the memory of Arctic winter rigour seemed to live for ever. Still, in spite of rock and swamp and icy winter, Yankee energy will triumph here as it has triumphed else where over kindred difficulties.

"There's got to be a Boss City hereaway on this end of the lake," said the captain of the little boat; and though he spoke with much labour of imprecation, both needless then and now, taking what might be termed a cursory view of the situation, he summed up the prospects of Duluth conclusively and clearly enough.

I cannot say I enjoyed a stay of two days in Duluth. Several new saloons (name for dram-shops, gaming-houses, and generally questionable places) were being opened for the first time to the public, and free drinks were consequently the rule. Now "free drinks" have generally a demoralizing tendency upon a community, but taken in connexion with a temperature of 98 degrees in the shade, they quickly develop into free revolvers and freer bowie-knives. Besides, the spirit of speculation was rampant in the hotel, and so many men had corner lots, dock locations, pine forests, and pre-empted lands to sell me, that nothing but flight prevented my becoming a large holder of all manner of Duluth securities upon terms that, upon the clearest showing, would have been ridiculously favourable to me. The principal object of my visit to Duluth was to discover if any settlement existed at the Vermilion Lakes, eighty miles to the north and not far from the track of the Expedition, a place which had been named to the military authorities in Canada as likely to form a base of attack for any filibusters who would be adventurous enough to make a dash at the communication of the expeditionary force. A report of the discovery of gold and silver mines around the Vermilion Lakes had induced a rush of miners there during the previous year; but the mines had all "bust up," and the miners had been blown away to other regions, leaving the plant and fixtures of quartz-crushing machinery standing drearily in the wilderness. These facts I ascertained from the engineer, who had constructed a forest track from Duluth to the mines, and into whose office I penetrated in quest of information. He, too, looked upon me as a speculator.

"Don't mind them mines," he said, after I had questioned him on all points of distance and road; "don't touch them mines; they're clean gone up. The gold in them mines don't amount to a row of pines, and there's not a man there now."

That evening there came a violent thunder-storm, which cleared and cooled the atmosphere; between ten o'clock in the morning and three in the afternoon the thermometer fell 30 degrees. Lake Superior had asserted its icy influence over the sun. Glad to get away from Duluth, I crossed the bay to Superior City, situated on the opposite, or Wisconsin shore of the lake. A curious formation of sand and shingle runs out from the shore of Duluth, forming a long narrow spit of land projecting far into Lake Superior. It bears the name of Minnesota Point, and has evidently been formed by the opposing influence of the east wind over the great expanse of the lake, and the current of the St. Louis River from the West. It has a length of seven miles, and is only a few yards in width. Close to the Wisconsin shore a break occurs in this long narrow spit, and inside this opening lies the harbour and city of Superior incomparably a better situation for a city and lake-port, level, sheltered, capacious; but, nevertheless, Superior City is doomed to delay, while eight miles off its young rival is rapidly rushing to wealth. This anomaly is easily explained. Duluth is pushed forward by the capital of the State of Minnesota, while the legislature of Wisconsin looks with jealous eye upon the formation of a second lake-port city which might draw off to itself the trade of Milwaukie.

In course of time, however, Superior City must rise, in spite of all hostility, to the very prominent position to which its natural advantages entitle it. I had not been many minutes in the hotel at Superior City before the trying and unsought character of land speculator was again thrust upon me.

"Now, stranger," said a long-legged Yankee, who, with his boots on the stove---the day had got raw and cold--and his knees considerably higher than his head, was gazing intently at me, "'I guess I've fixed you." I was taken aback by the sudden identification of my business, when he continued, "Yes, I've just fixed you. You air a Kanady speculator, ain't ye?" Not deeming it altogether wise to deny the correct ness of his fixing, I replied I had lived in Kanady for some time, but that I was not going to begin speculation until I had knocked round a little. An invitation to liquor soon followed. The disagreeable consequence resulting from this admission soon became apparent. I was much pestered towards evening by offers of investment in things varying from a sand-hill to a city-square, or what would infallibly in course of time develop into a city-square. A gentleman rejoicing in the name of Vose Palmer insisted upon inter viewing me until a protracted hour of the night, with a view towards my investing in straight drinks for him at the bar and in an extensive pine forest for myself some where on the north shore of Lake Superior. I have no doubt the pine forest is still in the market; and should any enterprising capitalist in this country feel disposed to enter into partnership on a basis of bearing all expenses himself, giving only the profits to his partner, he will find "Vose Palmer, Superior City, Wisconsin, United States," ever ready to attend to him.

Before turning our steps westward from this inland ocean of Superior, it will be well to pause a moment on its shore and look out over its bosom. It is worth looking at, for the world possesses not its equal. Four Hundred English miles in length, 50 miles across it, 600 feet above Atlantic level, 900 feet in depth-one vast spring of purest crystal water, so cold, that during summer months its waters are like ice itself, and so clear, that hundreds of feet below the surface the rocks stand out as distinctly as though seen through plate-glass. Follow in fancy the outpourings of this wonderful basin; seek its future course in Huron, Erie, and Ontario, in that wild leap from the rocky ledge which makes Niagara famous through the world. Seek it farther still, in the quiet loveliness of the Thousand Isles; in the whirl and sweep of the Cedar Rapids; in the silent rush of the great current under the rocks at the foot of Quebec. Ay, and even farther away still, down where the lone Laurentian Hills come forth to look again upon that water whose earliest beginnings they cradled along the shores of Lake Superior. There, close to the sounding billows of the Atlantic, 2000 miles from Superior, these hills--the only ones that ever last-guard the great gate by which the St. Lawrence seeks the sea.

There are rivers whose current, running red with the silt and mud of their soft alluvial shores, carry far into the ocean the record of their muddy progress; but this glorious river system, through its many lakes and various names, is ever the same crystal current, flowing pure from the fountain-head of Lake Superior. Great cities stud its shores; but they are powerless to dim the transparency of its waters. Steamships cover the broad bosom of its lakes and estuaries; but they change not the beauty of the water-no more than the fleets of the world mark the waves of the ocean. Any person looking at the map's of the region bounding the great lakes of North America will be struck by the absence of rivers flowing into Lakes Superior, Michigan, or Huron from the south; in fact, the drainage of the states bordering these lakes on the south is altogether carried off by the valley of the Mississippi-it follows that this valley of Mississippi is at a much lower level than the surface of the lakes. These lakes, containing an area of some 73,000 square miles, are therefore an immense reservoir held high over the level of the great Mississippi valley, from which they are separated by a barrier of slight elevation and extent.

It is not many years ago since an enterprising Yankee proposed to annihilate Canada, dry up Niagara, and "fix British creation" generally, by diverting the current of Lake Erie, through a deep canal, into the Ohio River; but should nature, in one of her freaks of earthquake, ever cause a disruption to this intervening barrier on the southern shores of the great northern lakes, the drying up of Niagara, the annihilation of Canada, and the divers disasters to British power, will in all probability be followed by the submersion of half of the Mississippi states under the waters of these inland seas.

On the 26th June I quitted the shores of Lake Superior and made my way back to Moose Lake. Without any exception, the road thither was the very worst I had ever travelled over--four horses essayed to drag a stage-waggon over, or rather, I should say, through, a track of mud and ruts impossible to picture. The stage fare amounted to $6, or 4s. for 34 miles. An extra dollar reserved the box-seat and gave me the double advantage of knowing what was coming in the rut line and taking another lesson in the idiom of the American stage-driver. This idiom consists of the smallest possible amount of dictionary words, a few Scriptural names rather irreverently used, a very large intermixture of "git-ups" and ejaculatory "his," and a general tendency to blasphemy all round. We reached Tom's shanty at dusk. As before, it was crowded to excess, and the memory of the express man's warning was still sufficiently strong to make me prefer the forest to "bunking in" with the motley assemblage; a couple of Eastern Americans shared with me the little camp. We made a fire, laid some boards on the ground, spread a blanket upon them, pulled the "mosquito bars" over our heads, and lay down to attempt to sleep. It was a vain effort; mosquitoes came out in myriads, little atoms of gnats penetrated through the netting of the "bars," and rendered rest or sleep impossible. At last, when the gnats seemed disposed to retire, two Germans came along, and, seeing our fire, commenced stumbling about our boards. To be roused at two o'clock a.m., when one is just sinking into obliviousness after four hours of useless struggle with unseen enemies, is provoking enough, but to be roused under such circumstances by Germans is simply unbearable.

At last daylight came. A bathe in the creek, despite the clouds of mosquitoes, freshened one up a little and made Tom's terrible table see less repulsive. Then came a long hot day in the dusty cars, until at length St. Paul was reached.

I remained at St. Paul some twelve days, detained there from day to day awaiting the arrival of letters from Canada relative to the future supply of the Expedition. This delay was at the time most irksome, as I too frequently pictured the troops pushing on towards Fort Garry while I was detained inactive in Minnesota; but one morning the American papers came out with news that the expeditionary forces had met with much delay in their first move from Thunder Bay; the road over which it was necessary for them to transport their boats, munitions, and supplies for a distance of forty-four miles from Superior to Lake Shebandowan was utterly impracticable, portions of it, indeed, had still to be made, bridges to be built, swamps to be corduroyed, and thus at the very outset of the Expedition a long delay became necessary. Of course, the American press held high jubilee over this check, which was represented as only the beginning of the end of a series of disasters. The British Expedition was never destined to reach Red River--swamps would entrap it, rapids would engulf it; and if, in spite of these obstacles, some few men did succeed in piercing the rugged wilderness, the trusty rifle of the Metis would soon annihilate the presumptive intruders. Such was the news and such were the comments I had to read day after day, as I anxiously scanned the columns of the newspapers for intelligence. Nor were these comments on the Expedition confined to prophecy of its failure from the swamps and rapids of the route: Fenian aid was largely spoken of by one portion of the press. Arms and ammunition, and hands to use them, were being pushed towards St. Cloud and the Red River to aid the free sons of the North-west to follow out their manifest destiny, which, of course, was annexation to the United States. But although these items made reading a matter of no pleasant description, there were other things to be done in the good city of St. Paul not without their special interest. The Falls of the Mississippi at St. Anthony, and the lovely little Fall of Minnehaha, lay only some seven miles distant. Minnehaha is a perfect little beauty; its bright sparkling waters, forming innumerable fleecy threads! of silk-like wavelets, seem to laugh over the rocky edge; so light and so lace-like is the curtain, that the sunlight streaming through looks like a lovely bride through some rich bridal veil. The Falls of St. Anthony are neither grand nor beautiful, and are utterly disfigured by the various sawmills that surround them.

The hotel in which I lodged at St. Paul was a very favourable specimen of the American hostelry; its proprietor was, of course, a colonel, so it may be presumed that he kept his company in excellent order. I had but few acquaintances in St. Paul, and had little to do besides study American character as displayed in dining-room, lounging-hall, and verandah, during the hot fine days; but when the hour of sunset came it was my wont to ascend to the roof of the building to look at the glorious panorama spread out before me-for sunset in America is of itself a sight of rare beauty, and the valley of the Mississippi never appeared to better advantage than when the rich hues of the western sun were gilding the steep ridges that over hang it.

CHAPTER SIX.

Our Cousins--Doing America--Two Lessons--St. Cloud--Sauk Rapids--"Steam Pudding or Pumpkin Pie?"--Trotting him out--Away for the Red River.

26

ENGLISHMEN who visit America take away with them two widely different sets of opinions. In most instances they have rushed through the land, note-book in hand, recording impressions and eliciting information. The visit is too frequently a first and a last one; the thirty-seven states are run over in thirty-seven days; then out comes the book, and the great question of America, socially and politically considered, is sealed for evermore. Now, if these gentlemen would only recollect that impressions, which are thus hastily collected must of necessity share the imperfection of all things done in a hurry, they would not record these hurriedly gleaned facts with such an appearance of infallibility, or, rather, they might be induced to try a second rush across the Atlantic before attempting that first rush into print. Let them remember that even the genius of Dickens was not proof against such error, and that a subsequent visit to the States caused no small amount of alteration in his impressions of America. This second visit should be a rule with every man who wishes to read aright, for his own benefit, or for that of others, the great book which America holds open to the traveller. Above all, the English traveller who enters the United States with a portfolio filled with letters of introduction will generally prove the most untrustworthy guide to those who follow him for information. He will travel from city to city, finding everywhere lavish hospitality and boundless kindness; at every hotel he will be introduced to several of "our leading citizens;" newspapers will report his progress, general-superintendents of railroads will pester him with free passes over half the lines in the Union; and he will take his departure from New York after a dinner at Delmonico's, the cartes of which will cost a dollar each. The chances are extremely probable that his book will be about as fair a representation of American social and political institutions as his dinner at Delmonico's would justly represent the ordinary cuisine throughout the Western States.

Having been fêted and free-passed through the Union, he of course comes away delighted with everything. If he is what is called a Liberal in politics, his political bias still further strengthens his favourable impressions of democracy and Delmonico; if he is a rigid Conservative, democracy loses half its terrors when it is seen across the Atlantic--just as widow-burning or Juggernaut are institutions much better suited to Bengal than they would be to Berkshire. Of course Canada and things Canadian are utterly beneath the notice of our traveller. He may, however, introduce them casually with reference to Niagara, which has a Canadian shore, or Quebec, which possesses a fine view; for the rest, America, past, present, and to come, is to be studied in New York, Boston, Cincinnati, St. Louis, and half a dozen other big places, and, with Niagara, Salt Lake City and San Francisco thrown in for scenic effect, the whole thing is complete. Salt Lake City is peculiarly valuable to the traveller, as it affords him much subject-matter for questionable writing. It might be well to recollect, however, that there really exists no necessity for crossing the Atlantic and travelling as far west as Utah in order to compose questionable books upon unquestionable subjects; similar materials in vast quantities exist much nearer home, and Pimlico and St. John's Wood will be found quite as prolific in "Spiritual Wives" and "Gothic" affinities as any creek or lake in the Western wilderness. Neither is it to be wondered at that so many travellers carry away with them a fixed idea that our cousins are cousins in heart as well as in relationship-the friendship is of the Delmonico type too. Those speeches made to the departing guest, those Pledges of brotherhood over the champagne glass, this "old lang syne" with hands held in Scotch fashion, all these are not worth much in the markets of brotherhood. You will be told that the hostility of the inhabitants of the United States towards England is confined to one class, and that class, though numerically large, is politically insignificant. Do not believe it for one instant: the hostility to England is universal; it is more deep rooted than any other feeling; it is an instinct and not a reason, and consequently possesses the dogged strength of unreasoning antipathy. I tell you, Mr. Bull, that were you pitted to-morrow against a race that had not one idea in kindred with your own, were you fighting a deadly struggle against a despotism the most galling on earth, were you engaged with an enemy whose grip was around your neck and whose foot was on your chest, that English-speaking cousin of yours over the Atlantic whose language is your language, whose literature is your literature, whose civil code is begotten from your digests of law would stir no hand, no foot, to save you, would gloat over your agony, would keep the ring while you were, being knocked out of all semblance of nation and power, and would not be very far distant when the moment came to hold a feast of eagles over your vast disjointed limbs. Make no mistake in this matter, and be not blinded by ties of kindred or belief. You imagine that because he is your cousin-sometimes even your very son-that he cannot hate you, and you nurse yourself in the belief that in a moment of peril the stars and stripes would fly alongside the old red cross. Listen one moment; we cannot go five miles through any State in the American Union without coming upon a square substantial building in which children are being taught one universal lesson-the history of how, through long years of blood and strife, their country came forth a nation from the bungling tyranny of Britain. Until five short years ago that was the one bit of history that went home to the heart of Young America, that Was the lesson your cousin learned, and still learns, in spite of later conflicts. Let us see what was the lesson your son had laid to heart. Well, your son learned his lesson, not from books, for too often he could not read, but he learned it in a manner which perhaps stamps it deeper into the mind than even letter-press or schoolmaster. He left you because you would not keep him, because you preferred grouse-moors and deer-forests in Scotland, or meadows and sheep-walks in Ireland to

27

him or his. He did not leave you as one or two from a household--as one who would go away and establish a branch connexion across the ocean; he went away by families, by clans, by kith and kin, for ever and for aye and he went away with hate in his heart and dark thoughts towards you who should have been his mother. It matters little that he has bettered himself and grown rich in the new land; that is his affair; so far as you were concerned, it was about even betting whether he went to the bottom of the Atlantic or to the top of the social tree-so, I say, to close this subject, that son and cousin owe you and give you, scant and feeblest love. You will find themn the firm friend of the Russian, because that Russian is likely to become your enemy in Herat, in Cabool, in Kashgar, or in Constantinople; you will find him the ally of the Prussian whenever Kaiser William, after the fashion of his tribe, orders his legions to obliterate the line between Holland and Germany, taking hold of that metaphorical pistol which you spent so many millions-to turn from your throat in the days of the first Napoleon. Nay, even should any woman-killing Sepoy put you to sore strait by indiscriminate and ruthless slaughter, he will be your cousin's friend, for the simple reason that he is your enemy.

But a study of American habits and opinions, however interesting in itself, was not calculated to facilitate in any way the solving of the problem which now beset me, namely, the further progress of my journey to the Northwest. The accounts which I daily received were not encouraging. Sometimes there came news that M. Riel had grown tired of his pre-eminence and was anxious to lay down his authority; at other times I heard of preparation made and making to oppose the Expedition by force, and of strict watch being maintained along the Pembina frontier to arrest and turn back all persons except such as were friendly to the Provisional Government.

Nor was my own position in St. Paul at all a pleasant one. The inquiries I had to make on subjects connected with the supply of the troops in Red River had made so many persons acquainted with my identity, that it soon became known that there was a British officer in the place--a knowledge which did not tend in any manner to make the days pleasant in themselves nor hopeful in the anticipation of a successful prosecution of my journey in the time to come. About the first week in July I left St. Paul for St. Cloud, seventy miles higher up on the Mississippi, having decided to wait no longer`` for instructions, but to trust to chance for further progress towards the North-west. "You will meet with no obstacle at this side of the line," said an American gentleman who was acquainted with the object of my journey, "but I won't answer for the other side;" and so, not knowing exactly how I was to get through to join the Expedition, but' determined to try it some way or other, I set out for Sauk Rapids and St. Cloud. Sauk Rapids, on the Mississippi River, is a city which has neither burst up nor gone on. It has thought fit to remain, without monument of any kind, where it originally located itself-on the left bank of the Mississippi, opposite the confluence of the Sauk River with the "Father of Waters." It takes its name partly from the Sauk River and partly from the rapids of the Mississippi which lie abreast of the town. Like many other cities, it had nourished feelings of the most deadly enmity. against its neighbours, and was to "kill creation" on every side; but these ideas of animosity have decreased considerably in lapse of time: Of course it possessed a newspaper--I believe it also possessed a church, but I did not see that edifice; the paper, however, I did see, and was much struck by the fact that the greater portion of the first page--the paper had only two-was taken up with a pictorial delineation of what Sauk Rapids would attain to in the future, when it had sufficiently developed its immense water-power; In the mean time previous to the development of said water-power-Sauk Rapids was not a bad sort of place: a bath at an hotel in St. Paul was a more expensive luxury than a dinner; but the Mississippi flowing by the door of the hotel at Sauk Rapids permitted free bathing in its waters. Any traveller in the United States will fully appreciate this condescension on the part of the great river. If a man wishes to be clean, he has to pay highly for the luxury. The baths which exist in the hotels are evidently meant for very rare and important occasions.

"I would like," said an American gentleman to a friend of mine travelling by railway, "I would like to show % you round our city, and I will call for you at the hotel."

"Thank you," replied my friend; "I have only to take a bath, and will be ready in half an hour."

"Take a bath!" answered the American; "why, you ain't sick, air you?"

There are not many commandments strictly adhered to in the United States; but had there ever existed a "Thou shalt not tub," the implicit obedience rendered to it would have been delightful, but perhaps, in that case, every American would have been a Diogenes.

The Russell House at Sauk Rapids was presided over by Dr. Chase. According to his card, Dr. Chase conferred more benefactions upon the human race for the very smallest remuneration than any man living. His hotel was situated in the loveliest portion of Minnesota, commanding the magnificent rapids of the Mississippi; his board and lodging were of the choicest description; horses and buggies were free, gratis, and medical attendance was also uncharged for. Finally, the card intimated that, upon turning over, still more astonishing revelations would meet the eye of the reader. Prepared for some terrible instance of humane abnegation on the part of Dr. Chase, I proceeded to do, as directed, and, turning over the card, read, "Present of a $500 greenback"!!! The gift of the green back was attended with some little drawback, inasmuch as it was conditional

28

upon paying to Dr. Chase the sum of $20,000 for the goodwill, etc., of his hotel, farm, and appurtenances, or procuring a purchaser for them at that figure, which was, as a matter of course, a ridiculously low one. Two damsels who assisted Dr. Chase in ministering to the wants of his guests at dinner had a very appalling manner of presenting to the frightened feeder his choice of viands. The solemn silence which usually pervades the dinner-table of an American hotel was nowhere more observable than in this Doctor's establishment; whether it was from the fact that each guest suffered under a painful knowledge of the superhuman efforts which the Doctor was making for his or her benefit, I cannot say; but I never witnessed the proverbially frightened appearance of the American people at meals to such a degree as at the dinner-table of the Sauk Hotel. When the damsels before alluded to commenced their peregrinations round the table, giving in terribly terse language the choice of meats, the solemnity of the proceeding could not have been exceeded. "Pork or beef?" "Pork," would answer the trembling feeder; "Beef or pork?" "Beef," would again reply the guest, grasping eagerly at the first name which struck upon his ear. But when the second course came round the damsels presented us with a choice of a very mysterious nature indeed. I dimly heard two names being uttered into the ears of my fellow-eaters, and I just had time to notice the paralyzing effect which the communication appeared to have upon them, when presently over my own shoulder I heard the mystic sound-I regret to say that at first these sounds entirely failed to present to my mind any idea of food or sustenance of known description, I therefore begged for a repetition of the words; this time there was no mistake about it, "Steam-pudding or pumpkin-pie?" echoed the maiden, giving me the terrible alternative in her most cutting tones; "Both!" I ejaculated, with equal distinctness, but, I believe, audacity unparalleled since the times of Twist. The female Bumble seemed to reel beneath the shock, and I noticed that after communicating her experience to her fellow waiting-woman, I was not thought of much account for the remainder of the meal.

Upon the day of my arrival at Sauk Rapids I had let it be known pretty widely that I was ready to become the purchaser of a saddle-horse, if any person had such an animal to dispose of. In the three following days the amount of saddle-horses produced in the neighbourhood was perfectly astonishing; indeed the fact of placing a saddle upon the back of any thing possessing four legs seemed to constitute the required animal; even a German--a "Dutchman'" came along with a miserable thing in horseflesh, sand-cracked and spavined, for which he only asked the trifling sum of $100. Two livery stables in St. Cloud sent up their superannuated stagers, and Dr. Chase had something to recommend of a very superior description. The end of it all was, that, declining to purchase any of the animals brought up for inspection, I found there was little chance of being able to get over the 400 miles which lay between St. Cloud and Fort Garry. It was now the 12th of July; I had reached the farthest limit of railroad communication, and before me lay 200 miles of partly settled country lying between the Mississippi and the Red River. It is true that a four-horse stage ran from St. Cloud to Fort Abercrombie on Red River, but that would only have conveyed me to about 300 miles distant from Fort Garry, and over that last 300 miles I could see no prospect of travelling. I had therefore determined upon procuring a horse and riding the entire way, and it was with this object that I had entered into these inspections of horseflesh already mentioned. Matters were in this unsatisfactory state on the 12th of July, when I was informed that the solitary steamboat which plied upon the waters of the Red River was about to make a descent to Fort Garry, and that a week would elapse before she would start from her moorings below Georgetown, a. station of the Hudson Bay Company situated 250 miles from St. Cloud. This was indeed the best of good news to me; I saw in it the long-looked-for chance of bridging this great stretch of 400 miles and reaching at last the Red River Settlement. I saw in it still more the prospect of joining at no very distant time the expeditionary force itself, after I had run the gauntlet of M. Riel and his associates, and although many obstacles yet remained to be overcome, and distances vast and wild had to be covered before that hope could be realized, still the prospect of immediate movement overcame every perspective difficulty; and glad indeed I was when from the top of a well-horsed stage I saw the wooden houses of St. Cloud disappear beneath the prairie behind me, and I bade good-bye for many a day to the valley of the Mississippi,

CHAPTER SEVEN.

North Minnesota--A beautiful Land--Rival Savages-Abercrombie--News from the North-Plans--A Lonely Shanty--The Red River--Prairies--Sunset-- Mosquitoes--Going North--A Mosquito Night--A Thunder-storm--A Prussian-- Dakota--I ride for it--The Steamer "International"--Pembina.

The stage-coach takes three days to run from St. Cloud to Fort Abercrombie, about 180 miles. The road was tolerably good, and many portions of the country were very beautiful to look at. On the second day one reaches the height of land between the Mississippi and Red Rivers, a region abounding in clear crystal lakes of every size and shape, the old home of the great Sioux nation, the true Minnesota of their dreams. Minnesota ("sky-coloured water"), how aptly did it describe that home which was no longer theirs! They have left it for ever; the

Norwegian and the Swede now call it theirs, and nothing remains of the red man save these sounding names of lake and river which long years ago he gave them. Along the margins of these lakes many comfortable dwellings nestle amongst oak openings and glades, and hill and valley are golden in summer with fields of wheat and corn, and little towns are springing up where twenty years ago the Sioux lodge-poles were the only signs of habitation; but one cannot look on this transformation without feeling, with Longfellow, the terrible surge of the white man, "whose breath, like the blast of the east wind, drifts evermore to the west the scanty smoke of the wigwams." What savages, too, are they, the successors of the old race--savages! not less barbarous because they do not scalp, or war-dance, or go out to meet the Ojibbeway in the woods or the Assineboine in the plains.

We had passed a beautiful sheet of water called Lake Osakis, and reached another lake not less lovely, the name of which I did not know.

"What is the name of this place?" I asked the driver who had stopped to water his horses.

"I don't know," he answered, lifting a bucket of water to his thirsty steeds; "some God-dam Italian name, I guess." This high rolling land which divides the waters flowing into the Gulf of Mexico from those of Hudson Bay lies at an elevation of 1600 feet above the sea level. It is rich in every thing that can make a country prosperous; and that portion of the "down-trodden millions," who "starve in the garrets of Europe," and have made their homes along that height of land, have no reason to regret their choice.

On the evening of the second day we stopped for the night at the old stockaded post of Pomme-de-Terre, not far from the Ottertail River. The place was foul beyond the power of words to paint it, but a "shake down" amidst the hay in a cow-house was far preferable to the society of man close by.

At eleven o'clock on the following morning we reached and crossed the Ottertail River, the main branch of the Red River, and I beheld with joy the stream upon whose banks, still many hundred miles distant, stood Fort Garry. Later in the day, having passed the great level expanse known as The Breckenridge Flats, the stage drew up at Fort Abercrombie, and I saw for the first time the yellow, muddy waters of the Red River of the North. Mr. Nolan, express agent, stage agent, and hotel keeper in the town of McAulyville, put me up for that night, and although the room which I occupied was shared by no less than five other individuals, he nevertheless most kindly provided me with a bed to myself. I can't say that I enjoyed the diggings very much. A person lately returned from Fort Garry detailed his experiences of that place and his interview with the President at some length. A large band of the Sioux Indians was ready to support the Dictator against all comers, and a vigilant watch was maintained upon the Pembina frontier for the purpose of excluding strangers who might attempt to enter from the United States; and altogether M. Riel was as securely established in Fort Garry as if there had not existed a red-coat in the universe. As for the Expedition, its failure was looked upon as a foregone conclusion; nothing had been heard of it excepting a single rumour, and that was one of disaster. An Indian coming from beyond Fort Francis, somewhere in the wilderness north of Lake Superior, had brought tidings to the Lake of the Woods, that forty Canadian soldiers had already been lost in one of the boiling rapids of the route. "Not a man will get through!" was the general verdict of society, as that body was represented at Mr. Nolan's hotel, and, truth' to say, society seemed elated at its verdict. All this, told to a roomful of Americans, had no very exhilarating effect upon me as I sat, unknown and unnoticed, on my portmanteau, a stranger to every one. When our luck seems at its lowest there is only one thing to be done, and that is to go on and try again. Things certainly looked badly, obstacles grew bigger as I got nearer to them--but that is a way they have, and they never grow smaller merely by being looked at; so I laid my plans for rapid movement. There was no horse or conveyance of any kind to be had from Abercrombie; but I discovered in the course of questions that the captain of the "International" steamboat on the Red River had gone to St. Paul a week before, and was expected to return to Abercrombie by the next stage, two days from this time; he had left a horse and Red River cart at Abercrombie, and it was his intention to start with this horse and cart for his steamboat immediately upon his arrival by stage from St. Paul. Now the boat "International" was lying at a part of the Red River known as Frog Point, distant by land 100 miles north from Abercrombie, and as I had no means of getting over this 100 miles, except through the agency of this horse and cart of the captain's, it became a question of the very greatest importance to secure a place in it, for, be it understood, that a Red River cart is a very limited conveyance, and a Red River horse, as we shall hereafter know, an animal capable of wonders, but not of impossibilities. To pen a brief letter to the captain asking for conveyance in his cart to Frog Point, and to despatch it-by the stage back towards St. Cloud, was the work of the following morning, and as two days had to elapse before the return stage could bring the captain, I set out to pass that time in a solitary house in the centre of the Breckenridge Prairie, ten miles back on the stage-road towards St. Cloud. This move withdrew me from the society of Fort Abercrombie, which for many reasons was a matter for congratulation, and put me in a position to intercept the captain on his way to Abercrombie. So-on the 13th of July I left Nolan's hotel, and, with dog and gun, arrived at the solitary house which was situated not very far from the junction of the Ottertail and Bois-des-Sioux River on the Minnesota shore, a small, rough settler's log-hut which stood out upon the level sea of grass and was visible miles and miles before one reached it. Here had rested one of those unquiet birds whose flight is ever westward, building himself a rude nest of such material as the oak-wooded "bays" of the Red River afforded, and multiplying--in spite of much opposition to the contrary. His eldest had been struck dead in his house only a few months before by the thunderbolt, which so frequently hurls destruction upon the valley of the Red River. The settler had seen many lands since his old home in Cavan had been left behind, and but for his name it would have been difficult to tell his Irish nationality. He had wandered up to Red River Settlement and wandered back again, had squatted in Iowa, and finally, like some bird which long wheels in circles ere it settles upon the earth, had pitched his tent on the Red River.

The Red River--let us trace it while we wait the coming captain who is to navigate us down its tortuous channel. Close to the Lake Ithaska, in which the great river Mississippi takes its rise, there is a small sheet of water known as Elbow Lake. Here, at an elevation of 1689 feet above the sea level, nine feet higher than the source of the Mississippi, the Red River has its birth. It is curious that the primary direction of both rivers should be in courses diametrically opposite to their afterlines; the Mississippi first running to the north, and the Red River first bending towards the south; in fact, it is only when it gets down here, near the Breckenridge Prairies, that it finally determines to seek a northern outlet to the ocean. Meeting the current of the Bois-des-Sioux, which has its source in Lac Travers, in which the Minnesota River, a tributary of the Mississippi, also takes its rise, the Red River hurries on into the level prairie and soon commences its immense windings. This Lac Travers discharges in wet seasons north and south, and is the only sheet of water on the Continent which sheds its waters into the tropics of the Gulf of Mexico and into the polar ocean of the Hudson Bay. In former times the whole system of rivers bore the name of the great Dakota nation the Sioux River and the title of Red River was only borne by that portion of the stream which flows from Red Lake to the forks of the Assineboine. Now, however, the whole stream, from its source in Elbow Lake to its estuary in Lake Winnipeg fully 900 miles by water, is called the Red River: people say that the name is derived from a bloody Indian battle which once took place upon its banks, tinging the waters with crimson dye. It certainly cannot be called red from the hue of the water, which is of a dirty-white colour. Flowing towards the north with innumerable twists and sudden turnings, the Red River divides the State of Minnesota, which it has upon its right, from the great territory of Dakota, receiving from each side many tributary streams which take their source in the Leaf Hills of Minnesota and in the Coteau of the Missouri. Its tributaries from the east flow through dense forests, those from the west wind through the vast sandy wastes of the Dakota Prairie, where trees are almost unknown. The plain through which Red River flows is fertile beyond description. At a little distance it looks one vast level plain through which the windings of the river are marked by a dark line of woods fringing the whole length of the stream--each tributary has also its line of forest--a line visible many miles away over the great sea of grass. As one travels on, there first rise above the prairie the summits of the trees; these gradually'! grow larger, until finally, after many hours, the river is reached. Nothing else breaks the uniform level. Standing upon the ground the eye ranges over many miles of grass, standing on a waggon, one doubles the area of vision, and to look over the plains from an elevation of twelve feet above the earth is to survey at a glance a space so vast that distance alone seems to bound its limits. The effect of sunset over these oceans of verdure is very beautiful; a thousand hues spread themselves upon the grassy plains; a thousand tints of gold are cast along the heavens, and the two oceans of the sky and of the earth intermingle in one great blaze of glory at the very gates of the setting sun. But to speak of sunsets now is only to anticipate. Here at the Red River we are only at the threshold of the sunset, its true home yet lies many days journey to the west: there, where the long shadows of the vast herds of bison trail slowly over the immense plains, huge and dark against the golden west; there, where the red man still sees in the glory of the setting sun the realization of his dream of heaven.

Shooting the prairie plover, which were numerous around the solitary shanty, gossiping with Mr. Connelly on Western life and Red River experiences--I passed the long July day until evening came to a close. Then came the time of the mosquito; he swarmed around the shanty, he came out from blade of grass and up from river sedge, from the wooded bay and the dusky prairie, in clouds and clouds, until the air hummed with his presence. My host "made a smoke," and the cattle came close around and stood into the very fire itself, scorching their hides in attempting to escape the stings of their ruthless tormentors. My friend's house was not a large one, but he managed to make me a shake-down on the loft overhead, and to it he led the way. To live in a country infested by mosquitoes ought to insure to a person the possession of health, wisdom, and riches, for assuredly I know of nothing so conducive to early turning in and early turning out as that most pitiless pest. On the present occasion I had not long turned in before I became aware of the presence of at least two other persons within the limits of the little loft, for only a few feet distant soft whispers became fintly audible. Listening attentively, I gathered the following dialogue:

"Do you think he has got it about him?"

"Maybe he has," replied the first speaker with the voice of a woman.

"Are you shure he has it at all at all?"

31

"Didn't I see it in his own hand?"

Here was a fearful position! The dark loft, the lonely shanty miles away from any other habitation, the mysterious allusions to the possession of property, all naturally combined to raise the most dreadful suspicions in the mind of the solitary traveller. Strange to say, this conversation had not the terrible effect upon me which might be supposed. It was evident that my old friends, father and mother of Mrs. C----, occupied the loft in company with me, and the mention of that most suggestive word, "crathure," was sufficient to neutralize all suspicions connected with the lonely surroundings of the place. It was, in fact, a drop of that much-desired "crathure" that the old couple were so anxious to obtain.

About three o'clock on the afternoon of Sunday the 17th July I left the house of Mr. Connelly, and journeyed back to Abercrombie in the stage waggon from St. Cloud. I had as a fellow-passenger the captain of the "International" steamboat, whose acquaintance was quickly made. He had received my letter at Pomme-de-Terre, and most kindly offered his pony and cart for our joint conveyance to George town that evening; so, having waited only long enough at Abercrombie to satisfy hunger and get ready the Red River cart, we left Mr. Nolan's door some little time before sunset, and turning north along the river held our way towards Georgetown. The evening was beautifully fine and clear; the plug trotted steadily on, and darkness soon wrapped its mantle around the prairie. My new acquaintance had many questions to ask and much information to impart, and although a Red River cart is not the easiest mode of conveyance to one who sits amidships between the wheels, still when I looked to the northern skies and saw the old pointers marking our course almost due north, and thought that at last I was launched fair on a road whose termination was the goal for which I had longed so earnestly, I little recked the rough jolting of the wheels whose revolutions brought me closer to my journey's end. Shortly after leaving Abercrombie we passed a small creek in whose leaves and stagnant waters mosquitoes were numerous.

"If the mosquitoes let us travel," said my companion, as we emerged upon the prairie again, "we should reach Georgetown to breakfast."

"If the mosquitoes let us travel?" thought I. "Surely he must be joking!"

I little knew then the significance of the captain's words. I thought that my experiences of mosquitoes in Indian jungles and Irrawaddy swamps, to say nothing of my recent wanderings by Mississippi forests, had taught me something about these pests; but I was doomed to learn a lesson that night and the following which will cause me never to doubt the possibility of anything, no matter how formidable or how unlikely it may appear, connected with mosquitoes. It was about ten o'clock at night when there rose close to the south-west a small dark cloud scarcely visible above the horizon. The wind, which was very light, was blowing from the north-east; so when my attention had been called to the speck of cloud by my companion I naturally concluded that it could in no way concern us, but in this I was grievously mistaken. In a very short space of time the little cloud grew bigger, the wind died away altogether, and the stars began to look mistily from a sky no longer blue. Every now and again my companion looked towards this increasing cloud, and each time his opinion seemed to be less favourable. But another change also occurred of a character altogether different. There came upon us, brought apparently by the cloud, dense swarms of mosquitoes, humming and buzzing along with us as we journeyed on, and covering our faces and heads with their sharp stinging bites. They seemed to come with us, after us, and against us, from above and from below, in volumes that ever increased. It soon began to dawn upon me that this might mean something akin to the "mosquitoes allowing us to travel," of which my friend had spoken some three hours earlier. Meantime the cloud had increased to large proportions; it was no longer in the south-west; it occupied the whole west, and was moving on towards the north. Presently, from out of the dark heavens, streamed liquid fire, and long peals of thunder rolled far away over the gloomy prairies. So sudden appeared the change that one could scarce realize that only a little while before the stars had been shining so brightly upon the ocean of grass. At length the bright flashes came nearer and nearer, the thunder rolled louder and louder, and the mosquitoes seemed to have made up their minds that to achieve the maximum of torture in the minimum of time was the sole end and aim of their existence. The captain's pony showed many signs of agony; my dog howled with pain, and rolled himself amongst the baggage in useless writhings.

"I thought it would come to this," said the captain. "We must unhitch and lie down."

It was now midnight. To loose the horse from the shafts, to put the oil-cloth over the cart, and to creep underneath the wheels did-not take my friend long. I followed his movements, crept in and drew a blanket over my head. Then came the crash; the fire seemed to pour out of the clouds. It was impossible to keep the blanket on, so raising it every now and again I. looked out from between the spokes of the wheel. During three hours the lightning seemed to run like a river of flame out of the clouds. Sometimes a stream would descend, then, dividing into two branches, would pour down on the prairie two distinct channels of fire. The thunder rang sharply, as though the metallic clash of steel was about it, and the rain descended in torrents upon the level prairies. At about three o'clock in the morning the storm seemed to lull a little. My companion crept out from underneath the cart; I followed. The plug, who had managed to improve the occasion by stuffing himself with grass, was soon in the shafts again, and just as dawn began to streak the dense low-lying clouds towards the east we were once more in motion. Still for a couple of hours more the rain came down in drenching torrents and the lightning flashed with angry fury over the long corn-like grass beaten flat by the rain-torrent. What a dreary prospect lay stretched around us when the light grew strong enough to show it! rain and cloud lying low upon the dank prairie.

Soaked through and through, cold, shivering, and sleepy, glad indeed was I when a house appeared in view and we drew up at the door of a shanty for Food and fire. The house belonged to a Prussian subject of the name of Probsfeld, a terribly self-opinionated North German, with all the bumptious proclivities of that thriving nation most fully developed.' Herr Probsfeld appeared to be a man who regretted that men in general should be persons of a very inferior order of intellect, but who accepted the fact as a thing not to be avoided under the existing arrangements of limitation regarding Prussia in general and Probsfelds in particular. While the Herr was thus engaged in illuminating our minds, the Frau was much more agreeably employed in preparing something for our bodily comfort. I noticed with pleasure that there appeared some hope for the future of the human race, in the fact that the generation of the Probsfelds seemed to be progressing satisfactorily. Many youthful Probsfelds were visible around, and matters appeared to promise a continuation of the line, so that the State of Minnesota and that portion of Dakota lying adjacent to it may still look confidently to the future. It is more than probable that Herr Probsfeld realized the fact, that just at that moment, when the sun was breaking out through the eastern clouds over the distant outline of the Leaf Hills, 700,000 of his countrymen were moving hastily toward the French frontier for the special furtherance of those ideas so dear to his mind-it is most probable, I say, that his self-laudation and cock-like conceit would have been in no ways lessened.

Our arrival at Georgetown had been delayed by the night storm on the prairie, and it was midday on the 18th when we reached the Hudson Bay Company Post which stood at the confluence of the Buffalo and Red Rivers. Food and fresh horses were all we required, and after these requisites had been obtained the journey was prosecuted with renewed vigour. Forty miles had yet to be traversed before the point at which the Steamboat lay could be reached, and for that distance the track ran on the left or Dakota side of the Red River. As we journeyed along the Dakota prairies the last hour of daylight overtook us, bringing with it a Scene of magical beauty. The sun resting on the rim of the prairie cast over the vast expanse of grass a flood of light. On the east lay the darker green of the trees of the Red River. The whole western sky was full of wild-looking thunder-clouds, through which the rays of sunlight shot upward in great trembling shafts of glory. Being on horseback and alone, for my companion had trotted on in his waggon, I had time to watch and note this brilliant spectacle; but as soon as the sun had dipped beneath the sea of verdure an ominous sound caused me to gallop on with increasing haste. The pony seemed to know the significance of that sound much better than its rider. He no longer lagged, nor needed the spur or whip to urge him to faster exertion, for darker and denser than on the previous night there rose around us vast numbers of mosquitoes--choking masses of biting insects, no mere cloud thicker and denser in one place than in another, but one huge wall of never-ending insects filling nostrils, ears, and eyes. Where they came from I cannot tell; the prairie seemed too small to hold them; the air too limited to yield them space. I had seen many vast accumulations of insect life in lands old and new, but never any thing that approached to this mountain of mosquitoes on the prairies of Dakota. To say that they covered the coat of the horse I rode would be to give but a faint idea of their numbers; they were literally six or eight deep upon his skin, and with a single sweep of the hand one could crush myriads from his neck. Their hum seemed to be in all things around. To ride for it was the sole resource. Darkness came quickly down, but the track knew no turn, and for seven miles I kept the pony at a gallop; my face, neck, and hands cut and bleeding.

At last in the gloom I saw, down in what appeared to be the bottom of a valley, a long white wooden building, with lights showing out through the windows. Riding quickly down this valley we reached, followed by hosts of winged pursuers, the edge of some water lying amidst tree-covered banks-the water was the Red River, and the white wooden building the steamboat "International."

Now one word about mosquitoes in the valley of the Red River. People will be inclined to say, "We know well what a mosquito is--very troublesome and annoying, no doubt, but you needn't make so much of what every one understands." People reading what I have written about this insect will probably say this. I would have said so myself before the occurrences of the last two nights, but I will never say so again, nor perhaps will my readers when they have read the following: It is no unusual event during a wet summer in that portion of Minnesota and Dakota to which I refer for oxen and horses to perish from the bites of mosquitoes. An exposure of a very few hours duration is sufficient to cause death to these animals. It is said, too, that not many years ago the Sioux were in the habit of sometimes killing their captives by exposing them at night to the attacks of the mosquitoes; and any person who has experienced the full intensity of a mosquito night along the American portion of the Red River will not have any difficulty in realizing how short a period would be necessary to cause death.

Our arrival at the "International" was the cause of no small amount of discomfort to the persons already on board that vessel. It took us but little time to rush over the gangway and seek safety from our pursuers within the precincts of the steamboat: but they were not to be baffled easily; they came in after us in millions; like Bishop Haddo's rats, they came "in at the windows and in at the doors," until in a very short space of time the interior of the boat became perfectly black with insects. Attracted by the light they flocked into the saloon, covering walls and ceiling in one dark mass. We attempted supper, but had to give it up. They got into the coffee, they stuck fast in the soft, melting butter, until at length, feverish, bitten, bleeding, and hungry, I sought refuge beneath the gauze curtains in my cabin, and fell asleep from sheer exhaustion.

And in truth there was reason enough for sleep independently of mosquitoes bites. By dint of hard travel we had accomplished 104 miles in twenty-seven hours. The midnight storm had lost us three hours and added in no small degree to discomfort. Mosquitoes had certainly caused but little thought to be bestowed upon fatigue during the last two hours; but I much doubt if the spur-goaded horse, when he stretches himself at night to rest his weary limbs, feels the less tired because the miles flew behind him all unheeded under the influence of the spur-rowel. When morning broke we were in motion. The air was fresh and cool; not a mosquito was visible. The green banks of Red River looked pleasant to the eye as the "International" puffed along between them, rolling the tranquil water before her in a great muddy wave, which broke amidst the red and grey willows on the shore. Now and then the eye caught glimpses of the prairies through the skirting of oak woods on the left, but to the right there lay an unbroken line of forest fringing deeply the Minnesota shore. The "International" was a curious craft; she measured about 130 feet in length, drew only two feet of water, and was propelled by an enormous wheel placed over her stern. Eight summers of varied success and as many winters of total inaction had told heavily against her river worthiness; the sun had cracked her roof and sides, the rigour of the Winnipeg winter left its trace on bows and hull. Her engines were a perfect marvel of patchwork--pieces of rope seemed twisted around crank and shaft, mud was laid thickly on boiler and pipes, little jets and spurts of steam had a disagreeable way of coming out from places not supposed to be capable of such outpourings. Her capacity for going on fire seemed to be very great; each gust of wind sent showers of sparks from the furnaces flying along the lower deck, the charred beams of which attested the frequency of the occurrence. Alarmed at the prospect of seeing my conveyance wrapped in flames, I shouted vigorously for assistance, and will long remember the look of surprise and pity with which the native regarded me as he leisurely approached with the water-bucket and cast its contents along the smoking deck.

I have already mentioned the tortuous course which the Red River has wound for itself through these level northern prairies. The windings of the river more than double the length of its general direction, and the turns are so sharp that after steaming a mile the traveller will often arrive at a spot not one hundred yards distant from where he started.

Steaming thus for one day and one night down the Red River of the North, enjoying no variation of scene or change of prospect, but nevertheless enjoying beyond expression a profound sense of mingled rest and progression, I reached at eight o'clock on the morning of the-20th of July the frontier post of Pembina.

And here, at the verge of my destination, on the boundary of the Red River Settlement, although making but short delay myself, I must ask my readers to pause awhile and to go back through long years into earlier times. For it would ill suit the purpose of writer or of reader if the latter were to be thus hastily introduced to the isolated colony of Assineboine without any preliminary-acquaintance with its history or its inhabitants.

CHAPTER EIGHT.

Retrospective--The North-west Passage--The Bay of Hudson--Rival Claims--The Old French Fur Trade--The North-west Company--How the Half-breeds came--The Highlanders defeated-Progress--Old Feuds.

WE who have seen in our times the solution of the long-hidden secret worked out amidst the icy solitudes of the Polar Seas cannot realize the excitement which for nigh 400 years vexed the minds of European kings and peoples--how they thought and toiled over this northern passage to wild realms of Cathay and Hindostan--how from every port, from the Adriatic to the Baltic, ships had sailed out in quest of this ocean strait, to find in succession portions of the great world which Columbus had given to the human race.

Adventurous spirits were these early navigators who thus fearlessly entered the great unknown oceans of the North in craft scarce larger than canal-boats. And how long and how tenaciously did they hold that some passage must exist by which the Indies could be reached! Not a creek, not a bay, but seemed to promise the long-sought-for opening to the Pacific.

Hudson and Frobisher, Fox, Baffin, Davis, and James, how little thought they of that vast continent whose presence was but an obstacle in the path of their discovery! Hudson had long perished in the ocean which bears his name before it was known to be a cul-de-sac. Two hundred years had passed away from the time of Columbus ere his dream of an open sea to the city of Quinsay in Cathay had ceased to find believers. This immense inlet of Hudson Bay must lead to the Western Ocean. So, at least, thought a host of bold navigators who steered their way through fog and ice into the great Sea of Hudson, giving those names to strait and bay and island, which we read in our school-days upon great wall-hung maps and never think or care about again. Nor were these anticipations of reaching the East held only by the sailors.

La Salle, when he fitted out his expeditions from the Island of Montreal for the West, named his point of departure La Chine, so certain was he that his canoes would eventually reach Cathay. And La Chine still exists to attest his object. But those who went on into the great continent, reaching the shores of vast lakes and the banks of mighty rivers, learnt another and a truer story. They saw these rivers flowing with vast volumes of water from the north-west; and, standing on the brink of their unknown waves, they rightly judged that such rolling volumes of water must have their sources far away in distant mountain ranges. Well might the great heart of De Soto sink within him when, after long months of arduous toil through swamp and forest, he stood at last on the low shores of the Mississippi and beheld in thought the enormous space which lay between him and the spot where such a river had its birth.

The East--it was always the East. Columbus had said the world was not so large as the common herd believed it, and yet when he had increased it by a continent he tried to make it smaller than it really was. So fixed were men's minds upon the East, that it was long before they would think of turning to account the discoveries of those early navigators. But in time there came to the markets of Europe the products of the New World. The gold and the silver of Mexico and the rich sables of the frozen North found their way into the marts of Western Europe. And while Drake plundered galleons from the Spanish Main, England and France commenced their career of rivalry for the possession of that trade in furs and peltries which had its sources round the icy shores of the Bay of Hudson. It was reserved however for the fiery Prince Rupert to carry into effect the idea of opening up the North-west. Through the ocean of Hudson Bay.

Somewhere about 200 years ago a ship sailed away from England bearing in it a company of adventurers sent out to form a colony upon the southern shores of James's Bay. These men named the new land after the Prince who sent them forth, and were the pioneers of that "Hon. Company of Adventurers from England trading into Hudson Bay."

More than forty years previous to the date of the charter by which Charles II. conferred the territory of Rupert's Land upon the London company, a similar grant had been made by the French monarch, Louis XIII, to "La Compagnie de la Nouvelle France." Thus there had arisen rival claims to the possession of this sterile region, and although treaties had at various times attempted to rectify boundaries or to rearrange watersheds, the question of the right of Canada or of the Company to hold a portion of the vast territory draining into Hudson Bay had never been legally solved.

For some eighty years after this settlement on James's Bay, the Company held a precarious tenure of their forts and factories. Wild-looking men, more Indian than French, marched from Canada over the height of land and raided upon the posts of Moose and Albany, burning the stockades and carrying off the little brass howitzers mounted thereon. The same wild-looking men, pushing on into the interior from Lake Superior, made their way into Lake Winnipeg, up the great Saskatchewan River, and across to the valley of the Red River; building their forts for war and trade by distant lake-shore and confluence of river current, and drawing off the valued trade in furs to France; until all of a sudden there came the great blow struck by Wolfe under the walls of Quebec, and every little far-away post and distant fort throughout the vast interior continent felt the echoes of the guns of Abraham. It might have been imagined that now, when the power of France was crushed in the Canadas, the trade which she had carried on with the Indian tribes of the Far West would lapse to the English company trading into Hudson Bay; but such was not the case.

Immediately upon the capitulation of Montreal, fur traders from the English cities of Boston and Albany appeared in Montreal and Quebec, and pushed their way along the old French route to Lake Winnipeg and into the valley of the Saskatchewan. There they, in turn, erected their little posts and trading-stations, laid out their beads and blankets, their strouds and cottons, and exchanged their long-carried goods for the beaver and marten and fisher skins of the Nadow, Sioux, Kinistineau, and Osinipoilles. Old maps of the North-west still mark spots along the shores of Winnipeg and the Saskatchewan with names of Henry's House, Finlay's House, and Mackay's House. These "houses" were the Trading-posts of the first English free-traders, whose combination in 1783 gave rise to the great North-west Fur Company, so long the fierce rival of the Hudson Bay. To picture here the jealous rivalry which during forty years raged throughout these immense territories would be to fill a volume with tales of adventure and discovery.

The zeal with which the North-west Company pursued the trade in furs quickly led to the exploration of the entire country. A Mackenzie penetrated to the Arctic Ocean down the immense river which bears his name--a

Frazer and a Thompson pierced the tremendous masses of the Rocky Mountains and beheld the Pacific rolling its waters against the rocks of New Caledonia. Based upon a system which rewarded the efforts of its employees by giving them a share in the profits of the trade, making them partners as well as servants, the North-west Company soon put to sore straits the older organization of the Hudson Bay. While the heads of both companies were of the same nation, the working men and voyageurs were of totally different races, the Hudson Bay employing Highlanders and Orkney men from Scotland, and the North-west Company drawing its recruits from the hardy French inhabitants of Lower Canada. This difference of nationality deepened the strife between them, and many a deed of cruelty and bloodshed lies buried amidst the oblivion of that time in those distant regions. The men who went out to the North-west as voyageurs and servants in the employment of the rival companies from Canada and from Scotland hardly ever returned to their native lands. The wild roving life in the great prairie or the trackless pine forest, the vast solitudes of inland lakes and rivers, the chase, and the camp-fire had too much of excitement in them to allow the voyageur to return again to the narrow limits of civilization. Besides, he had taken to himself an Indian wife, and although the ceremony by which that was effected was frequently wanting in those accessories of bell, book, and candle so essential to its proper well-being, nevertheless the voyageur and his squaw got on pretty well together, and little ones, who jabbered the smallest amount of English or French, and a great deal of Ojibbeway, or Cree, or Assineboine, began to multiply around them.

Matters were in this state when, in 1812, as we have already seen in an earlier chapter, the Earl of Selkirk, a large proprietor of the Hudson Bay Company, conceived the idea of planting a colony of Highlanders on the banks of the Red River near the lake called Winnipeg.

Some great magnate was intent on making a deer forest in Scotland about the period that this country was holding its own with difficulty against Napoleon. So, leaving their native parish of Kildonan in Sutherlandshire, these people established another Kildonan in the very heart of North America, in the midst of an immense and apparently boundless prairie. Poor people! they had a hard time of it-inundation and North-west Company hostility nearly sweeping them off their prairie lands. Before long matters reached a climax. The North-west Canadians and half-breeds sallied forth one day and attacked the settlers; the settlers had a small guard in whose prowess they placed much credence; the guard turned out after the usual manner of soldiers, the half-breeds and Indians lay in the long grass after the method of savages. For once the Indian tactics prevailed. The Governor of the Hudson Bay Company and the guard were shot down, the fort at Point Douglas on the Red River was taken, and the Scotch settlers driven out to the shores of Lake Winnipeg.

To keep the peace between the rival companies and the two nationalities was no easy matter, but at last Lord Selkirk came to the rescue; they were disbanding regiments after the great peace of 1815, and portions of two foreign corps, called De Muiron's and De Watteville's Regiments, were induced to attempt an expedition to the Red River.

Starting in winter from the shores of Lake Superior, these hardy fellows traversed the forests and frozen lakes upon snow-shoes, and, entering from the Lake of the Woods, suddenly appeared in the Selkirk Settlement, and took possession of Fort Douglas.

A few years later the great Fur Companies became amalgamated, or rather the North-west ceased to exist, and henceforth the Hudson Bay Company ruled supreme from the shores of the Atlantic to the frontiers of Russian America.

From that date, 1822, the progress of the little colony had been gradual but sure. Its numbers were constantly increased by the retired servants of the Hudson Bay Company, who selected it as a place of settlement when their period of active service had expired. Thither came the voyageur and the trader to spend the winter of their lives in the little world of Assineboine. Thus the Selkirk Settlement grew and flourished, caring little for the outside earth-"the world forgetting, by the world forgot."

But the old feelings which had their rise in earlier years never wholly died out. National rivalry still existed, and it required no violent effort to fan the embers into flame again. The descendants of the two nationalities dwelt apart; there were the French parishes and the Scotch and English parishes, and, although each nationality spoke the same mother tongue, still the spread of schools and churches fostered the different languages of the fatherland, and perpetuated the distinction of race which otherwise would have disappeared by lapsing into savagery. In an earlier chapter I have traced the events immediately pre ceding the breaking out of the insurrectionary movement among the French half-breeds, and in the foregoing pages I have tried to sketch the early life and history of the country into which I am about to ask the reader to follow me. Into the immediate sectional disputes and religious animosities of the present movement it is not my intention to enter; as I journey on an occasional arrow may be shot to the right or to the left at men and things; but I will leave to others the details of a petty provincial quarrel, while-I have before me, stretching far and wide, the vast solitudes which await in silence the footfall of the future.

CHAPTER NINE.

Running the Gauntlet--Across the Line--Mischief ahead-Preparations--A Night March--The Steamer captured--The Pursuit-Daylight--The Lower Fort--The Red-Indian at last--The Chief's Speech--A Big Feed--Making ready for the Winnipeg--A Delay--I visit Fort Garry--Mr. President Riel--The Final Start-Lake Winnipeg--The First Night out--My Crew.

THE steamer "International" made only a short delay at the frontier post of Pembina, but it was long enough to impress the on-looker with a sense of dirt and debauchery, which seemed to pervade the place. Some of the leading citizens came forth with hands stuck so deep in breeches' pockets, that the shoulders seemed to have formed an offensive and defensive alliance with the arms, never again to permit the hands to emerge into daylight unless it should be in the vicinity of the ankles.

Upon inquiring for the post-office, I was referred to the Postmaster himself, who, in his-capacity of leading citizen, was standing by. Asking if there were any letters lying at his office for me, I was answered in a very curt negative, the postmaster retiring immediately up the steep bank towards the collection of huts which calls itself Pembina. The boat soon cast off her moorings and steamed on into British territory. We were at length within the limits of the Red River Settlement, in the land of M. Louis Riel, President, Dictator, Ogre, Saviour of Society, and New Napoleon; as he was variously named by friends and foes in the little tea-cup of Red River whose tempest had cast him suddenly from dregs to surface. "I wasn't so sure that they wouldn't have searched the boat for you," said the captain from his wheel-house on the roof-deck, soon after we had passed the Hudson Bay Company's post, whereat M. Riel's frontier guard was supposed to hold its head-quarters. "Now, darn me, if them whelps had stopped the boat, but I'd have just rounded her back to Pembina and tied up under the American post yonder, and claimed protection as an American citizen." As the act of tying up under the American post would in no way have forwarded my movements, however consolatory it might have proved to the wounded feelings of the captain, I was glad that we had been permitted to proceed without molestation. But I had in my possession a document which I looked upon as an "open sesame" in case of obstruction from any of the underlings of the Provisional Government.

This document had been handed to me by an eminent ecclesiastic whom I met on the evening preceding my departure at St. Paul, and who, upon hearing that it was my intention to proceed to the Red River, had handed me, unsolicited, a very useful notification. So far, then, I had got within the outer circle of this so jealously protected settlement. The guard, whose presence had so often been the theme of Manitoban journals, the picquet line which extended from Pembina Mountain to Lake of the Woods (150 miles), was nowhere visible, and I. began to think that the whole thing was only a myth, and that the Red River revolt was as unsubstantial as the Spectre of the Brocken. But just then, as I stood on the high roof of the "International," from whence a wide view was obtained, I saw across the level prairie outside the huts of Pembina the figures of two horsemen riding at a rapid pace towards the north. They were on the road to Fort Garry. The long July day passed slowly away, and evening began to darken over the level land, to find us still steaming down the widening reaches of the Red River.

But the day had shown symptoms sufficient to convince me that there was some reality after all in the stories of detention and resistance, so frequently mentioned; more than once had the figures of the two horsemen been visible from the roof-deck of the steamer, still keeping the Fort Garry trail, and still forcing their horses at a gallop.

The windings of the river enabled these men to keep ahead of the boat, a feat which, from their pace and manner, seemed the object they had in view. But there were other indications of difficulty lying ahead: an individual connected with the working of our boat had been informed by persons at Pembina that my expected arrival had been notified to Mr. President Riel and the members of his triumvirate, as I would learn to my cost upon arrival at Fort Garry.

That there was mischief ahead appeared probable enough, and it was with no pleasant feelings that when darkness came I mentally surveyed the situation, and bethought me of some plan by which to baffle those who sought my detention.

In an hour's time the boat would reach Fort Garry. I was a stranger in a strange land, knowing not a feature in the locality, and with only an imperfect map for my guidance. Going down to my cabin, I spread out the map before me. I saw the names: of places familiar in imagination--the winding river, the junction of the Assineboine and the Red River, and close to it Fort Garry and the village of Winnipeg; then, twenty miles farther to the north, the Lower Fort Garry and the Scotch and English Settlement. My object was to reach this lower fort; but in that lay all the difficulty. The map showed plainly enough the place in which safety lay; but it showed no means by which it could be reached, and left me, as before, to my own resources. These were not large.

My baggage was small and compact, but weighty; for it had in it much shot and sporting gear for perspective swamp and prairie work at wild duck and sharp-tailed grouse. I carried arms available against man and beast a Colt's six-shooter and a fourteen-shot repeating carbine, both light, good, and trusty; excellent weapons when things came to a certain point, but useless before that point is reached.

Now, amidst perplexing prospects and doubtful expedients, one course appeared plainly prominent; and that was that there should be no capture by Riel. The baggage and the sporting gear might go, but, for the rest, I was bound to carry myself and my arms, together with my papers and a dog, to the Lower Fort and English Settlement. Having decided on this course, I had not much time to lose in putting it into execution. I packed my things, loaded my arms, put some extra ammunition into pocket, handed over my personal effects into the safe custody of the captain, and awaited whatever might turn up.

When these preparations were completed, I had still an hour to spare. There happened to be on board the same boat as passenger a gentleman whose English proclivities had marked him during the late disturbances at Red River as a dangerous opponent to M. Riel, and who consequently had forfeited no small portion of his liberty and his chattels. The last two days had made me acquainted-with his history and opinions, and, knowing that he could supply the want I was most in need of--a horse--I told him the plan I had formed for evading M. Ril, in case his minions should attempt my capture. This was to pass quickly from the steamboat on its reaching the landing-place and to hold my way across the country in the direction of the Lower Fort, which I hoped to reach before daylight. If stopped, there was but one course to pursue--to announce name and profession, and trust to the Colt and sixteen-shooter for the rest. My new acquaintance, however, advised a change of programme, suggested by his knowledge of the locality.

At the point of junction of the Assineboine and Red Rivers the steamer, he said, would touch the north shore. The spot was only a couple of hundred yards distant from Fort Garry, but it was sufficient in the darkness to conceal any movement at that point; we would both leave the boat and, passing by the flank of the fort, gain the village of Winnipeg before the steamer would reach her landing place; he would seek his home and, if possible, send a horse to meet me at the first wooden bridge upon the road to the Lower Fort. All this was simple enough, and supplied me with that knowledge of the ground which I required.

It was now eleven o'clock p.m., dark but fine. With my carbine concealed under a large coat, I took my station near the bows of the boat, watching my companion's movements. Suddenly the steam was shut off, and the boat began to round from the Red River into the narrow Assineboine. A short distance in front appeared lights and figures moving to and fro along the shore--the lights were those of Fort Garry, the figures those of Riel, O'Donoghue, and Lepine, with a strong body of guards.

A second more, and the boat gently touched the soft mud of the north shore. My friend jumped off to the beach; dragging the pointer by chain and collar after me, I too, sprang to the shore just as the boat began to recede from it. As I did so, I saw my companion rushing up a very steep and lofty bank. Much impeded by the arms and dog, I followed him up the ascent and reached the top. Around stretched a dead black level plain, on the left the fort, and figures were dimly visible about 200 yards away. There was not much time to take in all this, for my companion, whispering me to follow him closely, commenced to move quickly along an irregular path which led from the river bank. In a short time we: had reached the vicinity of a few straggling houses whose white walls showed distinctly through the darkness; this, he told me, was Winnipeg. Here was his residence, and here we were to separate. Giving me a few hurried directions for further guidance, he pointed to the road before me as a starting-point, and then vanished into the gloom. For a moment I stood at the entrance of the little village half irresolute what to do. One or two houses showed lights in single windows, behind gleamed the lights of the steamer which had now reached the place of landing. I commenced to walk quickly through the silent houses.

As I emerged from the farther side of the village I saw, standing on the centre of the road, a solitary figure. Approaching nearer to him, I found that he occupied a narrow wooden bridge which opened out upon the prairie. To pause or hesitate would only be to excite suspicion in the mind of this man, sentinel or guard, as he might be. So, at a sharp pace, I advanced towards him. He never moved; and without word or sign I passed him at arm's length. But here the dog, which I had unfastened when parting from my companion, strayed away, and, being loth to lose him, I stopped at the farther end of the bridge to call him back. This was evidently the bridge of which my companion had spoken, as the place where I was to await the horse he would send me.

The trysting-place seemed to be but ill-chosen-close to the village, and already in possession of a sentinel, it would not do. "If the horse comes," thought I, "he will be too late; if he does not come, there can be no use in waiting," so, giving a last whistle for the dog (which I never saw again), I turned and held my way into the dark level plain lying mistily spread around me. For more than an hour I walked hard along a black-clay track

38

bordered on both sides by prairie. I saw no one, and heard nothing save the barking of some stray dogs away to my right.

During this time the moon, now at its last quarter, rose above trees to the east, and enabled me better to discern the general features of the country through which I was passing. Another hour passed, and still I held on my way. I had said to myself that for three hours I must keep up the same rapid stride without pause or halt. In the meantime I was calculating for emergencies. If followed on horseback, I must become aware of the fact while yet my enemies were some distance away. The black capote flung on the road would have arrested their attention, the enclosed fields on the right of the track would afford me concealment, a few shots from the fourteen shooter fired in the direction of the party, already partly dismounted deliberating over the mysterious capote, would have occasioned a violent demoralization, probably causing a rapid retreat upon Fort Garry, darkness would have multiplied numbers, and a fourteen-shooter by day or night is a weapon of very equalizing tendencies.

When the three hours had elapsed I looked anxiously around for water, as I was thirsty in the extreme. A creek soon gave me the drink I thirsted for, and, once more refreshed, I kept on my lonely way beneath the waning moon. At the time when I was searching for water along the bottom of the Middle Creek my pursuers were close at hand--probably not five minutes distant--but in those things it is the minutes which make all the difference one way or the other.

We must now go back and join the pursuit, just to see what the followers of M. Riel were about.

Sometime during the afternoon preceding the arrival of the steamer at Fort Garry, news had come down by mounted express from Pembina, that a stranger was about to make his entrance into Red River.

Who he might be was not clearly discernible; some said he was an officer in Her Majesty's Service, and others, that he was somebody connected with the disturbances of the preceding winter who was attempting to revisit the settlement.

Whoever he was, it was unanimously decreed that he should be captured; and a call was made by M. Riel for "men not afraid to fight" who would proceed up the river to meet the steamer. Upon after-reflection, however, it was resolved to await the arrival of the boat, and, by capturing captain, crew, and passengers, secure the person of the mysterious stranger.

Accordingly, when the "International" reached the landing-place beneath the walls of Fort Garry a strange scene was enacted.

Messrs. Riel, Lepine, and O'Donoghue, surrounded by a body-guard of half-breeds and a few American adventurers, appeared upon the landing-place. A select detachment, I presume, of the "men not afraid to fight'" boarded the boat and commenced to ransack her from stem to stern. While the confusion was at its height, and doors, etc., were being broken open, it became known to some of the searchers that two persons had left the boat only a few minutes previously. The rage of the petty Napoleon became excessive, he sarcéed and stamped and swore, he ordered pursuit on foot and on horseback; and altogether conducted himself after the manner of rum-drunkenness and despotism based upon ignorance and "straight drinks."

All sorts of persons were made prisoners upon the spot. My poor companion was seized in his house twenty minutes after he had reached it, and, being hurried to the boat, was threatened with instant hanging. Where had the stranger gone to? and who was he? He had asserted himself to belong to Her Majesty's Service, and he had gone to the Lower Fort.

"After him!" screamed the President; "bring him in dead or alive."

So some half-dozen men, half-breeds and American filibusters, started out in pursuit. It was averred that the man who left the boat was of colossal proportions, that he carried arms of novel and terrible construction, and, more mysterious still, that he was closely followed by a gigantic dog.

People shuddered as they listened to this part of the story-a dog of gigantic size! What a picture, this immense man and that immense dog--stalking through the gloom-wrapped prairie, goodness knows where! Was it to be wondered at, that the pursuit, vigorously though it commenced, should have waned faint as it reached the dusky prairie and left behind the neighbourhood and the habitations of men? The party, under the leadership of Lepine the "Adjutant-general," was seen at one period of its progress besides the moments of starting and return. Just previous to daybreak it halted at a house known by the suggestive title of "Whisky Tom's," eight miles from the village of Winnipeg; whether it ever got farther on its way remains a mystery, but I am inclined to think that the many attractions of Mr. Tom's residence, as evinced by the prefix to his name, must have proved a powerful obstacle to such thirsty souls.

Daylight breaks early in the month of July, and I had been but little more than three hours on the march when the first sign of dawn began to glimmer above the tree tops of the Red River. When the light became strong enough to afford a clear view of the country, I found that I was walking along a road or track of very black soil with poplar groves at intervals on each side.

Through openings in these poplar groves I beheld a row of houses built apparently along the bank of the river, and soon the steeple of a church and a comfortable-looking glebe became visible about a quarter of a mile to the right. Calculating by my watch, I concluded that I must be some sixteen miles distant from Fort Garry, and therefore not more than four miles from the Lower Fort. However, as it was now quite light, I thought' I could not do better than approach the comfortable-looking glebe with a double view towards refreshment and information. I reached the gate and, having run the gauntlet of an evilly-intentioned dog, pulled a bell at the door.

Now it had never occurred to me that my outward appearance savoured not a little of the bandit--a poet has written about "the dark Suliote, in his shaggy capote" etc., conveying the idea of a very ferocious-looking fellow but I believe that my appearance fully realized the description, as far as outward semblance was concerned; so, evidently, thought the worthy clergyman when, cautiously approaching his hall-door, he beheld through the glass window the person whose reiterated ringing had summoned him hastily from his early slumbers. Half opening his door, he inquired my business.

"How far," asked I, "to the Lower Fort?"

"About four miles."

"Any conveyance thither?"

"None whatever."

He was about to close the door in my face, when I inquired his country, and he replied, "I am English."

"And I am an English officer, arrived last night in the Red River, and now making my way to the Lower Fort."

Had my appearance been ten times more disreputable than it was, had I carried a mitrailleuse instead of a fourteen-shooter, I would have been still received with open arms after that piece of information was given and received. The door opened very wide and the worthy clergyman's hand shut very close. Then suddenly there became apparent many facilities for reaching the Lower Fort not before visible, nor was the hour deemed too early to preclude all thoughts of refreshment.

It was some time before my host could exactly realize the state of affairs, but when he did, his horse and buggy were soon in readiness, and driving along the narrow road which here led almost uninterruptedly through little clumps and thickets of poplars, we reached the Lower Fort Garry not very long after the sun had begun his morning work of making gold the forest summits. I had run the gauntlet of the lower settlement; I was between the Expedition and its destination, and it was time to lie down and rest.

Up to this time no intimation had reached the Lower Fort of pursuit by the myrmidons of M. Riel. But soon there came intelligence. A farmer carrying corn to the mill in the fort had been stopped by a party of men some seven miles away, and questioned as to his having seen a stranger; others had also seen the mounted scouts. And so while I slept the sleep of the tired my worthy host was receiving all manner of information regarding the movements of the marauders who were in quest of his sleeping guest.

I may have been asleep some two hours, when I became aware of a hand laid on my shoulder and a voice whispering something into my ear. Rousing myself from a very deep sleep, I beheld the Hudson Bay officer in charge of the fort standing by the bed repeating words which failed at first to carry any meaning along with them.

"The French are after you," he reiterated.

"The French"-where was I, in France?

I had been so sound asleep, that it took some seconds to gather up-the different threads of thought where I had left them off a few hours before, and "the French" was at that time altogether a new name in my ears for the Red River natives. "The French are after you!" altogether it was not an agreeable prospect to open my eyes upon, tired, exhausted, and sleepy as I was. But, under the circumstances, breakfast seemed the best preparation for the siege, assault, and general battery which, according to all the rules of war, ought to have followed the announcement of the Gallic Nationality being in full pursuit of me.

Seated at breakfast, and doing full justice to a very excellent mutton chop and cup of Hudson Bay Company Souchong (and where does there exist such tea; out of China?), I heard a digest of the pursuit from the lips of my host. The French had visited him in his fort once before with evil intentions, and they might come again, so he proposed that we should drive down to the Indian Settlement, where the ever-faithful Ojibbeways would, if necessary, roll back the tide of Gallic pursuit, giving the pursuers a reception in which Pahaouza-tau-ka, or "The Great Scalp-taker," would play a prominent part.

40

Breakfast over, a drive of eight miles brought us to the mission of the Indian Settlement presided over by Archdeacon Cowley.

Here, along the last few miles of the Red River ere it seeks, through many channels, the waters of Lake Winnipeg, dwell the remnants of the tribes whose fathers in times gone by claimed the broad lands of the Red River; now clothing themselves, after the fashion of the white man, in garments and in religion, and learning a few of his ways and dealings, but still with many wistful hankerings towards the older era of the paint and feathers, of the medicine bag and the dream omen.

Poor red man of the great North-west, I am at last in your land! Long as I have been hearing of you and your wild doings, it is only here that I have reached you on the confines of the far-stretching Winnipeg. It is no easy task to find you now, for one has to travel far into the lone spaces of the Continent before the smoke of your wigwam or of your tepie blurs the evening air.

But henceforth we will be companions for many months, and through many varied scenes, for my path lies amidst the lone spaces which are still your own; by the rushing rapids where you spear the great "namha" (sturgeon) will we light the evening fire and lie down to rest, lulled by the ceaseless thunder of the torrent; the lone lake shore will give us rest for the midday meal, and from your frail canoe, lying like a sea-gull on the wave, we will get the "mecuhaga" (the blueberry) and the "wa-wa," (the goose) giving you the great medicine of the white man, the thé and suga in exchange. But I anticipate.

On the morning following my arrival at the mission house a strange sound greeted my ears as I arose. Looking through the window, I beheld for the first time the red man in his glory.

Filing along the outside road came some two hundred of the warriors and braves of the Ojibbeways, intent upon all manner of rejoicing. At their head marched Chief Henry Prince, Chief "Kechiwis" (or the Big Apron) "Sou Souse" (or Little Long Ears); there was also "We-we-tak-gum Na-gash" (or the Man who flies round the Feathers), and Pahaouza-tau-ka, if not present, was represented by at least a dozen individuals just as fully qualified to separate the membrane from the top of the head as was that most renowned scalp-taker.

Wheeling into the grass-plot in front of the mission house, the whole body advanced towards the door shouting, "Ho, ho!" and firing off their flint trading-guns in token of welcome. The chiefs and old men advancing to the front, seated themselves on the ground in a semi-circle, while the young men and braves remained standing or lying on the ground farther back in two deep lines. In front of all stood Henry Prince the son of Pequis, Chief of the Swampy tribe, attended by his interpreter and pipe-bearer.

My appearance upon the door-step was the signal for a burst of deep and long-rolling, "Ho, ho's," and then the ceremony commenced. There Was no dance or "pow wow;" it meant business at once. Striking his hand upon his breast the chief began; as he finished each sentence the interpreter took up the thread, explaining with difficulty the long rolling, words of the Indian.

"You see here," he said, "the most faithful children of the Great Mother; they have heard that you have come from the great chief who is bringing thither his warriors from the Kitchi-gami" (Lake Superior), "and they have come to bid you welcome, and to place between you and the enemies of the Great Mother their guns and their lives. But these children are sorely puzzled; they know not what to do. They have gathered in from the East, and the North, and the West, because bad men have risen their hands against the Great Mother and robbed her goods and killed her sons and put a strange flag over her fort. And these bad men are now living in plenty on what they have robbed, and the faithful children of the Great Mother are starving and very poor, and they wish to know what they are to do. It is said that a great chief is coming across from the big sea-water with many mighty braves and warriors, and much goods and presents for the Indians. But though we have watched long for him, the lake is still clear of his canoes, and we begin to think he is not coming at all; therefore we were glad when we were told that you had come, for now you will tell us what we are to do and what message the great Ogima has sent to the red children of the Great Mother."

The speech ended, a deep and prolonged "Ho!"--a sort of universal "thems our sentiments "--ran round the painted throng of warriors, and then they awaited my answer, each looking with stolid indifference straight before him.

My reply was couched in as few words as possible. "It was true what they had heard. The big chief was coming across from the Kitchi-gami at the head of many warriors. The arm of the Great Mother was a long one, and stretched far over'seas and forests; let them keep quiet, and when the chief would arrive, he would give them store of presents and supplies; he would reward them for their good behaviour. Bad men had set themselves against the Great Mother; but the Great Mother would feel angry if any of her red children moved against these men. The big chief would soon be with them, and all would be made right. As for myself, I was now on my way to meet the big chief and his warriors, and I would say to him how true had been the red children, and he would be made glad thereat. Meantime, they should have a present of tea, tobacco, flour, and pemmican; and with full stomachs their harts would feel fuller still."

41

A universal "Ho!" testified that the speech was good; and then the ceremony of hand-shaking began. I intimated, however, that time would only permit of my having that honour with a few of the large assembly--in fact, with the leaders and old men of the tribe.

Thus, in turns, I grasped the bony hands of the "Red Deer'" and the "Big Apron," of the "Old Englishman" and the "Long Claws," and the "Big Bird;" and, with the same "Ho, ho!" and shot-firing, they filed away as they had come, carrying with them my order upon the Lower Fort for one big feed and one long pipe, and, I dare say, many blissful visions of that life the red man ever loves to live-the life that never does come to him the future of plenty and of ease.

Meantime, my preparations for departure, aided by my friends at the mission, had gone on apace. I had got a canoe and five stout English half-breeds, blankets, pemmican, tea, flour, and biscuit. All were being made ready, and the Indian Settlement was alive with excitement on the subject of the coming man--now no longer a myth--in relation to a general millennium of unlimited pemmican and tobacco.

But just when all preparations had been made complete an unexpected event occurred which postponed for a time the date of my departure; this was the arrival of a very urgent message from the Upper Fort, with an invitation to visit that place before quitting the settlement. There had been an error in the proceedings on the night of my arrival, I was told, and, acting under a mistake, pursuit had been organized. Great excitement existed amongst the French half breeds, who were in reality most loyally disposed; it was quite a mistake to imagine that there was any thing approaching to treason in the designs of the Provisional Government and much more to the same effect. It is needless now to enter into the question of how much all this was worth: at that time so much conflicting testimony was not easily reduced into proper limits. But on three points, at all events, I could form a correct opinion for myself. Had not my companion been arrested and threatened with instant death? Was he not still kept in confinement? and had not my baggage undergone confiscation (it is a new name for an old thing)? And was there not a flag other than the Union Jack flying over Fort Garry? Yes, it was true; all these things were realities.

Then I replied, "While these things remain, I will not visit Fort Garry."

Then I was told that Colonel Wolseley had written, urging the construction of a road between Fort Garry and Lake of the Woods, and that it could not be done unless I visited the upper settlement.

I felt a wish, and a very strong one, to visit this upper Fort Garry and see for myself its chief and its garrison, if the thing could be managed in any possible way.

From many sources I was advised that it would be dangerous to do so; but those who tendered this counsel had in a manner grown old under the despotism of M. Riel, and had, moreover, begun to doubt that the expeditionary force would ever succeed in overcoming the terrible obstacles of the long route from Lake Superior. I knew better. Of Riel I knew nothing, or next to nothing; of the progress of the expeditionary force, I knew only that it was led by a man who regarded impossibilities merely in the light of obstacles to be cleared from his path; and that it was composed of soldiers who, thus led, would go any where, and do any thing, that men in any shape of savagery or of civilization can do or dare. And although no tidings had reached me of its having passed the rugged portage from the shore of Lake Superior to the height of land and launched itself fairly on the waters which flow from thence into Lake Winnipeg, still its ultimate approach never gave me one doubtful thought. I reckoned much on the Bishop's letter, which I had still in my possession, and on the influence which his last communication to the "President" would of necessity exercise; so I decided to visit Fort Garry, upon the conditions that my baggage was restored intact, Mr. Dreever set at liberty, and the nondescript flag taken down. My interviewer said he could promise the first two propositions, but of the third he was not so certain. He would, however, despatch a message to me with full information as to how they had been received. I gave him until five o'clock the following evening, at which hour, if his messenger had not appeared, I was to start for the Winnipeg River, en route for the Expedition.

Five o'clock came on the following day, and no messenger. Every thing was in readiness for my departure: the canoe, freshly pitched, was declared fit for the Winnipeg itself; the provisions were all ready to be put on board at a moment's notice. I gave half an hour's law, and that delay brought the messenger; so, putting off my intention of starting, I turned my face back towards Fort Garry. My former interviewer had sent me a letter; all was as I wished-Mr. Dreever had been set at liberty, my baggage given up, and he would expect me on the following morning.

The Indians were in a terrible state of commotion over my going. One of their chief medicine-men, an old Swampy named Bear, laboured long and earnestly to convince me that Riel had got on what he called "the track of blood," the devil's track, and that he could not get off of it. This curious proposition he endeavoured to illustrate by means of three small pegs of wood, which he set up on the ground. One represented Riel, another his Satanic Majesty, while the third was supposed to indicate myself.

He moved these three pegs about-very much after the fashion of a thimble-rigger; and I seemed to have, through my peg, about as bad a time of it as the pea under the thimble usually experiences. Upon the most conclusive testimony, Bear proceeded to show that I hadn't a chance between Riel and the devil, who, according to an equally clear demonstration, were about as bad as bad could be.

I had to admit a total inability to follow Bear in the reasoning which led to his deductions; but that only proved that I was not a "medicine-man," and knew nothing whatever of the peg theory.

So, despite of the evil deductions drawn by Bear from the three pegs, I set out for Fort Garry, and, journeying along the same road which I had travelled two nights previously, I arrived in sight of the village of Winnipeg before midday on the 23rd of July. At a little distance from the village rose the roof and flag-staffs of Fort Garry, and around in unbroken verdure stretched-the prairie lands of Red River.

Passing from the village along the walls of the fort, I crossed the Assineboine River and saw the "International" lying at her moorings below the floating bridge. The captain had been liberated, and waved his hand with a cheer as I crossed the bridge. The gate of the fort stood open, a sentry was leaning lazily against the wall, a portion of which leant in turn against nothing. The whole exterior of the place looked old and dirty. The muzzles of one or two guns protruding through the embrasures in the flanking bastions failed even to convey the idea of-fort or fortress to the mind of the beholder.

Returning from the east or St. Boniface side of the Red River, I was conducted by my companion into the fort. His private residence was situated within the walls, and to it we proceeded. Upon entering the gate I took in at a glance the surroundings-ranged in a semi-circle with their muzzles all pointing towards the entrance, stood some six or eight field-pieces; on each side and in front were bare looking, white-washed buildings. The ground and the houses looked equally dirty, and the whole aspect of the place was desolate and ruinous.

A few ragged-looking dusky men with rusty firelocks, and still more rusty bayonets, stood lounging about. We drove through without stopping, and drew up at the door of my companion's house, which was situated at the rear of the buildings I have spoken of. From the two flag-staffs flew two flags, one-the Union Jack in shreds and tatters, the other a well-kept bit of bunting having the fleur-de-lis and a shamrock on a white field. Once in the house, my companion asked me if I would see Mr. Riel.

"To call on him, certainly not," was my reply.

"But if he calls on you?"

"Then I will see him," replied I.

The gentleman who had spoken thus soon left the room. There stood in the centre of the apartment a small billiard table, I took up a cue and commenced a game with the only other occupant of the room-the same individual who had on the previous evening acted as messenger to the Indian Settlement. We had played some half a dozen strokes when the door opened, and my friend returned. Following him closely came a short stout man with a large head, a sallow, puffy face, a sharp, restless, intelligent eye, a square-cut massive forehead overhung by a mass of long and thickly clustering hair, and marked with well-cut eyebrows--altogether, a remarkable-looking face, all the more so, perhaps, because it was to be seen in a land where such things are rare sights.

This was M. Louis Riel, the head and front of the Red River Rebellion-the President, the little Napoleon, the Ogre, or whatever else he may be called. He was dressed in a curious mixture of clothing--a black frock-coat, vest, and trousers; but the effect of this somewhat clerical costume was not a little marred by a pair of Indian mocassins, which nowhere look more out of place than on a carpeted floor.

M. Riel advanced to me, and we shook hands with all that empressement so characteristic of hand-shaking on the American Continent. Then there came a pause. My companion had laid his cue down. I still retained mine in my hands, and, more as a means of bridging the awkward gulf of silence which followed the introduction, I asked him to continue the game--another stroke or two, and the mocassined President began to move nervously about the window recess. To relieve his burthened feelings, I inquired if he ever indulged in billiards; a rather laconic "Never," was his reply.

"Quite a loss," I answered, making an absurd stroke across the table; "a capital game."

I had scarcely uttered this profound sentiment when I beheld the President moving hastily towards the door, muttering as he went, "I see I am intruding here." There was hardly time to say, "Not at all," when he vanished.

But my companion was too quick for him; going out into the hall, he brought him back once more into the room, called away my billiard opponent, and left me alone with the chosen of the people of the new nation.

Motioning M. Riel to be seated, I took a chair myself, and the conversation began.

Speaking with difficulty, and dwelling long upon his words, Riel regretted that I should have shown such distrust of him and his party as to prefer the Lower Fort and the English Settlement to the Upper Fort and the society of the French. I answered, that if such distrust existed it was justified by the rumours spread by his sympathizers on the American frontier, who represented him as making active preparations to resist the approaching Expedition.

"Nothing," he said, "was more false than these statements. I only wish to retain power until I can resign it to a proper Government. I have done every thing for the sake of peace, and to prevent bloodshed amongst the people of this land. But they will find," he added passionately, "they will find, if they try, these people here, to put me out-they will find they cannot do it. I will keep what is mine until the proper Government arrives;" as he spoke he got up from his chair and began to pace nervously about the room.

I mentioned having met Bishop Taché in St. Paul and the letter which I had received from him. He read it attentively and commenced to speak about the Expedition.

"Had I come from it?"

"No; I was going to it."

He seemed surprised.

"By the road to the Lake of the Woods?"

"No; by the Winnipeg River," I replied.

"Where was the Expedition?"

I could not answer this question; but I concluded it could not be very far from the Lake of the Woods.

"Was it a large force?"

I told him exactly, setting the limits as low as possible, not to deter him from fighting if such was his intention. The question uppermost in his mind was one of which he did not speak, and he deserves the credit of his silence. Amnesty or no amnesty was at that moment a matter of very grave import to the French half-breeds, and to none so much as to their leader. Yet he never asked if that pardon was an event on which he could calculate. He did not even allude to it at all.

At one time, when speaking of the efforts he had made for the advantage of his country, he grew very excited, walking hastily up and down the room with theatrical attitudes and declamation, which he evidently fancied had the effect of imposing on his listener; but, alas! for the vanity of man, it only made him appear ridiculous; the mocassins sadly marred the exhibition of presidential power.

An Indian speaking with the solemn gravity of his race looks right manful enough, as with moose-clad leg his mocassined feet rest on prairie grass or frozen snow-drift; but this picture of the black-coated Metis playing the part of Europe's great soldier in the garb of a priest and the shoes of a savage looked simply absurd. At length M. Riel appeared to think he had enough of the interview, for stopping in front of me he said,

"Had I been your enemy you would have known it be fore. I heard you would not visit me, and, although I felt humiliated, I came to see you to show you my pacific inclinations."

Then darting quickly from the room he left me. An hour later I left the dirty ill-kept fort. The place was then full of half-breeds armed and unarmed. They said nothing and did nothing, but simply stared as I drove by. I had seen the inside of Fort Garry and its president, not at my solicitation but at his own; and now before me lay the solitudes of the foaming Winnipeg and the pathless waters of great inland seas.

It was growing dusk when I reached the Lower Fort. My canoe men stood ready, for the hour at which I was to have joined them had passed, and they had begun to think some mishap had befallen me. After a hasty supper and a farewell to my kind host of the Lower Fort, I stepped into the frail canoe of painted bark which lay restive on the swift current. "All right; away!" The crew, with paddles held high for the first dip, gave a parting shout, and like an arrow from its bow we shot out into the current. Overhead the stars were beginning to brighten in the intense blue of the twilight heavens; far away to the north, where the river ran between wooded shores, the luminous arch of the twilight bow spanned the horizon, merging the northern constellation into its soft hazy glow. Towards that north we held our rapid way, while the shadows deepened on the shores and the reflected stars grew brighter on the river.

We halted that night at the mission, resuming our course at sunrise on the following morning. A few miles below the mission stood the huts and birch-bark lodges Of the Indians. My men declared that it would be impossible to pass without the ceremony of a visit. The chief had given them orders on the subject, and all the Indians were expecting it; so, paddling in to the shore, I landed and walked up the pathway leading to the chief's hut.

It was yet very early in the morning, and most of the braves were lying asleep inside their wigwams, dogs and papooses seeming to have matters pretty much their own way outside.

The hut in which dwelt the son of Pequis was small, low, and ill-ventilated. Opening the latched door I entered stooping; nor was there much room to extend oneself when the interior was attained.

44

The son of Pequis had not yet been aroused from his morning's slumber; the noise of my entrance, however, disturbed him, and he quickly came forth from a small interior den, rubbing his eyelids and gaping profusely. He looked sleepy all over, and was as much disconcerted as a man usually is who has a visit of ceremony paid to him as he is getting out of bed.

Prince, the son of Pequis, essayed a speech, but I am constrained to admit that taken altogether it was a miserable failure. Action loses dignity when it is accompanied by furtive attempts at buttoning nether garments, and not even the eloquence of the Indian is proof against the generally demoralized aspect of a man just out of bed. I felt that some apology was due to the chief for this early visit; but I told him that being on my way to meet the great Ogima whose braves were coming from the big sea water, I could not pass the Indian camp without stopping to say good-bye.

Before any thing else could be said I shook Prince by the hand and walked back towards the river.

By this time, however, the whole camp was thoroughly aroused. From each lodge came forth warriors decked in whatever garments could be most easily donned.

The chief gave a signal, and a hundred trading-guns were held aloft and a hundred shots rang out on the morning air. Again and again the salutes were repeated, the whole tribe moving down to the water's edge to see me off. Putting out into the middle of the river, I discharged my four teen shooter in the air in rapid succession; a prolonged war whoop answered my salute, and paddling their very best, for the eyes of the finest canoers in the world were upon them, my men drove the little craft flying over the water until the Indian village and its still firing braves were hidden behind a river bend. Through many marsh-lined channels, and amidst a vast sea of reeds and rushes, the Red River of the North seeks the waters of Lake Winnipeg. A mixture of land and water, of mud, and of the varied vegetation which grows thereon, this delta of the Red River is, like other spots of a similar description, inexplicably lonely.

The wind sighs over it, bending the tall reeds with mournful rustle, and the wild bird passes and repasses with plaintive cry over the rushes which form his summer home.

Emerging from the sedges of the Red River, we shot out into the waters of an immense lake, a lake which stretched away into unseen spaces, and over whose waters the fervid July sun was playing strange freaks of mirage and inverted shore land.

This was Lake Winnipeg, a great lake even on a continent where lakes are inland seas. But vast as it is now, it is only a tithe of what it must have been in the earlier ages of the earth.

The capes and headlands of what once was a vast inland sea now stand far away from the shores of Winnipeg. Hundreds of miles from its present limits these great landmarks still look down on an ocean, but it is an ocean of grass. The waters of Winnipeg have retired from their feet, and they are now mountain ridges rising over seas of verdure. At the bottom of this bygone lake lay the whole valley of the Red River, the present Lakes Winnipegoos and Manitoba, and the prairie lands of the Lower Assineboine, 100,000 square miles of water. The water has long since been drained off by the lowering of the rocky channels leading to Hudson Bay, and the bed of the extinct lake now forms the richest prairie land in the world.

But although Winnipeg has shrunken to a tenth of its original size, its rivers still remain worthy of the great basin into which they once flowed. The Saskatchewan is longer than the Danube, the Winnipeg has twice the volume of the Rhine. 400,000 square miles of continent shed their waters into Lake Winnipeg; a lake as changeful as the ocean, but, fortunately for us, in its very calmest mood to-day. Not a wave, not a ripple on its surface; not a breath of breeze to aid the untiring paddles. The little canoe, weighed down by men and provisions, had scarcely three inches of its gunwale over the water, and yet the steersman held his course far out into the glassy waste, leaving behind the marshy headlands which marked the river's mouth.

A long low point stretching from the south shore of the lake was faintly visible on the horizon. It was past mid day when we reached it; so, putting in among the rocky boulders which lined the shore, we lighted our fire and cooked our dinner. Then, resuming our way, the Grande Traverse was entered upon. Far away over the lake rose the point of the Big Stone, a lonely cape whose perpendicular front was raised high over the water. The sun began to sink towards the west; but still not a breath rippled the surface of the lake, not a sail moved over the wide expanse, all was as lonely as though our tiny craft had been the sole speck of life on the waters of the world. The red sun sank into the lake, warning us that it was time to seek the shore and make our beds for the night. A deep sandy bay, with a high backing of woods and rocks, seemed to invite us to its solitudes. Steering in with great caution amid the rocks, we landed in this sheltered spot, and our boat upon the sandy beach. The shore yielded large store of drift-wood, the relics of many a northern gale. Behind us lay a trackless forest; in front the golden glory of the Western sky. As the night shades deepened around us and the red glare of our drift-wood fire cast its light upon the woods and the rocks, the scene became one of rare beauty.

As I sat watching from a little distance this picture so full of all the charms of the wild life of the voyageur and the Indian, I little marvelled that the red child of the lakes and the woods should be loth to quit such scenes for all the luxuries of our civilization. Almost as I thought with pity over his fate, seeing here the treasures of nature which were his, there suddenly emerged from the forest two dusky forms.' They were Ojibbeways, who came to share our fire and our evening meal. The land was still their own. When I lay down to rest that night on the dry sandy shore, I long watched the stars above me. As children sleep after a day of toil and play, so slept the dusky men who lay around me. It was my first night with these poor wild sons of the lone spaces; it was strange and weird, and the lapping of the mimic wave against the rocks close by failed to bring sleep to my thinking eyes. Many a night afterwards I lay down to sleep beside these men and their brethren--many a night by lake-shore, by torrent's edge, and far out amidst the measureless meadows of the West--but "custom stales" even nature's infinite variety, and through many wild bivouacs my memory still wanders back to that first night out by the shore of Lake Winnipeg.

At break of day we launched the canoe again and pursued our course for the mouth of the Winnipeg River. The lake which yesterday was all sunshine, to-day looked black and overcast--thunder-clouds hung angrily around the horizon, and it seemed as though Winnipeg was anxious to give a sample of her rough ways before she had done with us. While the morning was yet young we made a portage--that is, we carried the canoe and its stores across a neck of land, saving thereby a long paddle round a projecting cape. The portage was through a marshy tract covered with long grass and rushes. While the men are busily engaged in carrying across the boat and stores, I will introduce them to the reader. They were four in number, and were named as follows:-Joseph Monkman, cook and interpreter; William Prince, full Indian; Thomas Smith, ditto; Thomas Hope, ci-devant schoolmaster, and now self-constituted steersman. The three first were good men. Prince, in particular, was a splendid canoe-man in dangerous water. But Hope possessed the greatest capacity for eating and talking of any man I ever met. He could devour quantities of pemmican any number of times during the day, and be hungry still. What he taught during the period when he was schoolmaster I have never been able to find out, but he was popularly supposed at the mission to be a very good Christian. He had a marked disinclination to hard or continued toil, although he would impress an on looker with a sense of unremitting exertion. This he achieved by divesting himself of his shirt and using his paddle, as Alp used his sword, "with right arm bare." A fifth Indian was added to the canoe soon after crossing the portage.

A couple of Indian lodges stood on the shore along which we were coasting. We put in towards these lodges to ask information, and found them to belong to Samuel Henderson, full Swampy Indian. Samuel, who spoke excellent English, at once volunteered to come with me as a guide to the Winnipeg River; but I declined to engage him until I had a report of his capability for the duty from the Hudson Bay officer in charge of Fort Alexander, a fort now only a few miles distant. Samuel at once launched his canoe, said "Good-bye" to his wife and nine children, and started after us for the fort, where, on the advice of the officer, I finally engaged him.

CHAPTER TEN.

The Winnipeg River--The Ojibbeway's House--Rushing a Rapid--A Camp--No Tidings of the Coming Man--Hope in Danger--Rat Portage--A far-fetched Islington--"Like Pemmican".

WE entered the mouth of the Winnipeg River at midday and paddled up to Fort Alexander, which stands about a mile from the river's entrance. Here I made my final preparations for the ascent of the Winnipeg, getting a fresh canoe better adapted for forcing the rapids, and at five o'clock in the evening started on my journey Up the river. Eight miles above the fort the roar of a great fall of water sounded through the twilight. In surge and spray and foaming torrent the enormous volume of the Winnipeg was making its last grand leap on its way to mingle its waters with the lake. On the flat surface of an enormous rock which stood well out into the boiling water we made our fire and our camp.

The pine-trees which gave the fall its name stood round us, dark and solemn, waving their long arms to and fro in the gusty winds that swept the valley. It was a wild picture. The pine-trees standing in inky blackness the rushing water, white with foam-above, the rifted thunder-clouds. Soon the lightning began to flash and the voice of the thunder to sound above the roar of the cataract. My Indians made me a rough shelter with cross-poles and a sail-cloth, and, huddling themselves together under the upturned canoe, we slept regardless of the storm.

I was ninety miles from Fort Garry, and as yet no tidings of the Expedition.

A man may journey very far through the lone spaces of the earth without meeting with another Winnipeg River. In it nature has contrived to place her two great units of earth and water in strange and wild combinations. To say that the Winnipeg River has an immense volume of water, that it descends 360 feet in a distance of 160 miles, that it is full of eddies and whirlpools, of every variation of waterfall from chutes to cataracts, that it expands into lonely pine edged lakes and far-reaching island-studded bays, that its bed is cumbered with immense wave-polished rocks, that its vast solitudes are silent and its cascades ceaselessly active--to say all this is but to tell in bare items of fact the narrative of its beauty. For the Winnipeg by the multiplicity of its perils and the ever-changing beauty of its character, defies the description of civilized men as it defies the puny efforts of civilized travel. It seems part of the savage-fitted alone for him and for his ways, useless to carry the burden of man's labour, but useful to shelter the wild things of wood and water which dwell in its waves and along its shores. And the red man who steers his little birch-bark canoe through the foaming rapids of the Winnipeg, how well he knows its various ways! To him it seems to possess life and instinct, he speaks of it as one would of a high-mettled charger which will do any thing if he be rightly handled. It gives him his test of superiority, his proof of courage. To shoot the Otter Falls or the Rapids of the Barriere, to carry his canoe down the whirling eddies of Portage-de-l'Isle, to lift her from the rush of water at the Seven Portages, or launch her by the edge of the whirlpool below the Chute-à-Jocko, all this is to be a brave and a skilful Indian, for the man who can do all this must possess a power in the sweep of his paddle, a quickness of glance, and a quiet consciousness of skill, not to be found except after generations of practice. For hundreds of years the Indian has lived amidst these rapids; they have been the playthings of his boyhood, the realities of his life, the instinctive habit of his old age. What the horse is to the Arab, what the dog is to the Esquimaux, what the camel is to those who journey across Arabian deserts, so is the canoe to the Ojibbeway. Yonder wooded shore yields him from first to last the materials-he requires for its construction: cedar for the slender ribs, birch-bark to cover them, juniper to stitch together the separate pieces, red pine to give resin for the seams and crevices. By the lake or river shore, close to his wigwam, the boat is built;

"And the forest life is in it All its mystery and its magic, All the tightness of the birch-tree, All the toughness of the cedar, All the larch's supple sinews. And it floated on the river Like a yellow leaf in autumn, Like a yellow water-lily."

It is not a boat, it is a house; it can be carried long distances over land from lake to lake. It is frail beyond words, yet you can load it down to the water's edge; it carries the Indian by day, it shelters him by night; in it he will steer boldly out into a vast lake where land is unseen, or paddle through mud and swamp or reedy shallows; sitting in it, he gathers his harvest of wild rice and catches his fish or shoots his game; it will dash down a foaming rapid, brave a fiercely-rushing torrent, or lie like a sea-bird on the placid water.

For six months the canoe is the home of the Ojibbeway. While the trees are green, while the waters dance and sparkle, while the wild rice bends its graceful head in the lake and the wild duck dwells amidst the rush-covered mere, the Ojibbeway's home is the birch-bark canoe. When the winter comes and the lake and rivers harden beneath the icy breath of the north wind, the canoe is put carefully away; covered with branches and with snow, it lies through the long dreary winter until the wild swan and the wavy, passing northward to the polar seas, call it again from its long icy sleep.

Such is the life of the canoe, and such the river along which it rushes like an arrow.

The days that now commenced to pass were filled from dawn to dark with moments of keenest enjoyment, every thing was new and strange, and each hour brought with it some fresh surprise of Indian skill or Indian scenery.

The sun would be just tipping the western shores with his first rays when the canoe would be lifted from its ledge of rock and laid gently on the water; then the blankets and kettles, the provisions and the guns would be placed in it, and four Indians would take their seats, while one remained on the shore to steady the bark upon the water and keep its sides from contact with the rock; then when I had taken my place in the centre, the outside man would spring gently in, and we would glide away from the rocky resting-place. To tell the mere work of each day is no difficult matter: start at five o'clock a.m., halt for breakfast at seven o'clock, off again at eight, halt at one o'clock for dinner, away at two o'clock, paddle until sunset at 7:30; that was the work of each day. But how shall I attempt to fill in the details of scene and circumstance between these rough outlines of time and toil, for almost at every hour of the long summer day the great Winnipeg

WORKING UP THE WINNIPEG.

revealed some new phase of beauty and of peril, some changing scene of lonely grandeur? I have already stated that the river in its course from the Lake of the Woods to Lake Winnipeg, 160 miles, makes a descent of 360 feet. This descent is effected not by a continuous decline, but by a series of terraces at various distances from each other; in other words, the river forms innumerable lakes and wide expanding reaches bound together by rapids and perpendicular falls of varying altitude, thus when the voyageur has lifted his canoe from the foot of the Silver Falls and launched it again above the head of that rapid, he will have surmounted two-and-twenty feet of the ascent; again, the dreaded Seven Portages will give him a total rise of sixty feet in a distance of three miles. (How cold does the bare narration of these facts appear beside their actual realization in a small canoe manned by Indians!) Let us see if we can picture one of these many scenes. There sounds ahead a roar of falling water, and we see, upon rounding some pine-clad island or ledge of rock, a tumbling mass of foam and spray studded with projecting rocks and flanked by dark wooded shores; above we can see nothing, but below the waters, maddened by their wild rush amidst the rocks, surge and leap in angry whirlpools. It is as wild a scene of crag and wood and water as the eye can gaze upon, but we look upon it not for its beauty, because there is no time for that, but because it is an enemy that must be conquered. Now mark how these Indians steal upon this enemy before he is aware of it. The immense volume of water, escaping from the eddies and whirlpools at the foot of the fall, rushes on in a majestic sweep into calmer water; this rush produces along the shores of the river a counter or back-current which flows up sometimes close to the foot of the fall, along this back-water the canoe is carefully steered, being often not six feet from the opposing rush in the central river, but the back-current in turn ends in a whirlpool, and the canoe, if it followed this back-current, would inevitably end in the same place; for a minute there is no paddling, the bow paddle and the steersman alone keeping the boat in her proper direction as she drifts rapidly up the current. Amongst the crew not a word is spoken, but every man knows what he has to do and will be ready when the moment comes; and now the moment has come, for on one side there foams along a mad surge of water, and on the other the angry whirlpool twists and turns in smooth green hollowing curves round an axis of air, whirling round it with a strength that would snap our birch bark into fragments and suck us down into great depths below. All that can be gained by the back-current has been gained, and now it is time to quit it; but where? for there is often only the choice of the whirlpool or the central river. Just on the very edge of the eddy there is one loud shout given by the bow paddle, and the canoe shoots full into the centre of the boiling flood, driven by the united strength of the entire crew--the men work for their very lives, and the boat breasts across the river with her head turned full toward the falls; the waters foam and dash about her, the waves leap high over the gunwale, the Indians shout as they dip their paddles like lightning into the foam, and the stranger to such a scene holds his breath amidst this war of man against nature. Ha! the struggle is useless, they cannot force her against such a torrent, we are close to the rocks and the foam; but see, she is driven down by the current in spite of those wild fast strokes. The dead strength of such a rushing flood must prevail. Yes, it is true, the canoe has been driven back; but behold, almost in a second the whole thing is done-we float suddenly beneath a little rocky isle on the foot of the cataract. We have crossed the river in the face of the fall, and the portage landing is over this rock, while three yards out on either side the torrent foams its headlong course. Of the skill necessary to perform such things it is useless to speak. A single false stroke, and the whole thing would have failed; driven headlong down the torrent, another attempt would have to be made to gain this rock-protected spot, but now we lie secure here; spray all around us, for the rush of the river is on either side and you can touch it with an outstretched paddle. The Indians rest on their paddles and laugh; their long hair has escaped from its-fastening through their exertion, and they retie it while they rest. One is already standing upon the wet slippery rock holding the canoe in its place, then the others get out. The freight is carried up piece by piece and deposited on the flat surface some ten feet above; that done, the canoe is lifted out very gently, for a single blow against this hard granite boulder would shiver and splinter the frail birch-bark covering; they raise her very carefully up the steep face of the cliff and rest again on the top. What a view there is from this coigne of vantage! We are on the lip of the fall, on each side it makes its plunge, and below we mark at leisure the torrent we have just braved; above, it is smooth water, and away ahead we see the foam of another rapid. The rock on which we stand has been worn smooth by the washing of the water during countless ages, and from a cleft or fissure there springs a pine-tree or a rustling aspen. We have crossed the Petit Roches, and our course is onward still.

Through many scenes like this we held our way during the last days of July. The weather was beautiful; now and then a thunder-storm would roll along during the night, but the morning sun rising clear and bright would almost tempt one to believe that it had been a dream, if the pools of water in the hollows of the rocks and the dampness of blanket or oil-cloth had not proved the sun a humbug. Our general distance each day would be about thirty-two miles, with an average of six portages. At sunset we made our camp on some rocky isle or shelving shore, one or two cut wood, another got the cooking things ready, a fourth gummed the seams of the canoe, a fifth cut shavings from a dry stick for the fire--for myself, I generally took a plunge in the cool delicious water--and soon the supper hissed in the pans, the kettle steamed from its suspending stick, and the evening meal was eaten with appetites such as only the voyageur can understand.

Then when the shadows of the night had fallen around and all was silent, save the river's tide against the rocks, we would stretch our blankets on the springy moss of the crag and lie down to sleep with only the stars for a roof.

Happy, happy days were these--days the memory of which goes very far into the future, growing brighter as we journey farther away from them, for the scenes through which our course was laid were such as speak in whispers, only when we have left them--the whispers of the pine-tree, the music of running water, the stillness of great lonely lakes.

On the evening of the fifth day from leaving Fort Alexander we reached the foot of the Rat Portage, the twenty-seventh, and last, upon the Winnipeg River; above this portage stretched the Lake of the Woods, which here poured its waters through a deep rock-bound gorge with tremendous force. During the five days we had only encountered two solitary Indians; they knew nothing whatever about the Expedition, and, after a short parley and a present of tea and flour, we pushed on. About midday on the fourth day we halted at the Mission of the White Dog, a spot which some more than heathen missionary had named Islington in a moment of virtuous cockneyism. What could have tempted him to commit this act of desecration it is needless to ask.

Islington on the Winnipeg! O religious Gilpin, hadst thou fallen a prey to savage Cannibalism, not even Sidney Smith's farewell aspiration would have saved the savage who devoured you, you must have killed him.

The Mission of the White Dog had been the scene of Thomas Hope's most brilliant triumphs in the role of schoolmaster, and the youthful Ojibbeways of the place had formerly belonged to the band of hope. For some days past Thomas had been labouring under depression, his power of devouring pemmican had, it is true, remained unimpaired, but in one or two trying moments of toil, in rapids and portages, he had been found miserably wanting; he had, in fact, shown many indications of utter uselessness; he had also begun to entertain gloomy apprehensions of what the French would do to him when they caught him on the Lake of the Woods, and although he endeavoured frequently to prove that under certain circumstances the French would have no chance whatever against him, yet, as these circumstances were from the nature of things never likely to occur, necessitating, in the first instance, a presumption that Thomas would show fight, he failed to convince not only his hearers, but himself, that he was not in a very bad way. At the White Dog Mission he was, so to speak, on his own hearth, and was doubtless desirous of showing me that his claims to the rank of interpreter were well founded. No tidings whatever had reached the few huts of the Indians at the White Dog; the women and children, who now formed the sole inhabitants, went but little out of the neighbourhood, and the men had been away for many days in the forest, hunting and fishing. Thus, through the whole course of the Winnipeg, from lake to lake, I could glean no tale or tidings of the great Ogima or of his myriad warriors. It was quite dark when we reached, on the evening of the 30th July, the northern edge of the Lake of the Woods and paddled across its placid waters to the Hudson Bay Company's post at the Rat Portage. An arrival of a canoe with six strangers is no ordinary event at one of these remote posts which the great fur company have built at long intervals over their immense territory. Out came the denizens of a few Indian lodges, out came the people of the fort and the clerk in charge of it. My first question was about the Expedition, but here, as elsewhere, no tidings had been heard of it. Other tidings were however forthcoming which struck terror into the heart of Hope. Suspicious canoes had been seen for-some days past amongst the many islands of the lake; strange men had come to the fort at night, and strange fires had been seen on the islands-the French were out on the lake. The officer in charge of the post was absent at the time of my visit, but I had met him at Fort Alexander, and he had anticipated my wants in a letter which I myself carried to his son. I now determined to strain every effort to cross with rapidity the Lake of the Woods and ascend the Rainy River to the next post of the Company, Fort Francis, distant from Rat Portage about 1400 miles, for there I felt sure that I must learn tidings of the Expedition and bring my long solitary journey to a close. But the Lake of the Woods is an immense sheet of water lying 1000 feet above the sea level, and subject to violent gales which lash its bosom into angry billows. To be detained upon some island, storm-bound amidst the lake, %would never have answered, so I ordered a large keeled boat to be got ready by midday it only required a few trifling repairs of sail and oars, but a great feast had to be gone through in which my pemmican and flour were destined to play a very prominent part. As the word pemmican is one which may figure frequently in these pages, a few words explanatory of it may be useful. Pemmican, the favourite food of the Indian and the half-breed voyageur, can be made from the flesh of any animal, but it is nearly altogether composed of buffalo meat; the meat is first cut into slices, then dried either by fire or in the sun, and then pounded or beaten out into a thick flaky substance; in this state it is put into a large bag made from the hide of the animal, the dry pulp being soldered down into a hard solid mass by melted fat being poured over it-the quantity of fat is nearly half the total weight, forty pounds of fat going to fifty pounds of "beat meat;" the best pemmican generally has added to it ten pounds of berries and sugar, the whole composition forming the most solid description of food that man can make. If any person should feel inclined to ask, "What does pemmicau taste like?" I can only reply, "Like pemmican," there is nothing else in the world that bears to it the slightest resemblance. -Can I say any thing that Will give the reader an idea of its sufficing quality? Yes, I think I can. A dog that will eat from four to six pounds of raw fish a day when sleighing, will only devour two pounds: of pemmican, if he be fed upon that food; yet I have seen Indians and half-breeds eat four pounds of it in a single day-but this is anticipating. Pemmican can be prepared in many ways, and it is not easy to decide which method is the least objectionable. There is rubeiboo and richot, and pemmican plain and pemmican raw, this last method being the one most in vogue amongst voyageurs; but the richot, to me, seemed the best; mixed with a little flour and fried in a pan, pemmican in this form can be eaten, provided the appetite be sharp and there is nothing else to be had--this last consideration is, however, of importance.

CHAPTER ELEVEN.

The Expedition--The Lake of the Woods--A Night Alarm--A close Shave--Rainy River--A Night Paddle--Fort Francis--A Meeting--The Officer commanding the Expedition--The Rank and File--The 60th Rifles--A Windigo--Ojibbeway Bravery--Canadian Volunteers.

The feast having been concluded (I believe it had gone on all night, and was protracted far into the morning), the sails and oars were suddenly reported ready, and about midday on the 31st July we stood away from the Portages du Rat into the Lake of the Woods. I had added another man to my crew, which now numbered seven hands, the last accession was a French half-breed, named Morrisseau. Thomas Hope had possessed himself of a flint gun, with which he was to do desperate things should we fall in with the French scouts upon the lake. The boat in which I now found myself was a large, roomy craft, capable of carrying about three tons of freight; it had a single tall mast carrying a large square lug-sail, and also possessed of powerful sweeps, which were worked by the men in standing positions, the rise of the oar after each stroke making the oarsman sink back upon the thwarts only to resume again his upright attitude for the next dip of the heavy sweep.

This is the regular Hudson Bay Mackinaw boat, used for the carrying trade of the great Fur Company on every river from the Bay of Hudson to the Polar Ocean. It looks a big, heavy, lumbering affair, but it can sail well before a wind, and will do good work with the oars too.

That portion of the Lake of the Woods through which we now steered our way was a perfect maze and network of island and narrow channel; a light breeze from the north favoured us, and we passed gently along the rocky islet shores through unruffled water. In all directions there opened out innumerable channels, some narrow and winding, others straight and open, but all lying'-between shores clothed with a rich and luxuriant vegetation; shores that curved and twisted into mimic bays and tiny promontories, that rose in rocky masses abruptly from the water, that sloped down to meet the lake in gently swelling undulations, that seemed, in fine, to present in the compass of a single glance every varying feature of island scenery. Looking through these rich labyrinths of tree and moss-covered rock, it was difficult to imagine that winter could ever -stamp its frozen image upon such a soft summer scene. The air was balmy with the scented things which grow profusely upon the islands; the water was warm, almost tepid, and yet despite of this the winter frost would cover the lake with five feet of ice, and the thick brushwood of the islands would lie hidden during many months beneath great depths of snow.

As we glided along through this beautiful scene the men kept a sharp look-out for the suspicious craft whose presence had caused such alarm at the Portage-du-Rat. We saw no trace of man or canoe, and nothing broke the stillness of the evening except the splash of a sturgeon in the lonely bays. About sunset we put ashore upon a large rock for supper. While it was being prepared I tried to count the islands around. From a projecting point I could see island upon island to the number of over a hundred--the wild cherry, the plum, the wild rose, the raspberry, intermixed with ferns and mosses in vast variety, covered every spot around me, and from rock and crevice the pine and the poplar hung their branches over the water. As the breeze still blew fitfully from the north we again embarked and held our way through the winding channels--at times these channels would grow wider only again to close together; but there was no current, and the large high sail moved us slowly through the water. When it became dark a fire suddenly appeared on an island some distance ahead. Thomas Hope grasped his flint gun and seemed to think the supreme moment had at length arrived. During the evening I could tell by the gestures and looks of the men that the mysterious rovers formed the chief subject of conversation, and our latest accession painted so vividly their various suspicious movements, that Thomas was more than ever convinced his hour was at hand. Great then was the excitement when the fire was observed upon the island, and greater still when I told Samuel to steer full towards it. As we approached we could distinguish figures moving to and fro between us and the bright flame, but when we had got within a few hundred yards of the spot the light was suddenly extinguished, and the ledge of rock upon which it had been burning became wrapped in darkness. We hailed, but there was no reply. Whoever had been around the fire had vanished through the trees; launching their canoe upon the other side of the island, they had paddled away through the intricate labyrinth scared by our sudden appearance in front of their lonely bivouac. This apparent confirmation of his worst fears in no way served to reanimate the spirits of Hope, and though shortly after he lay down with the other men in the bottom of the boat, it was not without misgivings as to the events which lay before him in the darkness. One man only remained up to steer, for it was my intention to run as long as the breeze, faint though it was, lasted. I had been asleep about half an hour when I felt my arm quickly pulled, and, looking up, beheld Samuel bending over me, while with one hand he steered the boat. "Here they are," he whispered, "here they are." I looked over the gunwale and under the sail and beheld right on the course we were steering two bright fires burning close to the water's edge. We were running down a channel which seemed to narrow to a strait between two islands, and presently a third fire came into view on the other side of the strait, showing distinctly the narrow pass towards which we were steering, it did not appear to be more than twenty feet across it, and, from its exceeding narrowness and the position of the fires, it seemed as though the place had really been selected to dispute our outward passage. We were not more than two hundred yards from the strait and the breeze was holding well into it. What was to be done? Samuel was for putting the helm up; but that would Have been useless, because we were already in the channel, and to run on shore would only place us still more in the power of our enemies, if enemies they were, so I told him to hold his course and run right through the narrow pass. The other men had sprung quickly from their blankets, and Thomas was the picture of terror. When he saw that I was about to run the boat through the strait, he instantly made up his mind to shape for himself a different course. Abandoning his flint musket to any body who would take it, he clambered like a monkey on to the gunwale, with the evident intention of dropping noiselessly into the water, and seeking, by swimming on shore, a safety which he deemed denied to him on board. Never shall I forget his face as he was pulled back into the boat; nor is it easy to describe the sudden revulsion of feeling which possessed him when: a dozen different fires breaking into view showed at once that the forest was on fire, and that the imaginary bivouac of the French was only the flames of burning brushwood. Samuel laughed over his mistake, but Thomas looked on it in no laughing light, and, seizing his gun, stoutly maintained that had it really been the French they would have learnt a terrible lesson from the united volleys of the fourteen-shooter and his flint musket.

The Lake of the Woods covers a very large extent of country. In length it measures about seventy miles, and its greatest breadth is about the same distance; its shores are but little known, and it is only the Indian who can steer with accuracy through its labyrinthine channels. In its southern portion it spreads out into a vast expanse of open water, the surface of which is lashed by tempests into high-running seas.

In the early days of the French fur trade it yielded large stores of beaver and of martens, but it has long ceased to be rich in furs. Its shores and islands will be found to abound in minerals whenever civilization reaches them.

Among the Indians the lake holds high place as the favourite haunt of the Manitou. The strange water-worn rocks, the islands of soft pipe-stone from which are cut the bowls for many a calumet, the curious masses of ore resting on the polished surface of rock, the islands struck yearly by lightning, the islands which abound in lizards although these reptiles are scarce elsewhere--all these make the Lake of the Woods a region abounding in Indian legend and superstition. There are isles upon which he will not dare to venture, because the evil spirit has chosen them; there are promontories upon which offerings must be made to the Manitou when the canoe drifts by their lonely shores; and there are spots watched over by the great Kennebic, or Serpent, who is jealous of the treasures which they contain. But all these things are too long to dwell upon now; I must haste along my way.

On the second morning after leaving Rat Portage we began to leave behind the thickly-studded islands and to get out into the open waters. A thunder-storm had swept the lake during the night, but the morning was calm, and the heavy sweeps were not able to make much way. Suddenly, while we were halted for breakfast, the wind veered round to the north-west and promised us a rapid passage across the Grande Traverse to the mouth of Rainy River. Embarking hastily, we set sail for a strait known as the Grassy Portage, which the high stage of water in the lake enabled us to run through without touching ground. Beyond this strait there stretched away a vast expanse of water over which the white-capped waves were running in high billows from the west. It soon became so rough that we had to take on board the small canoe which I had brought with me from Rat Portage in case of accident, and which was towing astern. On we swept over the high-rolling billows with a double reef in the lug-sail. Before us, far away, rose a rocky promontory, the extreme point of which we had to weather in order to make the mouth of Rainy River. Keeping the boat as close to the wind as she would go, we reeled on over the tumbling seas. Our lee-way was very great, and for some time it seemed doubtful if we would clear the point; as we neared it we saw that there was a tremendous sea running against the rock, the white sprays shooting far up into the air When the rollers struck against it. The wind had now freshened to a gale and the boat laboured much, constantly shipping sprays. At last we were abreast of the rocks, close hauled, and yet only a hundred yards from the breakers. Suddenly the wind veered a little, or the heavy swell which was running caught us, for we began to drift quickly down into the mass of breakers. The men were all huddled together in the bottom of the boat, and for a moment or two nothing could be done. "Out with the sweeps!" I roared. All was confusion; the long sweeps got foul of each other, and for a second every thing went wrong. At last three sweeps were got to work, but they could do nothing against such a sea. We were close to the rocks, so close that one began to make preparations for doing something--one didn't well know what--when we should strike. Two more oars were out, and for an instant we hung in suspense as to the result. How they did pull! it was the old paddle-work forcing the rapid again; and it told; in spite of wave and wind, we were round the point, but it was only by a shade. An hour later we were running through a vast expanse of marsh and reeds into the mouth of Rainy River; the Lake of the Woods was passed, and now before me Lay eighty miles of the Rivière-de-la-Pluie.

A friend of mine once, describing the scenery of the Falls of the Cauvery in India, wrote that "below the falls there was an island round which there was water on every side:" this mode of description, so very true and yet so very simple in its character, may fairly-be applied to Rainy River; one may safely say that it is a river, and that it has banks on Either side of it; if one adds that the banks are rich, fertile, and well wooded, the description will be complete--such was the river up which I now steered to meet the Expedition. The Expedition, where was it? An Indian whom we met on the lake knew nothing about it; perhaps on the river we should hear some tidings. About five miles from the mouth of Rainy River there was a small out-station of the Hudson Bay Company kept by a man named Morrisseau, a brother of my boatman. As we approached this little post it was announced to us by an Indian that Morrisseau had that morning lost a child. It was a place so wretched looking that its name of Hungery Hall seemed well adapted to it.

When the boat touched the shore the father of the dead child came out of the hut, and shook hands with every one in solemn silence; when he came to his brother he kissed him, and the brother in his turn went up the bank and kissed a number of Indian women who were standing round; there was not a word spoken by any one; after awhile they all went into the hut in which the little body lay, and remained some time inside. In its way, I don't ever recollect seeing a more solemn exhibition of grief than this complete silence in the presence of death; there was no question asked, no sign given, and the silence of the dead seemed to have descended upon the living. In a little time several Indians appeared, and I questioned them as to the Expedition; had they seen or heard of it?

"Yes, there was one young man who had seen with his own eyes the great army of the white braves."

"Where?" I asked.

"Where the road slants down into the lake, was the interpreted reply.

"What were they like?" I asked again, half incredulous after so many disappointments.

He thought for awhile: "They were like the locusts," he answered, "they came on one after the other." There could be no mistake about it, he had seen British soldiers.

The chief of the party now came forward, and asked what I had got to say to the Indians; that he would like to hear me make a speech; that they wanted to know why all these men were coming through their country. To make a speech! it was a curious request. I was leaning with my back against the mast, and the Indians were seated in a line on the bank; every thing looked so miserable around, that I thought I might for once play the part of Chadband, and improve the occasion, and, as a speech was expected of me, make it. So I said, "Tell this old chief that I am sorry he is poor and hungry; but let him look around, the land on which he sits is rich and fertile, why does he not cut down the trees that cover it, and plant in their places potatoes and corn? then he will have food in the winter when the moose is scarce and the sturgeon cannot be caught." He did not seem to relish my speech, but said nothing. I gave a few plugs of tobacco all round, and we shoved out again into the river. "Where the road comes down to the lake" the Indian had seen the troops; where was that spot? No easy matter to decide, for lakes are so numerous in this land of the North-west that the springs of the earth seem to have found vent there. Before sunset we fell in with another Indian; he was alone in a canoe, which he paddled close along shore out of the reach of the strong breeze which was sweeping us fast up the river. While he was yet a long way off, Samuel declared that he had recently left Fort Francis, and therefore would bring us news from that place. "How can you tell at this distance that he has come from the fort?" I asked. "Because his shirt looks bright," he answered. And so it was; he had left the fort on the previous day and run seventy miles; he was old Monkman's Indian returning after having left that hardy voyageur at Fort Francis.

Not a soldier of the Expedition had yet reached the fort, nor did any man know where they were.

On again; another sun set and another sun rose, and we were still running up the Rainy River before a strong north wind which fell away towards evening. At sundown of the 3rd August I calculated that some four and twenty miles must yet lie between me and that fort at which, I felt convinced, some distinct tidings must reach me of the progress of the invading column. I was already 180 miles beyond the spot where I had counted upon falling in with them. I was nearly 400 miles from Fort Garry.

Towards evening on the 3rd it fell a dead calm, and the heavy boat could make but little progress against the strong running current of the river, so I bethought me of the little birch-bark canoe which I had brought from Rat Portage; it was a very tiny one, but that was no hindrance to the work I now\ required of it. We had been sailing all day, so my men were fresh. At supper I proposed that Samuel, Monkman, and William Prince should come on with me during the night, that we would leave Thomas Hope in command of the big boat and push on for the fort in the light canoe, taking with us only sufficient food for one meal. The three men at once assented, and Thomas was delighted at the prospect of one last grand feed all to himself, besides the great honour of being promoted to the rank and dignity of Captain of the boat. So we got the little craft out, and having gummed her all over, started once more on our upward way just as the shadows of the night began to close around the river. We were four in number, quite as many as the canoe could carry; she was very low in the water and, owing to some damage received in the rough waves of the Lake of the Woods, soon began to leak badly. Once we put ashore to gum and pitch her seams again, but still the water oozed in and we were wet. What was to be done? with these delays we never could hope to reach the fort by daybreak, and something told me instinctively, that unless I did get there that night I would find the Expedition already arrived. Just at that moment we descried smoke rising amidst the trees on the right shore, and soon saw the poles of Indian lodges. The men said they were very bad Indians. firom the American side--the left shore of Rainy River is American territory--but the chance of a bad Indian was better than the certainty of a bad canoe, and we stopped at the camp. A lot of half-naked redskins came out of the trees, and the pow-wow commenced. I gave them all tobacco, and then asked if they would give me a good canoe in exchange for my bad one, telling them that I would give them a present next day at the fort if one or two amongst them would come up there. After a short parley they assented, and a beautiful canoe was brought out and placed on the water. They also gave us a supply of dried sturgeon, and, again shaking hands all round, we departed on our way.

This time there was no mistake, the canoe proved as dry as a bottle, and we paddled bravely on through the mists of night. About midnight we halted for supper, making a fire amidst the long wet grass, over which we fried the sturgeon and boiled our kettle; then we went on again through the small hours of the morning. At times I could see on the right the mouths of large rivers which flowed from the west: it is down these rivers that the American Indians come to fish for sturgeon in the Rainy River. For nearly 200 miles the country is still theirs, and the Pillager and Red Lake branches of the Ojibbeway nation yet hold their hunting-grounds in the vast swamps of North Minnesota.

These Indians have a bad reputation, as the name of Pillager implies, and my Red River men were anxious to avoid falling in with them. Once during the night, opposite the mouth of one of the rivers opening to the west, we saw the lodges of a large party on our left; with paddles that were never lifted out of the water, we glided

53

noiselessly by, as silently as a wild duck would cleave the current. Once again during the long night a large sturgeon, struck suddenly by a paddle, alarmed us by bounding out of the water and landing full upon the gunwale of the Canoe, splashing back again into the water and wetting us all by his curious manoeuvre. At length in the darkness we heard the hollow roar of the great Falls of the Chaudiere sounding loud through the stillness. It grew louder and louder as with now tiring strokes my worn-out men worked mechanically at their paddles. The day was beginning to break. We were close beneath the Chaudiere and alongside of Fort Francis. The scene was wondrously beautiful. In the indistinct light of the early dawn the cataract seemed twice its natural height, the tops of pine trees rose against the pale green of the coming day, close above the falls the bright morning star hung, diamond-like, over the rim of the descending torrent; around the air was tremulous with the rush of water, and to the north the rose-coloured streaks of the aurora were woven into the dawn. My long solitary journey had nearly reached its close.

Very cold and cramped by the constrained position in which I had remained all night, I reached the fort, and, unbarring the gate, with my rifle knocked at the door of one of the wooden houses. After a little, a man opened the door in the costume, scant and unpicturesque, in which he had risen from his bed.

"Is that Colonel Wolseley?" he asked.

"No," I answered; "but that sounds well; he can't be far off."

"He will be in to breakfast," was the reply.

After all, I was not much too soon. When one has journeyed very far along such a route as the one I had followed since leaving Fort Garry in daily expectation of meeting with a body of men making their way from a distant point through the same wilderness, one does not like the idea of being found at last within the stockades of an Indian trading-post as though one had quietly taken one's ease at an inn. Still there were others to be consulted in the matter, others whose toil during the twenty-seven hours of our continuous travel had been far greater than mine.

After an hour's delay I went to the house where the men were lying down, and said to them, "The Colonel is close at hand. It will be well for us to go and meet him, and we will thus see the soldiers before they arrive at the Fort;" so getting the canoe out once more, we carried her above the falls, and paddled up towards the Rainy Lake, whose waters flow into Rainy River two miles above the fort.

It was the 4th of August-we reached the foot of the rapid which the river makes as it flows out of the Lake. Forcing up this rapid, we saw spreading out before us the broad waters of the Rainy Lake.

The eye of the half-breed or the Indian is of marvellous keenness; it. can detect the presence of any strange object long before that object will strike the vision of the civilized man; but on this occasion the eyes of my men were at fault, and the glint of something strange upon the lake first caught my sight. There they are! Yes, there they were. Coming along with the full swing of eight paddles, swept a large North-west canoe, its Iroquois paddlers timing their strokes to an old French chant as they shot down towards the river's source.

Beyond, in the expanse of the lake, a boat or two showed far and faint. We put into the rocky shore, and, mounting upon a crag which guarded the head of the rapid, I waved to the leading canoe as it swept along. In the centre sat a figure in uniform with forage-cap on head, and I could see that he was scanning through a field-glass the strange figure that waved a welcome from the rock. Soon they entered the rapid, and commenced to dip down its rushing waters. Quitting the rock, I got again into my canoe, and we shoved off into the current. Thus running down the rapid the two canoes drew together, until at its foot they were only a few paces apart.

Then the officer in the large canoe, recognizing a face he had last seen three months before in the hotel at Toronto, called out, "Where on earth have you dropped from?" and with a "Fort Garry, twelve days out, sir," I was in his boat.

The officer whose canoe thus led the advance into Rainy River was no other than the commander of the Expeditionary Force. During the period which had elapsed since that force had landed at Thunder Bay on the shore of Lake Superior, he had toiled with untiring energy to overcome the many obstacles which opposed the progress of the troops through the rock-bound fastnesses of the North. But there are men whose perseverance hardens, whose energy quickens beneath difficulties and delay, whose genius, like some spring bent back upon its base, only gathers strength from resistance. These men are the natural soldiers of the world; and fortunate is it for those who carry swords and rifles and are dressed in uniform when such men are allowed to lead them, for with such men as leaders the following, if it be British, will be all right--nay, if it be of any nationality on the earth, it will be all right too. Marches will be made beneath suns which by every rule of known experience ought to

WE PUT INTO THE ROCKY SHORE, AND, MOUNTING UPON A CRAG WHICH GUARDED THE
HEAD OF THE RAPID, I WAVED TO THE LEADING CANOE AS IT SWEPT ALONG.

prove fatal to nine-tenths of those who are exposed to them, rivers will be crossed, deserts will be traversed, and mountain passes will be pierced, and the men who cross and traverse and pierce them will only marvel that doubt or distrust should ever have entered into their minds as to the feasibility of the undertaking. The man who led the little army across the Northern wilderness towards Red River was well fitted in every respect for the work which was to be done. He was young in years but he was old in service; the highest professional training had developed to the utmost his ability, while it had left unimpaired the natural instinctive faculty of doing a thing from oneself, which the knowledge of a given rule for a given action so frequently destroys. Nor was it only by his energy, perseverance, and professional training that Wolseley was fitted to lead men upon the very exceptional service now required from them. Officers and soldiers will always follow when those three qualities are combined in the man who leads them; but they will follow with delight the man who, to these qualities, unites a happy aptitude for command, which is neither taught nor learned, but which is instinctively possessed.

Let us look back a little upon the track of this Expedition. Through a vast wilderness of wood and rock and water, extending for more than 600 miles, 1200 men, carrying with them all the appliances of modern war, had to force their way.

The region through which they travelled was utterly destitute of food, except such as the wild game afforded to the few scattered Indians; and even that source was so limited that whole families of the Ojibbeways had perished of starvation, and cases of cannibalism had been frequent amongst them. Once cut adrift from Lake Superior, no chance remained for food until the distant settlement of Red River had been reached. Nor was it at all certain that even there supplies could be obtained, periods of great distress had occurred in the settlement itself; and the disturbed state into which its affairs had lately fallen in no way promised to give greater habits of agricultural industry to a people who were proverbially roving in their tastes. It became necessary, therefore, in piercing this wilderness to take with the Expedition three month's supply of food, and the magnitude of the undertaking will be somewhat under stood by the outside world when this fact is borne in mind.

Of course it would have been a simple matter if the-boats which carried the men and their supplies had been able to sail through an unbroken channel into the bosom of Lake Winnipeg; but through that long 600 miles of lake and river and winding creek, the rocky declivities of cataracts and the wild wooded shores of rapids had to be traversed, and full forty-seven times between lake and lake had boats, stores, and ammunition, had cannon, rifles, sails, and oars to be lifted from the water, borne across long ridges of rock and swamp and forest, and placed again upon the northward rolling river. But other difficulties had to be overcome which delayed at the outset the movements of the Expedition. A road, leading from Lake Superior to the height by land (42 miles), had been rendered utterly impassable by fires which swept the forest and rains which descended for days in continuous torrents. A considerable portion of this road had also to be opened out in order to carry the communication through to Lake Shebandowan close to the height of land.

For weeks the whole available strength of the Expedition f had been employed in road-making and in hauling the boats up the rapids of the Kaministiquia River, and it was only on the 16th of July, after seven weeks of unremitting toil and arduous labour, that all these preliminary difficulties had been finally overcome and the leading detachments of boats set out upon their long and perilous journey into the wilderness. Thus it came to pass that on the morning of the 4th of August, just three weeks after that departure, the silent shores of the Rainy River beheld the advance of these pioneer boats who thus far had "marched on without impediment."

The evening of the day that witnessed my arrival at Fort Francis saw also my departure from it; and before the sun had set I was already far down the Rainy River. But I was no longer the solitary white man; and no longer the camp-fire had around it the swarthy faces of the Swampies. The woods were noisy with many tongues; the night was bright with the glare of many fires. The Indians, frightened by such a concourse of braves, had fled into the woods, and the roofless poles of their wigwams alone marked the camping-places where but the evening before I had seen the red man monarch of all he surveyed. The word had gone forth from the commander to push on with all speed for Red River, and I was now with the advanced portion of the 60th Rifles en route for the Lake of the Woods. Of my old friends the Swampies only one remained with me, the others had been kept at Fort Francis to be distributed amongst the various brigades of boats as guides to the Lake of the Woods and Winnipeg River; even Thomas Hope had got a promise of a brigade-in the mean time pork was abundant; and between pride and pork what more could even Hope desire?

In two days we entered the Lake of the Woods, and hoisting sail stood out across the waters. Never before had these lonely islands witnessed such a sight as they now beheld. Seventeen large boats close hauled to a splendid breeze swept in a great scattered mass through the high running seas, dashing the foam from their bows as they dipped and rose under their large lug-sails. Samuel Henderson led the way, proud of his new position, and looked upon by the soldiers of his boat as the very acme of an Indian. How the poor fellows enjoyed that day! no oar, no portage no galling weight over rocky ledges, nothing but a grand day's racing over the immense lake. They smoked-all day, balancing themselves on the weather-side to steady the boats as they keeled over into the heavy seas. I think they would have-given even Mr. Riel that day a pipeful of tobacco; but Heaven help him if they: had caught him two days later on the portages of the Winnipeg! he would have had a hard time of it.

There has been some Hungarian poet, I think, who has found a theme for his genius in the glories of the _private soldier. He had been a soldier himself, and he knew the wealth of the mine hidden in the unknown and unthought of Rank and File. It is a pity that the knowledge of that wealth should not be more widely circulated.

Who are the Rank and File? They are the poor wild birds whose country has cast them off, and who repay her by offering their lives for her glory; the men who take the shilling, who drink, who drill, who march to music, who fill the graveyards of Asia; the men who stand sentry at the gates of world-famous fortresses, who are old when their elder brothers are still young, who are bronzed and burned by fierce suns, who sail over seas packed in great masses, who watch at night over lonely magazines, who shout, "Who comes there?" through the darkness, who dig in trenches, who are blown to pieces in mines, who are torn by shot and shell, who have carried the flag of England into every land, who have made her name famous through the nations, who are the nation's pride in her hour of peril and her plaything-in her hour of prosperity--these are the rank and file. We are a curious nation; until lately we bought our rank, as we buy our mutton, in a market; and we found officers and gentlemen where other nations would have found thieves and swindlers. Until lately we flogged our files with a cat-o'-nine-tails, and found heroes by treating men like dogs. But to return to the rank and file.

The regiment-which had been selected for the work of piercing these solitudes of the American continent had peculiar claims for that service. In bygone times it had been composed exclusively of Americans, and there was not an Expedition through all the wars which England waged against France in the New World in which the 60th, or "Royal Americans," had not taken a prominent part. When Munro yielded to Montcalm the fort of William Henry, when Wolfe reeled back from Montmorenci and stormed Abraham, when Pontiac swept the forts from Lake Superior to the Ohio, the 60th, or Royal Americans, had ever been foremost in the struggle. Weeded now of their weak and sickly men, they formed a picked 'body, numbering 350 soldiers, of whom any nation on earth might well be proud. They were fit to do anything and to go any where; and if a fear lurked in the minds of any of them, it was that Mr. Riel would not show fight. Well led, and officered by men who shared with them every thing, from the portage-strap to a roll of tobacco, there was complete confidence from the highest to the lowest. To be wet seemed to be the normal condition of man, and to carry a pork-barrel weighing 200 pounds over a rocky portage was but constitutional and exhilarating exercise--such were the men with whom, on the evening of the 8th of August, I once more reached the neighbourhood' of the Rat Portage. In a little bay between many islands the flotilla halted just before entering the reach which led to the portage. Paddling on in front with Samuel in my little canoe, we came suddenly upon four large Hudson Bay boats with full crews of Red River half-breeds and Indians-they were on their way to meet the Expedition, with the object of rendering what assistance they could to the troops in the descent of the Winnipeg river. They had begun, to despair of ever falling in with it, and great was the excitement at the sudden meeting; the flint-gun was at once discharged into the air, and the shrill shouts began to echo through the islands. But the excitement on the side of the Expedition was quite as keen. The sudden shots and the wild shouts made the men in the boats in rear imagine that the fun was really about to begin, and that a skirmish through the wooded isles would be the evening's work. The mistake was quickly discovered. They were glad of course to meet their Red River friends; but somehow, I fancy, the feeling, of joy would certainly not have been lessened had the boats held the dusky adherents of the Provisional Government.

On the following morning the seventeen boats commenced the descent of the Winnipeg river, while I remained at the Portage-du-Rat to await the arrival of the chief of the Expedition from Fort Francis. Each succeeding day brought a fresh brigade of boats under the guidance of one of my late canoe-men; and finally Thomas Hope came along,-seemingly enjoying life to the utmost--pork was plentiful, and as for the French there was no need to dream of them, and he could sleep in peace in the midst of fifty white soldiers. During six days I remained at the little Hudson Bay Company's post at the Rat Portage, making short excursions into the surrounding lakes and rivers, fishing below the rapids of the Great Chute; and in the evenings listening to the Indian stories of the lake as told by my worthy host, Mr. Macpherson, a great portion of whose life had been spent in the vicinity.

One day I went some distance away from the fort to fish at the foot of one of the great rapids formed by the Winnipeg River as it runs from the Lake of the Woods. We carried our canoe over two or three portages, and at length reached the chosen spot. In the centre of the river an Indian was floating quietly in his canoe, casting every now and then a large hook baited with a bit of fish into the water. My bait consisted of a bright spinning piece of metal, which I had got in one of the American cities on my way through Minnesota. Its effect upon the fish of this lonely region was marvellous; they had never before been exposed to such a fascinating affair, and they rushed at it with avidity. Civilization on the rocks had certainly a better time of it, as far as catching fish went, than barbarism in the canoe. With the shining thing we killed three for the Indian's one. My companion, who was working the spinning bait while I sat on the rock, casually observed, pointing to the Indian, "He's a Windigo."

"A what?" I asked.

"A Windigo."

"What is that?"

"A man that has eaten other men."

"Has this man eaten other men?"

"Yes; a long time ago he and his band were starving, and they killed and ate forty other Indians who were starving with them. They lived through the winter on them, and in the spring he had to fly from Lake Superior because the others wanted to kill him in revenge; and so he came here, and he now lives alone near this place."

The Windigo soon paddled over to us, and I had a good opportunity of studying his appearance. He was a stout, low-sized savage, with coarse and repulsive features, and eyes fixed sideways in his head like a Tartar's. We had left our canoe some distance away, and my companion asked him to put us across to an island. The Windigo at once consented: we got into his canoe, and he ferried us over. I don't know the name of the island upon which he landed us, and very likely it has got no name, but in my mind, at least, the rock and the Windigo will always be associated with that celebrated individual of our early days, the King of the Cannibal Islands. The Windigo looked with wonder at the spinning bait, seeming to regard it as a "great medicine;" perhaps if he had possessed such a thing he would never have been forced by hunger to become a Windigo.

Of the bravery of the Lake of the Woods Ojibbeway I did not form a very high estimate. Two instances related to me by Mr. Macpherson will suffice to show that opinion to have been well founded. Since the days when the Bird of Ages dwelt on the Coteau-des-Prairies the Ojibbeway and the Sioux have warred against each other; but as the Ojibbeway dwelt chiefly in the woods and the Sioux are denizens of the great plains, the actual war carried on between them has not beena unusually destructive. The Ojibbeways dislike to go far into the open plains; the Sioux hesitate to pierce the dark depths of the forest, and the war is generally confined to the border land, where the forest begins to merge into the plains. Every now and again, however, it becomes necessary to go through the form of a war-party, and the young men depart upon the war-path against their hereditary enemies. To kill a Sioux and take his scalp then becomes the great object of existence. Fortunate is the brave who can return to the camp bearing with him the coveted trophy. Far and near spreads the glorious news that a Sioux scalp has been taken, and for many a night the camps are noisy with the shouts and revels of the scalp dance from Winnipeg to Rainy Lake. It matters little whether it be the scalp of a man, a woman, or a child; provided it be a scalp it is all right. There is the record of the two last war-paths from the Lake of the Woods.

Thirty Ojibbeways set out one fine day for the plains to war against the Sioux, they followed the line of the Rosseaui river, and soon emerged from the forest. Before them lay a camp of Sioux. The thirty braves, hidden in the thickets, looked at the camp of their enemies; but the more they looked the less they liked it. They called a council of deliberation; it was unanimously resolved to retire to the Lake of the Woods: but surely they must bring back a scalp, the women would laugh at them! What was to be done? At length the difficulty was solved. Close by there was a newly-made grave, a squaw had died and been buried. Excellent idea; one scalp was as good as another. So the braves dug up the buried squaw-, took the scalp, and departed for Rat Portage. There was a great dance, and it was decided that each and every one of the thirty Ojibbeways deserved well of his nation.

But the second instance is still more revolting. A very brave Indian departed alone from the Lake of the Woods to war against the Sioux; he wandered about, hiding in the thickets by day and coming forth at night. One evening, being nearly starved, he saw the smoke of a wigwam; he went towards it, and found that it was inhabited only by women and children, of whom there were four altogether. He went up and asked for food; they invited him to enter the lodge; they set before him the best food they had got, and they laid a buffalo robe for his bed in the warmest corner of the wigwam. When night came, all slept; when midnight came the Ojibbeway quietly arose from his couch, killed the two women, killed the two children, and departed for the Lake of the Woods with four scalps. Oh, he was a very brave Indian, and his name went far through the forest! I know somebody who would have gone very far to see him hanged.

Late on the evening of the 14th August the commander of the Expedition arrived from Fort Francis at the Portage-du-Rat. He had attempted to cross the Lake of the Woods in a gig manned by soldiers, the weather being too tempestuous to allow the canoe to put out, and had lost his way in the vast maze of islands already spoken of. As we had received intelligence at the Portage-du-Rat of his having set out from the other side of the lake, and as hour after hour passed without bringing his boat in sight, I got the canoe ready and, with two Indians, started to light a beacon-fire on the top of the Devil's Rock, one of the haunted islands of the lake, which towered high over the surrounding isles. We had not proceeded far, however, before we fell in with the missing gig bearing down for the portage under the guidance of an Indian who had been picked up en route.

On the following day I received orders to start at once for Fort Alexander at the mouth of the Winnipeg River to engage guides for the brigades of boats which had still to come--two regiments of Canadian Militia. And here let us not-forget the men who, following in the footsteps of the regular troops, were now only a few marches behind their more fortunate comrades. To the lot of these two regiments of Canadian Volunteers fell the same hard toil of oar and portage which we have already described. The men composing these regiments were stout athletic fellows, eager for service, tired of citizen life, and only needing the toil of a campaign to weld them into as tough and resolute a body of men as ever leader could desire.

CHAPTER TWELVE.

To Fort Garry--Down the Winnipeg--Her Majesty's Royal Mail--Grilling a Mail-bag--Running a Rapid--Up the Red River-A dreary Bivouac--The President bolts--The Rebel Chiefs--Departure of the Regular Troops.

I TOOK a very small canoe, manned by three Indians--father and two sons--and, with provisions for three days, commenced the descent of the river of rapids. How we shot down the hissing waters in that tiny craft! How fast we left the wooded shores behind us, and saw the-lonely isles flit by as the powerful current swept us like a leaf upon its bosom!

It was late of the afternoon of the 15th August when I left for the last time the Lake of the Woods. Next night our camp was made below the Eagle's Nest, seventy miles from the Portage-du-Rat. A wild storm burst upon us at night-fall, and our bivouac was a damp and dreary one. The Indians lay under the canoe; I sheltered as best I could beneath a huge pine-tree. My oil-cloth was only four feet in length-a shortcoming on the part of its feet which caused mine to suffer much discomfort. Besides, I had Her Majesty's royal mail to keep dry, and, with the limited liability of my oil-cloth in the matter of length, that became no easy task--two bags of letters and papers, home letters and papers, too, for the Expedition. They had been flung into my: canoe when leaving Rat Portage, and I had spent the first day in-sorting them as we swept along, and now they were getting wet in spite of every effort to the contrary. I made one bag into a pillow, but the rain came through the big pine-tree, splashing down through the branches, putting out my fire and drenching mail-bags and blankets.

Daylight came at last, but still the rain hissed down, making it no easy matter to boil our kettle and fry our bit of pork. Then we put out for the day's work on the river. How bleak and wretched it all was! After a while we found it was impossible to make head against the storm of wind and rain which swept the water, and we had to put back to the shelter of our miserable camp. About seven o'clock the wind fell, and we set out again. Soon the sun came forth drying and warming us all over. All day we paddled on, passing in succession the grand Chute-à-Jacquot, the Three Portages-des-Bois, the Slave Falls, and the dangerous rapids of the Barrière. The Slave Falls! who that has ever beheld that superb rush of water will forget it? Glorious, glorious Winnipeg! it may be that with these eyes of mine I shall never see thee again, for thou liest far out of the track of life, and man mars not thy beauty with ways of civilized travel; but I shall often see thee in imagination, and thy rocks and thy waters shall murmur in memory for life.

That night, the 17th of August, we made our camp on a little island close to the Otter Falls. It came a night of ceaseless rain, and again the mail-bags underwent a drenching. The old Indian cleared a space in the dripping vegetation, and made me a rude shelter with branches woven together; but the rain beat through, and drenched body, bag, and baggage. And yet how easy it all was, and how sound one slept! simply because one had to do it; that one consideration is the greatest expounder of the possible. I could not speak a word to my Indians, but we got on by signs, and seldom found the want of speech--"ugh, ugh" and "caween," yes and no, answered for any difficulty. To make a fire and a camp, to boil a kettle and fry a bit of meat are the home works of the Indian. His life is one long picnic, and it matters as little to him whether sun or rain, snow or biting frost, warm, drench, cover, or freeze him, as it does to the moose or the reindeer that share his forest life and yield him often his forest fare. Upon examining the letters in-the morning the interior of the bags presented such a pulpy and generally deplorable appearance that I was obliged to stop at one of the Seven Portages for the purpose of drying Her Majesty's mail. With this object we made a large fire, and placing cross-sticks above proceeded to toast and grill the dripping papers. The Indians sat around, turning the letters with little sticks as if they were baking cakes or frying sturgeon. Under their skilful treatment the pulpy mats soon attained the consistency, and in many instances the legibility, of a smoked herring, but as they had before presented a very fishy appearance that was not of much consequence.

This day was bright and fine. Notwithstanding the delay caused by drying the mails, as well as distributing them to the several brigades which we overhauled and passed, we ran a distance of forty miles and made no less than fifteen portages. The carrying or portaging power of the Indian is very remarkable. A young boy will trot away under a load which would stagger a strong European unaccustomed to such labour. The portages and the falls which they avoid bear names which seem strange and un meaning but which have their origin in some long-forgotten incident connected with the early history of the fur trade or of Indian war. Thus the great Slave Fall tells by its name the fate of two Sioux captives taken in some foray by the Ojibbeway; lashed together in a canoe, they were the only men who ever ran the Great Chute. The rocks around were black with the figures of the Ojibbeways, whose wild triumphant yells were hushed by the roar of the cataract; but the torture was a short one; the mighty rush, the wild leap, and the happy hunting-ground, where even Ojibbeways cease from troubling and Sioux warriors are at rest, had been reached. In Mackenzie's journal the fall called Galet-du-Bonnet is said to have been named by the Canadian voyageurs, from the fact that the Indians were in the habit of crowning the highest rock above the portage with wreaths of flowers and branches of trees. The Grand Portage, which is three quarters of a mile in length, is the great test of the strength of the Indian and half-breed; but, if Mackenzie speaks correctly, the voyageur has much degenerated since the early days of the fur trade, for he writes that seven pieces, weighing each ninety pounds, were carried over the Grand Portage by an Indian in one trip, 630 pounds borne three quarters of a mile by one man--the loads look big enough still, but 250 pounds is considered excessive now. These loads are carried in a manner which allows the whole strength of the body to be put into the work. A broad leather strap is placed round the forehead, the ends of the strap passing back over the shoulders support the pieces which, thus carried, lie along-the spine from the small of the back to the crown of the head. When fully loaded, the voyageur stands with his body bent forward, and with one hand steadying the "pieces," he trots briskly away over the steep and rock-strewn portage, his bare or mocassined feet enable him to pass nimbly over the slippery rocks in places where boots would infallibly send portager and pieces feet-foremost to the bottom.

In ascending the Winnipeg we have seen what exciting toil is rushing or breasting up a rapid. Let us now glance at the still more exciting operation of running a rapid. It is difficult-to find in life any event which so effectually condenses intense nervous sensation into the shortest possible space of time as does the work of shooting, or running an immense rapid. There is no toil, no heart-breaking labour about it, but as much coolness, dexterity, and skill as man can throw into the work of hand, eye, and head; knowledge of when to strike and how to do it; knowledge of water and of rock, and of the one hundred combinations which rock and watercan assume--for these two things, rock and water, taken in the abstract, fail as completely to convey any idea of their fierce embracings in the throes of a rapid as the fire burning quietly in a drawing-room fireplace fails to convey the idea of a house wrapped and sheeted in flames. Above the rapid all is still and quiet, and one cannot see what is going on below the first rim of the rush, but stray shoots of spray and the deafening roar of descending water tell well enough what is about to happen. The Indian has got some rock or mark to steer by, and knows well the door by which he is to enter the slope of water. As the canoe--never appearing so frail and tiny as when it is about to commence its series of wild leaps and rushes--nears the rim where the waters disappear from view, the bowsman stands up and, stretching forward his head, peers down the eddying rush'; in a second he is on his knees again; without turning his head he speaks a word or two to those who are behind him; then not quick enough to take in the rushing scene. There is a rock here and a big green cave of water there; there is a tumultuous rising and sinking and sinking of snow-tipped waves; there are places that are smooth-running for a moment and then yawn and open up into great gurgling chasms the next; there are strange whirls and backward eddies and rocks, rough and smooth and polished--and through all this the canoe glances like an arrow, dips like a wild bird down the wing of the storm, now slanting from a rock, now edging a green cavern, now breaking through a backward rolling billow, without a word spoken, but with every now and again a quick convulsive twist and turn of the bow-paddle to edge far off some rock, to put her full through some boiling billow, to hold her steady down the slope of some thundering chute which has the power of a thousand horses: for remember, this river of rapids, this Winnipeg, is no mountain torrent, no brawling brook, but over every rocky ledge and "wave-worn precipice" there rushes twice a vaster volume than Rhine itself pours forth. The rocks which strew the torrent are frequently the most trifling of the dangers of the descent, formidable though they appear to the stranger. Sometimes a huge boulder will stand full in the midst of the channel, apparently presenting an obstacle from which escape seems impossible. The canoe is rushing full towards it, and no power can save it--there is just one power that can do it, and the rock itself provides it. Not the skill of man could run the boat bows on to that rock. There is a wilder sweep of water rushing off the polished sides than on to them, and the instant that we touch that sweep we shoot away with redoubled speed. No, the rock is not as treacherous as the whirlpool and twisting billow.

On the night of the 20th of August the whole of the regular troops of the Expedition and the general commanding it and his staff had reached Fort Alexander, at the mouth of the Winnipeg River. Some accidents had occurred, and many had been the "close shaves" of rock and rapid, but no life had been lost; and from the 600 miles of wilderness there emerged 400 soldiers whose muscles and sinews, taxed and tested by continuous toil, had been developed to a pitch of excellence seldom equalled, and whose appearance and physique--browned, tanned, and powerful told: of the glorious climate of these Northern solitudes, It was near sunset when the large canoe touched the wooden pier opposite the Fort Alexander and the commander of the Expedition stepped on shore to meet his men, assembled for the first time together since Lake Superior's distant sea had been left behind. It-was a meeting not devoid of those associations which make such things memorable, and the cheer which went up from the soldiers who lined the steep bank to bid him welcome had in it a note of that sympathy which binds men together by the inward consciousness of difficulties shared in common and dangers--successfully overcome together. Next day the united fleet put out into Lake Winnipeg; and steered for the lonely shores of the Island of Elks, the solitary island of the southern portion of the lake. In a broad, curving, sandy bay the boats found that night a shelter; a hundred fires threw their lights far into the lake, and bugle-calls startled echoes that assuredly had never been rouse before by notes so strange. Sailing in a wide scattered mass before a favouring breeze, the fleet reached about noon the following day the mouth of the Red River, the river whose name was the name of the Expedition, and whose shores had so long been looked forward to as a haven of rest from portage and oar labour. There it was at last, seeking through its many mouths the waters of the lake. And now our course lay up along the reed fringed river and sluggish current to where the tree-tops began to rise over the low marsh-land-up to where my old friends the Indians had pitched their camp and given me the parting salute on the morning of my departure just one month before. It was dusk when we reached the Indian Settlement and made a camp upon the opposite shore, and darkness had quite set in when I reached the mission-house, some three miles higher up. My old friend the Archdeacon was glad indeed to welcome me back. News from the settlement there was none--news from the outside world there was plenty. "A great battle had been fought near the Rhine," the old man said, "and the French had been disastrously defeated."

Another day of rowing, poling, tracking, and sailing, and evening closed over the Expedition, camped within six miles of Fort Garry; but all through the day the river banks were enlivened with people shouting welcome to the soldiers, and church bells rang out peals of gladness as the boats passed by. This was through the English and Scotch Settlement, the people of which had long grown weary of the tyranny of the Dictator Riel. Riel--why, we have almost forgotten him altogether during these weeks on the Winnipeg! Nevertheless, he-had still held his own within the walls of Fort Garry, and still played to a constantly decreasing audience the part of the Little Napoleon.

During this day, the 23rd August, vague rumours reached us of terrible things to be done by the warlike President. He would suddenly appear with his guns from the woods? he would blow up the fort when the troops had taken possession--he would die in the ruins. These and many other schemes of a similar description were to be enacted by the Dictator in the last extremity of his despair. I had spent the day in the saddle, scouring the woods on the right bank of the river in advance of the fleet, while on the left shore a company of the 60th, partly mounted, moved on also in advance of the leading boats. But neither Riel nor his followers appeared to dispute the upward passage of the flotilla, and the woods through which I rode were silent and deserted. Early in the morning a horse had been lent to me by an individual rejoicing in the classical name of Tacitus Struthers. Tacitus had also assisted me to swim the steed across the Red River in order to gain the right shore, and, having done so, took leave of me with oft-repeated injunctions to preserve from harm the horse and his accoutrements, "For," said Tacitus, "that horse is a racer." Well, I suppose it must have been that fact that made the horse race all day through the thickets and oak woods of the right shore, but I rather fancy my spurs had something to say to it too.

When night again fell, the whole force had reached a spot six-miles from the rebel fort, and camp was formed for the last time on the west bank of the river. And what a night and storm then broke upon the Red River Expedition! till the tents flapped and fell and the drenched soldiers shiv'ered shelterless, waiting for the dawn. The occupants of tents which stood the pelting of the pitiless storm were no better off than those outside; the surface of the ground became ankle-deep in mud and water, and the men lay in pools during the last hours of the night. At length a dismal daylight dawned over the dreary scene, and the upward course was resumed. Still the rain came down in torrents, and, with water above, below, and around, the Expedition neared its destination. If the steed of Tacitus had had a hard day, the night had been less severe upon him than upon his rider. I had procured him an excellent stable at the other side of the river, and upon recrossing again in the morning I found him as ready to race as his owner could desire. Poor beast, he was a most miserable-looking animal, though belying his attenuated appearance by his performance. The only race which his generally forlorn aspect justified one in believing him capable of running was a race, and a hard one, for existence; but for all that he went well, and Tacitus himself might have envied the classical outline of his Roman nose.

About two miles north of Fort Garry the Red River makes a sharp bend to the east and, again turning round to the west, forms a projecting point or neck of land known as Point Douglas. This spot is famous in Red River history as the scene of the battle, before referred to in these pages, where the voyageurs and French half-breeds of the North west Fur Company attacked the retainers of the Hudson Bay, some time in 1813, and succeeded in putting to death by various methods of half-Indian warfare the governor of the rival company and about a score of his followers. At this point, where the usually abrupt bank of the Red River was less steep, the troops began to disembark from the boats for the final advance upon Fort Garry. The preliminary arrangements were soon completed, and the little army, with its two brass guns trundling along behind Red River carts, commenced its march across the mud-soaked prairie. How unspeakably dreary it all looked! the bridge, the wretched village, the crumbling fort, the vast level prairie, water soaked, draped in mist, and pressed down by low-lying clouds. To me the ground was not new--the bridge was the spot where only a month before I had passed the half reed sentry in my midnight march to the Lower Fort. Other things had changed since then besides the weather.

Preceded by skirmishers and followed by a rear-guard, the little force drew near Fort Garry. There was no sign of occupation; no flag on the flag-staff, no men upon the 4 walls; the muzzles of one or two guns showed through the bastions, but no sign of defence or resistance was visible about the place. The gate facing the north was closed, but the ordinary one, looking South upon the Assineboine River, was found open. As the skirmish line neared the northside two mounted men rode round the west face and entered at a gallop through the open gateway. On the top steps of the Government House stood a tall, majestic-looking man, who, with his horse beside him; alternately welcomed with uplifted hat the new arrivals and enounced in no stinted terms one or two miserable-looking men who seemed to cower beneath his reproaches. This was an officer of the Hudson Bay Company, ell known as one of the most intrepid amongst the many brave men who had sought for the lost Franklin in the darkness of the long polar night. He had been the first to enter the fort, some minutes in advance of the Expedition, and his triumphant imprecations, bestowed with unsparing vigour, had tended to accelerate the flight of M. Riel and the members of his government, who sought in rapid retreat the safety of the American frontier. How had the mighty fallen! With insult and derision the President and his colleagues fled from the scene of their triumph and their crimes. An officer in the service of the Company they had plundered hooted them as they went, but perhaps there was a still harder note of retribution in the "still small voice" which must have sounded from the bastion wherein the murdered Scott had been so brutally done to death. On the bare flag-staff in the fort the Union Jack was once more hoisted, and from the battery found in the square a royal salute of twenty-one guns told to settler and savage that the man who had been "elevated by the grace of Providence and the suffrage of his fellow-citizens to the highest position the Government of his country" had been ignominiously expelled from his high position. Still even in his fall we must not be too hard upon him. Vain, ignorant, and conceited though he was, he seemed to have been an implicit believer in his mission; nor can it be doubted that he possessed a fair share of courage too--courage not of the Red River type, which is a very peculiar one, but more in accordance with our European ideas of that virtue.

That he meditated opposition cannot be doubted. The muskets cast away by his guard were found loaded; ammunition had been served from the magazine on the morning of the flight. But muskets and ammunition are not worth much without hands and hearts to use them, and twenty hands with perhaps an aggregate of two and a half hearts among them were all he had to depend on at the last moment. The other members of his government appear to have been utterly devoid of a single redeeming quality. The Hon. W. B. O'Donoghue was one of those miserable beings who seem to inherit the Vices of every calling and nationality to which they can claim a kindred. Educated for some semi-clerical profession which he abandoned for the more congenial trade of treason rendered apparently secure by distance, he remained in garb the cleric, while he plundered his prisoners and indulged in the fashionable pastime of gambling with purloined property and racing with confiscated horses--a man whose revolting countenance at once suggested the hulks and prison garb, and who, in any other land save America, would probably long since have reached the convict level for which nature destined him. Of the other active member of the rebel council--Adjutant-General the Hon. Lepine--it is unnecessary to say much. He seems to have possessed all the vices of the Metis without any of his virtues or noble traits. A strange ignorance, quite in keeping with the rest of the Red River rebellion, seems to have existed among the members of the Provisional Government to the last moment with regard to the approach of the Expedition. It is said that it was only the bugle-sound of the skirmishers that finally convinced M. Riel of the proximity of the troops, and this note, utterly unknown in Red River, followed quickly by the arrival in hot haste of the Hudson Bay official, whose deprecatory language has been already alluded to, completed the terror of the rebel government, inducing a retreat so hasty, that the breakfast of Government House was found untouched. Thus that tempest in the tea-cup, the revolt of Red River, found a fitting conclusion in the President's untasted tea. A wild scene of drunkenness and debauchery amongst the voyageurs followed the arrival of the troops in Winnipeg'. The miserable-looking village produced, as if by magic, more saloons than any city of twice its size in the States could boast of. The vilest compounds of intoxicating liquors were sold indiscriminately to every one, and for a time it seemed as though the place had become a very Pandemonium. No civil authority had been given to the commander of the Expedition, and no civil power of any kind existed in the settlement. The troops alone were under control, but the populace were free to work what mischief they pleased. It is almost to be considered a matter of congratulation, that the terrible fire-water sold by the people of the village should have been of the nature that it was, for so deadly were its effects upon the brain and nervous system, that under its influence men became perfectly helpless, lying stretched upon the prairie for hours, as though they were bereft of life itself. I regret to say that Samuel Henderson was by no means an exception to the general demoralization that ensued. Men who had been forced to fly from the settlement during the reign of the rebel government now returned to their homes, and for some time it seemed probable that the sudden revulsion of feeling, unrestrained by the presence of a civil power, would lead to excesses against the late ruling faction; but, with one or two exceptions, things began to quiet down again, and soon the arrival of the civil governor, the Hon. Mr. Archibald, set matters completely to rights.

Before ten days had elapsed the regular troops had commenced their long return march to Canada, and the two regiments of Canadian militia had arrived to remain stationed for some time in the settlement. But what work it was to get the voyageurs away! The Iroquois were terribly intoxicated, and for a long time refused to get into the boats. There was a bear (a trophy from Fort Garry), and a terrible nuisance he proved at the embarkation; for a long-time previous to the start he had been kept quiet with un limited sugar, but at last he seemed to have had enough of that condiment, and, with a violent tug, he succeeded in snapping his chain and getting away up the bank. What a business it was! drunken Iroquois stumbling about, and the bear, with 100 men after him, scuttling in every direction. Then when the bear would be captured and put safely back into his boat, half a dozen of the Iroquois would get out and run a-muck through every thing. Louis (the pilot) would fall foul of Jacques Sitsoli, and commence to inflict severe bodily punishment upon the person of the unoffending Jacques, until, by the interference of the multitude, peace would be restored and both would be reconducted to their boats. At length they all got away down the river. Thus, during the first week of September, the whole of the regulars departed once more to try the torrents of the Winnipeg, and on the 10th of the month the commander also took his leave. I was left alone in Fort Garry. The Red River Expedition was over, and I had to find my way once more through the United States to Canada. My long journey seemed finished, but I was mistaken, for it was only about to begin.

CHAPTER THIRTEEN.

Westward--News from the Outside World--I retrace my Steps--An Offer--The West--The Kissaskatchewan--The Inland Ocean--Preparations-- Departure--A Terrible Plague--A lonely Grave-Digressive--The Assineboine River--Rossette.

One night, it was the 19th of September, I was lying out in the long prairie grass near the south shore of Lake Manitoba, in the marshes of which I had been hunting wild fowl for some days. It was apparently my last night in Red River, for the period of my stay there had drawn to its close. I had much to think about-that night, for only a few hours before a French half-breed named La Ronde had brought news to the lonely shores of Lake Manitoba--news such as men can hear but once in their lives: the whole of the French army and the Emperor had surrendered themselves prisoners at Sedan, and the Republic had been proclaimed in Paris.

So dreaming and thinking over these stupendous facts, I-lay-under the quiet stars, while around me my fellow travellers slept. The prospects of my own career seemed gloomy enough too. I was about to go back to old associations and life-rusting routine, and here was a nation, whose every feeling my heart had so long echoed a response to, beaten down and trampled under the heel of the German whose legions must already be gathering around the walls of Paris. Why not offer to France in the moment of her bitter adversity the sword and service of even one sympathizing friend--not much of a gift, certainly, but one which would be at least congenial to my own longing for a life of service, and my hopeless prospects in a profession in which wealth was made the test of ability. So as I lay there in the quiet of the starlit prairie, my mind, running in these eddying circles of thought, fixed itself upon this idea: I would go to Paris. I would seek through one well-known in other times the means of putting in execution my resolution. I felt strangely excited; sleep seemed banished altogether. I arose from the ground, and walked away into the stillness of the night. Oh, for a sign, for some guiding light in this uncertain hour of my life! I looked towards the north as this thought entered my brain. The aurora was burning faint in the horizon; Arcturus lay like a diamond above the ring of the dusky prairie. As I looked, a bright globe of light flashed from beneath the star and passed slowly along towards the west, leaving in its train a long track of rose-coloured light; in the uttermost bounds of the west it died slowly away. Was my wish answered? and did my path lie to the west, not east after all? or was it merely that thing which men call chance, and dreamers destiny?

A few days from this time I found myself at the frontier post of Pembina, whither the troublesome doings of the escaped Provisional leaders had induced the new governor Mr. Archibald to send me. On the last day of September I again reached, by the steamer "International," the Well-remembered Point of Frogs. I had left Red River for good. When the boat reached the landing-place a gentleman came on board, a well-known member of the Canadian bench.

"Where are you going?" he inquired of me.

"To Canada."

"Why?"

"Because there is nothing more to be done."

"Oh, you must come back."

"Why so?"

"Because we have a lot of despatches to send to Ottawa, and the mail is not safe. Come back now and you will be here again in ten days time."

Go back again on the steam-boat and come up next trip--would I?

There are many men who pride themselves upon their fixity of purpose, and a lot of similar fixidities and steadiness; but I don't. I know of nothing so fixed as the mole, so obstinate as the mule, or so steady as a stone wall, but I don't particularly care about making their general characteristics the rule of my life; and so I decided to go back to Fort Garry, just as I would have decided to start for the North Pole had the occasion offered.

Early in the second week of October I once more drew nigh the hallowed precincts of Fort Garry.

"I am so glad you have returned," said the governor, Mr. Archibald, when I met him on the evening of my arrival, "because I want to ask you if you will undertake a much longer journey than any thing you have yet done. I am going to ask you if you will accept a mission to the Saskatchewan Valley and through the Indian countries of the West. Take a couple of days to think over it, and let me know your decision."

"There is no necessity, sir," I replied, "to consider the matter, I have already made up my mind, and, if necessary, will start in half an hour."

This was on the 10th of October, and winter was already sending his breath over the yellow grass of the prairies.

And now let us turn our glance to this great North west whither my wandering steps are about to lead me. Fully 900 miles as bird would fly, and 1200 as horse can travel, west of Red River an immense range of mountains, eternally capped with snow, rises in rugged masses from a vast stream-seared plain. They who first beheld these grand guardians of the central prairies named them the Montagnes des Rochers; a fitting title for such vast accumulation of rugged magnificence. From the glaciers and ice valleys of this great range of mountains innumerable streams descend into the plains. For a time they wander, as if heedless of direction, through groves and glades and green spreading declivities; then, assuming greater fixidity of purpose, they gather up many a wandering rill, and start eastward upon a long journey. At length the many detached streams resolve themselves into two great water systems; through hundreds of miles these two rivers pursue their parallel courses, now approaching, now opening out from each other. Suddenly, the southern river bends towards the north, and at a point some 600 miles from the mountains pours its volume of water into the northern channel. Then the united river rolls in vast majestic curves steadily towards the north-east, turns once more towards the south, opens out into a great reed covered marsh, sweeps on into a large cedar-lined lake, and finally, rolling over a rocky ledge, casts its waters into the northern end of the great Lake Winnipeg, fully 1300 miles from the glacier cradle where it took its birth. This river, which has along it every diversity of hill and vale, meadow-land and forest, treeless plain and fertile hill-side, is called by the wild tribes who dwell-along its glorious shores the Kissaskatchewan, or Rapid-flowing River. But this Kissaskatchewan is not the only river which waters the great central region lying between Red River and the Rocky Mountains. The Assineboine or Stony River drains the rolling prairie lands 500 miles west from Red River, and many a smaller stream and rushing, bubbling brook carries into its devious channel the waters of that vast country which lies between the American boundary-line and the pine woods of the lower Saskatchewan.

So much for the rivers; and now for the land through which they flow. How shall we picture it? How shall we tell the story of that great, boundless, solitary waste of verdure?

The old, old maps which the navigators of the sixteenth century framed from the discoveries of Cabot and Cartier, of Varrazanno and Hudson, played strange pranks with the geography of the New World. The coast-line, with the estuaries of large rivers, was tolerably accurate; but the centre of America was represented as a vast inland sea whose shores stretched far into the Polar North; a sea through which lay the much-coveted passage to the long sought treasures of the old realms of Cathay. Well, the geographers of that period erred only in the description of ocean which they placed in the central continent, for an ocean there is, and an ocean through which men seek the treasures of Cathay, even in our own times. But the ocean is one of grass, and the shores are the crests of mountain ranges, and the dark pine forests of sub-Arctic regions. The great ocean itself does not present more infinite variety than does this prairie-ocean of which we speak. In winter, a dazzling surface-of purest snow; in early summer, a vast expanse of grass and pale pink roses; in autumn too often a-wild sea of raging-fire. No ocean of water in the world can vie with its gorgeous sunsets;--no solitude can equal the loneliness of a night-shadowed prairie: one feels the stillness, and hears the silence, the wail of the prowling wolf makes the voice of solitude audible, the stars look down through infinite silence upon a silence almost as intense. This ocean has no past--time has been nought to it; and men have come and gone, leaving behind them no track, no vestige, of their presence. Some French writer, speaking of these prairies, has said that the sense of this utter negation of life, this complete absence of history, has struck him with a loneliness oppressive and sometimes terrible in its intensity. Perhaps so; but, for my part, the prairies had nothing terrible in their aspect, nothing oppressive in their loneliness. One saw here the world as it had taken shape and form from the hands of the Creator. Nor did the scene look less beautiful because nature alone tilled the earth, and the unaided sun brought forth the flowers.

October had reached its latest week: the wild geese and swans had taken their long flight to the south, and their wailing cry no more descended through the darkness; ice had settled upon the quiet pools and was settling upon the quick-running streams; the horizon glowed at night with the red light of moving prairie fires. It was the close of the Indian summer, and winter was coming quickly down from his far northern home.

On the 24th of October I quitted Fort Garry, at ten o'clock at night, and, turning out into the level prairie, commenced a long journey towards the West. The night was cold and moonless, but a brilliant aurora flashed and trembled in many-coloured shafts across the starry sky. Behind me lay friends and news of friends, civilization, tidings of a terrible war, firesides, and houses; before me lay unknown savage tribes, long days of saddle-travel, long nights of chilling bivouac, silence, separation, and space!

I had as a companion for a portion of the journey an officer of the Hudson Bay Company's service who was returning to his fort in the Saskatchewan, from whence he had but recently come. As attendant I had a French half-breed from Red River Settlement--a tall, active fellow, by name Pierre Diome. My means of travel consisted of five horses and one Red River cart. For my personal use I had a small black Canadian horse, or pony, and an English saddle. My companion, the Hudson Bay officer, drove his own light spring-waggon, and had also his own horse. I was well found in blankets, deer-skins, and moccassins; all the appliances of half-breed apparel had been brought into play to fit me out, and I found myself possessed of ample stores of leggings, buffalo "mittaines" and capots, where with to face the biting breeze of the prairie and to stand at night the icy bivouac. So much for personal costume; now for official kit. In the first place, I was the bearer and owner of two commissions. By virtue of the first I was empowered to confer upon two gentlemen in the Saskatchewan the rank and status of Justice of the Peace; and in the second I was appointed to that rank and status myself. As to the matter of extent of jurisdiction comprehended under the name of Justice of the Peace for Rupert's Land and the North-west, I believe that the only parallel to be found in the world exists under the title of "Czar of all the Russias" and "Khan of Mongolia;" but the northern limit of all the Russias has been successfully arrived at, whereas the North-west is but a general term for every thing between the 49th parallel of north latitude and the North-Pole itself. But documentary evidence of unlimited jurisdiction over Blackfeet, Bloods, Big Bellies (how much better this name sounds in French!), Sircies, Peagins, Assineboines, Crees, uskegoes, Salteaux, Chipwayans, Loucheaux, and Dogribs, not including Esquimaux, was not the only cartulary carried by me into the prairies. A terrible disease had swept, for some months previous to the date of my journey, the Indian tribes of Saskatchewan. Small-pox, in its most aggravated type, had passed from tribe to tribe, leaving in its track depopulated wigwams and vacant council-lodges; thousands (and there are not many thousands, all told) had perished on the great sandy plains that lie between the Saskatchewan and the Missouri. Why this most terrible of diseases should prey with especial fury upon the poor red man of America has never been accounted for by, medical authority; but that it does prey upon him with a violence nowhere else to be found is an undoubted fact. Of all the fatal methods of destroying the Indians which his white brother has introduced into the West, this plague of small-pox is the most deadly. The history of its annihilating progress is written in too legible characters on the desolate expanses of untenanted wilds, where the Indian graves are the sole traces of the red man's former domination. Beneath this awful scourge whole tribes have disappeared the bravest and the best have vanished, because their bravery forbade that they should flee from the terrible infection, and, like soldiers in some square plunged through and rent with shot, the survivors only closed more despairingly together when the death-stroke fell heaviest among them. They knew nothing of this terrible disease; it had come from the white man and the trader; but its speed had distanced even the race for gold, and the Missouri Valley had been swept by the epidemic before the men who carried the firewater had crossed the Mississippi. For eighty years these vast regions had known at intervals the deadly presence of this disease, and through that lapse of time its history had been ever the same. It had commenced in the trading camp; but the white man had remained comparatively secure, while his red brothers were swept away by hundreds. Then it had travelled on, and every thing had gone down before it-the chief and the brave, the medicine-man, the squaw, the papoose. The camp moved away; but the dread disease clung to it--dogged it--with a perseverance more deadly than hostile tribe or prowling war-party; and far over the plains the track was marked with the unburied bodies and bleaching bones of the wild warriors of the West.

The summer which had just passed had witnessed one of the deadliest attacks of this disease. It had swept from the Missouri through the Blackfeet tribes, and had run the whole length of the North Saskatchewan, attacking indiscriminately Crees, half-breeds, and Hudson Bay employees. The latest news received from the Saskatchewan was one long record of death. Carlton House, a fort of the Hudson Bay Company, 600 miles north-west from Red River, had been attacked in August. Late in September the disease still raged among its few inhabitants. From farther west tidings had also come bearing the same message of disaster. Crees, half-breeds, and even the few Europeans had been attacked; all medicines had been expended, and the officer in charge at Carlton had perished of the disease.

"You are to ascertain as far as you can in what places and among what tribes of Indians, and what settlements of Whites, the small-pox is now prevailing, including the extent of its ravages, and every particular you can ascertain in connexion with the rise and the spread of the disease. You are to take with you such, small supply of medicines as shall be deemed by the Board of Health here suitable and proper for the treatment of small-pox, and you will obtain written instructions for the proper treatment of the disease, and will leave a copy thereof with the chief officer of each fort you pass, and with any clergyman or other intelligent person belonging to settlements outside the forts." So ran this clause in my instructions, and thus it came about that amongst many curious parts which a wandering life had caused me to play, that of physician in ordinary to the Indian tribes of the farthest west became the most original. The preparation of these medicines and the printing of the instructions and directions for the treatment of small-pox had consumed many days and occasioned considerable delay in my departure. At length the medicines were declared complete, and I proceeded to inspect them. Eight large cases met my astonished gaze. I was in despair; eight cases would necessitate slow progression and extra horses; fortunately a remedy arose. A medical officer was directed by the Board of Health to visit the Saskatchewan; he was to start at a later date. I handed over to him six of the eight cases, and with my two remaining ones and unlimited printed directions for small-pox in three stages, departed, as we have already seen. By forced marching I hoped to reach the distant station of Edmonton on the Upper Saskatchewan in a little less than one month, but much would depend upon the state of the larger rivers and upon the snow-fall en route. The first week in November is usually the period of the freezing in of rivers; but crossing large rivers partially frozen is a dangerous work, and many such obstacles lay between me and the mountains. If Edmonton was to be reached before the end of November delays would not be possible, and the season of my journey was one which made the question of rapid travel a question of the change of temperature of a single night. On the second day out we passed the Portage-la-prairie, the last settlement towards the West. A few miles farther on

65

we crossed the Rat Creek, the boundary of the new province of Manitoba, and struck out into the solitudes. The first sight was not a cheering one. Close beside the trail, just where it ascended from the ravine of the Rat Creek, stood a solitary newly-made grave. It was the grave of one who had been left to die only a few days before. Thrown away by his companions, who had passed on towards Red River, he had lingered for three days all exposed to dew and frost. At length death had kindly put an end to his sufferings, but three days more elapsed before any person would approach to bury the remains. He had died from smallpox brought from the Saskatchewan, and no one would go near the fatal spot. A French missionary, however, passing by stopped to dig a hole in the black, soft earth; and so the poor disfigured clay found at length its lonely resting-place. That night we made our first camp out in the solitudes. It was a dark, cold night, and the wind howled dismally through some bare thickets close by. When the fire flickered low and the wind wailed and sighed amongst the dry white grass, it was impossible to resist a feeling of utter loneliness. A long journey lay before me, nearly 3000 miles would have to be traversed before I could hope to reach the neighbourhood of even this lonely spot itself, this last verge of civilization; the terrific cold of a winter of which I had only heard, a cold so intense that travel ceases, except in the vicinity of the forts of the Hudson Bay Company-a cold which freezes mercury, and of which the spirit registers 80 degrees of frost-this was to be the thought of many nights, the ever-present companion of many days. Between this little camp-fire and the giant mountains to which my steps were turned, there stood in that long 1200 miles but six houses, and in these houses a terrible malady had swept nearly half the inhabitants out of life. So, lying down that night for the first time with all this before me, I felt as one who had to face not a few of those things from which is evolved that strange mystery called death, and looking out into the vague dark immensity around me, saw in it the gloomy shapes and shadowy outlines of the by gone which memory hides but to produce at such times. Men whose lot in life is cast in that mould which is so aptly described by the term of "having only their wits to depend on," must accustom themselves to fling aside quickly and at will all such thoughts and gloomy memories, for assuredly, if they do not so habituate themselves, they had better never try in life to race against those more favoured individuals who have things other than their wits to rely upon. The Wit will prove but a sorry steed unless its owner be ever ready to race it against those more substantial horses called Wealth and Interest, and if in that race, the prize of which is Success, Wit should have to carry its rider into strange and uncouth places, over rough and broken country, while the other two horses have only plain sailing before them, there is only all the more reason for throwing aside all useless weight and extra incumbrance; and, with these few digressive remarks, we will proceed into the solitudes.

The days that now commenced to pass were filled from dawn to dark with unceasing travel; clear, bright days of mellow sunshine followed by nights of sharp frost which almost imperceptibly made stronger the icy covering of the pools and carried farther and farther out into the running streams the edging of ice which so soon was destined to cover completely the river and the rill. Our route lay along the left bank of the Assineboine, but at a considerable distance from the river, whose winding course could be marked at times by the dark oak woods that fringed it. Far away to the south rose the outline of the Blue Hills of the Souris, and to the north the Riding Mountains lay faintly upon the horizon. The country was no longer level, fine rolling hills stretched away before us over which the wind came with a keenness that made our prairie-fare seem delicious at the close of a hard day's toil. 36, 22, 24, 20; such were the readings of my thermometer as each morning I looked at it by the fire-light as we arose from our blankets-before the dawn and shivered in the keen hoarfrost while the kettle was being boiled. Perceptibly getting colder, but still clear and fine, and with every Breeze laden with healthy and invigorating freshness, for four days we journeyed without seeing man or beast; but on the morning of the fifth day, while camped in a thicket on the right of the trail, we heard the noise of horses passing near us. A few hours afterwards we passed a small band of Salteaux encamped farther on; and later in the day overtook a half-breed trader on his way to the Missouri to trade with the Sioux. This was a celebrated French half breed named Chaumon Rossette. Chaumon had been undergoing a severe course of drink since he had left the settlement some ten days earlier, and his haggard eyes and swollen features revealed the incessant orgies of his travels. He had as companion and defender a young Sioux brave, whose handsome face also bore token to his having been busily employed in seeing Chaumon through it. M. Rossette was one of the most noted of the Red River bullies, a terrible drunkard, but tolerated for some stray tokens of a better nature which seemed at times to belong to him. When we came up to him he was camped with his horses and carts on a piece of rising ground situated between two clear and beautiful lakes.

"Well, Chaumon, going to trade again?"

"Oui, Captain."

"You had better not come to the forts, all liquor can be confiscated now. No more whisky for Indian-all stopped."

"I go very far out on Coteau to meet Sioux. Long before I get to Sioux I drink all my own liquor; drink all, trade none. Sioux know me very well, Sioux give me plenty horses; plenty things: I quite fond of Sioux."

Chaumon had that holy horror of the law and its ways which every wild or semi-wild man possesses. There is nothing so terrible to the savage as the idea of imprisonment; the wilder the bird the harder he will feel the cage. The next thing to imprisonment in Chaumon's mind was a Government proclamation--a thing all the more terrible because he could not read a line of it nor comprehend what it could be about. Chaumon's face was a study when I handed him three different proclamations and one copy of "The Small-pox in Three Stages." Whether he ever reached the Coteau and his friends the Sioux I don't know, for I soon passed on my way; but if that lively bit of literature, entitled "The Small-pox in Three Stages," had as convincing an impression on the minds of the Sioux as it had upon Chaumon, that he was doing something very reprehensible indeed, if he could only find out what it was, abject terror must have been carried far over the Coteau and the authority of the law fully vindicated along the Missouri.

On Sunday morning the 30th of October we reached a high bank overlooking' a deep valley through which rolled the Assineboine River. On the opposite shore, 300 feet above the current, stood a few white houses surrounded by a wooden palisade. Around, the country stretched away on all sides in magnificent expanses. This was Fort Ellice, near the junction of the Qu'Appelle and Assineboine Rivers, 230 miles west from Fort Garry. Fording the Assineboine, which rolled its masses of ice Swiftly against the shoulder and neck of my horse, we climbed the steep hill, and gained the fort. I had ridden that distance in five days and two hours.

CHAPTER FOURTEEN.

The Hudson Bay Company--Furs and Free Trade--Fort Ellice--Quick Travelling-Horses--Little Blackie--Touchwood Hills--A Snow-storm--The South Saskatchewan--Attempt to cross the River--Death of poor Blackie--Carlton.

IT may have occurred to some reader to ask, What is this company whose name so often appears upon these pages? Who are the men composing it, and what are the objects it has in view? You have glanced at its early history, its rivalries, and its discoveries, but now, now at this present time, while our giant rush of life roars and surges along, what is the work done by this Company of Adventurers trading into the Bay of Hudson? Let us see if we can answer. Of the two great monopolies which the impecuniosity of Charles II. gave birth to, the Hudson Bay Company alone survives, but to-day the monopoly is one of fact, and not of law. All men are now free to come and go, to trade and sell and gather furs in the great Northern territory, but distance and climate raise more formidable barriers against strangers than law or protection could devise. Bold would be the trader who would carry his goods to the far away Mackenzie River; intrepid would be the voyageur who sought a profit from the lonely shores of the great Bear Lake. Locked in their fastnesses of ice and distance, these remote and friendless solitudes of the North must long remain, as they are at present, the great fur preserve of the Hudson Bay Company. Dwellers within the limits of European states can ill comprehend the vastness of territory over which this Fur Company holds sway. I say holds sway, for the north of North America is still as much in the possession of the Company, despite all cession of title to Canada, as Crusoe was the monarch of his island, or the man must be the owner of the moon. From Pembina on Red River to Fort Anderson on the Mackenzie is as great a distance as from London to Mecca. From the King's Posts to the Pelly Banks is farther than from Paris to Samarcand, and yet today throughout that immense region the Company is king. And what a king! no monarch rules his subjects with half the power of this Fur Company. It clothes, feeds, and utterly maintains nine-tenths of its subjects. From the Esquimaux at Ungava to the Loucheaux at Fort Simpson, all live by and through this London Corporation. The earth possesses not a wilder spot than the barren grounds of Fort Providence; around lie the desolate shores of the great Slave Lake. Twice in the year news comes from the outside world-news many, many months old--news borne by men and dogs through 2000 miles of snow; and yet even there the gun that brings down the moose and the musk-ox has been forged in a London smithy; the blanket that covers the wild Indian in his cold camp has been woven in a Whitney loom; that knife is from Sheffield; that string of beads from Birmingham. Let us follow the ships that sail annually from the Thames bound for the supply of this vast region. It is early in June when she gets clear of the Nore; it is mid-June when the Orkneys and Stornaway are left behind; it is August when the frozen Straits of Hudson are pierced; and the end of the month has been reached when the ship comes to anchor off the sand-barred mouth of the Nelson River. For one year-the stores that she has brought lie in the warehouses of York factory; twelve months later they reach Red River; twelve months later again they reach Fort Simpson on the Mackenzie. That rough flint-gun, which might have done duty in the days of the Stuarts, is worth many a rich sable in the country of the Dogribs and the Loucheaux, and is bartered for skins whose value can be rated at four times their weight in gold; but the gun on the banks of the Thames and the gun in the pine woods of the Mackenzie are two widely different articles. The old rough flint, whose bent barrel the Indians will often straighten between the cleft of a tree or the crevice of a rock, has been made precious by the labour of many men; by the trackless wastes through which it has been carried; by winter-famine of those who have to vend it; by the years which elapse between its departure from the work shop and the return of that skin of sable or silver-fox for which it has been bartered. They are short-sighted men who hold that because the flint-gun and the sable possess such different values in London, these articles should also possess their relative values in North America, and argue from this that the Hudson Bay Company treat the Indians unfairly; they are short-sighted men, I say, and know not of what they speak. That old rough flint has often cost more to put in the hands of that Dogrib hunter than the best finished central fire of Boss or Purdey. But that is not all that has to be said about the trade of this Company. Free trade may be an admirable institution for some nations-making them, amongst other things, very-much more liable to national destruction; but it by no means follows that it should be adapted equally well to the savage Indian. Unfortunately for the universality of British institutions, free trade has invariably been found to improve the red man from the face of the earth. Free trade in furs means dear beavers, dear martens, dear minks, and dear otters; and all these "dears" mean whisky, alcohol, high wine, and poison, which in their turn mean, to the Indian, murder, disease, small-pox, and death. There is no need to tell me that these four dears and their four corollaries ought not to be associated with free trade, an institution which is so pre-eminently pure; I only answer that these things have ever been associated with free trade in furs, and I see no reason whatever to behold in our present day amongst traders, Indian, or, for that matter, English, any very remarkable reformation in the principles of trade. Now the Hudson Bay Company are in the position of men who have taken a valuable shooting for a very long term of years or for a perpetuity,-and who therefore are desirous of preserving for a future time the game which they hunt, and also of preserving the hunters and trappers who are their servants. The free trader is as a man who takes his shooting for the term of a year or two and wishes to destroy all he can. He has two objects in view; first, to get the furs himself, second, to prevent the other traders from getting them. "If I cannot get them, then he shan't. Hunt, hunt, hunt, kill, kill, kill; next year may take care of itself." One word more. Other companies and other means have been tried to carry on the Indian trade and to protect the interests of the Indians, but all have failed; from Texas to the Saskatchewan there has been but one result, and that result has been the destruction of the wild animals and the extinction, partial or total, of the Indian race.

I remained only long enough at Fort Ellice to complete a few changes in costume which the rapidly increasing cold rendered necessary. Boots and hat were finally discarded, the stirrup-irons were rolled in strips of buffalo skin,-the large moose-skin "mittaines" taken into wear, and immense moccasins got ready. These precautions were necessary, for before us there now lay a great open region with treeless expanses that were sixty miles across them-a vast tract of rolling hill and plain over which, for three hundred miles, there lay no fort or house of any kind.

Bidding adieu to my host, a young Scotch gentleman, at Fort Ellice, my little party turned once more towards the North-west and, fording the Qu'Appelle five miles above its confluence with the Assineboine, struck out into a lovely country. It was the last day of October and almost the last of the Indian summer. Clear and distinct lay the blue sky upon the quiet sun-lit prairie. The horses trotted briskly on under the charge of an English half-breed named Daniel. Pierre Diome had returned to Red River, and Daniel was to bear me company as far as Carlton on the North Saskatchewan. My five horses were now beginning to show the effect of their incessant work, but it was only in appearance, and the distance travelled each day was increased instead of diminished as we journeyed on. I would not have believed it possible that horses could travel the daily distance which mine did without breaking down altogether under it, still less would it have appeared possible upon the food which they had to eat. We had neither hay nor oats to give them; there was nothing--but the dry grass of the prairie, and no time to eat that but the cold frosty hours of the night. Still we seldom travelled less than fifty miles a-day, stopping only for one hour at midday, and going on again until night began to wrap her mantle around the shivering prairie. My horse was a wonderful animal; day after day would I fear that his game little limbs were growing weary, and that soon he must give out; but no, not a bit of it; his black coat roughened and his flanks grew a little leaner, but still he went on as gamely and as pluckily as ever.

ACROSS THE PLAINS IN NOVEMBER.

Often during the long day I would dismount and walk along leading him by the bridle, while the other two men and the six horses jogged on far in advance; when they had disappeared altogether behind some distant ridge of the prairie my little horse would commence to look anxiously around, whinnying and trying to get along after his comrades; and then how gamely he trotted on when I remounted, watching out for the first sign of his friends again, far-away little specks on the great wilds before us. When the camping place would be reached at nightfall the first care went to the horse. To remove saddle, bridle, and saddle-cloth, to untie the strip of soft buffalo leather from his neck and twist it well around his fore-legs, for the purpose of hobbling, was the work of only a few minutes, and then poor Blackie hobbled away to find over the darkening expanse his night's provender. Before our own supper of pemmican, half-baked bread, and tea had been discussed, we always drove the band of horses down to some frozen lake hard-by, and Daniel cut with the axe little drinking holes in the ever-thickening ice; then up would bubble the water and down went the heads-of the thirsty horses for a long pull at the too often bitter spring, for in this region between the Assineboine and the South Saskatchewan fully half the lakes and pools that lie scattered about in-vast variety are harsh with salt and alkalis. Three horses always ran loose while the other three worked in harness. These loose horses, one might imagine, would be prone to gallop away when they found themselves at liberty to do so: but nothing seems farther from their thoughts; they trot along by the side of their harnessed comrades apparently as though they knew all about it now and again they stop behind, to crop a bit of grass or tempting stalk of wild pea or vetches, but on they come again until the party has been reached, then, with ears thrown back, the jog-trot is resumed, and the whole band sweeps on over hill and plain. To halt and change horses is only the work of two minutes --out comes one horse, the other is standing close by and never stirs while the hot harness is being put upon him; in he goes into the rough shafts, and, with a crack of the half-breed's whip across his flanks, away we start again.

But my little Blackie seldom got a respite from the saddle; he seemed so well up to his work, so much stronger and better than any of the others, that day after day I rode him, thinking each day, "Well, to-morrow I will let him run loose;" but when to-morrow came he used to look so fresh and well, carrying his little head as high as ever, that again I put the saddle on his back, and another day's talk and companionship would still further cement our friendship, for I grew to like that horse as one only can like the poor dumb beast that serves us. I know not how it is, but horse and dog have worn themselves into my heart as few men have ever done in life and now, as day by day went by in one long scene of true companionship, I came to feel for little Blackie a friendship not the less sincere because all the service was upon his side, and I was powerless to make his supper a better one, or give him more cosy lodging for the night. He fed and lodged himself and he carried me--all he asks in return was a water-hole in the frozen lake, and that I cut for him. Sometimes the night came down upon us still in the midst of a great open treeless plain, without shelter, water, or grass, and then we would continue on in the inky darkness as though our march was to last eternally, and poor Blackie would step out as if his natural state was one of perpetual motion. On the 4th November we rode over sixty miles; and when at length the camp was made in the lea of a little clump of bare willows, the snow was lying cold upon the prairies, and

69

Blackie and his comrades went out to shiver through their supper in the bleakest scene my eyes had ever looked upon.

About midway between Fort Ellice and Carlton a sudden and well-defined change occurs in the character of the country; the light soil disappears, and its place is succeeded by a rich dark loam covered deep in grass and vetches. Beautiful hills swell in slopes more or less abrupt on all sides, while lakes fringed with thickets and clumps of good-sized poplar balsam lie lapped in their fertile hollows.

This region bears the name of the Touchwood Hills. Around it, far into endless space, stretch immense plains of bare and scanty vegetation, plains seared with the tracks of countless buffalo which, until a few years ago, were wont to roam in vast herds between the Assineboine and the Saskatchewan. Upon whatever side the eye turns when crossing these great expanses, the same wrecks of the monarch of the prairie lie thickly strewn over the surface. Hundreds of thousands of skeletons dot the short scant grass; and when fire has laid barer still the level surface, the bleached ribs and skulls of long-killed bison whiten far and near the dark burnt prairie. There is something unspeakably melancholy in the aspect of this portion of the North-west. From one of the westward jutting spurs of the Touchwood Hills the eye sees far away over an immense plain; the sun goes down, and as he sinks upon the earth the straight line of the horizon becomes visible for a moment across this blood red disc, but so distant, so far away, that it seems dream like in its immensity. There is not a sound in the air or on the earth; on every side lie spread the relics of the great fight waged by man against the brute creation: all is silent and deserted--the Indian and the buffalo gone, the settler not yet come. You turn quickly to the right or left; over a hill-top, close by, a solitary wolf steals away. Quickly the vast prairie begins to grow dim, and darkness forsakes the skies because they light their stars, coming down to seek in the utter solitude of the blackened plains a kindred spirit for the night.

On the night of the 4th November we made our camp long after dark in a little clump of willows far out in the plain which lies west of the Touchwood Hills. We had missed the only lake that was known to lie in this part of the plain, and after journeying far in the darkness halted at length, determined to go supperless, or next to supperless, to bed, for pemmican without that cup which nowhere tastes more delicious than in the wilds of the North-west would prove but sorry comfort, and the supper without tea would be only a delusion. The fire was made, the frying-pan taken out, the bag of dried buffalo meat and the block of pemmican got ready, but we said little in the presence of such a loss as the steaming kettle and the hot, delicious, fragrant tea. Why not have provided against this evil hour by bringing on from the last frozen lake some blocks of ice? Alas! why not? Moodily we sat down round the blazing willows. Meantime Daniel commenced to unroll the oil cloth cart cover-and lo, in the ruddy glare of the fire, out rolled three or four large pieces of thick, heavy ice, sufficient to fill our kettle three times over with delicious tea. Oh, what a joy it was! and how we relished that cup! for remember, cynical friend who may be inclined to hold such happiness cheap and light, that this wild life of ours is a curious leveller of civilized habits--a cup of water to a thirsty man can be more valuable than a cup of diamonds, and the value of one article over the other is only the question of a few hours privation. When the morning of the. 5th dawned we were covered deep in snow, a storm had burst in the night, and all around was hidden in a dense sheet of driving snow-flakes; not a vestige of our horses was to be seen, their tracks were obliterated by the fast-falling snow, and the surrounding objects close at hand showed dim and indistinct through the white cloud. After fruitless search, Daniel returned to camp with the tidings that the horses were nowhere to be found; so, when breakfast had been finished, all three set out in separate directions to look again for the missing steeds. Keeping the snow-storm on my left shoulder, I went along through little clumps of stunted bushes which frequently deceived me by their resemblance through the driving snow to horses grouped together. After awhile I bent round towards the wind and, making a long sweep in that direction, bent again so as to bring the drift upon my right shoulder. No horses, no tracks, any where--nothing but a waste of white drifting flake and feathery snow-spray. At last I turned away from the wind, and soon struck full on our little camp; neither of the others had returned. I cut down some willows and made a blaze. After a while I got on to the top of the cart, and looked out again into the waste. Presently I heard a distant shout; replying vigorously to it, several indistinct forms came into view; and Daniel soon emerged from the mist, driving before him the hobbled wanderers; they had been hidden under the lea of a thicket some distance off, all clustered together for shelter and warmth. Our only difficulty was now the absence of my friend the Hudson Bay officer. We waited some time, and at length, putting the saddle on Blackie, I started out in the direction he had taken. Soon I heard a faint far-away shout; riding quickly in the direction from whence it proceeded, I heard the calls getting louder and louder, and soon came up with a figure heading right away into the immense plain, going altogether in a direction opposite to where our camp lay. I shouted, and back came my friend no little pleased to find his road again, for a snowstorm is no easy thing to steer through, and at times it will even fall out that not the Indian with all his craft and instinct for direction will be able to find his way through its blinding maze. Woe betide the wretched man who at such a time finds himself alone upon the prairie, without fire or the means of making it; not even the ship-wrecked-sailor clinging to the floating mast is in a more pitiable strait. During the greater portion of this day it snowed hard, but our track was distinctly-marked across the plains, and we held on all day. I still rode Blackie; the little fellow had to keep his wits at work to avoid tumbling into the badger holes which the snow soon rendered invisible. These badger holes in this portion of the plains were very numerous; it is not always easy to avoid them when the ground is clear of snow, but riding becomes extremely difficult when once the winter has set in. The badger burrows straight down for two or three feet, and if a horse be travelling at any pace his fall is so sudden and violent that a broken leg is too often the result. Once or twice Blackie went in nearly to the shoulder, but he invariably scrambled up again all right-poor fellow, he was reserved for a worse fate, and his long journey was near its end! A clear cold day followed the day of snow, and for the first time the thermometer fell below zero.

Day dawned upon us on the 6th November camped in a little thicket of poplars some seventy miles from the South Saskatchewan; the thermometer stood 30 below zero, and as I drew the girths tight on poor Blackie's ribs that morning, I felt happy in the thought that I had slept for the first time under the stars with 35 degrees of frost lying on the blanket outside. Another long day's ride, and the last great treeless plain was crossed and evening found us camped near the Minitchinass, or Solitary Hill, some sixteen miles south-east of the South Saskatchewan. The grass again grew long and thick, the clumps of willow, poplar, and birch had reappeared, and the soil, when we scraped the snow away to make our sleeping place, turned up black and rich-looking under the blows of the axe. About midday on the 7th November, in a driving storm of snow, we suddenly emerged upon a high plateau. Before us, at a little distance, a great gap or valley seemed to open suddenly out, and farther off the white sides of hills and dark tree-tops rose into view. Riding to the edge of this steep valley I beheld a magnificent river flowing between great banks of ice and snow 300 feet below the level on which we stood. Upon each side masses of ice stretched out far into the river, but in the centre, between these banks of ice, ran a swift, black-looking current the sight of which for a moment filled us with dismay. We had counted upon the Saskatchewan being firmly locked in ice, and here was the river rolling along between its icy banks forbidding all passage. Descending to the low valley of the river, we halted for dinner, determined to try some method by which to cross this formidable barrier. An examination of the river and its banks soon revealed the difficulties before us. The ice, as it approached the open portion, was unsafe, rendering it impossible to get within reach of the running water.` An interval of some ten yards separated the sound ice from the current, while nearly 100 yards of solid ice lay between the true bank of the river and the dangerous portion; thus our first labour was to make a solid footing for ourselves from which to launch any raft or make-shift boat which we might construct. After a great deal of trouble and labour, we got the waggon-box roughly fashioned into a raft, covered over with one of our large oil-cloths, and Lashed together with buffalo leather. This most primitive looking craft we carried down over the ice to where the dangerous portion commenced; then Daniel,-wielding the axe with powerful dexterity, began to hew away at the ice until space enough was opened out to float our raft upon. Into this-we slipped the-waggon-box, and into the waggon-box we put the half-breed Daniel. It floated admirably, and on went the axe-man, hewing, as before, with might and main. It was cold, wet work, and, in spite of every thing, the water began to ooze through the oil-cloth into the waggon-box. We had to haul it up, empty it, and launch again; thus for some hours we kept on, cold, wet, and miserable, until night forced us to desist and make our camp on the tree-lined shore. So we hauled in the wagon and retired, baffled, but not beaten, to begin again next morning. There were many reasons to make this delay feel vexatious and disappointing; we had travelled a distance of 560 miles in twelve days; travelled only to find ourselves stopped by this partially frozen river at a point twenty miles distant from Carlton, the first great station on my journey. Our stock of provisions, too, was not such as would admit of much delay; pemmican and dried meat we had none, and flour, tea, and grease were all that remained to us. However, Daniel declared that he knew a most excellent method of making a combination of flour and fat which Would allay all disappointment-and I must conscientiously admit that a more hunger-satiating mixture than he produced out of the frying-pan it had never before been my lot to taste. A little of it went such a long way, that it would be impossible to find a parallel for it in portability; in fact, it went such a long way, that the person who dined off it found himself, by common reciprocity of feeling, bound to go a long way in return before he again partook of it; but Daniel was not of that opinion, for he ate the greater portion of our united shares, and slept peacefully when it was all gone. I would particularly recommend this mixture to the consideration of the guardians of the poor throughout the United Kingdom, as I know of nothing which would so readily conduce to the satisfaction of the hungry element in' our society. Had such a combination been known to Bumble. and his Board, the hunger of Twist would even have been satisfied by a single helping; but, perhaps, it might be injudicious to introduce into the sister island any condiment so antidotal in its nature to the removal of the Celt across the Atlantic--that "consummation so devoutly wished for" by the "leading journal."

Fortified by Daniel's delicacy, we set to work early next morning at raft-making and ice-cutting; but we made the attempt to cross at a portion of the river where the open water was narrower and the bordering ice sounded more firm to the testing blows of the axe. One part of the river had now closed in, but the ice over it was unsafe.

71

We succeeded in' getting the craft into the running water and, having strung together all the available line and rope we possessed, prepared for the venture. It was found that the waggon-boat would only carry one passenger, and accordingly I took my place in it, and with a make-shift paddle put out into the quick-running stream. The current had great power over the ill-shaped craft, and it was no easy-matter to keep her head at all against stream.

I had not got five yards out when the whole thing commenced to fill rapidly with water, and I had just time to get back again to ice before she was quite full. We hauled her out once more, and found the oil-cloth had been cut by the jagged ice, so there was nothing for it but to remove it altogether and put on another. This was done, and soon our waggon-box was once again afloat. This time I reached in safety the farther side; but there a difficulty arose which we had not foreseen. Along this farther edge of ice the current ran with great force, and as the leather line which was attached to the back of the boat sank deeper and deeper into the water, the drag upon it caused the boat to drift quicker and quicker downstream; thus, when I touched the opposite ice, I found the drift was so rapid that my axe failed to catch a hold in the yielding edge, which broke away at every stroke. After several ineffectual attempts to stay the rush of the boat, and as I was being borne rapidly into a mass of rushing water and huge blocks of ice, I saw it was all up, and shouted to the others to rope in the line; but this was no easy matter, because the rope had got foul of the running ice, and was caught underneath. At last, by careful handling, it was freed, and I stood once more on the spot from whence I had started, having crossed the River Saskatchevan to no purpose. Daniel now essayed the task, and reached the opposite shore, taking the precaution to work up the nearer side before crossing; once over, his vigorous use of the axe told on the ice, and he succeeded in fixing the boat against the edge. Then lhe quickly clove his way into the frozen mass, and, by repeated blows, finally reached a spot from which he got on shore.

This success of our long labour and exertion was announced to the solitude by three ringing cheers, which we gave from our side; for, be it remembered, that it was now our intention to use the waggon-boat to convey across all our baggage, towing the boat from one side to the other by means of our line; after which, we would force the horses to swim the river, and then cross ourselves in the boat. But all our plans were defeated by an unlooked-for accident; the line lay deep in the water, as before, and to raise it required no small amount of force. We hauled and hauled, until snap went the long rope somewhere underneath the water, and all was over. With no little difficulty Daniel got the boat across again to our side, and we all went back to camp wet, tired, and dispirited by so much labour and so many misfortunes. It froze hard that night, and in the morning the great river had its waters altogether hidden opposite our camp by a covering of ice. Would it bear? that was the question. We went on it early, testing with axe and sharp-pointed poles. In places it was very thin, but in other parts it rang hard and solid to the blows. The dangerous spot was in the very centre of the river, where the water had shown through in round holes on the previous day, but we hoped to avoid these bad places by taking a slanting course across the channel. After walking backwards and forwards several times, we determined to try a light horse. He was led out with a long piece of rope attached to his neck. In the centre of the stream the ice seemed to bend slightly as he passed over, but no break occurred, and in safety we reached the opposite side. Now came Blackie's turn. Somehow or other I felt uncomfortable about it and remarked that the horse ought to have his shoes removed before the attempt was made. My companion, however, demurred, and his experience in these matters had extended over so many years, that I was foolishly induced to allow him to proceed as he thought fit, even against my better judgment. Blackie was taken out, led as before, tied by a long line. I followed close behind him, to drive him if necessary. He did not need much driving, but took the ice quite readily. We had got to the centre of the river, when the surface suddenly bent downwards, and, to my horror, the poor horse plunged deep into black, quick-running water! He was not three yards in front of me when the ice broke. I recoiled involuntarily from the black, seething chasm; the horse, though he plunged suddenly down, never let his head under water, but kept swimming manfully round and round the narrow hole, trying all he could to get upon the ice. All his efforts were useless; a cruel wall of sharp ice struck his knees as he tried to lift them on the surface, and the current, running with immense velocity, repeatedly carried him back underneath. As soon as the horse had broken through, the man who held the rope let it go, and the leather line flew back about poor Blackie's head. I got up almost to the edge of the hole, and stretching out took hold of the line again; but that could do no good nor give him any assistance in his struggles. I shall never forget the way the poor brute looked at me--even now, as I write these lines, the whole scene comes back in memory with all the vividness of a picture, and I feel again the horrible sensation of being utterly unable, though almost within touching distance, to give him help in his dire extremity and if ever dumb animal spoke with unutterable eloquence, that horse called to me in his agony he turned to me as to one from whom he had a right to expect assistance. I could not stand the scene any longer. "Is there no help for him?" I cried to the other men. "None whatever," was the reply; "the ice is dangerous -all around."

Then I rushed back to the shore and up to the camp where my rifle lay, then back again to the fatal spot where the poor beast still struggled against his fate. As I raised the rifle he looked at me so imploringly that my hand shook and trembled. Another instant, and the deadly bullet crashed through his head, and, with one look never to be forgotten, he went down under the cold, unpitying ice!

It may have been very foolish, perhaps, for poor Blackie was only a. horse, but for all that I went back to camp, and, sitting down in the snow, cried like a child. With my own hand I had taken my poor friend's life; but if there should exist somewhere in the regions of space that happy Indian paradise where horses are never hungry and never tired, Blackie, at least, will forgive the hand that sent him there, if he can but see the heart that long regretted him.

Leaving Daniel in charge of the remaining horses, we crossed on foot the fatal river, and with a single horse set out for Carlton. From the high north bank I took one last look back at the South Saskatchewan-it lay in its broad deep valley glittering in one great band of purest 'snow; but I loathed the sight of it, while the small round open hole, dwarfed to a speck by distance, marked the spot where my poor horse had found his grave, after having carried me so faithfully through the long lonely wilds. We had travelled about six miles when a figure appeared in sight, coming towards us upon the same track. The new-comer proved to be a Cree Indian travelling to Fort Pelly. He bore the name of the Starving Bull. Starving Bull and his boy at once turned back With us towards Carlton. In a little while a party of horsemen hove in sight: they had come out from the fort to visit the South Branch, and amongst them was the Hudson Bay officer in charge of the station. Our first question had reference to the plague. Like a fire, it had burned itself out. There was no case then in the fort, but out of the little garrison of some sixty souls no fewer than thirty-two had perished! Four only had recovered of the thirty-six who had taken the terrible infection.

We halted for dinner by the edge of the Duck Lake; midway between the North and South Branches of the Saskatchewan. It was a rich, beautiful country, although the snow lay some inches deep. Clumps of trees dotted the undulating surface, and lakelets glittering in the bright sunshine spread out in sheets of dazzling whiteness. The Starving Bull set himself busily to work preparing our dinner. What it would have been under ordinary circumstances, I cannot state; but, unfortunately for its success on the present occasion, its preparation was attended with unusual drawbacks. Starving Bull had succeeded in killing a skunk during his journey. This performance, while highly creditable to his energy as a hunter, was by no means conducive to his success, as a cook. Bitterly did that skunk revente himself upon us who had borne no part in his destruction. Pemmican is at no time a delicacy; but pemmican flavoured with skunk was more than I could attempt. However, Starving Bull proved himself worthy of his name, and the frying-pan was-soon scraped clean under his hungry manipulations.

Another hour's ride brought us to a high bank, at the base of which lay the North Saskatchewan. In the low ground adjoining the river stood Carlton House, a large square enclosure, the wooden walls of which were more than twenty feet in height. Within these palisades some dozen or more houses stood crowded together. Close by, to the right, many snow-covered mounds with a few rough wooden crosses above them marked the spot where, only four weeks before, the last Victim of the epidemic had been laid. On the very spot where I stood looking at this sceiqe, a Blackfoot Indian, three years earlier, had stolen out from a thicket, fired at, and grievously wounded the Hudson Bay officer belonging to the fort, and now close to the same spot a small cross marked that officer's last resting-place. Strange fate! he had escaped the Blackfoot's bullet only to be the first to succumb to the deadly epidemic. I cannot say that Carlton was at all a lively place of sojourn. Its natural gloom was considerably deepened by the events of the last few months, and the whole place seemed to have received the stamp of death upon it. To add to the general depression, provisions were by no means abundant, the few Indians that had come in from the plains brought the same tidings of unsuccessful chase--for the buffalo were "far out" on the great prairie, and that phrase "far out," applied to buffalo, means starvation in the North-west.

CHAPTER FIFTEEN.

The Saskatchewan--Start from Carlton--Wild Mares--Lose our Way--A long Ride-Battle River--Mistawassis the Cree--A Dance.

Two things strike the new-comer at Carlton. First, he sees evidences on every side of a rich and fertile country; and, secondly, he sees by many signs that war is the normal condition of the wild men who have pitched their tents in the land of the Saskatchewan that land from which we have taken the Indian prefix Kis, without much improvement of length or euphony. It is a name but little known to the ear of the outside world, but destined one day or other to fill its place in the long list of lands whose surface yields back to man, in manifold, the toil of his brain and hand. Its boundaries are of the simplest description, and it is as well to begin with them. It has on the north a huge forest, on the west a huge mountain, on the south an immense desert, on the east an immense marsh. From the forest to the desert there lies a distance varying from 40 to 150 miles, and from the marsh to the mountain, 800 miles of land lie spread in every varying phase of undulating fertility. This is the Fertile Belt, the land of the Saskatchewan, the winter home of the buffalo, the war country of the Crees and Blackfeet, the future home of millions yet unborn. Few men have looked on this land--but the thoughts of many in the New World tend towards it, and crave for description and fact which in many instances can only be given to them at second-hand.

Like all things in this world, the Saskatchewan has its poles of opinion; there are those who paint it a paradise, and those who picture it a hell. It is unfit for habitation, it is to be the garden-spot of America--it is too cold, it is too dry--it is too beautiful; and, in reality, what is it? I answer in a few words. It is rich; it is fertile; it is fair to the eye. Man lives long in it, and the children of his body are cast in manly mould. The cold of winter is intense, the strongest heat of summer is not excessive. The autumn days are bright and-beautiful; the snow is seldom deep, the frosts are early to come and late to go. All crops flourish, though primitive and rude are the means by which they are tilled; timber is in places plentiful, in other places scarce; grass grows high, thick, and rich. Horses winter out, and are round-carcased, and fat in spring. The lake-shores are deep in hay; lakelets every where. Rivers close in mid-November and open in mid-April. The lakes teem with fish; and such fish! fit for the table of a prince, but disdained at the feast of the Indian. The river-heads lie all in a forest region; and it is midsummer when their water has reached its highest level. Through the land the red man stalks; war, his unceasing toil--horse-raiding, the pastime of his life. How long has the Indian thus warred?-since he has been known to the white man, and long before.

In 1776 the earliest English voyager in these regions speaks of war between the Assineboines and their trouble some western neighbours, the Snake and Blackfeet Indians. But war was older than the era of the earliest white man, older probably than the Indian himself; for, from what ever branch of the human race this stock is sprung, the lesson of warfare was in all cases the same to him. To say he fights is, after all, but to say he is a man; for whether it be in Polynesia or in Paris, in the Saskatchewan or in Sweden, in Bundelond or in Bulgaria, fighting is just the one universal "touch of nature which makes the whole world kin."

"My good brothers," said a missionary friend of mine, some little while ago, to an assemblage of Crees, "My good brothers--why do you carry on this unceasing war with the Blackfeet and Peaginoos, with Sircies and Bloods? It is not good, it is not right; the great Manitou does not like his children to kill each other, but he wishes them to live in peace and brotherhood."

To which the Cree chief made answer--"My friend, what you say is good; but look, you are white man and Christian, we are red men and worship the Manitou; but what is the news we hear from the traders and the black-robes? Is it not always the news of war? The Kitchi Mokamans (i.e. the Americans) are on the war-path against their brethren of the South, the English are fighting some tribes far away over the big lake; the French, and all the other tribes are fighting too! My brother, it is news of war, always news of war! and we--we go on the war-path in small numbers. We stop when we kill a few of our enemies and take a few scalps; but your nations go to war in countless thousands, and we hear of more of your braves killed in one battle than all our tribe numbers together. So, my brother, do not say to us that it is wrong to go on the war-path, for what is right for the white man cannot be wrong in his red brother. I have done!"

During the seven days which I remained at Carlton the winter was not idle. It snowed and froze, and looked dreary enough within the darkening walls of the fort. A French missionary had come down from the northern lake of Isle-à-la-Crosse, but, unlike his brethren, he appeared shy and uncommunicative. Two of the stories which he related, however, deserve record. One was a singular magnetic storm which took place at Isle-à-la-Crosse during the preceding winter. A party of Indians and half-breeds were crossing the lake on the ice when suddenly their hair stood up on end; the hair of the dogs also turned the wrong way, and the blankets belonging to the part even evinced signs of acting, in an upright manner. I will not pretend to account for this phenomenon, but merely tell it as the worthy père told it to me, and I shall rest perfectly satisfied if my readers hair does not follow the example of the Indians dogs and blankets and proceed generally after the manner of the "frightful porcupine." The other tale told by the père was of a more tragical nature. During a storm in the prairies near the South Branch of the Saskatchewan a rain of fire suddenly descended upon a camp of Cree Indians and burned everything around. Thirty-two Crees perished in the flames; the ground was burned deeply for a considerable distance, and only one or two of the party who happened to stand close to a lake were saved by throwing themselves into the water. "It was," said my informant, "not a flash of lightning, but a rain of fire which descended for some moments."

The increasing severity of the frost hardened into a solid mass the surface of the Saskatchewan, and on the morning of the 14th November we set out again upon our Western journey. The North Saskatchewan which I now crossed for the first time, is a river 400 yards in width, lying between banks descending steeply to a low alluvial valley. These outer banks are some 200 feet in height, and in some by-gone age were doubtless the boundaries of the majestic stream that then rolled between them. I had now a new-band of horses numbering altogether nine head, but three of them were wild brood mares that had never before been in harness, and laughable was the scene that ensued at starting. The snow was now sufficiently deep to prevent wheels running with ease, so we substituted two small horse-sleds for the Red River cart, and into these sleds the wild mares were put. At first they refused to move an inch--no, not an inch; then came loud and prolonged thwacking from a motley assemblage of Crees and half-breeds. Ropes, shanganappi, whips, and sticks were freely used; then, like an arrow out of a bow, away went the mare; then suddenly a dead stop, two or three plunges high in air, and down flat upon the ground. Againthe thwacking, and again suddenly up starts the mare and off like a rocket. Shanganappi harness is tough stuff and a broken sled is easily set to rights, or else we would have been in a bad way. But for all horses in the North-west there is the very simplest manner of persuasion: if the horse lies down, lick him until he gets up; if he stands up on his hind-legs, lick him until he reverts to his original position; if he bucks, jibs, or kicks, lick him, lick him, lick him; when you are tired of licking him, get another man to continue the process; if you can use violent language in three different tongues so much the better, but if you cannot imprecate freely at least in French, you will have a bad time of it. Thus we started from Carlton and, crossing the wide Saskatchewan, held our way south-west for the Eagle Hills. It was yet the dusk of the early morning, but as we climbed the steep northern bank the sun was beginning to lift himself above the horizon. Looking back, beneath lay the wide frozen river, and beyond the solitary fort still wrapped in shade, the trees glistened pure and white on the high-rolling bank beside me, and the untrodden snow stretched far away in dazzling brilliancy. Our course now lay to the south of west, and -our pace was even faster than it had been in the days of poor Blackie. About midday we entered upon a vast tract of burnt country, the unbroken snow filling the hollows of the ground beneath it. Fortunately, just at camping-time we reached a hill-side whose grass and tangled vetches had escaped the fire, and here we pitched our camp for the night. Around rose hills whose sides were covered with the traces of fire-destroyed' forests, and a lake lay close beside us, wrapped in ice and snow. A small winter-station had been established by the Hudson Bay Company at a point some ninety miles distant from Carlton, opposite the junction of the Battle River with the North Saskatchewan. There, it was said, a large camp of Crees had assembled, and to this post we were now directing our steps.

On the morning of the second day out from Carlton, the guide showed symptoms of haziness as to direction: he began to bend greatly to the south, and at sunrise he ascended a high hill for the purpose of taking a general survey of the surrounding country. From this hill the eye ranged over a vast extent of landscape, and although the guide failed altogether to correct his course, the hill-top yielded such a glorious view of sun rising from a sea of snow into an ocean of pale green barred with pink and crimson streaks, that I felt well repaid for the trouble of the long ascent. When evening closed around us that day, I found myself alone amidst a wild, weird scene. Far as the eye could reach in front and to the right a boundless, treeless plain stretched into unseen distance; to the left a range of steep hills rose abruptly from the plain; over all the night was coming down. Long before sunset I had noticed a clump of trees many miles ahead, and thought that in this solitary thicket we would make our camp for the night. Hours passed away, and yet the solitary clump seemed as distant as ever-- nay, more, it even appeared to grow smaller as I approached it. At last, just at dusk, I drew near the wished for camping-place; but lo! it was nothing but a single bush. My clump had vanished, my camping-place had gone, the mirage had been playing tricks with the little bush and magnifying it into a grove of aspens. When night fell there was no trace of camp or companions, but the snow marks showed that I was still upon the right track. On again for two hours in darkness often it was so dark that it was only by giving the horse his head that he was able to smell out the hoofs of his comrades in the partially covered grass of frozen swamp and moorland. No living thing stirred, save now and then a prairie owl flitting through the gloom added to the sombre desolation of the scene. At last the trail turned suddenly towards a deep ravine to the left. Riding to the edge of this ravine, the welcome glare of a fire glittering through a thick screen of bushes struck my eye. The guide had hopelessly lost his way, and after thirteen hours hard riding we were lucky to find this cosy nook in the tree-sheltered valley. The Saskatchewan was close beside us, and the dark ridges beyond were the Eagle Hills of the Battle River.

Early next forenoon we reached the camp of Crees and the winter post of the Hudson Bay Company some distance above the confluence of the Battle Riverwith the Saskatchewan. A wild scene of confusion followed our entry into the camp; braves and squaws, dogs and papooses crowded round, and it was difficult work to get to the door of the little shanty where the Hudson Bay officer dwelt. Fortunately, there was no small-pox in this crowded camp, although many traces of its effects were to be seen in the seared and disfigured faces around, and in none more than my host, who had been one of the four that had recovered at Carlton. He was a splendid specimen of a half-breed, but his handsome face was awfully marked by the terrible scourge. This assemblage of Crees was under the leadership of Mistawassis, a man of small and slight stature, but whose bravery had often been tested in fight against the Blackfeet. He was a man of quiet and dignified manner, a good listener, a fluent speaker, as much at his ease and as free from restraint as any lord in Christendom. He hears the news I have to tell him through the interpreter, bending his head in assent to every sentence; then he pauses a bit and speaks. "He wishes to know if aught can be done against the Blackfeet; they are troublesome, they are fond of war; he has seen war for many years, and he would wish for peace; it is only the young men, who want scalps and the soft words of the squaws, who desire war." I tell him that "the Great Mother wishes her red children to live at peace; but what is the use? do they not themselves break the peace when it is made, and is not the war as often commenced by the Crees as by the Blackfeet?" He says that "men have told them that the white man was coming to take their lands, that the white braves were coming to the country, and he wished to know if it was true." "If the white braves did come," I replied, "it would be to protect the red man, and to keep peace amongst all. So dear was the red man to the heart of the chief whom the Great Mother had sent, that the sale of all spirits had been stopped in the Indian country, and henceforth, when he saw any trader bringing whisky or fire-water into the camp, he could tell his young men to go and take the fire-water by force from the trader."

"That is good," he repeated twice, "that is good!" but whether this remark of approval had reference to the stoppage of the fire-water or to the prospective seizure of liquor by his braves, I cannot say. Soon after the departure of Mistawassis from the hut, a loud drumming outside was suddenly struck up, and going to the door I found the young men had assembled to dance the dance of welcome in my honour; they drummed and danced in different stages of semi-nudity for some time, and at the termination of the performance I gave an order for tobacco all round. When the dancing-party had departed, a very garrulous Indian presented himself, saying that he had been informed that the Ogima was possessed of some "great medicines," and that he wished to see them. I have almost forgotten to remark that my store of drugs and medicines had under gone considerable delapidation from frost and fast travelling. An examination held at Carlton into the contents of the two cases had revealed a sad state of affairs. Frost had smashed many bottles; powders badly folded up had fetched way in a deplorable manner; tinctures had proved their capability for the work they had to perform by tincturing every thing that came within their reach; hopeless confusion reigned in the department of pills. A few glass-stoppered bottles had indeed resisted the general demoralization; but, for the rest, it really seemed as though blisters, pills, powders, scales, and disinfecting fluids had been wildly bent upon blistering, pilling, powdering, weighing, and disinfecting one another ever since they had left Fort Garry. I deposited at Carlton a considerable quantity of a disinfecting fluid frozen solid, and as highly garnished with pills as the exterior of that condiment known as a chancellor's pudding is resplendent with raisins. Whether this conglomerate really did disinfect the walls of Carlton I cannot state, but from its appearance and general medicinal aspect I should say that no disease, however virulent, had the slightest chance against it. Having repacked the other things as safely as possible into one large box, I still found that I was the possessor of medicine amply sufficient to poison a very large extent of territory, and in particular I had a small leather medicine-chest in which the glass-stoppered bottles had kept intact. This chest I now produced for the benefit of my garrulous friend; one very strong essence of smelling-salts particularly delighted him; the more it burned his nostrils the more he laughed and hugged it, and after a time declared that there could be no doubt whatever as to that article,--for it was a very "great medicine" indeed.

CHAPTER SIXTEEN.

The Red Man--Leave Battle River--The Red Deer Hills--A long Ride--Fort Pitt--The Plague--Hauling by the Tail--A pleasant Companion--An easy Method of Divorce--Reach Edmonton.

EVER, towards the setting sun drifts the flow of Indian migration; ever nearer and nearer to that glorious range of snow-clad peaks which the red man has so aptly named "the Mountains of the Setting Sun." It is a mournful task to trace back through the long list of extinct tribes the history of this migration. Turning over the leaves of books belonging to that "old colonial time" of which Longfellow speaks, we find strange names of Indian tribes now utterly unknown, meetings of council and treaty making with Mohawks and Oneidas and Tuscaroras.

They are gone, and scarcely a trace remains of them. Others have left in lake and mountain-top the record of their names. Erie and Ottawa, Seneca and Cayuga tell of forgotten or almost forgotten nations which a century ago were great and powerful. But never at any time since first the white man was welcomed on the newly-discovered shores of the Western Continent by his red brother, never has such disaster and destruction overtaken these poor wild, wandering sons of nature as at the moment in which we write. Of yore it was the pioneers of France, England, and Spain with whom they had to contend, but now the whole white world is leagued in bitter strife against the Indian. The American and Canadian are only names that hide beneath them the greed of united Europe. Terrible deeds have been wrought out in that western land; terrible heart-sickening deeds of cruelty and rapacious infamy--have been, I say? no, are to this day and hour, and never perhaps more sickening than now in the full blaze of nineteenth-century civilization. If on the long line of the American frontier, from the Gulf of Mexico to the British boundary, a Single life is taken by an Indian, if even a horse or ox be stolen from a settler, the fact is chronicled in scores of-journals throughout the United States, but the reverse of the story we never know. The countless deeds of perfidious robbery, of ruthless murder done by white savages out in these Western wilds never find the light of day. The poor red man has no telegraph, no newspaper, no type, to tell his sufferings and his woes. My God, what a terrible tale could I not tell of these dark deeds done by the white savage against the far nobler red man! From southernmost Texas to most northern Montana there is but one universal remedy for Indian difficulty--kill him. Let no man tell me that such is not the case. I answer, I have heard it hundreds of times: "Never trust a redskin unless he be dead." "Kill every buffalo you see," said a Yankee colonel to me one day in Nebraska; "every buffalo dead is an Indiaan gone;" such things are only trifles. Listen to this cute feat of a Montana trader. A store-keeper in Helena City had some sugar stolen from him. He poisoned the sugar next night and left his door open. In the morning six Indians were found dead outside the town. That was a cute notion, I guess; and yet there are other examples worse than that, but they are too revolting to tell. Never mind; I suppose they have found record somewhere else if not in this world, and in one shape or another they will speak in due time. The Crees are perhaps the only tribe of prairie Indians who have as yet suffered no injustice at the hands of the white man. The land is still theirs, the hunting-rounds remain almost undisturbed; but their days are numbered, and already the echo of the approaching wave of Western immigration is sounding through the solitudes of the Cree country.

It is the same story from the Atlantic to the Pacific. First the White man was the welcome guest, the honoured visitor; then the greedy hunter, the death-dealing vender of fire-water and poison; then the settler and exterminator--every where it has been the same story.

This wild man who first welcomed the new-comer is the only perfect socialist or communist in the world. He holds all things in common with his tribe--the land, the bison, the river, and the moose. He is starving, and the rest of the tribe want food. Well, he kills a moose, and to the last bit the coveted food is shared by all. That war-party has taken one hundred horses in the last raid into Blackfoot or Peagin territory; well, the whole tribe are free to help themselves to the best and fleetest steeds before the captors will touch one out of the band. There is but a scrap of beaver, a thin rabbit, or a bit of sturgeon in the lodge; a stranger comes, and he is hungry; give him his share and let him be first served and best attended to. If one child starves in an Indian camp you may know that in every lodge scarcity is universal and that every stomach is hungry. Poor, poor fellow! his virtues are all his own; crimes he may have, and plenty, but his noble traits spring from no book-learning, from no school-craft, from the preaching of no pulpit; they come from the instinct of good which the Great Spirit has taught him; they are the whisperings from that lost world whose glorious shores beyond the Mountains of the Setting Sun are the long dream of his life. The most curious anomaly among the race of man, the red man of America, is passing away beneath our eyes into the infinite solitude. The possession of the same noble qualities which we affect to reverence among our nations makes us kill him. If he would be as the African or the Asiatic it would be all right for him; if he would be our slave he might live, but as he won't be that, won't toil and delve and hew for us, and will persist in hunting, fishing, and roaming over the beautiful prairie land which the Great Spirit gave him; in a word, since he will be free we kill him. Why do I call this wild child the great anomaly of the human race? I will tell you. Alone amongst savage tribes he has learnt the lesson which the great mother Nature teaches to her sons through the voices of the night, the forest, and the solitude. This river, this mountain, this measureless meadow speak to him in a language of their own. Dwelling with them, he learns their varied tongues, and his speech becomes the echo of the beauty that lies spread around him. Every name for lake or river, for mountain or meadow, has its peculiar significance, and to tell the Indian title of such things is generally to tell the nature of them also. Ossian never spoke with the voice of the mist-shrouded mountain or the wave-beat shores of the isles more thoroughly than does this chief of the Blackfeet or the Sioux speak the voices of the things of earth and air amidst which his wild life is cast.

I know that it is the fashion to hold in derision and mockery the idea that nobility, poetry, or eloquence exist in the wild Indian. I know that with that low brutality which has ever made the Anglo-Saxon race deny its enemy the possession of one atom of generous sensibility, that dull enmity which prompted us to paint the Maid of Orleans a harlot, and to call Napoleon the Corsican robber--I know that that same instinct glories in degrading the savage, whose chief crime is that he prefers death to slavery; glories in painting him devoid of every trait of manhood, worthy only to share the fate of the wild beast of the wilderness--to be shot down mercilessly when seen. But those bright spirits who have redeemed the America of to-day from the dreary waste of vulgar greed and ignorant conceit which we in Europe have flung so heavily upon her; those men whose writings have come back across the Atlantic, and have become as household words among us--Irving, Cooper, Longfellow--have they not found in the rich store of Indian poetry the source of their choicest thought? Nay, I will go farther, because it may be said that the a poet would be prone to drape with poetry every subject on which his fancy lighted, as the sun turns to gold and crimson the dullest and the dreariest clouds: but Search the books of travel amongst remote Indian tribes, from Columbus to Catlin, from Charlevoix to Carver, from Bonneville to Palliser the story is ever the same. The traveller is welcomed and made much of; he is free to come and go; the best food is set before him; the lodge is made warm and bright; he is welcome to stay his lifetime if he pleases. "I swear to your majesties," writes Columbus--alas! the red man's greatest enemy--"I swear to your majesties that there is not in the world a better people than these, more affectionate, affable, or mild."

"At this moment," writes an American officer only ten years back, "it is certain a man can go about throughout the Blackfoot territory without molestation, except in the contingency of being mistaken at night for an Indian." No, they are-fast going, and soon they will be all gone, but in after-times men will judge more justly the poor wild creatures whom to-day we kill and vilify; men will go back again to those old books of travel, or to those pages of "Hiawatha" and "Mohican," to find that far away from the border-land of civilization the wild red man, if more of the savage, was infinitely less of the brute than was the white ruffian who destroyed him.

I quitted the camp at Battle River on the 17th November, with a large band of horses and a young Cree brave who had volunteered his services for some reason of his own which he did not think necessary to impart to us. The usual crowd of squaws, braves in buffalo robes, naked children, and howling dogs assembled to see us start. The Cree led the way mounted on a ragged-looking pony, then came the baggage-sleds, and I brought up the rear on a tall horse belonging to the Company. Thus we held our way in a north-west direction over high-rolling plains along the north bank of the Saskatchewan towards Fort Pitt.

On the morning of the 18th we got away from our camping thicket of poplars long before the break of day. There was no track to guide us, but the Cree went straight as an arrow over hill and dale and frozen lake. The hour that preceded the dawn was brilliant with the flash and glow of meteors across the North-western sky. I lagged so far behind to watch them that when day broke I found myself alone, miles from the party. The Cree kept the pace so well that it took me some hours before I again Caught sight of them. After a hard ride of six-and-thirty miles, we halted for dinner on the banks of English Creek. Close beside our camping-place a large clump of spruce-pine stood in dull contrast to the snowy surface. They looked like old friends to me--friends of the Winnipeg and the now distant Lake of the Woods; for from Red River to English Creek, a distance of 750 miles, I-had seen but a solitary pine-tree. After a short dinner We resumed our rapid way, forcing the pace with a view of making Fort Pitt by night-fall. A French half-breed declared he knew a short cut across the hills of the Red Deer, a wild rugged tract of country lying on the north of the Saskatchewan. Crossing these hills, he said, we would strike the river at their farther side, and then, passing over on the ice, cut the bend which the Saskatchewan makes to the north, and, emerging again opposite Fort Pitt, finally re-cross the river at that station. So much for the plan, and now for its fulfilment.

We entered the region of the Red Deer Hills at about two o'clock in the afternoon, and continued at a very rapid pace in a westerly direction for three hours. As we proceeded the country became more broken, the hills rising steeply from narrow V-shaped valleys, and the ground in many places covered with fallen and decaying trees--the wrecks of fire and tempest. Every where throughout this wild region lay the antlers and heads of moose and elk; but, with the exception of an occasional large jackass-rabbit, nothing living moved through the silent hills. The ground was free from badger-holes; the day, though dark, was fine; and, with a good horse under me, that two hours gallop over, the Red Deer Hills was glorious work. It wanted yet an hour of sunset when we came suddenly upon the Saskatchewan flowing in a deep narrow valley between steep and lofty hills, which were bare of trees and bushes and clear of snow. A very wild desolate scene it looked as I surveyed it from a projecting spur upon whose summit I rested my blown horse. I was now far in advance of the party who occupied a parallel ridge behind me. By signs they intimated that our course now lay to the north; in fact, Daniel had steered very much too ar south, and we had struck the Saskatchewan river a long, distance below the intended place of crossing. Away we went again to the north, soon losing sight of the party; but as I kept the river on my left far below in the valley I knew they could not cross without my being aware of it. Just before sun set they appeared again in sight, making signs that they were about to descend into the valley and to cross the river. The valley here was five hundred feet in depth, the slope being one of the steepest I had ever seen. At the bottom of this steep descent the Saskatchewan lay in its icy bed, a large majestic-looking river three hundred yards in width. We crossed on the ice without accident, and winding up the steep southern shore gained the level plateau above. The sun was going down, right on our forward track. In the deep valley below the Cree and an English half-breed were getting the horses and baggage-sleds over the river. We made signs to them to camp in the valley, and we ourselves turned our tired horses towards the west, determined at all hazards to reach the fort that night. The Frenchman led the way riding, the Hudson Bay officer followed in a horse-sled, I brought up the rear on horseback. Soon it got quite dark, and we held on over a rough and bushless plateau seamed with deep gullies into which we descended at hap hazard forcing our weary horses with difficulty up the opposite sides. The night got later and later, and still no sign of Fort Pitt; riding in rear I was able to mark the course taken by our guide, and it soon struck me that he was steering wrong; our correct course lay west, but he seemed to be heading gradually to the North, and finally, began to veer even towards the East. I called out to the Hudson Bay man that I had serious doubts as to Daniel's knowledge of the track, but I was assured that all was correct. Still we went on, and still no sign of fort or river. At length the Frenchman suddenly pulled Up and asked us to halt while he rode on and surveyed the country, because he had lost the track, and didn't know where he had got to. Here was a pleasant prospect! without food, fire, or covering, out on the bleak plains, with the thermometer at 20 degrees of frost! After some time the Frenchman returned and declared that he had altogether lost his way, and that there was nothing for it but to camp where we were, and wait for daylight to proceed. I looked around in the darkness. The ridge on which we stood was bare and bleak, with the snow drifted off into the valleys. A few miserable stunted willows were the only signs of vegetation, and the wind whistling through their ragged branches made up as dismal a prospect as man could look at. I certainly felt in no very amiable mood with the men who had brought me into this predicament, because I had been overruled in the matter of leaving our baggage behind and in the track we had been pursuing. My companion, however, accepted the situation with apparent resignation, and I saw him commence to unharness his horse from the sled with the aspect of a man who thought a bare hill-top without food, fire, or clothes was the normal state of happiness to which a man might reasonably aspire at the close of an eighty-mile march, with out laying himself open to the accusation of being over effeminate.

Watching this for some seconds in silence, I determined to shape for myself a different course. I dismounted, and taking from the sled a shirt made of deer-skin, mounted again my poor weary horse and turned off alone into the darkness. "Where are you going to?" I heard my companions calling out after me. I was half inclined not to answer, but turned in the saddle and holloaed back, "To Fort Pitt, that's all." I heard behind me a violent bustle, as though they were busily engaged in yoking up the horses again, and then I rode off as hard as my weary horse could go. My friends took a very short time to harness up again, and they were soon powdering along through the wilderness. I kept on for about half an hour, steering by the stars due west; suddenly I came out upon the edge of a deep valley, and by the broad white band beneath recognized the frozen Saskatchewan again. I have at least found the river, and Fort Pitt, we knew, lay somewhere upon the bank. Turning away from the river, I held on in a south-westerly direction for a considerable distance, passing up along a bare snow-covered valley and crossing a high ridge at its end. I could hear my friends behind in the dark. But they had got, I think, a notion that I had taken leave of my senses, and they were afraid to call out to me. After a bit I bent my course again to the west, and steering by my old guides, the stars, those truest and most unchanging friends of the wanderer, I once more struck the Saskatchewan, this time descending to its level and crossing it on the ice.

As I walked along, leading my horse, I must admit to experiencing a sensation not at all pleasant. The memory of the crossing of the South Branch was still too strong to admit of over-confidence in the strength of the ice, and as every now and again my tired horse broke through the upper crust of snow and the ice beneath cracked, as it always will when weight is placed on it for the first time, no matter how strong it may be, I felt by no means as comfortable as I would have wished. At last the long river was passed, and there on the opposite shore lay the cart track to Fort Pitt. We were close to Pipe-stone Creek, and only three miles from the Fort.

It was ten o'clock when we reached the closely-barred gate of this Hudson Bay post, the inhabitants of which had gone to bed. Ten o'clock at night, and we had started at six o'clock in the morning. I had been fifteen hours in the saddle, and no less than ninety miles had passed under my horse's hoofs, but so accustomed had I grown to travel that I felt just as ready to set out again as though only twenty miles had been traversed. The excitement of the last few hours steering by the stars in an unknown country, and its most successful denouement, had put fatigue and weariness in the background; and as we sat down to a well-cooked supper of buffalo steaks and potatoes, with the brightest eyed little lassie, half Cree, half Scotch, in the North-west to wait upon us, while a great fire of pine wood blazed and crackled on the open hearth, I couldn't help saying to my companions, "Well, this is better than your hill-top and the fireless bivouac in the rustling willows."

Fort Pitt was free from small-pox, but it had gone through a fearful ordeal: more than one hundred Crees had perished close around its stockades. The unburied dead lay for days by the road-side, till the wolves, growing bold with the impunity which death among the hunters ever gives to the hunted, approached and fought over the decay ing bodies. From a spot many marches to the south the Indians had come to the fort in midsummer, leaving behind them a long track of dead and dying men over the waste of distance. "Give us help," they cried, "give us help, our medicine-men can do nothing against this plague; from the white man We got it, and it is only the white man who can take it away from us."

But there was no help to be given, and day by day the wretched band grew less. Then came another idea into the red man's brain: "If we can only give this disease to the white man and the trader in the fort," thought they, "we will cease to suffer from it ourselves;" so they came into the houses dying and disfigured as they were, horrible beyond description to look at, and sat down in the entrances of the wooden houses, and stretched themselves on the floors and spat upon the door-handles. It was no use, the fell disease held them in a grasp from which there was no escape, and just six weeks before my arrival the living remnant fled away in despair.

Fort Pitt stands on the left or north shore of the Saskatchewan River, which is here more than four hundred yards in width. On the opposite shore immense bare, bleak hills raise their wind-swept heads seven hundred feet above the river level. A few pine-trees show their tops some distance away to the north, but no other trace of wood is to be seen in that vast amphitheatre of dry grassy hill in which the fort is built. It is a singularly wild-looking scene, not without a certain beauty of its own, but difficult of association with the idea of disease orepidemic, so pure and bracing is the air which sweeps over those great grassy uplands.

On the 20th November I left Fort Pitt, having exchanged some tired horses for fresher ones, but still keeping the same steed for the saddle, as nothing, better could be procured from the band at the fort. The snow had now almost disappeared from the ground, and a Red River cart was once more taken into use for the baggage. Still keeping along the north shore of the Saskatchewan, we now held our way towards the station of Victoria, a small half-breed settlement situated at the most northerly bend which the Saskatchewan makes in its long course from the mountains to Lake Winnipeg. The order of march was ever the same; the Cree, wrapped in a loose blanket, with his gun balanced across the shoulder of his pony, jogged on in front, then came a young half-breed named Batte notte, who will be better known perhaps to the English reader when I say that he was the son of the Assineboine guide who conducted Lord Milton and Dr. Cheadle through the pine forests of the Thompson River. This youngster employed himself by continually shouting the name of the horse he was driving--thus "Rouge!" would be vigorously yelled out by his tongue, and Rouge at the same moment would be vigorously belaboured by his whip; "Noir!" he would again shout, when that most ragged animal would be within the shafts; and as Rouge and Noir invariably had this ejaculation of their respective titles coupled with the descent of the whip upon their respective backs, it followed that after a while the mere mention of the name conveyed to the animal the sensation of being licked. One horse, rejoicing in the title of "Jean l'Hereux," seemed specially selected for this mode of treatment. He was a brute of surpassing obstinacy, but, as he bore the name of his former owner, a French semi-clerical maniac who had fled from Canada and joined the Blackfeet, and who was regarded by the Crees as one of their direst foes, I rather think that the youthful Battenotte took out on the horse some of the grudges that he owed to the man. Be that as it may, Jean l'Hereux got many a trouncing as he laboured along the sandy pine-covered ridges which rise to the north-west of Fort Pitt.

On the night of the 21st November we reached the shore of the Eggo Lake, and made our camp in a thick clump of aspens. About midday on the following day we came in sight of the Saddle Lake, a favourite camping-ground of the Crees, owing to its inexhaustible stores of finest fish. Nothing struck me more as we thus pushed on rapidly along the Upper Saskatchewan than the absence of all authentic information from stations farther west. Every thing was rumour, and the most absurd rumour. "If you meet an old Indian named Pinguish and a boy without a name at Saddle Lake," said the Hudson Bay officer at Fort Pitt to me, "they may give you letters from Edmonton, and you may get some news from them, because they lost letters near the lake three weeks ago, and perhaps they may have found them by the time you get there." It struck me very forcibly, after a little while, that this "boy without a name" was a most puzzling individual to go in search of. The usual interrogatory question of "What's your name?" would not be of the least use to find such a personage, and to ask a man if he had no name, as a preliminary question, might be to insult him. I therefore fell back upon Pinguish, but could obtain no intelligence of him whatever. Pinguish had apparently never been heard of. It then occurred to me that the boy without the name might perhaps be a remarkable character in the neighbourhood, owing to his peculiar exception from the lot of humanity; but no such negative person had ever been known, and I was constrained to believe that Pinguish and his mysterious partner had fallen victims to the small-pox or had no existence; for at Saddle Lake the small-pox had worked its direst fury, it was still raging in two little huts close to the track, and when we halted for dinner near the south end of the lake the first man who approached was marked and seared by the disease. It was fated that this day we were to be honoured by peculiar company at our dinner. In addition to the small-pox man, there came an ill-looking fellow of the name of Fayel, who at once proceeded to make himself at his ease beside us. This individual bore a deeper brand than that of small-pox upon him, inasmuch as a couple of years before he had foully murdered a comrade in one of the passes of the Rocky Mountains when returning from British Columbia. But this was not the only intelligence as to my companions that I was destined to receive upon my arrival on the following day at Victoria.

"You have got Louis Battenotte, with you, I see," said the Hudson Bay officer in charge.

"Yes," I replied.

"Did he tell you any thing about the small-pox?"

"Oh yes; a great deal; he often spoke about it."

"Did he say he had had it himself?"

"No."

"Well, he had," continued ny host, "only a month ago, and the coat and trousers that he now wears were the same articles of clothing in which he lay all the time he had it," was the pleasant reply.

After this little revelation concerning Battenotte and his habiliments, I must admit that I was not quite as ready to look with pleasure upon his performance of the duties of cook, chambermaid, and general valet as I had been in the earlier stage of our acquaintance; but a little reflection made the hole thing right again, convincing one of the fact that travelling, like misery, "makes one acquainted with strange bedfellows," and that luck has more to do with our lives than we are wont to admit. After leaving Saddle Lake we entered a very rich and beautiful country, completely clear of snow and covered deep in grass and vetches. We travelled hard, and reached at nightfall a thick wood of pines and spruce-trees, in which we made a cosy camp. I had brought with me a bottle of old brandy from Red River in case of illness, and on this evening, not feeling all right, I drew the cork while the Cree was away with the horses, and drank a little with my companion. Before we had quite finished, the Cree returned to camp, and at once declared that he smelt grog. He became very lively at this discovery. We had taken the precaution to rinse out the cup that had held the spirit, but he nevertheless commenced a series of brewing which appeared to give him infinite satisfaction. Two or three times did he fill the empty cup with water and drain it to the bottom, laughing and rolling his head each time with delight, and in order to be sure that he had got the right one he proceeded in the same manner with every cup we possessed; then he confided to Battenotte that he had not tasted grog for a long time before, the last occasion being one on which he had divested himself of his shirt and buffalo robe, in other words, gone naked, in order to obtain the coveted fire-water.

The weather had now become beautifully mild, and on the 23rd of November the thermometer did not show even one degree of frost. As we approached the neighbourhood of the White Earth River the aspect of the country became very striking: groves of spruce and pine crowned the ridges; rich, well-watered valleys lay between, deep in the long white grass of the autumn. The track wound in and out through groves and wooded declivities, and all nature looked bright and beautiful. Some of the ascents from the river bottoms were so steep that the united efforts of Battenotte and the Cree were powerless to induce Rouge or Noir, or even Jean l'Hcreux, to draw the cart to the summit. But the Cree was equal to the occasion. With a piece of shanganappi he fastened L'Hereux's tail to the shafts of the cart-shafts which had already between them the redoubted Noir. This new method of harnessing had a marked effect upon L'Hereux; he strained and hauled with a persistency and vigour which I feared must prove fatal to the permanency of his tail in that portion of his body in which nature had located it, but happily such was not the case, and by the united efforts of all parties the summit was reached.

I only remained one day at Victoria, and the 25th of November found me again en route for Edmonton. Our Cree had, however, disappeared. One night when he was eating his supper with his scalping-knife--a knife, by the way, with which he had taken, he informed us, three Black feet scalps --I asked him why he had come away with us from Battle River. Because he wanted to get rid of his wife, of whom he was tired, he replied. He had come off without saying any thing to her. "And what will happen to the wife?" I asked. "Oh, she will marry another brave when she finds me gone," he answered, laughing at the idea. I did not enter into the previous domestic events which had led to this separation, but I presume they were of a nature similar to those which are not altogether unknown in more civilized society, and I make no hesitation in offering to our legislators the example of my friend the Cree as tending to simplify the solution, or rather the dissolution, of that knotty point, the separation of couples who, for reasons best known to themselves, have ceased to love. Whether it was that the Cree found in Victoria a lady suitad to his fancy, or whether he had heard of a war-party against the Sircies, I cannot say, but he vanished during the night of our stay in the fort, and we saw him no more.

As we journeyed on towards Edmonton the country maintained its rich and beautiful appearance, and the weather continued fine and mild. Every where nature had written in unmistakable characters the story of the fertility of the soil over which we rode--every where the eye looked upon panoramas filled with the beauty of lake and winding river, and grassy slope and undulating woodland. The whole face of the country was indeed one vast park. For two days we passed through this beautiful land,-and on the evening of the 28th November drew near to Edmonton. My party had been increased by the presence of two gentlemen from Victoria, a Wesleyan minister and the Hudson Bay official in charge of the Company's post at that place. Both of these gentlemen had resided long in the Upper Saskatchewan, and were intimately acquainted with the tribes who inhabit The vast territory from the Rocky Mountains to Carlton House. It was late in the evening, just one month after I had started from the banks of the Red River, that I approached the high palisades of Edmonton. As one who looks back at evening from the summit of some lofty ridge over the long track which he has followed since the morning, so now did my mind travel back over the immense distance through which I had ridden in twenty-two days of actual travel and in thirty-three of the entire journey-that distance could not have been less than 1000 miles; and as each camp scene rose again before me, with its surrounding of snow and storm-swept prairie and lonely clump of aspens, it seemed as though something like infinite space stretched between me and that far-away land which one word alone can picture, that one word in which so many others centre--Home.

CHAPTER SEVENTEEN.

Edmonton--The Ruffian Tahakooch--French Missionaries--Westward still--A beautiful Land--The Blackfeet-Horses--A "Bellox" Soldier--A Blackfoot Speech--The Indian Land--First Sight of the Rocky Mountains--The Mountain House--The Mountain Assineboines--An Indian Trade--M. la Combe--Fire-water--A Night Assault.

EDMONTON, the head-quarters of the Hudson Bay Company's Saskatchewan trade, and the residence of a chief factor of the corporation, is a large five-sided fort with the usual flanking bastions and high stockades. It has within these stockades many commodious and well-built wooden houses, and differs in the cleanliness and order of its arrangements from the general run of trading forts in the Indian country. It stands on a high level bank 100 feet above the Saskatchewan River, which rolls below in a broad majestic stream, 300 yards in width. Farming operations, boat-building, and flour-milling are carried on extensively at the fort, and a blacksmith's forge is also kept going. My business with the officer in charge of Edmonton was soon concluded. It principally consisted in conferring upon him, by commission, the same high judicial functions which I have already observed had been entrusted to me before setting out for the Indian territories. There was one very serious drawback, however, to the possession of magisterial or other authority in the Saskatchewan, in as much as there existed no means whatever of putting that authority into force.

The Lord High Chancellor of England, together with the Master of the Rolls and the twenty-four judges of different degrees, would be perfectly useless if placed in the Saskatchewan to put in execution the authority of the law. The Crees, Blackfeet, Peagins, and Sircies would doubtless have come to the conclusion that these high judicial functionaries were "very great medicines;" but beyond that conclusion, which they would have drawn more from the remarkable costume and head-gear worn by those exponents of the law than from the possession of any legal acumen, much would not have been attained. These considerations somewhat mollified the feelings of disappointment with which I now found myself face to face with the most desperate set of criminals, while I was utterly unable to enforce against them the majesty of my commission.

First, there was the notorious Tahakooch-murderer, robber, and general scoundrel of deepest dye; then there was the sister of the above, a maiden of some twenty summers, who had also perpetrated the murder of two Black foot children close to Edmonton; then there was a youthful French half-breed who had killed his uncle at the settlement of Grand Lac, nine miles to the north-west; and, finally, there was my dinner companion at Saddle Lake, whose crime I only became aware of after I had left that locality. But this Tahakooch was a ruffian too desperate. Here was one of his murderous acts. A short time previous to my arrival two Sircies came to Edmonton. Tahakooch and two of his brothers were camped near the fort. Tahakooch professed friendship for the Sircies, and they went to his lodge. After a few days had passed the Sircies thought it was time to return to their tribe. Rumour said that the charms of the sister of Tahakooch had captivated either one or both of them, and that she had not been insensible to their admiration. Be this as it may, it was time to go; and so they prepared for the journey. An Indian will travel by night as readily as by day, and it was night when these men left the tent of Tahakooch.

"We will go to the fort," said the host, "in order to get provisions for your journey."

The party, three in number, went to the fort, and knocked at the gate for admittance. The man on watch at the gate, before unharring, looked from the bastion over the stockades, to see who might be the three men who sought an entrance. It was bright moonlight, and he noticed the shimmer of a gun-barrel under the blanket of Tahakooch. The Sircies were provided with some dried meat, and the party went away. The Sircies marched first in single file, then followed Tahakooch close behind them; the three formed one line. Suddenly, Tahakooch drew from beneath his blanket a short double-barrelled gun, and discharged both barrels into the back of the nearest Sircie. The bullets passed through one man into the body of the other, killing the nearest one instantly. The leading Sircie, though desperately wounded, ran fleetly along the moonlit path until, faint and bleeding, he fell. Tahakooch was close behind; but the villain's hand shook, and four times his shots missed the wounded wretch upon the ground. Summoning up all his strength, the Sircie sprung upon his assailant; a hand-to-hand struggle ensued; but the desperate wound was too much for him, he grew faint in his efforts, and the villain Tahakooch passed his knife into his victim's body. All this took place in the same year during which I reached Edmonton, and within sight of the walls of the fort. Tahakooch lived only a short distance away, and was a daily visitor at the fort.

But to recount the deeds of blood enacted around the wooden walls of Edmonton Would be to fill a volume. Edmonton and Fort Pitt both stand within the war country of the Crees and Blackfeet, and are consequently the scenes of many conflicts between these fierce and implacable enemies. Hitherto my route has led through the Cree country, hitherto we have seen only the prairies and woods through which the Crees hunt and camp; but my wanderings are yet far from their end. To the south-west, for many and many a mile, lie the wide regions of the Blackfeet and the mountain Assineboines; and into these regions I am about to push my way. It is a wild, lone land guarded by the giant peaks of mountains whose snow-capped summits lift themselves 17,000 feet above the sea level. It is the birth-place of waters which seek in four mighty streams the four distant oceans--the Polar Sea, the Atlantic, the Gulf of Mexico, and the Pacific.

A few miles north-west of Edmonton a settlement composed exclusively of French half-breeds is situated on the shores of a rather extensive lake which bears the name of the Grand Lac, or St. Albert. This settlement is presided over by a mission of French Roman Catholic clergymen of the order of Oblates, headed by a bishop of the same order and nationality. It is a curious contrast to find in this distant and strange land men of culture and high mental excellence devoting their lives to the task of civilizing the wild Indians of the forest and the prairie--going far in advance of the settler, whose advent they have but too much cause to dread. I care not what may be the form of belief which the on-looker may hold--whether it be in unison or in antagonism with that faith preached by these men; but he is only a poor semblance of a man who can behold such a sight through the narrow glass of sectarian feeling, holding' opinions foreign to his own. He who has travelled through the vast colonial empire of Britain--that empire which covers one third of the entire habitable surface of the globe and probably half of the lone lands of the world must often have met with men dwelling in the midst of wild, savage peoples whom they tended with a strange and mother-like devotion. If you asked who was this stranger who dwelt thus among wild men in these Lone places, you were told he was the French missionary; and if you sought him in his lonely hut, you found ever the same surroundings, the same simple evidences of a faith which seemed more than human. I do not speak from hearsay or book-knowledge. I have myself witnessed the scenes I now try to recall. And it has ever been the same, East and West, far in advance of trader or merchant, of sailor or soldier, has gone this dark-haired, fragile man, whose earliest memories are thick with sunny scenes by bank of Loire or vine-clad slope of Rhone or Garonne, and whose vision in this life, at least, is never destined to rest again upon these oft-remembered places. Glancing through a pamphlet one day at Edmonton, a pamphlet which recorded the progress of a Canadian Wesleyan Missionary Society, I read the following extract from the letter of a Western missionary:--"These representatives of the Man of Sin, these priests, are hard-workers; summer and winter they follow the camps, suffering great privations. They are indefatigable in their efforts to make converts, but their converts," he adds, "have never heard of the Holy Ghost." "The man of sin "--which of us is without it? To these French missionaries at Grand Lac I was the bearer of terrible tidings. I carried to them the story of Sedan, the overwhelming rush of armed Germany into the heart of France, the closing of the high-schooled hordes of Teuton savagery around Paris; all that was hard home news to: hear. Fate had leant heavily upon their little congregation; out of 900 souls more than 300 had perished of small-pox up to the date of my arrival, and others were still sick in the huts along the lake. Well might the bishop and his priests bow their heads in the midst of such manifold tribulations of death and disaster.

By the last day of November my preparations for further travel into the regions lying west of Edmonton were completed, and at midday on the 1st December I set out for the Rocky Mountain House. This station, the most Western and southern held by the Hudson Bay Company in the Saskatchewan, is distant from Edmonton about 180 miles by horse trail, and 211 miles by river. I was provided with five fresh horses, two good guides, and I carried letters to merchants in the United States, should fortune permit me to push through the great stretch of Blackfoot country lying on the northern borders of the American territory; for it was my intention to leave the Mountain House as soon as possible, and to endeavour to cross by rapid marches the 400 miles of plains to some of the mining cities of Montana or Idaho; the principal difficulty lay, however, in the reluctance of men to come with me into the country of the Blackfeet. At Edmonton only one man spoke the Blackfoot tongue, and the offer of high wages failed to induce him to attempt the journey. He was a splendid specimen of a half-breed; he had married a Blackfoot squaw, and spoke the difficult language with fluency; but he had lost nearly all his relations in the fatal plague, and his answer was full of quiet thought when asked to be my guide.

"It is a work of peril," he said, "to pass the Blackfoot country all' pitching along the foot of the mountains; they will see our trail in the snow, follow it, and steal our horses, or perhaps worse still. At another time I would attempt it, but death has been too heavy upon my friends, and I don't feel that I can go."

It was still possible, however, that at the Mountain House I might find a guide ready to attempt the journey, and my kind host at Edmonton provided me with letters to facilitate my procuring all supplies from his subordinate officer at that station. Thus fully accoutred and prepared to meet the now rapidly increasing severity of the winter, I started on the 1st December for the mountains. It-was a bright, beautiful day. I was alone with my two retainers; before me lay an uncertain future, but so many curious scenes had been passed in safety during the last six months of my life, that I recked little of what was before me, drawing a kind of blind confidence from the thought that so much could not have been in vain. Crossing the now fast-frozen Saskatchewan, we ascended the southern bank and entered upon a rich country watered with many streams and wooded with park-like clumps of aspen and pine. My two retainers were first-rate fellows. One spoke English very fairly: he was a brother of the bright-eyed little beauty at Fort Pitt. The other, Paul Foyale, was a thick,

83

stout-set man, a good voyageur, and excellent-in camp. Both were noted travellers, and both had suffered severely in the epidemic of the small-pox. Paul had lost his wife and child, and Rowland's children had all had the disease, but had recovered. As for any idea about taking infection from men coming out of places where that infection existed, that would have been the merest foolishness; at least, Paul and Rowland thought so, and as they were destined to be my close companions for some days, cooking for me, tying up my blankets, and sleeping beside me, it was just as well to put a good face upon the matter and trust once more to the glorious doctrine of chance. Besides, they were really such good fellows, princes among voyayeurs, that, small-pox or no small-pox, they were first-rate company for any ordinary mortal. For two days we jogged merrily along. The Musquashis or Bears Hill rose before us and faded away into blue distance behind us. After sundown on the 2nd we camped in a thicket of large aspens by the high bank of the Battle River, the same stream at whose mouth nearly 400 miles away I had found the Crees a fortnight before. On the 3rd December we crossed this river, and, quitting the Blackfeet trail, struck in a south-westerly direction through a succession of grassy hills with partially wooded valleys and small frozen lakes. A glorious country to ride over--a country in which the eye ranged across miles and miles of fair-lying hill and long-stretching valley; a silent, beautiful land upon which summer had stamped so many traces, that December had so far been powerless to efface their beauty. Close by to the south lay the country of the great Blackfeet nation--that wild, restless tribe whose name has been a terror to other tribes and to trader and trapper for many and many a year. Who and what are these wild dusky men who have held their own against all comers, sweeping like a whirlwind over the sand deserts of the central continent? They speak a tongue distinct from all other Indian tribes; they have ceremonies and feasts wholly different, too, from the feasts and ceremonies of other nations; they are at war with every nation that touches the wide circle of their boundaries; the Crows, the Flatheads, the Kootenies, the Rocky Mountain Assineboines, the Crees, the Plain Assineboines, the Minnitarrees, all are and have been the inveterate enemies of the five confederate nations which form together the great Blackfeet tribe. Long years ago, when their great forefather crossed the Mountains of the Setting Sun and settled along the sources of the Missouri and the South Saskatchewan, so runs the legend of their old chiefs, it came to pass that a chief had three sons, Kenna, or The Blood, Peaginou, or The Wealth, and a third who was nameless. The two first were great hunters, they brought to their father's lodge rich store of moose and elk meat, and the buffalo fell before their unerring arrows; but the third, or nameless one, ever returned empty-handed from the chase, until his brothers mocked him for his want of skill. One day the old chief said to this unsuccessful hunter, "My son, you cannot kill the moose, your arrows shun the buffalo, the elk is too fleet for your footsteps, and your brothers mock you because you bring no meat into the lodge; but see, I will make you a great hunter." And the old chief took from the lodge-fire a piece of burnt stick, and, wetting it, he rubbed the feet of his son with the blackened charcoal, and he named him Sat-Sia-qua, or The Blackfeet, and evermore Sat-Sia-qua was a mighty hunter, and his arrows flew straight to the buffalo, and his feet moved swift in the chase. From these three sons are descended the three tribes of Blood, Peaginou, and Blackfeet, but in addition, for many generations, two other tribes or portions of tribes have been admitted into the confederacy; These are the Sircies, on the north, a branch, or offshoot from the Chipwayans of the Athabasca; and the Gros Ventres, or Atsinas, on the southeast, a branch from the Arrapahoe nation who dwelt along the sources of the Platte. How these branches became detached from the parent stocks has never been determined, but to this day they speak the languages of their original tribe in addition to that of the adopted one. The parent tongue of the Sircies is harsh and guttural, that of the Blackfeet is rich and musical; and while the Sircies always speak Blackfeet in addition to their own tongue, the Blackfeet rarely master the language of the Sircies.

War, as we have already said, is the sole toil and thought of the red man's life. He has three great causes of fight: to steal a horse, take a scalp, or get a wife. I regret to have to write that the possession of a horse is valued before that of a wife-and this has been the case for many years. "A horse," writes McKenzie, "is valued at ten guns, a woman is only worth one gun;" but at that time horses were scarcer than at present. Horses have been a late importation, comparatively speaking, into the Indian country. They travelled rapidly north from Mexico, and the prairies soon became covered with the Spanish mustang, for whose possession the red man killed his brother with singular pertinacity. The Indian to-day believes that the horse has ever dwelt with him on the Western deserts, but that such is not the case his own language undoubtedly tells. It is curious to compare the different names which the wild men gave the new-comer who was destined to work such evil among them. In Cree, a dog is called "Atim," and a horse, "Mistatim," or the "Big Dog." In the Assineboine tongue the horse is called "Sho-a-th-in-ga," "Thongatch shonga," a great dog. In Blackfeet, "Po-no-ka-mi-taa" signifies the horse; and "Po-no-ko" means red deer, and "Emita," a dog--the "Red-deer Dog." But the Sircies made the best name of all for the new-comer; they called him the "Chistli" "Chis," seven, "Li," dogs "Seven Dogs." Thus we have him called the big dog, the great dog, the red-deer dog, the seven dogs, and the red dog, or "It-shou-ma-shungu," by the Gros Ventres. The dog was their universal beast of burthen, and so they multiplied the name in many ways to enable it to define the Superior powers of the new beast.

But a far more formidable enemy than Crow or Cree has lately come in contact with the Blackfeet--an enemy before whom all his stratagem, all his skill with lance or arrow, all his dexterity of horsemanship is of no avail. The "Moka-manus" (the Big-knives), the white men, have pushed up the great Missouri River into the heart of the Blackfeet country, the fire-canoes have forced their way along the muddy waters, and behind them a long chain of armed posts have arisen to hold in check the wild roving races of Dakota and the Montana. It is a useless struggle that which these Indians wage against their latest and most deadly enemy, but nevertheless it is one in which the sympathy of any brave heart must lie on the side of the savage. Here, at the head-waters of the great River Missouri which finds its outlet into the Gulf of Mexico-here, pent up against the barriers of the "Mountains of the Setting Sun," the Blackfeet offer a last despairing struggle to the ever-increasing tide that hems them in. It is not yet two years since a certain citizen soldier of the United States made a famous raid against a portion of this tribe at the head-waters of the Missouri. It so happened that I had the opportunity of hearing this raid described from the rival points of view of the Indian and the white man, and, if possible, the brutality of the latter--brutality which was gloried in--exceeded the relation of the former. Here is the story of the raid as told me by a miner whose "pal" was present in the scene. "It was a little afore day when the boys came upon two redskins in a gulch near-away to the Sun River" (the Sun River flows into the Missouri, and the forks lie below Benton). "They caught the darned red devils and strapped them on a horse, and swore that if they didn't just lead the way to their camp that they'd blow their b---- brains out; and Jim Baker wasn't the coon to go under if he said he'd do it--no, you bet he wasn't. So the red devils showed the trail, and soon the boys came out on a wide gulch, and saw down below the lodges of the Pagans. Baker just says, 'Now, boys, says he, 'thar's the devils, and just you go in and clear them out. No darned prisoners, you know; Uncle Sam ain't agoin' to keep prisoners, I guess. No darned squaws or young uns, but just kill'em all, squaws and all; it's them squaws what breeds'em, and them young uns will only be horse-thieves or hair-lifters when they grows up; so just make a clean shave of the hull brood. Wall, mister, ye see, the boys jist rode in among the lodges afore daylight, and they killed every thing that was able to come out of the tents, for, you see, the redskins had the small-pox bad, they had, and a heap of them couldn't come out nohow; so the boys jist turned over the lodges and fixed them as they lay on the ground. Thar was up to 170 of them Pagans wiped out that mornin', and thar was only one of the boys sent under by a redskin firing out at him from inside a lodge. I say, mister, that Baker's a bell-ox among sodgers, you bet."

One month after this slaughter on the Sun River a band of Peagins were met on the Bow River by a French missionary priest, the only missionary whose daring spirit has carried him into the country of these redoubled tribes. They told him of the cruel loss their tribe had suffered at the hands of the "Long-knives;" but they spoke of it as the fortune of war, as a thing to be deplored, but to be also revenged: it was after the manner of their own war, and it did not strike them as brutal or cowardly; for, alas! they knew no better. But what shall be said of these heroes--the outscourings of Europe--who, under the congenial guidance of that "bell-ox" soldier Jim Baker, "wiped out them Pagan redskins"? This meeting of the missionary with the Indians was in: its way singular. The priest, thinking that the loss of so many lives would teach the tribe how useless must be a war carried on against-the Americans, and how its end must inevitably be the complete destruction of the Indians, asked the chief to assemble his band to listen to his counsel and advice. They met together in the council-tent, and then the priest began. He told them that "their recent loss was only the beginning of their destruction, that the Long knives had countless braves, guns and rifles beyond number, fleet steeds, and huge war-canoes, and that it was useless for the poor wild man to attempt to stop their progress through the great Western solitudes." He asked them "why were their faces black and their hearts heavy? was it not for their relatives and friends so lately killed, and would it not be better to make peace while yet they could do it, and thus save the lives of their remaining friends?"

While thus he spoke there reigned a deep silence through the council-tent, each one looked fixedly at the ground before him; but when the address was over the chief rose quietly, and, casting around a look full of dignity, he asked, "My brother, have you done, or is there aught you would like yet to say to us?"

To this the priest made answer that he had no more to say.

"It is well," answered the Indian; "and listen now to what I say to you; but first," he said, turning to his men, "you, my brethren, you, my sons, who sit around me, if there should be aught in my words from which you differ, if I say one word that you would not say yourselves, stop me, and say to this black-robe I speak with a forked tongue." Then, turning again to the priest, he continued, "You have spoken true, your words come straight; the Long-knives are too many and too strong for us; their guns shoot farther than ours, their big guns shoot twice" (alluding to shells which exploded after they fell); "their numbers are as the buffalo were in the days of our fathers. But what of all that? do you want us to starve on the land which is ours? to lie down as slaves to the white man, to die away one by one in misery and hunger? It is true that the long-knives must kill us, but I say still, to my children and to my tribe, fight on, fight on, fight on! go on fighting to the very last man; and let that last man go on fighting too, for it is better to die thus, as a brave man should die, than to live a little time and then die like a coward. So now, my brethren, I tell you, as I have told you before, keep fighting still. When you see these men coming along the river, digging holes in the ground and looking for the little bright sand" (gold), "kill them, for they mean to kill you; fight, and if it must be, die, for you can only die once, and it is better to die than to starve."

He ceased, and a universal hum of approval running through the dusky warriors told how truly the chief had spoken the thoughts of his followers; Again he said, "What does the white man want in our land? You tell us he is rich and strong, and has plenty of food to eat; for what then does he come to our land? We have only the buffalo, and he takes that from us. See the buffalo, how they dwell with us; they care not for the closeness of our lodges, the smoke of our camp-fires does not fright them, the shouts of our young men will not drive them away; but behold how they flee from the sight, the sound, and the smell of the white man! Why does he take the land from us? who sent him here? He puts up sticks, and he calls the land his land, the river his river, the trees his trees. Who gave him the ground, and the water, and the trees? was it the Great Spirit? No; for the Great Spirit gave to us the beasts and the fish, and the white man comes to take the waters and the ground where these fishes and these beasts live--why does he not take the sky as well as the ground? We who have dwelt on these prairies ever since the stars fell" (an epoch from which the Blackfeet are fond of dating, their antiquity) "do not put sticks over the land and say, Between these sticks this land is mine; you shall not come here or go there."

Fortunate is it for these Blackfeet tribes that their hunting grounds lie partly on British territory--from where our midday camp was made on the 2nd December to the boundary-line at the 49th parallel, fully 180 miles of plain knows only the domination of the Blackfeet tribes. Here, around this midday camp, lies spread a fair and fertile land; but close by, scarce half a day's journey to the south, the sandy plains begin to supplant the rich grass-covered hills, and that immense central desert commences to spread out those ocean-like expanses which find their southern limits far down by the waters of the Canadian River, 1200 miles due south of the Saskatchewan. This immense central sandy plateau is the true home of the bison. Here were raised for countless ages these huge herds whose hollow tramp shook the solid roof of America during the countless cycles which it remained unknown to man. Here, too, was the true home of the Indian: the Commanche, the Apache, the Kiowa, the Arapahoe, the Shienne, the Crow, the Sioux, the Pawnee, the Omahaw, the Mandan, the Manatarree, the Blackfeet, the Cree, and the Assineboine divided between them the immense region, warring and wandering through the vast expanses until the white race from the East pushed their way into the land, and carved out states and territories from the Mississippi to the Rocky Mountains. How it came to pass in the building of the world that to the north of that great region of sand and waste should spread out suddenly the fair country of the Saskatchewan, I must leave to the guess-work of other and more scientific writers; but the fact remains, that alone, from Texas to the sub-Arctic forest, the Saskatchewan Valley lays its fair length for 800 miles in mixed fertility.

But we must resume our Western way. The evening of the 3rd December found us crossing a succession of wooded hills which divide the water system of the North from that of the South Saskatchewan. These systems come so close together at this region, that while my midday kettle was filled with water which finds its way through Battle River into the North Saskatchewan, that of my evening meal was taken from the ice of the Pas-co-pee, or Blindman's; River, whose waters seek through Red Deer River the South Saskatchewan.

It was near sunset when we rode by the lonely shores of the Gull Lake, whose frozen surface stretched beyond the horizon to the north. Before us, at a distance of some ten miles, lay the abrupt line of the Three Medicine Hills, from whose gorges the first view of the great range of the Rocky Mountains was destined to burst upon my sight; But not on this day was I to behold that long-looked-for vision. Night came quickly down upon the silent wilderness; and it was long after dark when we made our camps by the bank of the Pas-co-pee, or Blindman's River, and turned adrift the weary horses to graze in a well-grassed meadow lying in one of the curves of the river. We had ridden more than sixty miles that day.

About midnight a heavy storm of snow burst upon us, and daybreak revealed the whole camp buried deep in snow. As I threw back the blankets from my head (one always lies covered up completely), the wet, cold mass struck chillily upon my face. The snow was wet and sticky, and therefore things were much more wretched than if the temperature had been lower; but the hot tea made matters seem brighter, and about breakfast-time the snow ceased to fall and the clouds began to clear away. Packing our wet blankets together, we set out for the three Medicine Hills, through whose defiles our course lay; the snow was deep in the narrow valleys, making travelling slower and more laborious than before. It was midday when, having rounded the highest of the three hills, we entered a narrow gorge fringed with a fire-ravaged forest. This gorge wound through the hills, preventing a far-reaching view ahead; but at length its western termination was reached, and there lay before me a sight to be long remembered. The great chain of the Rocky Mountains rose their snow-clad sierras in endless succession. Climbing one of the eminences, I gained a vantage-point on the summit from which some by-gone fire had swept the trees. Then, looking west, I beheld the great range in unclouded glory. The snow had cleared the atmosphere, the sky was coldly bright. An immense plain stretched from my feet to the mountain--a plain so vast that every object of hill and wood and lake lay dwarfed into one continuous level, and at the back of this level, beyond the pines and the lakes and the river-courses, rose the giant range, solid, impassable, silent--a mighty barrier rising-midst an immense land, standing sentinel over the plains and prairies of America, over the measureless solitudes of this Great Lone Land. Here, at last, lay the Rocky Mountains.

THE ROCKY MOUNTAINS AT THE SOURCES OF THE SASKATCHEWAN.

Leaving behind the Medicine Hills, we descended into the plain and held our way until sunset towards the west. It was a calm and beautiful evening; far away objects stood out sharp and distinct in the pure atmosphere of these elevated regions. For some hours we had lost sight of the mountains, but shortly before sunset the summit of a long ridge was gained, and they burst suddenly into view in greater magnificence than at midday. Telling my men to go on and make the camp at the Medicine River, I rode through some fire-wasted forest to a lofty grass-covered height which the declining sun was bathing in floods of glory. I cannot hope to put into the compass of words the scene which lay rolled beneath from this sunset-lighted eminence; for, as I looked over the immense plain and watched the slow descent of the evening sun upon the frosted crest of these lone mountains, it seemed as if the varied scenes of my long journey had woven themselves into the landscape, filling with the music of memory the earth, the sky, and the mighty panorama of mountains. Here at length lay the barrier to my onward wanderings, here lay the boundary to that 4000 miles of unceasing travel which had carried me by so many varied scenes so far into the lone-land; and other thoughts were not wanting. The peaks on which I gazed were no pigmies; they stood the culminating monarchs of the mighty range of the Rocky Mountains. From the estuary of the Mackenzie to the Lake of Mexico no point of the American continent reaches higher to the skies. That eternal crust of snow seeks in summer widely-severed oceans. The Mackenzie, the Columbia, and the Saskatchewan spring from the peaks whose teeth-like summits lie grouped from this spot into the compass of a single glance. The clouds that cast their moisture upon this long line of upheaven rocks seek again the ocean which gave them birth in its far-separated divisions of Atlantic, Pacific, and Arctic. The sun sank slowly behind the range and darkness began to fall on the immense plain, but aloft on the topmost edge the pure white of the jagged crest-line glowed for an instant in many-coloured silver, and then the lonely peaks grew dark and dim.

As thus I watched from the silent hill-top this great mountain-chain, whose summits slept in the glory of the sunset, it seemed no stretch of fancy which made the red man place his paradise beyond their golden peaks. The "Mountains of the Setting Sun," the "Bridge of the World," Thus he has named them, and beyond them the soul first catches a glimpse of that mystical land where the tents are pitched midst everlasting verdure and countless herds and the music of ceaseless streams.

That night there came a frost, the first of real severity that had fallen upon us. At daybreak next morning, the 5th December, my thermometer showed 22 degrees below zero, and, in spite of buffalo boots and moose "mittaines," the saddle proved a freezing affair; many a time I got down and trotted on in front of my horse until feet and hands, cased as they were, began to be felt again. But the morning, though piercingly cold, was bright with sunshine, and the snowy range was lighted up in many a fair hue, and the contrasts of pine wood and snow and towering wind-swept cliff showed in rich beauty. As the day wore on we entered the pine forest which stretches to the base of the mountains, and emerged suddenly upon the high banks of the Saskatchewan. The river here ran in a deep, wooded valley, over the western extremity of which rose the Rocky Mountains; the windings of the river showed distinctly from the height on which we stood; and in mid-distance the light blue smoke of the Mountain House curled in fair contrast from amidst a mass of dark green pines.

Leaving my little party to get my baggage across the Clear Water River, I rode on ahead to the fort. While yet a long way off we had been descried by the watchful eyes of some Rocky Mountain Assineboines, and our arrival had been duly telegraphed to the officer in charge. As usual, the excitement was intense to know what the strange party could mean. The denizens of the place looked upon themselves as closed up for the winter, and the arrival of a party with a baggage-cart at such a time betokened something unusual. Nor was this excitement at all lessened when in answer to a summons from the opposite bank of the Saskatchewan I announced my name and place of departure. The river was still open, its rushing waters had resisted so far the efforts of the winter to cover them up, but the ice projected a considerable distance from either shore; the open water in the centre was, however, shallow, and when the rotten ice had been cut away on each side I was able to force my horse into it. In he went with a great splash, but he kept his feet nevertheless; then at the other side the people of the fort had cut away the ice too, and again the horse scrambled safely up. The long ride to the West was over; exactly forty-one days earlier I had left Red River, and in twenty-seven days of actual travel I had ridden 1180 miles.

The Rocky Mountain House of the Hudson Bay Company stands in a level meadow which is clear of trees, although dense forest lies around it at some little distance. It is indifferently situated with regard to the Indian trade, being too far from the Plain Indians, who seek in the American posts along the Missouri a nearer and more profitable exchange for their goods; while the wooded district in which it lies produces furs of a second-class quality, and has for years been deficient in game. The neighbouring forest, however, supplies a rich store of the white spruce for boat-building, and several full-sized Hudson Bay boats are built annually at the fort. Coal of very fair quality is also plentiful along the river banks, and the forge glows with the ruddy light of a real coal fire--a friendly sight when one has not seen it during many months. The Mountain House stands within the limits of the Rocky Mountain Assineboines, a branch of-the once famous Assineboines of the Plains whose wars in times not very remote made them the terror of the prairies which lie between the middle Missouri and the Saskatchewan. The Assineboines derive their name, which signifies "stone-heaters," from a custom in vogue among them before the advent of the traders into their country. Their manner of boiling meat was as follows: a round hole was scooped in the earth, and into the hole was sunk a piece of raw hide; this was filled with water, and the buffalo meat placed in it, then a fire was lighted close by and a number of round stones made red hot; in this state they were dropped into, or held in, the water, which was thus raised to boiling temperature and the meat cooked. When the white man came he sold his kettle to the stone-heaters, and henceforth the practice disappeared, while the name it had given rise to remained--a name which long after the final extinction of the tribe will still exist in the River Assineboine and its surroundings. Nothing testifies more conclusively to the varied changes and vicissitude's Indian tribes than the presence of this branch of the Assineboine nation in the pine forests of the Rocky Mountains. It is not yet a hundred years since the "Ossinepoilles" were found by one of the earliest traders inhabiting the country between the head of the Pasquayah or Saskatchewan and the country of the Sioux, a stretch of territory fully 900 miles in length.

Twenty years later they still were numerous along the whole line of the North Saskatchewan, and their lodges were at intervals seen along a river line of 800 miles in length, but even then a great change had come upon them. In 1780 the first epidemic of small-pox swept over the Western plains, and almost annihilated the powerful Assineboines. The whole central portion of the tribe was destroyed, but the outskirting portions drew together and again made themselves a terror to trapper and trader. In 1821 they were noted for their desperate forays, and for many years later a fierce conflict raged between them and the Blackfeet; under the leadership of a chief still famous in Indian story--Tehatka, or the "Left-handed;" they for a long time more than held their own against these redoubtable warriors. Tehatka was a medicine-man of the first order, and by the exercise of his superior cunning and dream power he was implicitly relied on by his followers; at length fortune deserted him, and he fell in a bloody battle with the Gros Ventres near the Knife River, a branch of the Missouri, in 1837. About the same date small-pox again swept the tribe, and they almost disappeared from the prairies. The Crees too pressed down from the North and East, and occupied a great-portion of their territory; the Blackfeet smote them hard on the south-west frontier; and thus, between foes and disease, the Assineboines of to-day have dwindled down into far-scattered remnants of tribes. Warned by the tradition of the frightful losses of earlier times from the ravages of small-pox, the Assineboines this year kept far out in the great central prairie along the coteau, and escaped the infection altogether, but their cousins, the Rocky Mountain Stonies, were not so fortunate, they lost some of their bravest men during the pre ceding summer and autumn. Even under the changed circumstances of their present lives, dwelling amidst the forests and rocks instead of in the plains and open country, these Assineboines of the Mountains retain many of the better characteristics of their race; they are brave and skilful men, good hunters of red deer, moose, and big horn, and are still held in dread by the Blackfeet, who rarely venture into their country. They are well acquainted with the valleys and passes through the mountains, and will probably take a horse over as rough ground as any men in the creation.

At the ford on the Clear Water River, half a mile from the Mountain House, a small clump of old pine-trees stands on the north side of the stream. A few years ago a large band of Blood Indians camped round this clump of pines during a trading expedition to the Mountain House. They were under the leadership of two young chiefs, brothers. One evening a dispute about some trifling matter arose, words ran high, there was a flash of a scalping-knife, a plunge, and one brother reeled back with a fearful gash in his side, the other stalked slowly to his tent, and sat down silent and impassive. The wounded man loaded his gun, and keeping the fatal wound closed together with one hand walked steadily to his brothers tent; pulling back the door-casing, he placed the muzzle of his gun to the heart of the man who sat immovable all the time, and shot him dead, then, removing his hand from his own mortal wound, he fell lifeless beside his brother's body. They buried the two brothers in the same grave by the shadow of the dark pine-trees. The band to which the chiefs belonged broke up and moved away into the great plains--the reckoning of blood had been paid, and the account was closed. Many tales of Indian war and revenge could I tell--tales gleaned from trader and missionary and voyageur, and told by camp-fire or distant trading post, but there is no time to recount them now, a long period of travel lies before me and I must away to enter upon it; the scattered thread must be gathered up and tied together too quickly, perhaps, for the success of this wandering story, but not an hour too soon for the success of another expedition into a still farther and more friendless region. Eight days passed pleasantly at the Mountain House; rambles by day into the neighbouring hills, stories of Indian life and prairie scenes at the evening fire filled up the time, and it was near mid-December before I thought of moving my quarters.

The Mountain House is perhaps the most singular specimen of an Indian trading post to be found in the wide territory of the Hudson Bay Company. Every precaution known to the traders has been put in force to prevent the possibility of surprise during "a trade." Bars and bolts and places to fire down at the Indians who are trading abound in every direction; so dreaded is the name borne by the Black feet, that it is thus their trading post has been constructed. Some fifty years ago the Company had a post far south on the Bow River in the very heart of the Blackfeet country. Despite of all precautions it was frequently plundered And at last burnt down by the Blackfeet, and since that date no attempt has ever been made to erect another fort in their country.

Still, I believe the Blackfeet and their confederates are not nearly so bad as they have been painted, those among the Hudson Bay Company who are best acquainted with them are of the same opinion, and, to use the words of Pe to-pee, or the Perched Eagle, to Dr. Hector in 1857, "We see but little of the white man," he said, "and our young men do not know how to behave; but if you come among us, the chiefs will restrain the young men, for we have power over them. But look at the Crees, they have long lived in the company of white men, and nevertheless they are just like dogs, they try to bite when your head is turned--they have no manners; but the Blackfeet have large hearts and they love to show hospitality." Without going the length of Pe-to-pee in this estimate of the virtues of his tribe, I am still of opinion that under proper management these wild wandering men might be made trusty friends. We have been too much inclined to believe all the bad things said of them by other tribes, and, as they are at war with every nation around them, the wickedness of the Blackfeet'has grown into a proverb among men. But to go back to the trading house. When the Blackfeet arrive on a trading visit to the Mountain House they usually come in large numbers, prepared for a brush with either Crees or Stonies. The camp is formed at some distance from the fort, and the braves, having piled their robes, leather, and provisions on the backs of their wives or their horses, approach in long cavalcade. The officer goes out to meet them, and the gates are closed. Many speeches are made, and the chief, to show his "big heart," usually piles on top of a horse a heterogeneous mass of buffalo robes, pemmican, and dried meat, and hands horse and all he carries over to the trader. After such a present no man can possibly enter tain for a moment a doubt upon the subject of the big-heartedness of the donor, but if, in the trade which ensues: after this present has been made, it should happen that fifty horses are bought by the Company, not one of all the band will cost so dear as that which demonstrates the large heartedness of the brave.

Money-values are entirely unknown in these trades. The values of articles are computed by "skins;" for instance, a horse will be reckoned at 60 skins; and these 60 skins will be given thus: a gun, 15 skins; a capote, 10 skins; a blanket, 10 skins; ball and powder, 10 skins; tobacco, 15 skins total, 60 skins. The Bull Ermine, or the Four Bears, or the Red Daybreak, or whatever may be the brave's name, hands over the horse, and gets in return a blanket, a gun, a capote, ball and powder, and tobacco. The term "skin" is a very old one in the fur trade; the original standard, the beaver skin or, as it was called, "the made beaver" was the medium of exchange, and every other skin and article of trade was graduated upon the scale of the beaver; thus a beaver, or a skin, was reckoned equivalent to 1 mink skin, one marten was equal to 2 skins, one black fox 20 skins, and so on; in the same manner, a blanket, a capote, a gun, or a kettle had their different values in skins. This being explained, we will now proceed with the trade.

Sapoomaxica, or the Big Crow's Foot, having demonstrated the bigness of his heart, and received in return a tangible proof of the corresponding size of the trader's, addresses his braves, cautioning them against violence or rough behaviour. The braves, standing ready with their peltries, are in a high state of excitement to begin the trade. Within the fort all the preparations have been completed, communication cut off between the Indian room and the rest of the buildings, guns placed up in the loft overhead, and men all get ready for any thing that might turn up; then the outer gate is thrown open, and a large throng enters the Indian room. Three or four of the first-comers are now admitted through a narrow passage into the trading-shop, from the shelves of which most of the blankets, red cloth, and beads have been removed, for the red man brought into the presence of so much finery would unfortunately behave very much after the manner of a hungry boy put in immediate juxtaposition to bath-buns, cream-cakes, and jam-fritters, to the complete collapse of profit upon the trade to the Hudson Bay Company. The first Indians admitted hand in their peltries through a wooden grating, and receive in exchange so many blankets, beads, or strouds. Out they go to the large hall where their comrades are anxiously awaiting their turn, and in rush another batch, and the doors are locked again. The reappearance of the fortunate braves with the much-coveted articles of finery adds immensely to the excitement. What did they see inside? "Oh, not much, only a few dozen blankets and a few guns, and a little tea and sugar;" this is terrible news for the outsiders, and the crush to get\in increases tenfold, under the belief that the good things will all be gone. So the trade progresses, until at last all the peltries and provisions have changed hands, and there is nothing more to be traded; but some times things do not run quite so smoothly. Sometimes, when the stock of pemmican or robes is small, the braves object to see their "pile" go for a little parcel of tea or sugar. The steelyard and weighing-balance are their especial objects of dislike. "What for you put on one side tea or sugar, and on the other a little bit of iron?" they say; "we don't know what that medicine is-but, look here, put on one side of that thing that swings a bag of pemmican, and put on the other side blankets and tea and sugar, and then, when the two sides stop swinging, you take the bag of pemmican and we will take the blankets and the tea: that would be fair, for one side will be as big as the other." This is a very bright idea on the part of the Four Bears, and elicits universal satisfaction all round. Four Bears and his brethren are, however, a little bit put out of conceit when the trader observes, "Well, let be as you say. We will make the balance swing level between the bag of pemmican and the blankets, but we will carry out the idea still further. You will put your marten skins and your otter and fisher skins on one side, I will put against them on the other my blankets, and my gun and ball and powder; then, when both sides are level, you will take the ball and powder and the blankets, and I will take the marten and the rest of the fine furs." This proposition throws a new light upon the question of weighing-machines and steelyards, and, after some little deliberation, it is resolved to abide by the old plan of letting the white trader decide the weight himself in his own way, for it is clear that the steelyard is a great medicine which no brave can understand, and which can only be manipulated by a white medicine-man.

This white medicine-man was in olden times a terrible demon in the eyes' of the Indian. His power reached far into the plains; he possessed three medicines of the very highest order: his heart could sing, demons sprung from the light of his candle, and he had a little box stronger than the strongest Indian. When a large band of the Blackfeet would assemble at Edmonton, years ago, the Chief Factor would-win-dup his musical box, get his magic lantern ready, and take out his galvanic battery. Imparting with the last-named article a terrific shock to the frame of the Indian chief, he would warn him that far out in the plains he could at will inflict the same medicine upon him if he ever behaved badly. "Look," he would say, "now my heart beats for you," then the spring of the little musical box concealed under his coat would be touched, and lo! the heart of the white trader would sing with the strength of his love for the Blackfeet. "To-morrow I start to cross the mountains against the Nez Perces," a chief would say, "what says my white brother, don't he dream that my arm will be strong in battle, and that the scalps and horses of the Nez Perces will be ours?" "I have dreamt that you are to draw one of these two little sticks which I hold in my hand. If you draw the right one, your arm will be strong, your eye keen, the horses of the Nez Perces will be yours; but, listen, the fleetest horse must come to me; you will have to give me the best steed in the band of the Nez Perces. Woe betide you if you should draw the wrong stick!" Trembling with fear, the Blackfoot would approach and draw the bit of wood. "My brother, you are a great chief, you have drawn the right stick--your fortune is assured, go." Three weeks later a magnificent horse, the pride of some Nez Perce chief on the lower Columbia, would be led into the fort on the Saskatchewan, and when next the Blackfoot chief came to visit the white medicine-man a couple of freshly taken scalps would dangle from his spear shaft.

In former times, when rum was used in the trade, the most frightful scenes were in the habit of occurring in the Indian room. The fire-water, although freely diluted with water soon reduced the assemblage to a state of wild hilarity, quickly followed by stupidity and sleep. The fire-water for the Crees was composed of three parts

90

of water to one of spirit, that of the Blackfeet, seven of water to one of spirit, but so potent is the power which alcohol in any shape his well-diluted liquor, was wont to become helplessly intoxicated. The trade usually began with a present of-fire water all round--then the business went on apace. 'Horses, robes, tents, provisions, all would be proffered for one more drink at the beloved poison. Nothing could exceed the excitement inside the tent, except it was the excitement outside. There the anxious crowd could only learn by hearsay what was going on within. Now and then a brave, with an amount of self-abnegation worthy of a better cause, would issue from the tent with his cheeks distended and his mouth full of the fire-water, and going along the ranks of his friends he would squirt a little of the liquor into the open mouths of his less fortunate brethren.

But things did not always go so smoothly. Knives were wont to flash, shots to be fired--even-now the walls of the Indian rooms at Fort Pitt and Edmonton show many traces of bullet marks and knife hacking done in the wild fury of the intoxicated savage. Some ten years ago this most baneful distribution was stopped by the Hudson Bay Company in the Saskatchewan district, but the free traders still continued to employ alcohol as a means of acquiring the furs belonging to the Indians. I was the bearer of an Order in Council from the Lieutenant-Governor prohibiting, under heavy penalties, the sale, distribution, or possession of alcohol, and this law, if hereafter enforced, will do much to remove at least one leading source of Indian demoralization.

The universal passion for dress is strangely illustrated in the Western Indian. His ideal of perfection is the English costume of some forty years ago. The tall chimney-pot hat with round narrow brim, the coat with high collar going up over the neck, sleeves tight-fitting, waist narrow. All this is perfection, and the chief who can array himself in this ancient garb struts out of the fort the envy and admiration of all beholders. Sometimes the tall felt chimney-pot is graced by a large feather which has done duty in the turban of a dowager thirty years ago in England. The addition of a little gold tinsel to the coat collar is of considerable consequence, but the presence of a nether garment is not at all requisite to the completeness of the general get-up. For this most ridiculous-looking costume a Blackfeet chief will readily exchange his beautifully-dressed deerskin Indian shirt embroidered with porcupine quills and ornamented with the raven locks of his enemies--his head-dress of ermine skins, his flowing buffalo robe: a dress in which he looks every inch a savage king for one in which he looks every inch a foolish savage. But the new dress does not long survive--bit by bit it is found unsuited to the wild work which its: owner has to perform; and although it never loses the high estimate originally set upon it, it, nevertheless, is discarded by virtue of the many inconveniences arising out of running buffalo in'a tall beaver,-or fighting in a tail coat against Crees.

During the days spent in the Mountain House I enjoyed the society of the most enterprising and best informed missionary in the Indian countries-M. la Combe. This gentleman, a native of Lower Canada, has devoted himself for more than twenty years to the Blackfeet and Crees of the far-West, sharing their sufferings, their hunts, their summer journeys, and their winter camps--sharing even, unwillingly, their war forays and night assaults. The devotion which he has evinced towards these poor wild warriors has not been thrown away upon them, and Pèere la Combe is the only man who can pass and repass from Blackfoot camp to Cree camp with perfect impunity when these long-lasting enemies are at war. On one occasion he was camped with a small party of Blackfeet south of the. Red Deer River. It was night, and the lodges were silent and dark, all save one, the lodge of the chief, who had invited the black-robe to his tent for the night and was conversing with him as they lay on the buffalo robes, while the fire in the centre of the lodge burned clear and bright. Every thing was quiet, and no thought of war-party or lurking enemy was entertained. Suddenly a small dog put his head into the lodge. A dog is such an ordinary and inevitable nuisance in the camp of the Indians, that the missionary never even noticed the partial intrusion. Not so the Indian; he hissed out, "It is a Cree dog. We are surprised! run!" then, catching his gun in one hand and dragging his wife by the other, he darted from his tent into the darkness. Not one second too soon, for instantly there crashed through the leather lodge some score of bullets, and the wild war-whoop of the Crees broke forth through the sharp and rapid detonation of many muskets. The Crees were upon them in force. Darkness, and the want of a dashing leader on the part of the Crees, Saved the Blackfeet from total destruction, for nothing could have helped them had their enemies charged home; but as soon as the priest had reached the open which he did when he saw how matters stood-he called loudly to the Blackfeet not to run, but to stand and return the fire of their attackers. This timely advice checked the onslaught of the Crees, who were in numbers nmore than sufficient to make an end of the Blackfeet party in a few minutes. Mean time, the Blackfeet Women delved busily in the earth with knife and finger, while the men fired at random into the darkness. The lighted, semi-transparent tent of the chief had given a mark for the guns of the Crees; but that was quickly overturned, riddled' with balls and although the Crees continued to fire without intermission, their shots generally went high. Sometimes the Crees would charge boldly up to within a few feet of their enemies, then fire and rush back again, yelling all the time, and taunting their enemies. The père spent the night in attending to the wounded Blackfeet. When day dawned the Crees drew off to count their losses; but it was afterwards ascertained that eighteen of their braves had been killed or wounded, and of the small party of Blackfeet twenty had fallen--but who cared? Both sides kept their scalps, and that was every thing.

This battle served not a little to increase the reputation in which the missionary was held as a "great medicine-man." The Blackfeet ascribed to his "medicine" what was really due to his pluck; and the Crees, when they learnt that he had been with their enemies during the fight, at once found in that fact a satisfactory explanation for the want of courage they had displayed.

But it is time to quit the Mountain House, for winter has run on into mid-December, and 1500 miles have yet to be travelled, but not travelled towards the South. The most trusty guide, Piscan Munro, was away on the plains; and as day after day passed by, making the snow a little deeper and the cold a little colder, it was evident that the passage of the 400 miles intervening between the Mountain House and the nearest American Fort had become almost an impossibility.

CHAPTER EIGHTEEN.

Eastward--A beautiful Light.

On the 12th of December I said "Good-bye" to my friends at the Mountain House, and, crossing the now ice-bound torrent of the Saskatchewan, turned my steps, for the first time during many months towards the East. With the same two men, and eight horses, I passed quickly through the snow-covered country. One day later I looked my last look at the far-stretching range of the Rocky Mountains from the lonely ridges of the Medicine Hills. Henceforth there would be no mountains. That immense region through which I had traveled--from Quebec to these Three Medicine Hills--has not a single mountain ridge in its long 3000 miles; woods, streams, and mighty rivers, ocean-lakes, rocks, hills, and prairies, but no mountains, no rough cloud-seeking summit on which to rest the eye that loves the bold outlined of peak and precipice.

"Ah! doctor, dear," Said an old Highland woman, dying in the Red River Settlement long years after she had left her Highland home--"Ah! doctor, dear, if I could but see a wee bit of hill I thinking I might get well again."

Camped that night near a beaver lodge on the Pas-co-pe, the conversation turned upon the mountains we had just left.

"Are they the greatest mountains in the world?" asked Paul Foyale.

"No, there are others nearly as big again."

"Is the Company there, too?" again inquired the faithful Paul.

I was obliged to admit that the Company did not exist in the country of these very big mountains, and I rather fear that the admission somewhat detracted from the altitude of the Himalayas in the estimation of my hearers.

About an hour before daybreak on the 16th of December a Very remarkable light was visible for some time in the zenith, A central orb, or heart of red and crimson light, became suddenly visible a little to the north of the zenith; around this most luminous centre was a great ring, or circle of bright light, and from this outer band there flashed innumerable rays far-into the surrounding darkness. As I looked at it, my thoughts traveled far away to the proud city by the Seine. Was she holding herself bravely against the German hordes? In olden times these weird lights of the sky were supposed only to flash forth when "kings or heroes" fell. Did the sky mirror the earth, even as the ocean mirrors the sky? While I looked at the gorgeous spectacle blazing above me, the great heart of France was red with the blood of her sons, and from the circles of the German league there flashed the glare of cannon round the doomed but defiant city.

CHAPTER NINETEEN.

I start from Edmonton with Dogs--Dog-travelling--The Cabri Sack--A Cold Day--Victoria--"Sent to Rome"--Reach Fort Pitt--The blind Cree--A Feast or a Famine--Death of Pe-na-koam the Blackfoot.

I was now making my way back to Edmonton, with the intention of there exchanging my horses for dogs, and then endeavouring to make the return journey to Red River upon the ice of the River Saskatchewan. Dog travelling was a novelty. The cold had more than reached the limit at which the saddle is a safe mode of travel, and the horses suffered so much in pawing away the snow to get within reach of the grass lying underneath, that I longed to exchange them for the train of dogs, the painted cariole, and little baggage-sled. It took me four days to complete the arrangements necessary for my new journey; and, on the afternoon of the 20th December, I set out upon a long journey, with dogs, down the valley of the Saskatchewan. I little thought then of the distance before me; of the intense cold through which I was destined to travel during two entire months of most rigorous winter; how day by day the frost was to harden, the snow to deepen, all nature to sink more completely under the breath of the ice-king. And it was well that all this was hidden from me at the time, or perhaps I should have been tempted to remain during the winter at Edmonton, until the spring had set free once more the rushing waters of the Saskatchewan.

Behold me then on the 20th of December starting from Edmonton with three trains of dogs--one to carry myself, the other two to drag provisions, baggage, and blankets and all the usual paraphernalia of winter travel. The cold which, with the exception of a few nights severe frost, had been so long-delayed now seemed determined to atone for lost time by becoming suddenly intense. On the night of the 21st December we reached, just at dusk, a magnificent clump of large pine-trees on the right bank of the river. During the afternoon the temperature had fallen below zero; a keen wind blew along-the frozen river, and the dogs and men were glad to clamber up the steep clayey bank into the thick shelter of the pine bluff, amidst whose dark-green recesses a huge fire was quickly alight. While here we sit in the ruddy blaze: of immense dry pine logs it will be well to say a few words on dogs and dog driving.

Dogs in the territories of the North-west have but one function--to haul. Pointer, setter, lurcher, foxhound, greyhound, Indian mongrel, miserable cur or beautiful Esquimaux, all alike are destined to pull a sled of some kind or other during, the months of snow and ice: all are destined to howl under the driver's lash; to tug wildly at the moose-skin collar; to drag until they can drag no more, and then to die. At what age a dog is put to haul I could never satisfactorily ascertain, but I have seen dogs doing some kind of hauling long be fore the peculiar expression of the puppy had left their countenances. Speaking now with the experience of nearly fifty days of dog travelling, and the knowledge of some twenty different trains of dogs of all sizes, ages, and degrees, watching them closely on the track and in the camp during 1300 miles of travel, I may claim, I think, some right to assert that I possess no inconsiderable insight into the habits, customs, and thoughts (for a dog thinks far better than many of his masters) of the hauling dog. When I look back again upon the long list of "Whiskies," "Brandies," "Chocolats," "Corbeaus," "Tigres," "Tete Noirs," "Cerf Volants," "Pilots," "Capitaines," "Cariboos," "muskymotes," "Coffees," and "Nichinassis" who individually and collectively did their best to haul me and my baggage over that immense waste of snow and ice, what a host of sadly resigned faces rises up in the dusky light of the fire! faces seared by whip-mark and blow of stick, faces mutely conscious that that master for whom the dog gives up every thing in this life was treating him in a most brutal manner. I do not for an instant mean to assert that these dogs were not, many of them, great rascals and rank imposters; but Just as slavery produces certain vices in the slave which it would be unfair to hold him accountable for, so does this perversion of the dog from his true use to that of a beast of burthen produce in endless variety traits of cunning and deception in the hauling-dog. To be a thorough expert in dog-training a man must be able to imprecate freely and with considerable variety in at least three different languages. But whatever number of tongues the driver may speak, one is indispensable to perfection in the art, and that is French: curses seem useful adjuncts in any language, but curses delivered in French will get a train of dogs through or over any thing. There is a good story told which illustrates this peculiar feature in dog-training. It is said that a high dignitary of the Church was once making a winter tour through his missions in the North-west. The driver, out of deference for his freight's profession, abstained from the use of forcible language to his dogs, and the hauling was very indifferently performed. Soon the train came to the foot of a hill, and notwithstanding all the efforts of the driver with whip and stick the dogs were unable to draw the cariole to the summit.

"Oh," said the Church dignitary, "this is not at all as good a train of dogs as the one you drove last year; why, they are unable to pull me up this hill!"

"No, monseigneur," replied the owner of the dogs, "but I am driving them differently; if you will only permit me to drive them in the old way you will see how easily they will pull the cariole to the top of this hill; they do not understand my new method."

"By all means," said the bishop; "drive them then in the usual manner."

Instantly there rang out a long string of "sacré chien," "sacré diable," and still more unmentionable phrases. The effect-upon the dogs was magical; the cariole flew to the summit; the progress of the episcopal tour was undeniably expedited, and a-practical exposition was given of the poet's thought, "From seeming evil still aducing good."

Dogs in the Hudson Bay territories haul in various ways. The Esquimaux in the far North run their dogs abreast. The natives of Labrador and along the shores of Hudson Bay harness their dogs by many separate lines in a kind of band or pack, while in the Saskatchewan, and Mackenzie River territories the dogs are put one after the other, in tandem fashion. The usual number allowed to a complete train is four, but three, and sometimes even two are used. The train of four dogs is harnessed to the 'cariole, or sled, by means of two long traces; between these traces the dogs stand one after the other, the head of one dog being about a foot behind the tail of the dog in front of him. They are attached to the traces by a round collar which slips on over the head and ears and then lies close on the swell of the neck; this collar buckles on each side to the traces, which are kept from touching the ground by a back-band of leather buttoned under the dog's ribs or stomach. This back band is generally covered with little brass bells; the collar is also hung with larger bells, and tufts of gay-coloured ribbons or fox-tails are put upon it. Great pride is taken in turning out a train of dogs in good style. Beads, bells, and embroidery are freely used to bedizen the poor brutes, and a most comical effect is produced by the appearance of so much finery upon the woefully frightened dog, who, when he is first put into his harness, usually looks the picture of fear. The fact is patent that in hauling the dog is put to a work from which his whole nature revolts, that is to say the ordinary dog; with the beautiful dog of the Esquimaux breed the case is very different. To haul is as natural to him as to point is natural to the pointer. He alone looks jolly over the work and takes to it kindly, and consequently he alone of all dogs is the best and most lasting hauler; longer than any other dog will his clean firm feet hold tough over the trying ice, and although other dogs will surpass him in the speed which they will maintain for a few days, he alone can travel his many hundreds of miles and finish fresh and hearty after all. It is a pleasure to sit behind such a train of dogs; it is a pain to watch the other poor brutes toiling at their traces. But, after all it is the same with dog-driving as with every other thing; there are dogs and there -are dogs, and the distance from one to the other is as, great as that between a Thames barge and a Cowes schooner.

The hauling-dogs day is a long tissue of trial. While yet the night is in its small hours, and the aurora is beginning to think of hiding its trembling lustre in the earliest dawn, the hauling-dog has his slumber rudely broken by the summons of his driver. Poor beast! All night long he has lain curled up in the roundest of round balls hard by the camp; there, in the lea of tree-stumps or snow-drift, he has dreamt the dreams of peace and comfort. If the night has been one of storm, the fast-falling flakes have added to his sense of warmth by covering him completely beneath them. Perhaps, too, he will remain unseen by the driver when the fatal moment comes for harnessing-up. Not a bit of it. He lies ever so quiet under the snow, but the rounded hillock betrays his hiding place; and he is dragged forth to the gaudy gear of bells and moose-skin lying ready to receive him. Then comes the start. The pine or aspen bluff is left behind, and under the grey starlight we plod along through the snow. Day dawns, sun rises, morning wears into midday, and it is time to halt for dinner; then on again in Indian file, as before. If there is no track in the snow a man goes in front on snow-shoes, and the leading dog, or "foregoer," as he is called, trots close behind him. If there should be a track, however faint, the dog-will follow it himself; and when sight fails to show it, or storm has hidden it beneath drifts, his sense of smell will enable him to keep straight. Thus through the long waste we journey on, by frozen lakelet, by willow copse, through pine forest, or over treeless prairie, until the winter's day draws to its close and the darkening landscape bids us seek some resting-place for the night. Then the hauling-dog is taken out of the harness, and his day's work is at an end; his whip-marked face begins to look less rueful, he stretches and rolls in the dry powdery snow, and finally twists himself a bed and goes fast asleep. But the real moment of pleasure is still in store for him When our supper is over the chopping of the axe, on the block of pemmican, or the unloading of the frozen white-fish

LEAVING A COSY CAMP AT DAWN.

from the provision-sled, tells him that his is about to begin. He springs lightly up and watches eagerly these preparations for his supper. On the plains he receives a daily ration of 2 lbs. of pemmican. In the forest and lake country, where fish is the staple food, he gets two large white-fish raw. He prefers fish to meat, and will work better on it too. His supper is soon over; there is a short after-piece of growling and snapping at hungry comrade, and then he lies down out in the snow to dream that whips have been abolished and hauling is discarded for ever, sleeping peacefully until morning, unless indeed some band of wolves should prowl around and, scenting campfire, howl their long chorus to the midnight skies.

And now, with this introductory digression on dogs, let us return to our camp in the thick pine-bluff on the river bank.

The night fell very cold. Between supper and bed there is not much time when present cold and perspective early-rising are the chief features of the night and morning. I laid down my buffalo robe with more care than usual, and got into my sack of deer-skins with a notion that the night was going to be one of unusual severity. My sack of deer-skins--so far it has been scarcely mentioned in this journal, and yet it played no insignificant part in the nightly programme. Its origin and construction were simply these. Before leaving Red River I had received from a gentleman, well known in the Hudson Bay Company, some most useful suggestions as to winter travel. His residence of many years in the coldest parts of Labrador, and his long journey into the interior of that most wild and sterile land, had made him acquainted with all the vicissitudes of northern travel. Under his direction I had procured a number of the skins of the common cabri, or small deer, had them made into a large sack of some seven feet in length and three in diameter. The skin of this deer is very light, but possesses, for some reason with which I am unacquainted, a power of giving great warmth to the person it covers. The sack was made with the hair turned inside, and was covered on the outside with canvass. To make my bed, therefore, became a very simple operation: lay down a buffalo robe, unroll the sack, and the thing was done. To get into bed was simply to get into the sack, pull the hood over one's head, and go to sleep. Remember, there was no tent, no outer covering of any kind, nothing but the trees--sometimes not many of them--the clouds, or the stars.

During the journey with horses I had generally found the bag too warm, and had for the most part slept on it, not in it; but now its time was about to begin, and this night in the pine-bluff was to record a signal triumph for the sack principle applied to shake-downs.

About three o'clock in the morning the men got up, unable to sleep on account of the cold, and set the fire going. The noise soon awoke me, but I lay quiet inside the bag, knowing what was going on outside. Now, amongst its other advantages, the sack possessed one of no small value. It enabled me to tell at once on awaking what the cold was doing outside; if it was cold in the sack, or if the hood was fastened down by frozen breath to the opening, then it must be a howler outside; then it was time to get ready the greasiest breakfast and put on the thickest duffel-socks and mittens. On the morning of the 22nd all these symptoms were manifest; the bag was not warm, the hood was frozen fast against the opening, and one or two smooth-haired dogs were shivering close beside my feet and on top of the bag. Tearing under the frozen mouth of the sack, I got out into the open. Beyond a doubt it was cold; I don't mean cold in the ordinary manner, cold such as you can localize to your feet, or your fingers, or your nose, but cold all over, crushing cold. Putting on coat and moccasins as close to the fire as possible, I ran to the tree on which I had hung the thermometer on the previous evening; it stood at 37 below zero at 3:30 in the morning. I had slept well; the cabri sack was a very Ajax among roosts; it defied the elements. Having eaten a tolerably fat breakfast and swallowed a good many cups of hot tea, we packed the sleds, harnessed the dogs, and got away from the pine bluff two hours before daybreak. Oh, how biting cold it was! On in the grey snow light with a terrible wind sweeping up the long reaches of the river; nothing spoken, for such cold makes men silent, morose, and savage. After four hours travelling, we stopped to dine. It was only 9:30, but we had breakfasted six hours before. We were some time before we could make fire, but at length it was set going, and we piled the dry driftwood fast upon the flames. Then I set up my thermometer again; it registered 39 below zero, 71 degrees of frost. What it must have been at day break I cannot say; but it was sensibly colder than at ten o'clock, and I do not doubt must have been 45 below zero. I had never been exposed to any thing like this cold before. Set full in the sun at eleven o'clock, the thermometer rose only to 26 below zero, the sun seemed to have lost all power of warmth; it was very low in the heavens, the day being the shortest in the year; in fact, in the centre of the river the sun did not show above the steep south bank, while the wind had full sweep from the north-east. This portion of the Saskatchewan is the farthest north reached by the river in its entire course. It here runs for some distance a little north of the 51th parallel of north latitude, and its elevation above the sea is about 1801 feet. During the whole day we journeyed on, the wind still kept dead against us, and at times it was impossible to face its terrible keenness. The dogs began to tire out; the ice cut their feet, and the white surface was often speckled with the crimson icicles that fell from their wounded toes. Out of the twelve dogs composing my cavalcade, it would have been impossible to select four good ones. Coffee, Tête Noir, Michinass, and another whose name I forget, underwent repeated whalings at the hands of my driver, a half-breed from Edmonnton named Frazer. Early in the afternoon the head of Tête Noir was reduced to shapeless pulp from tremendous thrashings. Michinass, or the "Spotted One," had one eye wherewith to watch the dreaded driver, and coffee had devoted so much strength to wild lurches and sudden springs in order to dodge the descending whip, that he had none whatever to bestow upon his legitimate toil of hauling me. At length, so useless did he become, that he had to be taken out altogether from the harness and left to his fate on the river. "And this," I said to myself, "is dog-driving; this inhuman thrashing and varied cursing, this frantic howling of dogs, this bitter, terrible cold is the long-talked of mode of winter travel!" To say that I was disgusted and stunned by the prospect of such work for hundreds of Miles would be-only to speak a portion of what I felt. Was the cold always to be so crushing? were the dogs always to be the same wretched creatures? Fortunately, no; but it was only when I reached Victoria that night, long after dark, that I learned that the day had been very exceptionally severe, and that my dogs were unusually miserable ones.

As at Edmonton so in the fort at Victoria the small-pox had again broken out; in spite of cold and frost the infection still lurked in many places, and in none more fatally than in this little settlement where, during the autumn, it had wrought so much havoc among the scanty community. In this distant settlement I spent the few days of Christmas; the weather had become suddenly milder, although the thermometer still stood below zero.

Small-pox had not been the only evil from which Victoria had suffered during the year which was about to close; the Sircies had made many raids upon it during the summer, stealing-down the sheltering banks of a small creek which entered the Saskatchewan at the opposite side, and then swimming the broad river during the night and lying hidden at day in the high corn-fields of the mission. Incredible though it may appear, they continued this practice at a time when they were being; swept away by the small-pox; their bodies were found in one instance dead upon the bank of the river they had crossed by swimming when the fever of the disease had been at its height. Those who live their lives quietly at home, who sleep in beds, and lay up when sickness comes upon them, know but little of what the human frame is capable of enduring if put to the test. With us, to be ill is to lie down; not so with the Indian; he is never ill with the casual illnesses of our civilization: when he lies down it is to sleep for a few hours, or-for ever. Thus these Sircies had literally kept the war-trail till they died. When the corn-fields were being cut around the mission, the reapers found unmistakable traces of how these wild men had kept the field undaunted by disease. Long black hair was found where it had fallen from the head of some brave in the lairs from which he had watched the horses of his enemies; the ruling passion had been strong in death. In the end, the much-coveted horses were carried off by the few survivors, and the mission had to bewail the loss of some of its best steeds. One, a mare belonging to the missionary himself, had returned to her home after an absence of a few days, but she carried in her flank a couple of Sircie arrows. She had broken away from the band, and the braves had sent their arrows after her in an attempt to kill what they could not keep. To add to the-misfortunes of the settlement, the buffalo were far out in the great plains; so between disease, war, and famine, Victoria had had a hard time of it.

In the farmyard of the mission-house there lay-a curious block of metal of immense weight'; it was ringed,- deeply indented, and polished on the outer edges of the indentations by the wear and friction of many years. Its history was a curious one. Longer than any man could say, it had lain on the summit of a hill far out in the southern prairies. It had been a medicine-stone of surpassing virtue among the Indians over a vast territory. No tribe or portion of a tribe would pass in the vicinity without paying a visit to this great-medicine: it was said to be increasing yearly in weight. Old men remembered having heard old men say that they had once lifted it easily from the ground. Now no single man could carry it. And it was no wonder that this metallic stone should be a Manito-stone and an object of intense veneration to the Indian; it had come down from heaven; it did not belong to the earth, but had descended out of the sky; it was, in fact an aerolite. Not very long before my, visit this curious stone had been removed from the hill upon which it had so long rested and brought to the Mission of Victoria by some person from that place: When the Indians found that it had been taken away, they were loud in the expression of their regret. The old medicine men declared that its removal would lead to great misfortunes and that war, disease, and dearth of buffalo would afflict the tribes of the Saskatchewan. This was not a prophecy made after the occurrence of the plague of small-pox, for in a magazine published by the Wesleyan Society in Canada there appears a letter from the missionary, setting forth the predictions of the medicine-men a year prior to my visit. The letter concludes with an expression of thanks that their evil prognostications had not been attended with success. But a few months later brought all the three evils upon the Indians; and never, probably, since the first trader had reached the country had so many afflictions of war, famine, and plague fallen upon the _Crees and the Blackfeet as during the year which succeeded the useless removal of their Manito-stone from the lone hill-top upon which the skies had cast it.

I spent the evening of Christmas Day in the house of the missionary. Two of his daughters sang very sweetly to the music of a small melodian. Both song and strain were sad--sadder, perhaps, than the words or music could make them; for the recollection of the two absent ones, whose newly-made graves, covered with their first snow, lay close outside, mingled with the hymn and deepened the melancholy of the music.

On the day after Christmas Day I left Victoria, with three trains of dogs, bound for Fort Pitt. This time the drivers were all English half-breeds, and that tongue was chiefly used to accelerate the dogs. The temperature had risen considerably, and the snow was soft and clammy, making the "hauling" heavy upon the dogs. For my own use I had a very excellent train, but the other two were of the useless class.` As before, the beatings were incessant, and I witnessed the first example of a very common occurrence in dog-driving--I beheld the operation known as "sending a dog to Rome." This consists simply of striking him over the head with a large stick until he falls perfectly senseless to the ground; after a little he revives, and, with memory of the awful blows that took his consciousness away full upon him, he pulls frantically at his load. Oftentimes a dog is "sent to Rome" because he will not allow the driver to arrange some hitch in the harness; then, while he is insensible, the necessary alteration is carried out, and when the dog recovers he receives a terrible lash of the whip to set him going again. The half-breeds are a race easily offended, prone to sulk if reproved; but at the risk of causing delay and inconvenience I had to interfere' with a peremptory order that "sending to Rome" should be at once discontinued in my trains. The wretched "Whisky," after his voyage to the Eternal City, appeared quite overcome with what he had there seen, and continued to stagger along the trail, making feeble efforts to keep straight. This tendency to wobble caused the half-breeds to indulge in funny remarks, one of them calling the track a "drunken trail." Eventually, "Whisky" was abandoned to his fate. I had never been a believer in the pluck and courage of the men who are the descendants of mixed European and Indian parents. Admirable as guides, unequalled as voyageurs, trappers, and hunters, they nevertheless are wanting in those qualities which give courage or true manhood. "Tell me your friends and I will tell you what you are ": is a sound proverb, and in no sense more true than when the bounds of man's friendships are stretched Wide. enough to admit those dumb companions, the horse and the dog. I never knew a man yet, or for that matter a woman, worth much who did not like dogs and horses, and I would always feel inclined to suspect a man who was shunned by a dog. The cruelty so systematically practised upon dogs by their half-breed drivers is utterly unwarrantable. In winter the poor brutes become more than ever the benefactors of man, uniting in themselves all the services of horse and dog--by day they work, by night they watch, and the man must be a very cur in nature who would inflict, at such a time, needless cruelty upon the animal that renders him so much assistance. On this day, the 29th December, we made a night march in the hope of reaching Fort Pitt. For four hours we walked on through the dark until the trail led us suddenly into the midst of an immense band of animals, which commenced to dash around us in a high state of alarm. At first we fancied in the indistinct moonlight that they were buffalo, but another instant sufficed to prove them horses. We had, in fact, struck into the middle of the Fort Pitt band of horses, numbering some ninety or a hundred head. We were, however, still a long way from the fort, and as the trail was utterly lost in the confused medley of tracks all round us, we were compelled to halt for the night near midnight. In a small clump of willows we made a hasty camp and lay down to sleep. Daylight next morning showed that conspicuous landmark called the Frenchman's Knoll rising north-east; and lying in the snow close beside us was poor "Whisky." He had followed on during the night from the place where he had been abandoned on the previous day, and had come up again with his persecutors while they lay asleep; for, after all, there was one fate worse than being "sent to Rome," and that was being left to starve. After a few hours run we reached Fort Pitt, having travelled about 150 miles in three days and a half.

Fort Pitt was destitute of fresh dogs or drivers, and consequently a delay of some days became necessary before my onward journey could be resumed. In the absence of dogs and drivers Fort Pitt, however, offered small-pox to its visitors. A case had broken out a few days previous to my arrival impossible to trace in any way, but probably the result of some infection conveyed into the fort during the terrible visitation of the autumn. I have already spoken of the power which the Indian possesses of continuing the ordinary avocations of his life in the presence of disease. This power he also possesses under that most terrible affliction-the loss of sight. Blindness is by no means an uncommon occurrence among the tribes of the Saskatchewan. The blinding glare of the snow-covered plains, the sand in summer, and, above all, the dense smoke of the tents, where the fire of wood, lighted in the centre, fills the whole lodge with a smoke which is peculiarly trying to the sight-all these causes render ophthalmic affections among the Indians a common misfortune. Here is the story of a blind Cree who arrived at Fort Pitt one day weak with starvation: From a distant camp he had started five days before, in company with his wife. They had some skins to trade, so they loaded their dog and set out on the march--the woman led the way, the blind man followed next, and the dog brought up the rear. Soon they approached a plain upon which buffalo were feeding. The dog, seeing the buffalo, left the trail, and, carrying the furs with him, gave chase. Away out of sight he went, until there was nothing for it but to set out in pursuit of him. Telling her husband to wait in this spot until she returned, the woman now started after the dog. Time passed,--it was growing late, and the wind swept coldly over the snow. The blind man began to grow uneasy; "She has lost her way," he said to himself; "I will go on, and we may meet." He walked on--he called aloud, but there was no answer; go back he could not; he knew by the coldness of the air that night had fallen on the plain, but day and night were alike to him. He was alone--he was lost. Suddenly he felt against his feet the rustle of long sedgy grass--he stooped down and found that he had reached the margin of a frozen lake. He was tired, and it was time to rest; so with his knife he cut a quantity of long dry grass, and, making a bed for himself on the margin of the lake, lay down and slept. Let us go back to the woman. The dog had led her a long chase, and it was very late when she got back to the spot where she had left her husband-he was gone, but his tracks in the snow were visible, and she hurried after him. Suddenly the wind arose, the light powdery snow began to drift in clouds over the surface of the plain, the track was speedily obliterated and night was coming on. Still she followed the general direction of the footprints, and at last came to the border of the same lake by which her husband was lying asleep, but it was at some distance from the spot. She too was tired, and, making a fire in a thicket, she lay down to sleep. About the middle of the night the man awoke and set out again on his solitary way. It snowed all night: the morning came, the day passed, the night closed again--again the morning dawned, and still he wandered on. For three days he travelled thus over an immense plain, without food, and having only the snow wherewith to quench his thirst. On the third day he walked into a thicket; he felt around, and found that the timber was dry; with his axe he cut down some wood, then struck a light and made a fire. When the fire was alight he laid his gun down beside it, and went to gather more wood; but fate was heavy against him, he was unable to find the fire which he had lighted, and by which he had left his gun. He made another fire, and again the same result. A third time he set to work; and now, to make certain of his getting back, again, he tied a line to a tree close beside his fire, and then set on to gather wood. Again the fates smote him-his line broke, and he had to grope his way in weary search. But chance, tired of ill-treating him so long, now stood his friend--he found the first fire, and with it his gun and blanket. Again he travelled on, but now his strength began to fail, and for the first time his heart sank within him--blind, starving, and utterly lost, there seemed no hope on earth for him. "Then," he said, "I thought of the Great Spirit of whom the white men speak, and I called aloud to him, 'O Great Spirit! have pity on me, and show me the path! and as I said it I heard close by the calling of a crow, and I knew that the road was not far off. I followed the call; soon I felt the crusted snow of a path under my feet, and the next day reached the fort." He had been five days without food.

No man can starve better than the Indian--no man can feast better either. For long days and nights, he will go without sustenance of any kind; but see him when the buffalo are near, when the cows are fat; see him then if you want to know what quantity of food it is possible for a man to consume at a sitting. Here is one bill of fare:--Seven men in thirteen days consumed two buffalo bulls, seven cabri, 40 lbs. of pemmican, and a great many ducks and geese, and on the last day there was nothing to eat. I am perfectly aware that this enormous quantity could not have weighed less than 1600 lbs. at the very lowest estimate, which would give a daily ration to each man of 18 lbs.; but, incredible as this may appear, it is by no means impossible. During the entire time I remained at Fort Pitt the daily ration issued to each man was 10 lbs. of beef. Beef is so much richer and coarser food than buffalo meat, that 10 lbs. of the former would be equivalent-to 15lbs. or 16 lbs. of the latter, and yet every scrap of that 10 lbs. was eaten by the man who received it. The women got 5 lbs., and the children, no matter how small, 3 lbs. each. Fancy a child in arms getting 3 lbs. of beef for its daily sustenance! The old Orkney men of the Hudson Bay Company servants must have seen in such a ration the realization of the poet's lines, "O Caledonia, stern and wild! Meet nurse for a poetic child," etc. All these people at Fort Pitt were idle, and therefore were not capable of eating as much as if they had been on the plains. The wild hills that surround Fort Pitt are frequently the scenes of Indian ambush and attack, and on more than one occasion the fort itself has been captured by the Blackfeet. The region in which Fort Pitt stands is a favourite camping-ground of the Crees, and the Blackfeet cannot be persuaded that the people of the fort are not the active friends and allies of their enemies in fact, Fort Pitt and Carlton are looked upon by them as places belonging to another company altogether from the one which rules at the Mountain House and at Edmonton. "If it was the same company," they-say, "how could they give our enemies, the Crees, guns and powder; for do they not give us guns and powder too?" This mode of argument, which refuses to recognize that species of neutrality so dear to the English heart, is eminently calculated to lay Fort Pitt open to Blackfeet raid. It is only a few years since the place was plundered by a large band, but the general forbearance displayed by the Indians on that occasion is nevertheless remarkable. Here is the story:

One morning the people in the fort beheld a small party of Blackfeet on a high hill at the opposite side of the Saskatchewan. The usual flag carried by the chief was waved to denote a wish to trade, and accordingly the officer in charge pushed off in his boat to meet and hold converse with the party. When he reached the other side he found the chief and a few men drawn up to receive him.

"Are there Crees around the fort?" asked the chief.

"No," replied the trader; "there are none with us."

"You speak with a forked tongue," answered the Blackfoot--dividing his fingers as he spoke to indicate that the-other was speaking falsely.

Just at that moment something caught the traders eye in the bushes along the river bank; he looked again and saw, close alongside, the willows swarming with naked Blackfeet. He made one spring back into his boat, and called to his men to shove off; but it was too late. In an instant two hundred braves rose out of the grass and willows and rushed into the water; they caught the boat and brought her back to the shore; then, filling her as full as she would hold with men, they pushed off for the other side. To put as good a face upon matters as possible, the trader commenced a trade, and at first the batch that had crossed, about forty in number, kept quiet enough, but some-of their number took the boat back again to the south shore and brought over the entire band; then the wild work commenced, bolts and bars were broken open, the trading-shop was quickly cleared out, and in the highest spirits, laughing loudly at the glorious fun they were having, the braves commenced to enter the houses, ripping up the feather beds to look for guns and tearing down calico curtains for finery. The men of the fort were nearly all away in the plains, and the women and children were in a high state of alarm. Sometimes the Indians would point their guns at the women, then drag them off the beds on which they were sitting and rip open bedding and mattress, looking for concealed weapons; but no further violence was attempted, and the whole thing was accompanied by such peals of laughter that it was evident the braves had not enjoyed such a "high old time" for a very long period. At last the chief, thinking, perhaps, that things had gone quite far enough, called out, in a loud voice, "Crees! Crees!" and, dashing out of the fort, was quickly followed by the whole band.

Still in high good humour, the braves recrossed the river, and, turning round on the farther shore, fired a volley to Wards the fort; but as the distance was at least 500 yards, this parting salute was simply as a bravado. This band was evidently bent on mischief. As they retreated south to their own country they met the carts belonging to the fort on their way from the plains; the men in charge ran off with the fleetest horses, but the carts were all captured and ransacked, and an old Scotchman, a servant of the Company, who stood his ground, was reduced to a state bordering upon nudity by the frequent demands of his captors.

The Blackfeet chiefs exercise great authority over their braves; some of them are men of considerable natural abilities, and all-must be brave and celebrated in battle. To disobey the mandate of a chief is at times to court instant death at his hands. At the present time the two most formidable chiefs of the Blackfeet nations are Sapoo-max-sikes, or "The Great Crow's Claw;" and Oma-ka-pee-mulkee-yeu, or "The Great Swan." These men are widely different in their characters; the Crow's Claw being a man whose word once given can be relied on to the death, but the other is represented as a man of colossal size and savage disposition, crafty and treacherous.

During the year just past death had struck heavily among the Blackfeet chiefs. The death of one of their greatest men, Pe-na-koam, or "The Far-off Dawn," was worthy of a great brave. When he felt that his last night had come, he ordered his best horse to be brought to the door of the tent, and mounting him he rode slowly around the camp; at each corner he halted and called out, in a loud voice to his people, "The last hour of Pe-na-koam has come; but to his people he says, Be brave; separate into small parties, so that this disease will have less power to kill you; be strong to fight our enemies the Crees, and be able to destroy them. It is no matter now that this disease has come upon us, for our enemies have got it too, and they will also die of it. Pe-na-koam tells his people before he dies to live so that they may fight their enemies, and be strong." It is said that, having spoken thus, he died quietly. Upon the top of a lonely hill they laid the body of their chief beneath a tent hung round with scarlet cloth; beside him they put six revolvers and two American repeating rifles, an at the door of his tent twelve horses were slain, so that their spirits would carry him in the green prairies of the happy hunting-grounds; four hundred blankets were piled around as offerings to his memory, and then the tribe moved away from the spot, leaving the tomb of their dead king to the winds and to the wolves.

CHAPTER TWENTY.

The Buffalo--His Limits and favourite Grounds--Modes of Hunting--A Fight --His inevitable End--I become a Medicine-man--Great Cold-Carlton--Family Responsibilities.

WHEN the early Spanish adventurers penetrated from the sea-board of America into the great central prairie region, they beheld for the first time a strange animal whose countless numbers covered the face of the country. When De Soto had been buried in the dark waters of the Mississippi, the remnant of his band, pursuing their western way, entered the "Country of the Wild Cows." When in the same year explorers pushed their way northward from Mexico into the region of the Rio-del-Norte, they looked over immense plains black with moving beasts. Nearly 100 years later settlers on the coasts of New England heard from westward-hailing Indians of huge beasts on the shores of a great lake not many days journey to the north-west. Naturalists in Europe, hearing of the new animal, named it the bison; but the colonists united in calling it the buffalo, and, as is usual in such cases, although science clearly demonstrated that it was a bison, and was not a buffalo, scientific knowledge had not a chance against practical ignorance, and "buffalo" carried the day. The true home of this animal lay in the great prairie region between the Rocky Mountains, the Mississippi, the Texan forest, and the Saskatchewan River and although undoubted evidence exists to show that at some period the buffalo reached in his vast migrations the shores of the Pacific and the Atlantic; yet since the party of De Soto only entered the Country of the Wild Cows after they had crossed the Mississippi, it may fairly be inferred that the Ohio River and the lower Mississippi formed the eastern boundaries to the wanderings of the herds since the New World has been known to the white man. Still even within this immense region, a region not less than 1,000,000 of square miles in area, the havoc worked by the European has been terrible. Faster even than the decay of the Indian has gone on the destruction-of the bison and only a few years must elapse before this noble beast, hunted down in the last recesses of his breeding-grounds, will have taken his place in the long list of those extinct giants which once dwelt in our world. Many favourite spots had this huge animal throughout the great domain over which he roamed-many beautiful scenes where, along river meadows, the grass in winter was still succulent and the wooded "bays" gave food and shelter, but-no more favourite ground than this valley of the Saskatchewan; thither he wended his way from the bleak plains of the Missouri in herds that passed and passed for days and nights in seemingly never-ending numbers. Along the countless creeks and rivers that add their tribute to the great stream, along the banks of the Battle River and the Vermilion River, along the many White Earth Rivers and Sturgeon Creeks of the upper and middle Saskatchewan, down through the willow copses and aspen thickets of the Touchwood Hills and the Assineboine, the great beasts dwelt in all the happiness of calf-rearing and connubial felicity. The Indians who then occupied these regions killed only what was required for the supply of the camps-a mere speck in the dense herds that roamed up to the very doors of the wigwams; but when the trader pushed his adventurous way into the fur regions of the North, the herds of the Saskatchewan plains began to experience a change in their surroundings. The meat, pounded down` and mixed with fat into "pemmican," was found to supply a most excellent food for transport service, and accordingly vast numbers of buffalo were destroyed to supply the demand of the fur traders. In the border-land between the wooded country and the plains, the Crees, not satisfied with the ordinary methods of destroying the buffalo, devised a plan by which great multitudes could be easily annihilated. This method of hunting, consists in the erection of strong wooden enclosures called pounds, into which the buffalo are guided by the supposed magic power of a medicine-man. Sometimes for two days the medicine-man will live with the herd, which he half guides and half drives into the enclosures; sometimes he is on the right, sometimes on the left, and sometimes, again, in rear of the herd, but never to windward of them. At last they approach the pound, which is usually concealed in a thicket of wood. For many miles from the entrance to this pound two gradually diverging lines of tree-stumps and heaps of snow lead out into the plains. Within these lines the buffalo are led by the medicine-man, and as the lines narrow towards the entrance, the herd, finding itself hemmed in on both sides, becomes more and more alarmed, until at length the great beasts plunge on into the pound itself, across the mouth of which ropes are quickly thrown and barriers raised. Then commences the slaughter. From the wooded fence around arrows and bullets are poured into the dense plunging mass of buffalo careering wildly round the ring. Always going in one direction, with the sun, the poor beasts race on until not a living thing is left; then, when there is nothing more to kill, the cutting-up commences, and pemmican-making goes on.

Widely different from this indiscriminate slaughter is the fair hunt on horseback in the great open plains. The approach, the cautious survey over some hill-top, the wild charge on the herd, the headlong flight, the turn to bay, the flight and fall--all this contains a large share of that excitement which we call by the much abused term sport. It is possible, however, that many of those who delight in killing placid pheasants and stoical partridges might enjoy the huge battue of an Indian "pound" in preference to the wild charge over the sky bound prairie, but, for my part, not being of the privileged few who breed pheasants at the expense of peasants (what a difference the "h" makes in Malthusian theories!), I have been compelled to seek my sport in hot climates instead of in hot corners, and in the sandy bluffs of Nebraska and the Missouri have drawn many an hour of keen enjoyment from the long chase of the buffalo. One evening, shortly before sunset, I was steering my way through the sandy hills of the Platte Valley, in the State of Nebraska, slowly towards Fort Kearney; both horse and rider were tired after a long day over sand-bluff and meadow-land, for buffalo were plenty, and five tongues dangling to the saddle told that horse, man, and rifle had not been idle. Crossing a grassy ridge, I suddenly came in sight of three buffalo just emerging from the broken bluff. Tired as was my horse, the sight of one of these three animals urged me to one last chase. He was a very large bull, whose black shaggy mane and dewlaps nearly brushed the short prairie grass beneath him. I dismounted behind the hill, tightened the saddle-girths, looked to rifle and cartridge touch, and then remounting rode slowly over the intervening ridge. As I came in view of the three beasts thus majestically stalking their way towards the Platte for the luxury of an evening drink, the three shaggy heads were thrown up--one steady look given, then round went the animals and away for the bluffs again. With a whoop and a cheer I gave chase, and the mustang, answering gamely to my call, launched himself well over the prairie. Singling out the large bull, I urged the horse with spur and voice, then, rising in the stirrups I took a snap-shot at my quarry. The bullet struck him in the flanks, and quick as lightning he wheeled down upon me. It was now my turn to run. I had urged the horse with voice and spur to close with the buffalo, but still more vigorously did I endeavour, under the altered position of affairs, to make him increase the distance lying between us. Down the sandy incline thundered the huge beast, gaining on us at every stride. Looking back over my shoulder, I saw him close to my horse's tail, with head lowered and eyes flashing furiously-under their shaggy covering. The horse was tired; the buffalo was fresh, and it seemed as though another instant must bring pursuer and pursued into wild collision. Throwing back my rifle over the crupper; I laid it at arm's length, with muzzle full upon the buffalo's head. The shot struck the centre of his forehead, but he only shook his head when he received it; still it seemed to check his pace a little, and as we had now reached level ground the horse began to gain something upon his pursuer. Quite as suddenly as he had charged the bull now changed his tactics. Wheeling off he followed his companions, who by this time had vanished into the bluffs. It never would have done to lose him after such a fight, so Ii brought the mustang round again, and gave chase. This time a shot fired low behind the shoulder brought my fierce friend to bay. Proudly he turned upon me, but now his rage was calm and stately, he pawed the ground, and blew with short angry snorts the sand in clouds from the plain; moving thus slowly towards me, he looked the incarnation of strength and angry pride. But his doom was sealed. I remember so vividly all the wild surroundings of the scene--the great silent waste, the two buffalo watching from a hill-top the fight of their leader, the noble beast himself stricken but defiant, and beyond, the thousand glories of the prairie sunset. It was only to last an instant, for the giant bull, still with low-bent head and angry snorts, advancing slowly towards his puny enemy, sank quietly to the plain and stretched his limbs in death. Late that night I reached the American fort with six tongues hanging to my saddle, but never since that hour, though often but a two days ride from buffalo, have I sought to take the life of one of these noble animals. Too soon will the last of them have vanished from the great central prairie land; never again will those countless herds roam from the Platte to the Missouri, from the Missouri to the Saskatchewan; chased for his robe, for his beef, for sport, for the very pastime of his death, he is rapidly vanishing from the land. Far in the northern forests of the Athabasca a few buffaloes may for a time bid defiance to man, but they, too, must disappear and nothing be left of this giant beast save the bones that for many an age will whiten the prairies over which the great herds roamed at will in times before the white man came.

It was the 5th of January before the return of the dogs from an Indian trade enabled me to get away from Fort Pitt. During the days I had remained in the fort the snow covering had deepened on the plains and winter had got a still firmer grasp upon the river and meadow. In two days travel we ran the length of the river between Fort Pitt and Battle River, travelling rapidly over the ice down the centre of the stream. The dogs were good ones, the drivers well versed in their work, and although the thermometer stood at 20 degrees below zero on the evening of the 6th, the whole run tended in no small degree to improve the general opinion which I had previously formed upon the delights of dog-travel. Arrived at Battle River, I found that the Crees had disappeared since my former visit; the place was now tenanted only by a few Indians and half-breeds. It seemed to be my fate to encounter cases of sickness at every post on my return journey. Here a woman was lying in a state of complete unconsciousness with intervals of convulsion and spitting of blood. It was in vain that I represented my total inability to deal with such a case. The friends of the lady all declared that it was necessary that I should see her, and accordingly I was introduced into the miserable hut in which she lay. She was stretched upon a low bed in one corner of a room about seven feet square; the roof approached so near the ground that I was unable to stand straight in any part of the place; the rough floor was crowded with women squatted thickly upon it, and a huge fire blazed in a corner, making the heat something terrible. Having gone through the ordinary medical programme of pulse feeling, I put some general questions to the surrounding bevy of women which, being duly interpreted into Cree, elicited the fact that the sick woman had been engaged in carrying a very heavy load of wood on her back for the use of her lord and master, and that while she had been thus employed she was seized with convulsions and became senseless. "What is it?" said the Hudson Bay man, looking at me in a manner which seemed to indicate complete confidence in my professional sagacity. "Do you think it's small-pox?" Some acquaintance with this disease enabled me to state my deliberate conviction that it was not small-pox, but as to what particular form of the many "ills that flesh is heir to" it really was, I could not for the life of me determine. I had not even that clue which the Yankee practitioner is said to have established for his guidance in the case of his infant patient, whose puzzling ailment he endeavoured to diagnosticate by administering what he termed "a convulsion powder," being a whale at the treatment of convulsions. In the case now before me convulsions were unfortunately of frequent occurrence, and I could not lay claim to the high powers of pathology which the Yankee had asserted himself to be the possessor of. Under all the circumstances I judged it expedient to forego any direct opinion upon the case, and to administer a compound quite as innocuous in its nature as the "soothing syrup" of infantile notoriety. It was, how ever, a gratifying fact to learn next morning that--whether owing to the syrup or not, I am not prepared to state the patient had shown decided symptoms of rallying, and took my departure from Battle River with the reputation of being a "medicine-man" of the very first order.

I now began to experience the full toil and labour of a winter journey. Our course lay across a bare, open region on which for distances of thirty to forty miles not one tree or bush was visible; the cold was very great, and the snow, lying loosely as it had fallen, was so soft that the dogs sank through the drifts as they pulled slowly at their loads. On the evening of the 10th January we reached a little clump of poplars on the edge of a large plain on which no tree was visible. It was piercingly cold, a bitter wind swept across the snow, making us glad to find even this poor shelter against the coming night. Two hours after dark the thermometer stood at minus 38 degrees, or 70 degrees of frost. The wood was small and poor; the wind howled through the scanty thicket, driving the smoke into our eyes as we cowered over the fire. Oh, what misery it was! and how blank seemed the prospect before me! 900 miles still to travel, and to-day I had only made about twenty miles, toiling from dawn to dark through blinding drift and intense cold. On again next morning over the trackless plain, thermometer at minus 20 in morning, and minus 12 at midday, with high wind, snow, and heavy drift. One of my men, a half-breed in name, an Indian in reality, became utterly done up from cold and exposure-the others would have left him behind to make his own way through the snow, or most likely to lie down and die, but I stopped the doggs until he came up, and then let him lie on one of the sleds for the remainder of the day. He was a miserable-looking wretch, but he ate enormous quantities of pemmican at every meal. After four days of very arduous travel we reached Carlton at sunset on the 12th January. The thermometer had kept varying between 20 and 38 degrees below zero every night, but on the night of the 12th surpassed any thing I had yet experienced. I spent that night in a room at Carlton, a room in which a fire had been burning until midnight, nevertheless at daybreak on the 13th the thermometer showed -20 degrees on the table close to my bed. At half-past ten o'clock, when placed outside, facing north, it fell to -44 degrees, and I afterwards ascertained that an instrument kept at the mission of Prince Albert, 60 miles east from Carlton, showed the enormous amount of 51 degrees below zero at daybreak that morning, 83 degrees of frost. This was the coldest night during the winter, but it was clear, calm, and fine. I now determined to leave the usual winter route from Carlton to Red River, and to strike out a new line of travel, which, though very much longer than the trail via Fort Pelly, had several advantages to recommend it to my choice. In the first place, it promised a new line of country down the great valley of the Saskatchewan River to its expansion into the sheet of water called Cedar Lake, and from thence across the dividing ridge into the Lake Winnipegosis, down the length of that water and its southern neighbour, the Lake Manitoba, until the boundary of the new province would be again reached, fully 700 miles from Carlton. It was a long, cold travel, but it promised the novelty of tracing to its delta in the vast marshes of Cumberland and the Pasquia, the great river whose foaming torrent I had forded at the Rocky Mountains, and whose middle course I had followed for more than a month of wintry travel.

Great as Were the hardships and privations of this Winter journey, it had nevertheless many moments of keen pleasure, moments filled with those instincts of that long-ago time before our civilization and its servitude had commenced--that time when, like the Arab and the Indian, we were all rovers over the earth; as a dog on a drawing-room carpet twists himself round and round before he lies down to sleep--the instinct bred in him in that time when bhis ancestors thus trampled smooth their beds in the long grasses of the primeval prairies--so man, in the midst of his civilization, instinctively goes back to some half-hidden reminiscence of the forest and the wilderness in which his savage forefathers dwelt. My lord seeks his highland moor, Norvegian salmon river, or more homely coverside; the retired grocer, in his snug retreat at Tooting, builds himself an arbour of rocks and mosses, and, by dint of strong imagination and stronger tobacco, becomes a very Kalmuck in his back-garden; and it is by no means improbable that the grocer in his rockery and the grandee at his rocketers draw their instincts of pleasure from the same long-ago time "When wild in woods the noble savage ran." But be this as it may, -this long journey of mine, despite its excessive cold, its nights under the wintry heavens, its days of ceaseless travel, had not as yet grown monotonous or devoid of pleasure, and although there were moments long before daylight when the shivering scene around the camp-fire froze one to the marrow, and I half feared to ask myself how many more mornings like this will I have to endure? how many more miles have been taken from that long total of travel? still, as the day wore on and the hour of the midday meal came round, and, warmed and hungry by exercise, I would relish with keen appetite the plate of moose steaks and the hot delicious tea, as camped amidst the snow, with buffalo robe spread out before the fire, and the dogs watching the feast with perspective ideas of bones and pan-licking, then the balance would veer back again to the side of enjoyment; and I could look forward to twice 600 miles of ice and snow without one feeling of despondency. These icy nights, too, were often filled with the strange meteors of the north. Hour by hour have I watched the many-hued shafts of the aurora trembling from their northern home across the starlight of the zenith, till their lustre lighted up the silent landscape of the frozen river with that weird light which the Indians name "the dance of the dead spirits." At times, too, the "sun dogs" hung about the sun so close, that it was not always easy to tell which was the real sun and which the mock one; but wild weather usually followed the track of the sun dogs; and whenever I saw them in the heavens I looked for deeper snow and colder bivouacs.

Carlton stands on the edge of the great forest region whose shores, if we may use the expression, are washed by the waves of the prairie ocean lying south of it; but the waves are of fire, not of water. Year by year the great torrent of flame moves on deeper and deeper into the dark ranks of the solemn-standing pines; year by year a wider region is laid open to the influences of sun and shower, and soon the traces of the conflict are hidden beneath the waving grass, and clinging vetches, and the clumps of tufted prairie roses. But another species of vegetation also springs up in the track of the fire; groves of aspens and poplars grow out of the burnt soil, giving to the country that park-like appearance already spoken of. Nestling along the borders of the innumerable lakes that stud the face of the Saskatchewan region, these poplar thickets sometimes attain large growth, but the fire too frequently checks their progress, and many of them stand bare and dry to delight the eye of the traveller with the assurance of an ample store of bright and warm firewood for his winter camp when the sunset bids him begin to make all cosy against the night.

After my usual delay of one day, I set out from Carlton, bound for the pine woods of the Lower Saskatchewan. My first stage was to be a short one. Sixty miles east from Carlton lies the small Presbyterian mission called Prince Albert. Carlton being destitute of dogs, I was obliged to take horses again into use; but the distance was only a two days march, and the track lay all the way upon the river. The wife of one of the Hudson Bay officers, desirous of visiting the mission, took advantage of my escort to travel to Prince Albert; and thus a lady, a nurse, and an infant aged eight months, became suddenly added to my responsibilities, with the thermometer varying between 70 and 80 degrees of frost I must candidly admit to having entertained very grave feelings at the contemplation of these family liabilities. A baby at any period of a man's life is a very serious affair, but a baby below zero is something appalling.

The first night passed over without accident.` I resigned my deerskin bag to the lady and her infant, and Mrs. Winslow herself could not have desired a more peaceful state of slumber than that enjoyed by the youthful traveller. But the second night was a terror long to be remembered; the cold was intense. Out of the inmost recesses of my abandoned bag came those dire screams which result from infantile disquietude. Shivering, under my blanket, I listened to the terrible commotion going on in the interior of that cold-defying construction that so long had stood my warmest friend.

At daybreak, chilled to the marrow, I rose, and gathered the fire together in speechless agony: no wonder, the thermometer stood at 40 degrees below zero; and yet, can it be believed? the baby seemed to be perfectly oblivious to the benefits of the bag, and continued to howl unmercifully. Such is the perversity of human nature even at that early age! Our arrival at the mission put an end to my family responsibilities, and restored me once more to the beloved bag; but the warm atmosphere of a house soon revealed the cause of much of the commotion of the night. "Wasn't-it-its-mother's-pet" displayed two round red marks upon its chubby countenance! "Wasn't-it-its-mother's-pet" had, in fact, been frost-bitten about the region of the nose and cheeks, and hence the hubbub. After a delay of two days at the mission, during which the thermometer always showed more than 60 degrees of frost in the early morning, I continued my journey towards the east, crossing over from the North to the South Branch of the Saskatchewan at a point some twenty miles from the junction of the two rivers--a rich and fertile land, well wooded and watered, a region destined in the near future to hear its echoes wake to other sounds than those of moose-call or wolf-howl. It was dusk in the evening of the 19th of January when we reached the high ground which looks down upon the "forks" of the Saskatchewan River. On some low ground at the farther side of the North Branch a camp-fire glimmered in the twilight. On the ridges beyond stood the dark pines of the Great Sub-Arctic Forest, and below lay the two broad converging rivers whose immense currents; hushed beneath the weight of ice, here merged into the single channel of the Lower Saskatchewan--a wild, weird scene it looked as the shadows closed around it. We descended with difficulty the steep bank and crossed the river to the camp-fire on the north shore. Three red-deer hunters were around it; they had some freshly killed elk meat, and potatoes from Fort-à-la-Corne, eighteen miles below the forks; and with so many delicacies our supper à-la-fourchette, despite a snow-storm, was a decided success.

THE FORKS OF THE SASKATCHEWAN.

CHAPTER TWENTY-ONE.

The Great Sub-Arctic Forest--The "Forks" of the Saskatchewan--An Iroquois --Fort-à-la-Corne--News from the outside World--All haste for Home--The solitary Wigwam--Joe Miller's Death.

At the "forks" of the Saskatchcwan the traveller to the east enters the Great Sub-Arctic Forest. Let us look for a moment at this region where the earth dwells in the perpetual gloom of the pine-trees. Travelling north from the Saskatchewan River at any portion of its course From Carlton to Edmonton, one enters on the second day's journey this region of the Great Pine Forest. We have before compared it to the shore of an ocean, and like a shore it has its capes and promontories which stretch far into the sea-like prairie, the indentations caused by the fires sometimes forming large bays and open spaces won from the domain of the forest by the fierce flames which beat against it in the dry days of autumn. Some 500 or 600 miles to the north this forest ends, giving place to that most desolate region of the earth, the barren grounds of the extreme north, the lasting home of the musk-ox and the summer haunt of the reindeer; but along the valley of the Mackenzie River the wooded tract is continued close to the Arctic Sea, and on the shores of the great Bear Lake a slow growth of four centuries scarce brings a circumference of thirty inches to the trunks of the white spruce. Swamp and lake, muskeg, and river rocks of the earliest formations, wild wooded tracts of impenetrable wilderness combine to make this region the great preserve of the rich fur-bearing animals whose skins are rated in the marts of Europe at four times their weight in gold. Here the darkest mink, the silkiest sable, the blackest otter are trapped and traded; here are bred these rich furs whose possession women prize as second only to precious stones. Into the extreme north of this region only the fur trader and the missionary have as yet penetrated. The sullen Chipwayan, the feeble Dogrib, and the fierce and warlike Kutchin dwell along the systems which carry the waters of this vast forest into Hudson Bay and thee Arctic Ocean.

This place, the "forks" of the Saskatchewan, is destined at some time or other to be an important centre of commerce and civilization. When men shall have cast down the barriers which now intervene between the shores of Lake Winnipeg and Lake Superior, what a highway will not these two great river Systems of the St. Lawrence and the Saskatchewan offer to the trader! Less than 100 miles of canal through low alluvial soil have only to be built to carry a boat from the foot of the Rocky Mountains to the head of Rainy Lake, within 100 miles of Lake Superior. With inexhaustible supplies of water held at a level high above the current surface of the height of land, it is not too much to say, that before many years have rolled by, boats will float from the base of the Rocky Mountains to the harbour of Quebec. But long before that time the Saskatchewan must have risen to importance from its fertility, its beauty, and its mineral wealth. Long before the period shall arrive when the Saskatchewan will ship its products to the ocean, another period will have come, when the mining populations of Montana and Idaho will seek in the fertile lands of the middle Saskatchewan a supply of those necessaries of life which the arid soil of the central States is powerless to yield. It is impossible that the wave of life which rolls so unceasingly into America can leave unoccupied this great fertile tract; as the river valleys farther east have all been peopled long before settlers found their way into the countries lying at the back, so must this great valley of the Saskatchewan, when once brought within the reach of the emigrant, become the scene of numerous settlements. As I stood in twilight looking down on the silent rivers merging into the great single stream which here enters the forest region, the mind had little difficulty in seeing another picture, when the river forks would be a busy scene of commerce, and man's labour would waken echoes now answering only to the wild things of plain and forest. At this point, as I have said, we leave the plains and the park-like country. The land of the prairie Indian and the buffalo-hunter lies behind us-of the thick-wood Indian and moose-hunter before us.

As far back as 1780 the French had pushed their Way into the Saskatchewan and established forts along its banks. It is generally held that their most western post was situated below the junction of the Saskatchewans, at a place called Nippoween; but I am of opinion that this is an error, and That their pioneer settlements had even gone west of Carlton. One of the earliest English travellers into the country, in 1776, speaks of Fort-des-Prairies as a post twenty-four days journey from Cumberland on the lower river, and as the Hudson Bay Company only moved west of Cumberland in 1774, it is only natural to suppose that this Fort-des Prairies had originally been a French post. Nothing proves more conclusively that the whole territory of the Saskatchewan was supposed to have belonged by treaty to Canada, and not to England, than does the fact that it was only at this date--1774-- that the Hudson Bay Company took possession of it.

During the bitter rivalry between the North-west and the Hudson Bay Companies a small colony of Iroquois indians was brought from Canada to the Saskatchewan and planted near the forks of the river. The descendants of these men are still to be found scattered over different portions of the country; nor have they lost that boldness and skill in all the wild works of Indian life which made their tribe such formidable warriors in the early contests of the French colonists; neither, have they lost that gift of eloquence which was so much prized in the days of Champlain and Frontinac. Here are the concluding words of a speech addressed by an Iroquois against the establishment of a missionary station near the junction of the Saskatchewan:

"You have spoken of your Great Spirit," said the Indian; "you have told us He died for all men--for the red tribes of the West as for the white tribes of the East; but did He not die with His arms stretched forth in different directions, one hang towards the rising sun and the other towards the setting sun?"

"Well, it is true."

"And now say, did He not mean by those outstretched arms that for evermore the white tribes should dwell in the East and the red tribes in the West? when the Great Spirit could not speak, did He not still point out where His children should live?" What a curious compound must be the man who is capable of such a strange, beautiful metaphor and yet remain a savage!

Fort-à-la-Corne lies some twenty miles below the point of junction of the rivers. Towards Fort-à-la-Corne I bent my steps with a strange anxiety, for at that point I was to intercept the "Winter Express" carrying from Red River its burden of news to the far-distant forts of the Mackenzie River. This winter packet had left Fort Garry in mid-December, and travelling by way of Lake Winnipeg, Norway House and Cumberland, was due at Fort-à-la-Corne about the 21st January. Anxiously then did I press on to the little fort, where I expected to get tidings of that strife whose echoes during the past month had been powerless to pierce the solitudes of this lone land. With tired dogs whose pace no whip or call could accelerate, we reached the fort at midday on the 21st. On the river, 'close by, an old Indian met us. Has the packet arrived? "Ask him if the packet has come," I said. He only stared blankly at me and shook his head. I had forgotten, what was the packet to him? the capture of a musk-rat was of more consequence than the capture of Metz. The packet had not come, I found when we reached the fort, but it was hourly expected, and I determined to await its arrival.

Two days passed away in wild storms of snow. The wind howled dismally through the pine woods, but within the logs crackled and flew, and the board of my host was always set with moose steaks and good things, although outside, and far down the river, starvation had laid his hand heavily upon the red man. It had fallen dark some hours on the evening of the 22nd January when there came a knock at the door of our house; the raised latch gave admittance to an old travel-worn Indian who held in his hand a small bundle of papers. He had cached the packet, he said, many miles down the river, for his dogs were utterly tired out and unable to move; he had come on himself with a few papers for the fort: the snow was very deep to Cumberland. He had been eight days in travelling 200 miles; he was tired and starving, and white with drift and storm. Such was his tale. I tore open the packet--it was a paper of mid-November. Metz had surrendered; Orleans been retaken; Paris, starving, still held out; for the rest, the Russians had torn to pieces the Treaty of Paris, and our millions and our priceless blood had been spilt and spent in vain on the Peninsula of the Black Sea--perhaps, after all, we would fight? So the night drew itself out, and the pine-tops began to jag the horizon before I ceased to read.

Early on the following morning, the express was hauled from its cache and brought to the fort; but it failed to throw much later light upon the meagre news of the previous evening. Old Adam was tried for verbal intelligence, but he too proved a failure. He had carried the packet from Norway House on Lake Winnipeg to Carlton for more than a score of winters, and, from the fact of his being the bearer of so much news in his lifetime, was looked upon by his compeers as a kind of condensed electric telegraph; but when the question of war was fairly put to him, he gravely replied that at the forts he had heard there was war, and "England," he added, "was gaining the day." This latter fact was too much for me, for I was but too well aware that had war been declared in November, an army organization based upon the Parliamentary system was not likely to have "gained the day" in the short space of three weeks.

To cross with celerity the 700 miles lying between me and Fort Garry Became now the chief object of my life. I lightened my baggage as much as possible, dispensing with many comforts of clothing and equipment, and on the morn ing of the 23rd January started for Cumberland. I will not dwell on the seven days that now ensued, or how from long before dawn to verge of evening we toiled down the great silent river. It was the close of January, the very depth of winter. With heads bent down to meet the crushing blast, we plodded on, oft times as silent as the river and the forest, from whose bosom no sound ever came, no ripple ever broke, no bird, no beast, no human face, but ever the same great forest-fringed river whose majestic turns bent always to the north-east. To tell, day after day, the extreme of cold that now seldom varied would be to inflict on the reader a tiresome record; and, in truth, there would be no use in attempting it; 40 below zero means so many things impossible to picture or to describe, that it would be a hopeless task to enter upon its delineation. After one has gone through the list of all those things that freeze; after one has spoken of the knife which burns the hand that would touch its blade, the tea that freezes while it is being dlrunk, there still remains a sense of having said nothing; a sense which may perhaps be better understood by saying that 40 degrees below zero means just one thing more than all these items--it means death, in a period whose duration would expire in the hours of a winter's daylight, if there was no fire or means of making it on the track.

Conversation round a camp-fire in the North-west is limited to one Subject--dogs and dog-driving. To be a good driver of dogs, and to be able to run fifty miles in a day with ease, is to be a great man. The fame of a noted dog-driver spreads far and wide. Night after night would I listen to the prodigies of running performed by some Ba'tiste or Angus, doughty champions of the rival races. If Ba'tiste dwelt at Cumberland, I Would begin to hear his name mentioned 200 miles from that place, and his fame would still be talked of 200 miles beyond it. With delight would I hear the name of this celebrity dying gradually away in distance, for by the disappearance of some oft-heard name and the rising of some new constellation of dog-driver, one could mark a stage of many hundred miles on the long road upon which I was travelling.

On the 29th January we reached the shore of Pine Island Lake, and saw in our track the birch lodge of an Indian. It was before sunrise, and we stopped the dogs to warm our fingers over the fire of the wigwam. Within sat a very old Indian and two or three women and children. The old man was singing to himself a low monotonous chant; beside him some reeds, marked by the impress of a human form, were spread upon the ground; the fire burned brightly in the centre of the lodge, while the smoke escaped and the light entered through the same round aperture in the top of the conical roof. When we had entered and seated ourselves, the old man still continued his song. "What is he saying?" I asked, although the Indian etiquette forbids abrupt questioning. "He is singing for his son," a man answered, "who died yesterday, and whose body they have taken to the fort last night." It was even so. A French Canadian who had dwelt in Indian fashion for some years, marrying the daughter of the old man, had died from the effects of over-exertion in running down a silver fox, and the men from Cumberland had taken away the body a few hours before. Thus the old man mourned, while his daughter the widow, and a child sat moodily looking at the flames. "He hunted for us; he fed us," the old man said. "I am too old to hunt; I can scarce see the light; I would like to die too." Those old words which the presence of the great mystery forces from our lips-those words of consolation which some one says are "chaff well meant for grain"--were changed into their Cree equivalents and duly rendered to him, but he he only shook his head, as though the change of language had not altered the value of the commodity. But the name of the dead hunter was a curious anomaly-Joe Miller. What a strange antithesis appeared this name beside the presence of the childless father, the fatherless child, and the mateless woman! One service the death of poor Joe Miller conferred on me--the dog-sled that had carried his body had made a track over the snow-covered lake, and we quickly glided along it to the Fort of Cumberland.

CHAPTER TWENTY-TWO.

Cumberland---We bury poor Joe--A good Train of Dogs--The great Marsh--Mutiny--Chicag the Sturgeon-fisher--A Night with a Medicine-man-- Lakes Winnipegoosis and Manitoba--Muskeymote eats his Boots--We reach the Settlement--From the Saskatchewan to the Seine.

CUMBERLAND HOUSE, the oldest post of the Company in the interior, stands on the south shore of Pine Island Lake; the waters of which seek the Saskatchewan by two channels--Tearing River and Big-stone River. These two rivers form, together with the Saskatchewan and the lake, a large island, upon which stands Cumberland. Time moves slowly at such places as Cumberland, and change is almost unknown. To-day it is the same as it was 100 years ago. An old list of goods sent to Cumberland, from England in 1783 had precisely the same items as one of 1870. Strouds, cotton, beads, and trading-guns are still the wants of the Indian, and are still traded for marten and musquash. In its day Cumberland has had distinguished visitors. Franklin; in 1819, wintered at the fort, and a sun-dial still stands in rear of the house, a gift from the great explorer. We buried Joe Miller in the pine-shadowed graveyard near the fort. Hard work it was with pick and crowbar to prise up the ice-locked earth and to get poor Joe that depth which the frozen clay would seem to grudge him. It was long after dark when his bed was ready, and by the light of a couple of lanterns we laid him down in the great rest. The graveyard and the funeral had few of those accessories of the modern mortuary which are supposed to be the characteristics of civilized sorrow. There was no mute, no crape, no parade--nothing of that imposing array of hat-bands and horses by which man, even` in the face of the mighty mystery, seeks still to glorify the miserable conceits of life; but the silent snow-laden pine-trees, the few words of prayer read in the flickering light of the lantern, the hush of nature and of night, made accessions full as fitting, as all the muffled music and craped sorrow of church and city.

At Cumberland I beheld for the first time a genuine train of dogs. There was no mistake about them in shape or form, from fore-goer to hindermost hauler. Two of them were the pure Esquimaux breed, the bush-tailed, fox-headed, long-furred, clean-legged animals whose ears, sharp-pointed and erect, sprung from a head embedded in thick tufts of woolly hair; Pomeranians multiplied by four; the other two were a curious compound of Esquimaux and Athabascan, with hair so long that eyes were scarcely 'visible. I had suffered so long from the wretched condition and description of the dogs of the Hudson Bay Company, that I determined to become the possessor of those animals, and, although I had to pay considerably more than had ever been previously demanded as the price of a train of dogs in the North, I was still glad, to get them at any figure. Five hundred miles yet lay between me and Red River-five hundred miles of marsh and frozen lakes, the delta of the Saskatchewan and the great Lakes Winnipegoosis and Manitoba.

It was the last day of January when I got away from Cumberland with this fine train of dogs and another 2 serviceable set which belonged to a Swampy Indian named Bear, who had agreed to accompany me to Red River. Bear was the son of the old man whose evolutions with the three pegs had caused so much commotion among the Indians at Red River on the occasion of my visit to Fort Garry eight months earlier. He was now to be my close companion during many days and nights, and it may not be out of place here to anticipate the verdict of three weeks, and to award him as a voyageur, snow-shoer and camp-maker a place second to none in the long list of my employees. Soon after quitting Cumberland we struck the Saskatchewan River, and, turning eastward along it, entered the great region of marsh and swamp. During five days our course lay through vast expanses of stiff frozen reeds, whose corn-like stalks rattled harshly against the parchment sides of the cariole as the dog-trains wound along through their snow-covered roots. Bleak and dreary beyond expression stretched this region of frozen swamp for fully 100 miles. The cold remained all the time at about the same degree--20 below zero. The camps were generally poor and miserable ones. Stunted willow is the chief timber of the region, and fortunate did we deem ourselves when at nightfall a low line of willows would rise above the sea of reeds to bid us seek its shelter for the night. The snow became deeper as we proceeded. At the Pasquia three feet lay level over the country, and the dogs sank deep as they toiled along. Through this great marsh the Saskatchewan winds in tortuous course, its flooded level in summer scarce lower than the alluvial shores that line it. The bends made by the river would have been too long to follow, so we held a straight track through the marsh, cutting the points as we travelled. It was difficult to imagine that this many-channelled, marsh-lined river could be the same noble stream whose mountain birth I had beheld far away in the Rocky Mountains, and whose central course had lain for so many miles through the bold precipitous bank of the Western prairies.

On the 7th February we emerged from this desolate region of lake and swamp, and saw before us in the twilight a ridge covered with dense woods. It was the west shore of the Cedar Lake, and on the wooded promontory towards which we steered some Indian sturgeon-fishers had pitched their lodges. But I had not got thus far without much trouble and vexatious resistance. Of the three men from Cumberland, one had utterly knocked up, and the other two had turned mutinous. What cared they for my anxiety to push on for Red River?

What did it matter if the whole world was at war? Nay, must I not be the rankest of impostors; for if there was war away beyond the big sea, was that not the very reason why any man possessing a particle of sense should take his time over the journey, and be in no hurry to get back again to his house?

One night I reached the post of Moose Lake a few hours before daybreak, having been induced to make the flank march by representations of the wonderful train of dogs at that station, and being anxious to obtain them in addition to my own: It is almost needless to remark that these dogs had no existence except in the imagination of Bear and his companion. Arrived at Moose Lake (one of the most desolate spots-I had' ever looked upon), I found out that the dog-trick was not the only one my men intended playing upon me, for a message was sent in by Bear to the effect that his dogs were unable to stand the hard travel of the past week, and that he could no longer accompany me. Here was a pleasant prospect--stranded on the wild shores of the Moose Lake with one train of dogs, deserted and deceived! There was but one course to pursue, and fortunately it proved the right one. "Can you give me a guide to Norway House?" I asked the Hudson Bay Company's half-breed clerk. "Yes." "Then tell Bear that he can go," I said, "and the quicker he goes the better. I will start for Norway House with my single train of dogs, and though it will add eighty miles to my journey I will get from thence to Red River down the length of Lake Winnipeg. Tell Bear he has the whole North-west to choose from except Red River. He had better not go there; for if I have to wait for six months For his arrival, I'll wait, just to put him in prison for breach of contract." What a glorious institution is the law! The idea of the prison, that terrible punishment in the eyes of the wild man, quelled the mutiny, and I was quickly assured that the whole thing was a mistake, and that Bear and his dogs were still at my service. Glad was I then, on the night of the 7th, to behold the wooded shores of the Cedar Lake rising out of the reeds of the great marsh, and to know that by another sunset I would have reached the Winnipegoosis and looked my last upon the valley of the Saskatchewan.

The lodge of Chicag the sturgeon-fisher was small; one entered almost on all-fours, and once inside matters were not much bettered. To the question, "Was Chicag at home?" one of his ladies replied that he was attending a medicine-feast close by, and that he would soon be in. A loud and prolonged drumming corroborated the statement of the medicine, and seemed to indicate that Chicag was putting on the steam with the Manito, having got an inkling of the new arrival. Meantime I inquired of Bear as to the ceremony which was being enacted. Chicag, or the "Skunk," I was told, and his friends were bound to devour as many sturgeon and to drink as much sturgeon oil as it was possible to contain. When that point had been attained the ceremony might be considered over, and if the morrow's dawn did not show the sturgeon nets filled with fish, all that could be said upon the matter was that the Manito was oblivious to the efforts of Chicag and his comrades. The drumming now reached a point that seemed to indicate that either Chicag or the sturgeon was having a bad time of it. Presently the noise ceased, the low door opened, and the "Skunk" entered, followed by some ten or a dozen of his friends and relations. How they all found room in the little hut remains a mystery, but its eight-by-ten of superficial space held some eighteen persons, the greater number of whom were greasy with the oil of the sturgeon. Meantime a supper of sturgeon had been prepared for me, and great was the excitement to watch me eat it. The fish was by no means bad; but I have reason to believe that my performance in the matter of eating it was not at all a success. It is true that stifling atmosphere, in tense heat, and many varieties of nastiness and nudity are not promoters of appetite; but even had I been given a clearer stage and more favourable conducers towards voracity, I must still have proved but a mere nibbler of sturgeon in the eyes of such a whale as Chicag.

Glad to escape from the suffocating hole, I emptied my fire-bag of tobacco among the group and got out into the cold night-air. What a change! Over the silent snow-sheeted lake, over the dark isles and the cedar shores, the moon was shining amidst a deep blue sky. Around were grouped a few birch-bark wigwams. My four dogs, now well known and trusty friends, were holding high carnival over the heads and tails of Chicag's feast. In one of the wigwams, detached from the rest, sat a very old man wrapped in a tattered blanket. He was splitting wood into little pieces, and feeding a small fire in the centre of the lodge, while he chattered to himself all the time. The place was clean, and as I watched the little old fellow at his work I decided to make my bed in his lodge. He was no other than Parisiboy, the medicine-man of the camp, the quaintest little old savage I had ever encountered. Two small white mongrels alone shared his wigwam. "See," he said, "I have no one with me but these two dogs." The curs thus alluded to felt themselves bound to prove that they were cognizant of the fact by shoving forward their noses one on each side of old Parisiboy, an impertinence on their part which led to their sudden expulsion by being pitched headlong out of the door. Parisiboy now commenced a lengthened exposition of his woes. "His blanket was old and full of holes, through which the cold found easy entrance. He was a very great medicine-man, but he was very poor, and tea was a luxury which he seldom tasted." I put a handful of tea into his little kettle, and his bright eyes twinkled with delight under their shaggy brows. "I never go to sleep," he continued; "it is too cold to go to sleep; I sit up all night splitting wood and smoking and keeping the fire alight; if I had tea I would never lie down at all." As I made my bed he continued to sing to himself, chatter and laugh with a peculiar low chuckle, watching me all the time. His first brew of tea was quickly made; hot and strong, he poured it into a cup, and drank it with evident delight; then in went more water on the leaves and down on the fire again went the little kettle.` But I was not permitted to lie down without interruption. Chicag headed a deputation of his brethren, and grew loud over the recital of his grievances. Between the sturgeon and the Company he appeared to think himself victim, but I was unable to gather whether the balance of ill-treatment lay on the side of the fish or of the corporation. Finally I got rid of the lot, and crept into my bag. Parisiboy sat at the other side of the fire, grinning and chuckling and sipping his tea. All night long I heard through my fitful sleep his harsh chuckle and his song. Whenever I opened my eyes, there was the little old man in the same attitude, crouching over the fire, which he sedulously kept alight. How many brews of tea he made, I can't say; but when daylight came he was still at the work, and as I replenished the kettle the old leaves seemed well-nigh bleached by continued boilings.

That morning I got away from the camp of Chicag, and crossing one arm of Cedar Lake reached at noon the Mossy Portage. Striking into the cedar Forest at this point, I quitted for good the Saskatchewan. Just three Months earlier I had struck its waters at the South Branch, and since that day fully 1600 miles of travel had carried me far along its shores. The Mossy Portage is a low swampy ridge dividing the waters of Cedar Lake from those of Lake Winnipegoosis. From one lake to the other is a distance of about four miles. Coming from the Cedar Lake the portage is quite level until it reaches the close vicinity of the Winnipegoosis, when there is a steep descent of some forty feet to gain the waters of the latter lake. These two lakes are supposed to lie at almost the same level, but I shall not be surprised if a closer examination of their respective heights proves the Cedar to be some thirty feet higher than its neighbour the Winnipegoosis. The question is one of considerable interest, as the Mossy Portage will one day or other form the easy line of communication between the waters of Red River and those of Saskatchewan.

It was late in the afternoon when we got the dogs on the broad bosom of Lake Winnipegoosis, whose immense surface spread out south and west until the sky alone bounded the prospect. But there were many islands scattered over the sea of ice that lay rolled before us; islands dark with the pine-trees that covered them, and standing out in strong relief from the dazzling whiteness amidst which they lay. On one of these islands we camped, spreading the robes under a large pine-tree and building up a huge fire from the wrecks of bygone storms. This Lake Winnipegoosis, or the "Small Sea,"' is a very large expanse of water measuring about 120 miles in length and some 30 in width. Its shores and islands are densely wooded with the white spruce, the juniper, the banksian pine, and the black spruce, and as the traveller draws near the southern shores he beholds again the dwarf white-oak which here reaches its northern limit. This growth of the oak-tree may be said to mark at present the line between civilization and savagery. Within the limit of the oak lies the country of the white man; without lies that Great Lone Land through which my steps have wandered so far. Descending the Lake Winnipegoosis to Shoal Lake, I passed across the belt of forest which. Lies between the two lakes, and emerging again upon Winnipegosis crossed it in a long day's journey to the Waterhen River. This river carries the surplus water of Winnipegosis into the large expanse of Lake Manitoba. For another hundred miles this lake lays its length towards the south, but here the pine-trees have vanished, and birch and poplar alone cover the shores. Along the whole line of the western shores of these lakes the bold ridges of the Pas, the Porcupine, Duck, and Riding Mountains rise over the forest-covered swamps which lie immediately along the water. These four mountain ranges never exceed an elevation of 1600 feet above the sea. They are wooded to the summits, and long ages ago their rugged cliffs formed, doubtless, a fitting shore-line to that great lake whose fresh-water billows were nursed in a space twice larger than even Superior itself can boast of; but, as has been stated in an earlier chapter, that inland ocean has long since shrunken into the narrower limits of Winnipeg, Winnipegoosis, and Manitoba-the Great Sea, the Little Sea, and the Straits of the God.

I have not dwelt upon the days of travel during which we passed down the length of these lakes. From the camp of Chicag I had driven my own train of dogs; with Bear the sole companion of the journey. Nor were these days on the great lakes by any means the dullest of the journey, Cerf Volant, Tigre, Cariboo, and Muskeymote gave ample occupation to their driver. Long before Manitoba was reached they had learnt a new lesson-that men were not all cruel to dogs in camp or on the road. It is true that in the learning of that lesson some little difficulty was occasioned by the sudden loosening and disruption of ideas implanted by generations of cruelty in the dog-mind of my train. It is true that Muskeymote, in particular, long held aloof from offers of friendship, and then suddenly passed from the excess of caution to the extreme of imprudence, imagining, doubtless, that the millennium had at length arrived, and that dogs were henceforth no more to haul. But Muskeymote was soon set right upon that point, and showed no inclination to repeat his mistake. Then there was Cerf Volant, that most perfect Esquimaux. Cerf Volant entered readily into friendship, upon an under-standing of an additional half-fish at supper every evening. No alderman ever loved his turtle better than did Cerf Volant love his white fish; but I rather think that the white fish was better earned than the turtle--however we will let that be matter of opinion. Having satisfied his hunger, which, by the way, is a luxury only allowed to the hauling-dog once a day, Cerf Volant would generally establish himself in close proximity to my feet, frequently on the top of the bag, from which coigne of vantage he would exchange fierce growls with any dog who had the temerity to approach us. None of our dogs were harness-eaters, a circumstance that saved us the nightly trouble of placing harness and cariole in the branches of a tree. On one or two occasions Muskeymote, however, ate his boots. "Boots!" the reader will exclaim; "how came Muskeymote to possess boots? We have heard of a puss in boots, but a dog, that is something new." Nevertheless Muskeymote had his boots, and ate them, too. This is how a dog is put in boots. When the day is very cold--I don't mean in your reading of that word, reader, but in its North-west sense--when the morning, then, comes very cold, the dogs travel fast, the drivers run to try and restore the circulation, and noses and cheeks which grow white beneath the bitter blast are rubbed with snow caught-quickly from the ground without pausing in the rapid stride; on such mornings, and they are by no means uncommon, the particles of snow which adhere to the feet of the dog form sharp icicles between his toes, which grow larger and larger as he travels. A nowing old hauler will stop every now and then, and tear out these icicles with his teeth, but a young dog plods wearily along leaving his footprints in crimson stains upon the snow behind him. When he comes into camp, he lies down and licks his poor wounded feet, but the rest is only for a short time, and the next start makes them worse than before. Now comes the time for boots. The dog-boot is simply a fingerless glove drawn on over the toes and foot, and tied by a running string of leather round the wrist or ankle of the animal; the boot itself is either made of leather or strong white cloth. Thus protected, the dog will travel for days and days with wounded feet, and get no worse, in fact he will frequently recover while still on the journey. Now Muskeymote, being a young dog, had not attained to that degree of wisdom which induces older dogs to drag the icicles from their toes, and consequently Muskeymote had to be duly booted every morning--a cold operation it was too, and many a run had I to make to the fire while it was being performed, holding my hands into the blaze for a moment and then back again to the dog. Upon arrival in camp these boots should always be removed from the dogs feet, and hung up in the smoke of the fire, with moccasins of the men, to dry. It was on an occasion when this custom had been forgotten that Muskeymote performed the feat we have already mentioned, of eating his boots.

The night-camps along the lakes were all good ones; it took some time to clear away the deep snow and to reach the ground, but wood for fire and young spruce tops for bedding were plenty, and fifteen minutes axe work sufficed to fell as many trees as our fire needed for night and morning. From wooded point to wooded point we journeyed on over the frozen lakes; the snow lying packed into the crevices and uneven places of the ice formed a compact level surface, upon which the dogs scarce marked the impress of their feet, and the sleds and cariole bounded briskly after the train, jumping the little wavelets of hardened snow to the merry jingling of innumerable bells. On snow such as this dogs will make a run of forty miles in a day, and keep that pace for many days in succession, but in the soft snow of the woods or the river thirty miles will form a fair day's work for continuous travel.

On the night of the 19th of February we made our last camp on the ridge to the south of Lake Manitoba, fifty miles from Fort Garry. Not without a feeling of regret was the old work gone through for the last time--the old work of tree-cutting, and fire-making, and supper-frying, and dog-feeding. Once more I had reached those confines of civilization on whose limits four months earlier I had made my first camp on the shivering Prairie of the Lonely Grave; then the long journey lay before me, now the unnumbered scenes of nigh 3000 miles of travel were spread out in that picture which memory sees in the embers of slow-burning fires, when the night-wind speaks in dreamy tones to the willow branches and waving grasses. And if there be those among my readers who can il comprehend such feelings, seeing only in this return the escape from savagery to civilization--from the wild Indian to the Anglo-American, from the life of toil and hardship to that of rest and comfort-then words would be useless to throw light upon the matter, or to better enable such men to understand that it was possible to look back with keen regret to the wild days of the forest and the prairie. Natures, no matter how we may mould them beneath the uniform pressure of the great machine called civilization, are not all alike, and many men's minds echo in some shape or other the voice of the Kirghis woman, which says, "Man must keep moving; for, behold, sun, moon, stars, water, beast, bird, fish, all are in movement: it is but the dead and the earth that remain in one place."

There are many who have seen a prisoned lark sitting on its perch, looking listlessly through the bars, from some brick wall against which its cage was hung; but at times, when the spring comes round, and a bit of grassy earth is put into the narrow cage, and, in spite of smoke and mist, the blue sky looks a moment on the foul face of the city, the little prisoner dreams himself free, and, with eyes fixed on the blue sky and feet clasping the tiny turf of green sod, he pours forth into the dirty street those notes which nature taught him in the never-to-be-forgotten days of boundless freedom. So I have seen an Indian, far down in Canada, listlessly watching the vista of a broad river whose waters and whose shores once owned the dominion of his race; and when I told him of regions where his brothers still built their lodges midst the wandering herds of the stupendous wilds, far away towards that setting sun upon 'which his eyes were fixed, there came a change over his listless look, and when he spoke in answer there was in his voice an echo from that bygone time when the Five Nations were a mighty power on the shores of the Great Lakes. Nor are such as these the only prisoners of our civilization. He who has once tasted the unworded freedom of the Western wilds must ever feel a sense of constraint within the boundaries of civilized life. The Russian is not the only man who has the Tartar close underneath his skin. That Indian idea of the earth being free to all men catches quick and lasting hold of the imagination--the mind widens out to grasp the reality of the lone space and cannot shrink again to suit the requirements of fenced divisions. There is a strange fascination in the idea, "Wheresoever my horse wanders there is my home;" stronger perhaps is that thought than any allurement of wealth, or power, or possession given us by life. Nor can after-time ever wholly remove it; midst the smoke and hum of cities, midst the prayer of churches, in street or salon, it needs but little cause to recall again to the wanderer the image of the immense meadows where, far away at the portals of the setting sun, lies the Great Lone Land.

It is time to close. It was my lot to shift the scene of life with curious rapidity. In a shorter space of time than it had taken to traverse the length of the Saskatchewan, I stood by the banks of that river whose proud city had just paid the price of conquest in blood and ruin--yet I witnessed a still heavier ransom than that paid to German robbers. I saw the blank windows of the Tuileries red with the light of flames fed from five hundred years of history, and the flagged courtyard of La Roquette running deep in the blood of Frenchmen spilt by France, while the common enemy smoked and laughed, leaning on the ramparts of St. Denis.

APPENDIX.

GOVERNOR ARCHIBALD'S INSTRUCTIONS.

Fort Garry, 10th October, 1870.

W. F. Butler, Esq., 69th Regiment.

SIR,--Adverting to the interviews between his honour the Lieutenant-Governor and yourself on the subject of the proposed mission to the Saskatchewan, I have it now in command to acquaint you with the objects his honour has in view in asking you to undertake the mission, and also to define the duties he desires you to perform.

In the first place, I am to say that representations have been made from various quarters that within the last two years much disorder has prevailed in the settlements along the line of the Saskatchewan, and that the local authorities are utterly powerless for the protection of life and property within that region. It is asserted to be absolutely necessary for the protection, not only of the Hudson Bay Company's Forts, but for the safety of the settlements along the river, that a small body of troops should be sent to some of the forts of the Hudson Bay Company, to assist the local authorities in the maintenance of peace and order.

I am to enclose you a copy of a communication on this subject from Donald A. Smith, Esq., the Governor of the Hudson Bay Company, and also. an extract of a letter from W. J. Christie, Esq., a chief factor stationed at Fort Carlton, which will give you some of the facts which have been adduced to show the representations to be well grounded.

The statements made in these papers come from the officers of the Hudson Bay Company, whose views may be supposed to be in some measure affected by their pecuniary interests.

It is the desire of the Lieutenant-Governor that you should examine the matter entirely from an independent point of view, giving his honour for the benefit of the Government of Canada your views of the state of matters on the Saskatchewan in reference to the necessity of troops being sent there, basing your report upon what you shall find by actual examination.

You will be expected to report upon the whole question of the existing state of affairs in that territory, and to state your views on what may be necessary to be done in the interest of peace and order.

Secondly, you are to ascertain, as far as you can, in what places and among what tribes of Indians, and what settlements of whites, the small-pox is now prevailing, including the extent of its ravages and every particular you can ascertain in connexion with the rise and the spread of the disease. You are to take with you such small supply of medicines as shall be considered by the Board of Health here suitable and proper for the treatment of small-pox, and you will obtain written instructions for the proper treatment of the disease, and will leave a copy thereof with the chief officer of each fort you pass, and with any clergyman or other intelligent person belonging to settlements outside the forts.

You will also ascertain, as far as in your power, the number of Indians on the line between Red River and the Rocky Mountains; the different nations and tribes into which they are divided and the particular locality inhabited, and the language spoken, and also the names of the principal chiefs of each tribe.

In doing this you will be careful to obtain the information without in any manner leading the Indians to suppose you are acting under authority, or inducing them to form any expectations based on your inquiries.

You will also be expected to ascertain, as far as possible, the nature of the trade in furs conducted upon the Saskatchewan, the number and nationality of the persons employed in what has been called the Free Trade there, and what portion of the supplies, if any, come from the United States territory, and what portion of the furs are sent thither; and generally to make such inquiries as to the source of trade in that region as may enable the Lieutenant-Governor to form an accurate idea of the commerce of the Saskatchewan.

You are to report from time to time as you proceed westward, and forward your communications by such opportunities as may occur. The Lieutenant-Governor will rely upon your executing this mission with all reasonable despatch.

(Signed) S. W. HILL, P. Secretary.

LIEUTENANT BUTLER'S REPORT.

INTRODUCTORY.

The Hon. Adams G. Archibald, Lieut.-Governor, Manitoba.

SIR,--Before entering into the questions contained in the written instructions under which I acted, and before attempting to state an opinion upon the existing situation of affairs in the Saskatchewvan, I will briefly allude to the time occupied in travel, to the route followed, and to the general circumstances attending my journey.

Starting from Fort Garry on the 25th October, I reached Fort Ellice at junction of Qu'Appelle and Assineboine Rivers on the 30th of the same month. On the following day I continued my journey towards Carlton, which place was reached on the 9th November, a detention of two days having occurred upon the banks of the South Saskatchewan River, the waters of which were only partially frozen. After a delay of five days in Carlton, the North Branch of the Saskatchewan was reported fit for the passage of horses, and on the morning of the 14th November I proceeded on my western journey towards Edmonton. By this time snow had fallen to the depth of about six inches over the country, which rendered it necessary to abandon the use of wheels for the transport of baggage, substituting a light sled in place of the cart which had hitherto been used, although I still retained the same mode of conveyance, namely the saddle, for personal use. Passing the Hudson Bay Company Posts of Battle River, Fort Pitt and Victoria, I reached Edmonton on the night of the 26th November. For the last 200 miles the country had become clear of snow, and the frosts, notwithstanding the high altitude of the region, had decreased in severity. Starting again on the afternoon of the 1st December, I recrossed the Saskatchewan River below Edmonton and continued in a south-westerly direction towards the Rocky Mountain House, passing through a country which, even at that advanced period of the year, still retained many traces of its summer beauty. At midday on the 4th December, having passed the gorges of the Three Medicine Hills, I came in sight of the Rocky Mountains, which rose from the western extremity of an immense plain and stretched their great snow-clad peaks far away to the northern and southern horizons.

Finding it impossible to procure guides for the prosecution of my journey south to Montana, I left the Rocky Mountain House on the 12th December and commenced my return travels to Red River along the valley of the Saskatchewan. Snow had now fallen to the depth of about a foot, and the cold had of late begun to show symptoms of its winter intensity. Thus on the morning of the 5th December my thermometer indicated 22 degrees below zero, and again on the 13th 16 below zero, a degree of cold which in itself was not remarkable, but which had the effect of rendering the saddle by no means a comfortable mode of transport.

Arriving at Edmonton on the 16th December, I exchanged my horses for dogs, the saddle for a small cariole, and on the 20th December commenced in earnest the winter journey to Red River. The cold, long delayed, now\ began in all its severity. On the 22nd December my thermometer at ten o'clock in the morning indicated 39 degrees below zero, later in the day a biting wind swept the long reaches of the Saskatchewan River and rendered travelling on the ice almost insupportable. To note here the long days of travel down the great valley of the Saskatchewan, at times on the frozen river and at times upon the neighbouring plains, would prove only a tiresome record. Little by little the snow seemed to deepen, day by day the frost to obtain a more lasting power and to bind in a still more solid embrace all visible Nature. No human voice, no sound of bird or beast, no ripple of stream to break the intense silence of these vast solitudes of the Lower Saskatchewan. At length, early in the month of February, I quitted the valley of Saskatchewan at Cedar Lake, crossed the ridge which separates that sheet of water from Lake Winnipegoosis, and, descending the latter lake to its outlet at Waterhen River, passed from thence to the northern extremity of the Lake Manitoba. Finally, on the 18th February, I reached the settlement of Oak Point on south shore of Manitoba, and two days later arrived at Fort Garry.

In following the river and lake route from Carlton, I passed in succession the Mission of Prince Albert, Forts-à-la-Corne and Cumberland, the Posts of the Pas, Moose Lake, Shoal River and Manitoba House, and, with a few exceptions, travelled upon ice the entire way.

The journey from first to last occupied 119 days and embraced a distance of about 2700 miles.

I have now to offer the expression of my best acknowledgements to the officers of the various posts of the Hudson Bay Company passed en route. To Mr. W. J. Christie, of Edmonton, to Mr. Richard Hardistry, of Victoria, as well as to Messrs. Hackland, Sinclair, Ballenden, Trail, Turner, Belanger, Matheison, McBeath, Munro, and MacDonald, I am indebted for much kindness and hospitality, and I have to thank Mr. W. J. Christie for information of much value regarding statistics connected with his district. I have also to offer to the Rev. Messrs. Lacombe, McDougall, and Nisbet the expression of the obligations which I am under towards them for uniform kindness and hospitality.

GENERAL REPORT.

Having in the foregoing pages briefly alluded to the time occupied in travel, to the route followed, and to the general circumstances attending my journey, I now propose entering upon the subjects contained in the written instructions under which I acted, and in the first instance to lay before you the views which I have formed upon the important question of the existing state of affairs in the Saskatchewan.

The institutions of Law and Order, as understood in civilized communities, are wholly unknown in the regions of the Saskatchewan, insomuch as the country is without any executive organization, and destitute of any means to enforce the authority of the law.

I do not mean to assert that crime and outrage are of habitual occurrence among the people of this territory, or that a state of anarchy exists in any particular portion of it, but it is an undoubted fact that crimes of the most serious nature have been committed, in various places, by persons of mixed and native blood, without any vindication of the law being possible, and that the position of affairs rests at the present moment not on the just power of an executive authority to enforce obedience, but rather upon the passive acquiescence of the majority of a scant population who hitherto have lived in ignorance of those conflicting interests which, in more populous and civilized communities, tend to anarchy and disorder.

But the question may be asked, If the Hudson Bay Company represent the centres round which the half-breed settlers have gathered, how then does it occur that that body should be destitute of governing power, and unable to repress crime and outrage? To this question I would reply that the Hudson Bay Company, being a commercial corporation, dependent for its profits on the suffrages of the people, is of necessity cautious in the exercise of repressive powers; that, also, it is exposed in the Saskatchewan to the evil influence which free trade has ever developed among the native races; that, furthermore, it is brought in contact with tribes long remarkable for their lawlessness and ferocity; and that, lastly, the elements of disorder in the whole territory of Saskatchewan are for many causes, yearly on the increase. But before entering upon the subject into which this last-consideration would lead me, it will be advisable to glance at the various elements which comprise the population of this Western region. In point of numbers, and in the power which they possess of committing depredations, the aboriginal races claim the foremost place among the inhabitants of the Saskatchewan. These tribes, like the Indians of other portions of Rupert's Land and the North-west, carry on the pursuits of hunting, bringing the produce of their hunts to barter for the goods of the Hudson Bay Company; but, unlike the Indians of more northern regions, they subsist almost entirely upon the buffalo, and they carry on among themselves an unceasing warfare which has long become traditional. Accustomed to regard murder as honourable war, robbery and pillage as the traits most ennobling to man hood, free from all restraint, these warring tribes of Crees, Assineboines, and Blackfeet form some of the most savage among even the races of Western America.

Hitherto it maybe said that the Crees have looked upon the white man as their friend, but latterly indications have not been wanting to foreshadow a change in this respect--a change which I. have found many causes to account for, and which, if the Saskatchewan remains in its present condition, must, I fear, deepen into more positive enmity. The buffalo, the red man's sole means of subsistence, is rapidly disappearing; year by year the prairies, which once shook beneath the tread of countless herds of bisons, are becoming denuded of animal life, and year by year the affliction of starvation comes with an ever-increasing intensity upon the land. There are men still living who remember to have hunted buffalo on the shores of Lake Manitoba. It is scarcely twelve years since Fort Ellice, on the Assineboine River, formed one of the principal posts of supply for the Hudson Bay Company; and the vast prairies which flank the southern and western spurs of the Touchwood Hills, now utterly silent and deserted, are still white with the bones of the migratory herds which, until lately, roamed over their surface.

Nor is this absence of animal life confined to the plains of the Qu'Appelle and of the Upper Assineboine--all along the line of the North Saskatchewan, from Carlton to Edmonton House, the same scarcity prevails; and if further illustration of this decrease of buffalo be wanting, I would state that, during the present winter, I have traversed the plains from the Red River to the Rocky Mountains without seeing even one solitary animal upon 1200 miles of prairie. The Indian is not slow to attribute this lessening of his principal food to the presence of the white and half-breed settlers, whose active competition for pemmican (valuable as supplying the transport service of the Hudson Bay Company) has led to this all but total extinction of the bison.

Nor does he fail to trace other grievances--some real, some imaginary-to the same cause. Wherever the half-breed settler or hunter has established himself he has resorted to the use of poison as a means of destroying the wolves and foxes which were numerous on the prairies. This most pernicious practice has had the effect of greatly embittering the Indians against the settler, for not only have large numbers of animals been uselessly destroyed, inasmuch as fully one-half the animals thus killed are lost to the trapper, but also the poison is frequently communicated to the Indian dogs, and thus a very important mode of winter transport is lost to the red man. It is asserted, too, that horses are sometimes poisoned by eating grasses which have become tainted by the presence of strychnine; and although this latter assertion may not be true, yet its effects are the same, as the Indian fully believes it. In consequence of these losses a threat has been made, very generally, by the natives against the half-breeds, to the effect that if the use of poison was persisted in, the horses belonging to the settlers would be shot.

Another increasing source of Indian discontent is to be found in the policy pursued by the American Government in their settlement of the countries lying south of the Saskatchewan. Throughout the territories of Dakota and Montana a state of hostility has long existed between the Americans and the tribes of Sioux, Black feet, and Peagin Indians. This state of hostility has latterly degenerated on the part of the Americans, into a war of extermination; and the policy of "clearing out" the red man has now become a recognized portion of Indian warfare. Some of these acts of extermination find their way into the public records, many of them never find publicity. Among the former, the attack made during the spring of 1870 by a large party of troops upon a camp of Peagin Indians close to the British boundary-line will be fresh in the recollection of your Excellency. The tribe thus attacked was suffering severely from small-pox, was surprised at daybreak by the soldiers, who, rushing in upon the tents, destroyed 170 men, women, and children in a few moments. This tribe forms one of the four nations comprised in the Blackfeet league, and have their hunting-grounds partly on British and partly on American territory. I have mentioned the presence of small-pox in connexion with these Indians. It is very generally believed in the Saskatchewan that this disease was originally communicated to the Blackfeet tribes by Missouri traders with a view to the accumulation of robes; and this opinion, monstrous though it may appear, has been somewhat terrified by the Western press when treating of the epidemic last year. As I propose to enter at some length into the question of this disease at a later portion of this report, I now only make allusion to it as forming one of the grievances which the Indian affirms he suffers at the hands of the white man.

In estimating the causes of Indian discontent as bearing upon the future preservation of peace and order in the Saskatchewan, and as illustrating the growing difficulties which a commercial corporation like the Hudson Bay Company have to contend against when acting in an executive capacity, I must now allude to the subject of Free Trade. The policy of a free trader in furs is essentially a short-sighted one-he does not care about the future--the continuance and partial well-being of the Indian is of no consequence to him. His object is to obtain possession of all the furs the Indian may have at the moment to barter, and to gain that end he spares no effort. Alcohol, discontinued by the Hudson Bay Company in their Saskatchewan district for many years, has been freely used of late by free traders from Red River; and, as great competition always exists between the traders and the employees of the Company, the former have not hesitated to circulate among the natives the idea that they have suffered much injustice in their intercourse with the Company. The events which took place in the Settlement of Red River during the winter of '69 and '70 have also tended to disturb the minds of the Indians--they have heard of changes of Government, of rebellion and pillage of property, of the occupation of forts belonging to the Hudson Bay Company, and the stoppage of trade and ammunition. Many of these events have been magnified and distorted--evil-disposed persons have not been wanting to spread abroad among the natives the idea of the downfall of the Company, and the threatened immigration of settlers to occupy the hunting-grounds and drive the Indian from the land. All these rumours, some of them vague and wild in the extreme, have found ready credence by camp-fires and in council-lodge, and thus it is easy to perceive how the red man, with many of his old convictions and beliefs rudely shaken, should now be more disturbed and discontented than he has been at any former period.

In endeavouring to correctly estimate the present condition of Indian affairs in the Saskatchewan the efforts and influence of the various missionary bodies must not be overlooked. It has only been during the last twenty years that the Plain Tribes have been brought into contact with the individuals whom the contributions of European and Colonial communities have sent out on missions of religion and civilization. Many of these individuals have toiled with untiring energy and undaunted perseverance in the work to which they have devoted themselves, but it is unfortunately true that the jarring interests of different religious denominations have sometimes induced them to introduce into the field of Indian theology that polemical rancour which so unhappily distinguishes more civilized communities.

114

To fully understand the question of missionary enterprise, as bearing upon the Indian tribes of the Saskatchewan valley, I must glance for a moment at the peculiarities in the mental condition of the Indians which render extreme caution necessary in all inter course between him and the white man. It is most difficult to make the Indian comprehend the true nature of the foreigner with whom he is brought in contact, or rather, I should say, that having his own standard by which he measures truth and falsehood, misery and happiness, and all the accompaniments of life, it is almost impossible to induce him to look at the white man from any point of view but his own. From this point of view every thing is Indian. English, French, Canadians, and Americans are so many tribes inhabiting various parts of the world, whose land is bad, and who are not possessed of buffalo-- for this last desideratum they (the strangers) send goods, missions, etc., to the Indians of the Plains. "Ah!" they say, "if it was not for our buffalo where would you be? You would starve, your bones would whiten the prairies." It is useless to tell them that such is not the case, they answer, "Where then does all the pemmican go to that you take away in your boats and in your carts?" With the Indian, seeing is believing, and his world is the visible one in which his wild life is cast. This being understood, the necessity for caution in communicating with the native will at once be apparent-yet such caution on the part of those who seek the Indians as missionaries is not always observed. Too frequently the language suitable for civilized society has been addressed to the red man. He is told of governments, and changes in the political world, successive religious systems are laid before him by their various advocates. To-day he is told to believe one religion, to-morrow to have faith in another. Is it any wonder that, applying his own simple tests to so much conflicting testimony, he becomes utterly confused, unsettled, and suspicious? To the white man, as a white man, the Indian has no dislike; on the contrary, he is pretty certain to receive him with kindness and friendship, provided always that the new-comer will adopt the native system, join the hunting-camp, and live on the plains; but to the white man as a settler, or hunter on his own account, the Crees and Blackfeet are in direct antagonism. Ownership in any particular portion of the soil by an individual is altogether foreign to men who, in the course of a single summer, roam over 500 miles of prairie. In another portion of this report I hope to refer again to the Indian question, when treating upon that clause in my instructions which relates exclusively to Indian matters. I have alluded here to missionary enterprise and to the Indian generally, as both subjects are very closely connected with the state of affairs in the Saskatchewan.

Next in importance to the native race is the half-breed element in the population which now claims our attention.

The persons composing this class are chiefly of French descent originally of no fixed habitation, they have, within the last few years, been induced by their clergy to form scattered settlements along the line of the North Saskatchewan. Many of them have emigrated from Red River, and others are either the discharged servants of the Hudson Bay Company or the relatives of persons still in the employment of the Company. In contradistinction to this latter class they bear the name of "free men" and if freedom from all restraint, general inaptitude for settled employment, and love for the pursuits of hunting be the characteristics of free men, then they are eminently entitled to the name they bear. With very few exceptions, they have preferred adopting the exciting but precarious means of living, the chase, to following the more certain` methods of agriculture. Almost the entire summer is spent by them upon the plains, where they carry on the pursuit of the buffalo in large and well organized bands, bringing the produce of their hunt to trade with the Hudson Bay Company.

In winter they generally reside at their settlements, going to the nearer plains in small parties and dragging the frozen buffalo meat for the supply of the Company's posts. This preference for the wild life of the prairies, by bringing them more in contact with their savage brethren, and by removing them from the means of acquiring knowledge and civilization, has tended in no small degree to throw them back in the social scale, and to make the establishment of a prosperous colony almost an impossibility--even starvation, that most potent inducement to toil, seems powerless to promote habits of industry and agriculture. During the winter season they frequently undergo periods of great privation, but, like he Indian, they refuse to credit the gradual extinction of the buffalo, and persist in still depending on that animal for their food. Were I to sum up the general character of the Saskatchewan half-breed population, I would say: They are gay, idle, dissipated, unreliable, and ungrateful, in a measure brave, hasty to form conclusions and quick to act upon them, possessing extra ordinary power-of endurance, and capable of undergoing immense fatigue, yet scarcely-ever to be depended on in critical moments, superstitious and ignorant, having a very deep-rooted distaste to any fixed employment, opposed to the Indian, yet widely separated from the white man--altogether a race presenting, I fear, a hopeless prospect to those who would attempt to frame, from such materials, a future nationality. In the appendix will be found a statement showing the population and extent of the half-breed settlements in the West. I will here merely remark that the principal settlements are to be found in the Upper Saskatchewan, in the vicinity of Edmonton House, at which post their trade is chiefly carried on.

Among the French half-breed population there exists the same political feeling which is to be found among their brethren in Manitoba, and the same sentiments which produced the outbreak of 1869-70 are undoubtedly existing in the small communities of the Saskatchewan. It is no easy matter to understand how the feeling of distrust towards Canada, and a certain hesitation to accept the Dominion Government, first entered into the mind of the half-breed, but undoubtedly such distrust and hesitation have made themselves apparent in the Upper Saskatchewan, as in Red River, though in a much less formidable degree; in fact, I may fairly close this notice of the half-breed population by observing that an exact counterpart of French political feeling in Manitoba may be found in the territory of the Saskatchewan, but kept in abeyance both by the isolation of the various settlements, as well as by a certain dread of Indian attack which presses equally upon all classes.

The next element of which I would speak is that composed of the white settler, European and American,` not being servants of the Hudson Bay Company. At the present time this class is numerically insignificant, and were it not that causes might at any moment arise which would rapidly develop it into consequence, it would not now claim more than a passing notice. These causes are to be found in the existence of gold throughout a large extent of the territory lying at the eastern base of the Rocky Mountains, and in the effect which the discovery of gold-fields would have in inducing a rapid movement of miners from the already over-worked fields of the Pacific States and British Columbia. For some years back indication of gold, in more or less quantities, have been found in almost every river running east from the mountains. On the Peace, Athabasca, McLeod, and Pembina Rivers, all of which drain their waters into the Arctic Ocean, as well as on the North Saskatchewan, Red Beer, and Bow Rivers, which shed to Lake Winnipeg, gold has been discovered. The obstacles which the miner has to contend with are, however, very great, and preclude any thing but the most partial examination of the country. The Blackfeet are especially hostile towards miners, and never hesitate to attack them, nor is the miner slow to retaliate; indeed he has been too frequently the aggressor, and the records of gold discovery are full of horrible atrocities committed upon the red man. It has only been in the neighbourhood of the forts of the Hudson Bay Company that continued washing for gold could be carried on. In the neighbourhood of Edmonton from three to twelve dollars of gold have frequently been "washed" in a single day by one man; but the miner is not satisfied with what he calls "dirt washing," and craves for the more exciting work in the dry diggings where, if the "strike" is good, the yield is sometimes enormous. The difficulty of procuring provisions or supplies of any kind has also prevented "prospecting" parties from examining the head-waters of the numerous streams which form the sources of the North and South Saskatchewan. It is not the high price of provisions that deters the miner from penetrating these regions, but the absolute impossibility of procuring any. Notwithstanding the many difficulties which I have enumerated, a very determined effort will in all probability be made, during the coming summer, to examine the head-waters of the North Branch of the Saskatchewan. A party of miners, four in number, crossed the mountains late in the autumn of 1870, and are now wintering between Edmonton and the Mountain House, having laid in large supplies for the coming season. These men speak with confidence of the existence of rich diggings in some portion of the country lying within the outer range of the mountains. From conversations which I have held with these men, as well as with others who have partly investigated the country, I am of opinion that there exists a very strong probability of the discovery of gold-fields in the Upper Saskatchewan at no distant period. Should this opinion be well founded, the effect which it will have upon the whole Western territory will be of the utmost consequence.

Despite the hostility of the Indians inhabiting the neighbourhood of such discoveries, or the plains or passes leading to them, a general influx of miners will take place into the Saskatchewan, and in their track will come the waggon or pack-horse of the merchant from the towns of Benton or Kootenais, or Helena. It is impossible to say what effect such an influx of strangers would have upon the plain Indians; but of one fact we may rest assured, namely, that should these tribes exhibit their usual spirit of robbery and murder they would quickly be exterminated by the miners.

Every where throughout the Pacific States and along the central territories of America, as well as in our own colony of British Columbia, a war of extermination has arisen, under such circum stances, between the miners and the savages, and there is good reason to suppose that similar results would follow contact with the proverbially hostile tribe of Blackfeet Indians.

Having in the foregoing remarks reviewed the various elements which compose the scanty but widely extended population of the Saskatchewan, outside the circle of the Hudson Bay Company, I have now to refer to that body, as far as it is connected with the present condition of affairs in the Saskatchewan.

As a governing body the Hudson Bay Company has ever had to contend against the evils which are inseparable from monopoly of trade combined with monopoly of judicial power, but so long as the aboriginal inhabitants were the only people with whom it came in contact its authority could be preserved; and as it centred within itself whatever knowledge and enlightenment existed in the country, its officials were regarded by the aboriginals as persons of a superior nature, nay, even in bygone times it was by no means unusual for the Indians to regard the possession of some of the most ordinary inventions of civilization on the part of the officials of the Company as clearly demonstrating a close affinity between these gentlemen and the Manitou, nor were these attributes of divinity altogether distasteful to the officers, who found them both remunerative as to trade and conducive to the exercise of authority. When, however, the Free Traders and the missionary reached the Saskatchewan this primitive state of affairs ceased-with the enlightenment of the savage came the inevitable discontent of the' Indian, until there arose the condition of things to which I have already alluded. I am aware that there are persons who, while admitting the present unsatisfactory state of the Saskatchewan, ascribe its evils more to mistakes committed by officers of the Company, in their management of the Indians, than to any material change in the character of the people; but I believe such opinion to be founded in error. It would be impossible to revert to the old management of affairs. The Indians and the half-breeds are aware of their strength, and openly speak of it; and although I am far from asserting that a more determined policy on the part of the officer in charge of the Saskatchewan District would not be attended by better results, still it is apparent that the great isolation of the posts, as well as the absence of any fighting element in the class of servants belonging to the Company, render the forts on the Upper Saskatchewan, in a very great degree, helpless, and at the mercy of the people of that country. Nor are the engaged servants of the Company a class of persons with whom it is at all easy to deal. Recruited principally from the French half-breed population, and exposed, as I have already shown, to the wild and lawless life of the prairies, there exists in reality only a very slight distinction between them and their Indian brethren, hence it is not surprising that acts of insubordination Should be of frequent occurrence among these servants, and that personal violence towards superior officers should be by no means an unusual event in the forts of the Saskatchewan; indeed it has only been by the exercise of manual force on the part of the officials in charge that the semblance of authority has sometimes been preserved. This tendency towards insubordination is still more observable among the casual servants or "trip men" belonging to the Company. These persons are in the habit of engaging for a trip or journey, and-frequently select the most critical moments to demand an increased rate of pay, or to desert en masse.

At Edmonton House, the head-quarters of the Saskatchewan District, and at the posts of Victoria and Fort Pitt, this state of lawlessness is more apparent than on the lower portion of the river. Threats are frequently made use of by the Indians and half-breeds as a means of extorting favourable terms from the officers in charge, the cattle belonging to the posts are uselessly killed, and altogether the Hudson Bay Company may be said to retain their tenure of the Upper Saskatchewan upon a base which appears insecure and unsatisfactory.

In the foregoing remarks I have entered at some length into the question of the materials comprising the population of the Saskatchewan, with a, view to demonstrate that the condition of affairs in-that territory is the natural result of many causes, which have been gradually developing themselves, and which must of necessity undergo still further developments if left in their present state. I have endeavoured to point out how from the growing wants of the aboriginal inhabitants, from the conflicting nature of the interests of the half-breed and Indian population, as well as from the natural constitution of the Hudson Bay Company, a state of society has arisen in the Saskatchewan which threatens at no distant day to give rise to grave complications; and which now has the effect of rendering life and property insecure and preventing the settlement of those fertile regions which in other respects are so admirably suited to colonization.

As matters at present rest, the region of the Saskatchewan is without law, order, or security for life or property; robbery and murder for years have gone unpunished; Indian massacres are unchecked even in the close vicinity of the Hudson Bay Company's posts, and all civil and legal institutions are entirely unknown.

I now enter upon that portion of your Excellency's instructions which has reference to the epidemic of small-pox in the Saskatchewan. It is about fifty years since the first great epidemic of small pox swept over the regions of the Missouri and the Saskatchewan, committing great ravages among the tribes of Sioux, Gros-Ventres, and Flatheads upon American territory; and among the Crees and Assineboines of the British. The Blackfeet Indians escaped that epidemic, while, on the other hand, the Assineboines, or Stonies of the Qu'Appelle Plains, were almost entirely destroyed. Since that-period the disease appears to have visited some of the tribes at intervals of greater or less duration; but until this and the previous year its ravages were confined to certain localities and did not extend universally throughout the country. During the summer and early winter of '69 and '70 reports reached the Saskatchewan of the prevalence of small-pox of a very malignant type among the South Peagin Indians, a branch of the great Blackfeet nation. It was hoped, however, that the disease would be confined to the Missouri River, and the Crees who, as usual, were at war with their traditional enemies, were warned by Missionaries and others that the prosecution of their predatory expeditions into the Blackfeet country would in all probability carry the infection into the North Saskatchewan. From the South Peagin tribes, on the head-waters of the Missouri, the disease spread rapidly through the kindred tribes of Blood, Blackfeet, and Lucee Indians, all which new tribes have their hunting-grounds north of the boundary-line. Unfortunately for the Crees, they failed to listen to the advice of those persons who had recommended a suspension of hostilities. With the opening of spring the war-parties commenced their raids; a band of seventeen Crees penetrated, in the month of April, into the Blackfeet country, and coming upon a deserted camp of their enemies in which a tent was still standing, they proceeded to ransack it, This tent contained the dead bodies of some Blackfeet, and although these bodies presented a very revolting spectacle, being in an advanced stage of decomposition, they were nevertheless-subjected to the usual process of mutilation, the scalps and clothing being also carried away.

For this act the Crees paid a terrible penalty; scarcely had they reached their own country before the disease appeared among them, in its most virulent and infectious form. Nor were the consequences of this raid less disastrous to the whole Cree nation. At the period of the-year to which I allude, the early summer, these Indians usually assemble together from different directions in large numbers, and it was towards one of those numerous assemblies that the returning war-party, still carrying the scalps and clothing of the Blackfeet, directed their steps. Almost immediately upon their arrival the disease broke out amongst them in its most malignant form. Out of the seventeen men who took part in the raid, it is asserted that not one escape the infection, and only two of the number appear to have survived. The disease, once-introduced into the camp, spread with the utmost rapidity; numbers of men, women, and children fell victims to it during the month of June; the cures of the medicine-men were found utterly-unavailing to arrest it, and, as a last resource, the camp broke up into small parties, some directing their march towards Edmonton, and others to Victoria, Saddle Lake, Fort Pitt, and along the whole line of the North Saskatchewan. Thus, at the same period, the beginning of July, small-pox of the very worst description was spread throughout some 500 miles of territory, appearing almost simultaneously at the Hudson Bay Company's posts from the Rocky Mountain House to Carlton.

It is difficult to imagine, a state of pestilence more terrible than that which kept pace with these moving parties of Crees during the summer months of 1870. By streams and lakes, in willow copses,'! and upon bare hill-sides, often shelterless from the fierce rays of the summer sun and exposed to the rains and dews of night, the poor plague-stricken wretches lay down to die--no assistance of any kind, for the ties of family were quickly loosened, and mothers abandoned their helpless children upon the wayside, fleeing onward to some fancied place of safety. The district lying between Fort Pitt and Victoria, a distance of about 140 miles, was perhaps the scene of the greatest suffering.

In the immediate neighbourhood of Fort Pitt two camps of Crees established themselves, at first in the hope of obtaining medical assistance, and failing in that--for the officer in charge soon exhausted his slender store--they appear to have endeavoured to convey the infection into the fort, in the belief that by doing so they would cease to suffer from it themselves. The dead bodies were left unburied close to the stockades, and frequently Indians in the worst stage of the disease might be seen trying to force an entrance into the houses, or rubbing portions of the infections matter from their persons against the door-handles and window-frames of the dwellings. It is singular that only three persons within the fort should have been infected with the disease, and I can only attribute the comparative immunity enjoyed by the residents at that post to the fact that Mr. John Sinclair had taken the precaution early in the summer to vaccinate all the persons residing there, having obtained the vaccine matter from a Salteaux Indian who had been vaccinated at the Mission of Prince Albert, presided over by Rev. Mr. Nesbit, sometime during the spring. In this matter of vaccination a very important difference appears to have existed between the Upper and Lower Saskatchewan. At the settlement of St. Albert, near Edmonton, the opinion prevails that vaccination was of little or no avail to check-the spread of the disease, while, on the contrary, residents on the lower portion of the Saskatchewan assert that they cannot trace a single case in which death had ensued after vaccination had been properly performed. I attribute this difference of opinion on the benefits resulting from vaccination to the fact that the vaccine matter used at St. Albert and Edimonton was of a spurious description, having been brought from Fort Benton, on the Missouri River, by traders during the early summer, and that also it was used when the disease had reached its height, while, on the other hand, the vaccination carried on from Mr. Nesbit's Mission appears to have been commenced early in the spring, and also to have been of a genuine description.

At the Mission of St. Albert, called also "Big Lake," the disease assumed a most malignant form; the infection appears to have been introduced into the settlement from two different sources almost at the same period. The summer hunting-party met the Blackfeet on the plains and visited the Indian camp (then infected with small-pox) for the purpose of making peace and trading. A few days later the disease appeared among them and swept off half their number in a very short space of time. To such a degree of helplessness were they reduced that when the prairie fires broke out in the neighbourhood of their camp they were unable to do any thing towards arresting its progress or saving their property. The fire swept through the camp, destroying a number of horses, carts, and tents, and the unfortunate people returned to their homes at Big Lake carrying the disease with them. About the same time some of the Crees also reached the settlement, and the infection thus communicated from both quarters spread with amazing rapidity. Out of a total population numbering about 900 souls, 600 caught the disease, and up to the date of my departure from Edmonton (22nd December) 311 deaths had occurred. Nor is this enormous percentage of deaths very much to be wondered at when we consider the circumstances attending this epidemic. The people, huddled together in small hordes, were destitute of medical assistance or of even the most ordinary requirements of the hospital. During the period of delirium incidental to small-pox, they frequently wandered forth at night into the open air, and remained exposed for hours to dew or rain; in the latter stages of the disease they took no precautions against cold, and frequently died from relapse produced by exposure; on the other hand, they appear to have suffered but little pain after the primary fever passed away. "I have frequently," says Père André, "asked a man in the last stages of small pox,-whose end was close at hand, if he was suffering much pain; and the almost invariable reply was, None whatever." They seem also to have died without suffering, although the fearfully swollen appearance of the face, upon which scarcely a feature was visible, would lead to the supposition that such a condition must of necessity be accompanied by great pain.

The circumstances attending the progress of the epidemic at Carlton House are worthy of notice, both on account of the extreme virulence which characterized the disease at that post, and also as no official record of this visitation of small-pox would be complete which failed to bring to the notice of your Excellency the undaunted: heroism displayed by a young officer of the Hudson Bay Company who was in temporary charge of the station. At the breaking out of the disease, early in the month of August, the population of Carlton: numbered about seventy souls. Of these thirty-two persons caught the infection, and twenty-eight persons died. Throughout the entire period of the epidemic the officer already alluded to, Mr. Wm. Traill, laboured with untiring perseverance in ministering to the necessities of the sick, at whose bedsides he was to be found both day and night, undeterred by the fear of infection, and undismayed by the unusually loathsome nature of the disease. To estimate with any thing like accuracy the losses caused among the Indian tribes is a matter of considerable difficulty. Some tribes and portions of tribes suffered much more severely than others. That most competent authority, Père Lacombe, is of opinion that neither the Blood nor Blackfeet Indians had, in proportion to their numbers, as many casualties as the Crees, whose losses may be safely stated at from 600 to 800 persons. The Lurcees, a small tribe in close alliance with the Blackfeet, suffered very severely, the number of their tents being reduced from fifty to twelve. On the.' other hand, the Assineboines, or Stonies of the Plains, warned by the memory of the former epidemic, by which they were almost annihilated, fled at the first approach of the disease, and, keeping far out in the south-eastern prairies, escaped the infection altogether. The very heavy loss suffered by the Lurcees to which I have just alluded was, I apprehend, due to the fact that the members of this tribe have long been noted as persons possessing enfeebled constitutions, as evidenced by the prevalence of goitre almost universally amongst them. As a singular illustration of the intractable nature of these Indians, I would mention that at the period when the small-pox was most destructive among them they still continued to carry on their horse-stealing raids against the Crees and half-breeds in the neighbourhood of Victoria Mission. It was not unusual to come upon traces of the disease in the corn-fields around the settlement, and even the dead bodies of some Lurcees were discovered in the vicinity of a river which they had been in the habit of swimming while in the prosecution of their predatory attacks. The Rocky Mountain Stonies are stated to have lost over fifty souls. The losses sustained by the Blood, Blackfeet, and Peagin tribes are merely conjectural; but, as their loss in leading men or chiefs has been heavy, it is only reasonable to presume that the casualties suffered generally by those tribes have been proportionately severe. Only three white persons appear to have fallen victims to the disease, one an officer of the Hudson Bay Company service at Carlton, and two members of the family of the Rev. Mr. McDougall, at Victoria. Altogether, I should be inclined to estimate the entire loss along the North Saskatchewan, not including Blood, Blackfeet, or Peagin Indians, at about 1200 persons. At the period of my departure from the Saskatchewan, the beginning of-the present year, the disease which committed such terrible havoc among the scanty population of that region still lingered in many localities. On my upward journey to the Rocky Mountains I had found the forts of the Hudson Bay Company free from infection: On my return journey I found cases of small-pox in the Forts, of Edmonton, Victoria, and Pitt--cases which, it is true, were of a milder description than those of the autumn and summer, but which, nevertheless, boded ill for the hoped for disappearance of the plague beneath the snows and cold of winter. With regard to the supply of medicine sent by direction of the Board of Health in Manitoba to the Saskatchewan, I have only to remark that I conveyed to Edmonton the portion of the supply destined for that station. It was found, however, that many of the bottles had been much injured by frost, and I cannot in any way favourably notice either the composition or general selection of these supplies.

Amongst the many sad traces of the epidemic existing in the Upper Saskatchewan I know of none so touching as that which is to be found in an assemblage of some twenty little orphan children gathered together beneath the roof of the sisters of charity at the settlement of St. Albert. These children are of all races, and even in some instances the sole survivors of what was lately a numerous family. They are fed, clothed, and taught at the expense of the Mission; and when we consider that the war which is at present raging in France has dried up the sources of charity from whence the Missions of the North-west derived their chief support, and that the present winter is one of unusual scarcity and distress along the North Saskatchewan, then it will be perceived what a fitting object for the assistance of other communities is now existing in this distant orphanage of the North.

I cannot close this notice of the epidemic without alluding to the danger which will arise in the spring of introducing the infection into Manitoba. As soon as the prairie route becomes practicable there will be much traffic to and from the Saskatchewan--furs and robes will be introduced into the settlement despite the law which prohibits their importation. The present quarantine establishment at Rat Creek is situated too near to the settlement to admit of a strict enforcement of the sanitary regulations. It was only in the month of October last year that a man coming direct from Carlton died at-this Rat Creek, while his companions, who were also from the same place, and from whom he caught the infection, passed on into the province. If I might suggest the course which appears to me to be the most efficacious, I would say that a constable stationed at Fort Ellice during the spring and summer months who would examine freighters and others, giving them bills of health to enable them to enter the province, would effectually meet the requirements of the situation. All persons coming from the West are obliged to pass close to the neighbourhood of Fort Ellice. This station is situated about 170 miles west of the provincial boundary, and about 300 miles south-east of the South Saskatchewan, forming the only post of call upon the road between Carlton and Portage la-Prairie. I have only to add that, unless vaccination is made compulsory among the half-breed inhabitants, they will, I fear, be slow to avail themselves of it. It must not be forgotten that with the disappearance of the snow from the plains a quantity of infected matter--clothing, robes, and portions of skeletons--will again be come exposed to the atmosphere, and also that the skins of wolves, etc., collected during the present winter will be very liable to contain infection of the most virulent description.

The portion of-your Excellency's instructions which has reference to the Indian tribes of the Assineboine and Saskatchewan regions now claims my attention.

The aboriginal inhabitants of the country lying between Red River and the Rocky Monntains are divided into tribes of Salteaux, Swampies, Crees, Assineboines, or Stonies of the Plains, Blackfeet and Assineboines of the Mountains. A simpler classification, and one which will be found more useful when estimating the relative habits of these tribes, is to divide them into two great classes of Trairie Indians and Thickwood Indians--the first comprising the Blackfeet with their kindred tribes of Bloods, Lurcees, and Peagins, as also the Crees of the Saskatchewan and the Assineboines of the Qu'Appelle; and the last being composed of the Rocky Mountain Stonies, the Swampy Crees, and the Salteaux of the country lying between Manitoba and Fort Ellice. This classification marks in reality the distinctive characteristics of the Western Indians. On the one hand, we find the Prairie tribes subsisting almost entirely upon the buffalo, assembling together in large camps, acknowledging the leadership and authority of men conspicuous by their abilities in war or in the chase, and carrying on a perpetual state\of warfare with the other Indians of the plains. On the other hand, we find the Indians of the woods subsisting by fishing and by the pursuit of moose and deer, living together in small parties, admitting only a very nominal authority on the part of one man, professing to entertain hostile feelings towards certain races, but rarely developing such feelings into positive hostilities--altogether a much more peacefully disposed people, because less exposed to the dangerous influence of large assemblies.

Commencing with the Salteaux, I find that they extend westward from Portage-la-Prairie to Fort Ellice, and from thence north to Fort Pelly and the neighbourhood of Fort-à-la-Corne, where they border and mix with the kindred race of Swampy or Muskego Crees. At Portage-la-Prairie and in the vicinity of Fort Ellice a few Sioux have appeared since the outbreak in Minnesota and Dakota in 1862. It is probable that the number of this tribe on British territory will annually increase with the prosecution of railroad enterprise and settlement in the northern portion of the United States. At present, however, the Sioux are strangers at Fort Ellice, and have not yet assumed those rights of proprietorship which other tribes, longer resident, arrogate to themselves. The Salteaux, who inhabit the country lying west of Manitoba, partake partly of the character of Thickwood, and partly of Prairie Indians--the buffalo no longer exists in that portion of the country, the Indian camps are small, and the authority of the chief merely nominal. The language spoken by this tribe is the same dialect of the Algonquin tongue which is used in the Lac-la-Pluie District and throughout the greater portion of the settlement.

Passing north-west from Fort Ellice, we enter the country of the Cree Indians, having to the north and east the Thickwood Crees, and to the south and west the Plain Crees. The former, under the various names of Swampies or Muskego Indians, inhabit the country west of Lake Winnipeg, extending as far as Forts Pelly and à-la-Corne, and from, the latter place, in a north-westerly direction, to Carlton and Fort Pitt. Their language, which is similar to that spoken by their cousins, the Plain Crees, is also a dialect of the Algonquin tongue. They are seldom found in large numbers, usually forming camps of from four to ten families. They carry on the pursuit of the moose and red deer, and are, generally speaking, expert hunters and trappers.

Bordering the Thickwood Crees on the south and west lies the country of the Plain Crees--a land of vast treeless expanses, of high rolling prairies, of wooded tracts lying in valleys of many-sized streams, in a word, the land of the Saskatchewan. A line running direct from the Touchwood Hills to Edmonton House would measure 500 miles in length, yet would lie altogether within the country of the Plain Crees. They inhabit the prairies which extend from the Qu'Appelle to the South Saskatchewan, a portion of territory which was formerly the land of the Assineboine, but which became the country of the Crees through lapse of time and chance of war. From the elbow of the South Branch of the Saskatchewan the Cree nation extends in a west and north-west direction to the vicinity of the Peace Hills, some fifty miles south of Edmonton. Along the entire line there exists a state of perpetual warfare during the months of summer and autumn, for here commences the territory over which roams the great Blackfeet tribe, whose southern boundary lies be yond the Missouri River, and whose western limits are guarded by the giant peaks of the Rocky Mountains. Ever since these tribes became known to the fur-traders of the North-west and Hudson Bay Companies there has existed this state of hostility amongst them. The Crees, having been the first to obtain fire-arms from the white traders, quickly-extended their boundaries, and moving from the Hudson Bay and the region of the lakes overran the plains of the Upper Saskatchewan. Fragments of other tribes scattered at long intervals through the present country of the Crees attest this conquest, and it is-probable that the whole Indian territory lying between the Saskatchewan and the American boundary-line would have been dominated over by this tribe had they not found themselves opposed by the great Blackfeet nation, which dwelt along the sources of the Missouri.

Passing west from Edmonton, we enter the country of the Rocky Mountain Stonies, a small tribe of Thickwood Indians dwelling along the source of the North Saskatchewan and in the outer ranges of the Rocky Mountains,-a fragment, no doubt, from the once-powerful Assineboine nation which has found a refuge amidst the forests and mountains of the West. This tribe is noted as possessing hunters and mountain guides of great energy and skill. Although at war with the Blackfeet, collisions are not frequent between them, as the Assineboines never go upon war-parties; and the Blackfeet rarely venture into the wooded country.

Having spoken in detail of the Indian tribes inhabiting the line of fertile country lying between Red River and the Rocky Mountains, it only remains for me to allude to the Blackfeet with the confederate tribes of Blood, Lurcees and Peagins. These tribes inhabit the great plains lying between the Red Deer River and the Missouri, a vast tract of country, which, with few exceptions, is treeless, and sandy--a portion of the true American desert, which extends from the fertile belt of the Saskatchewan to the borders of Texas. With the exception of the Lurcees, the other confederate tribes speak the same language--the Lurcees, being a branch of the Chipwayans of the North, speak a language peculiar to themselves, while at the same time understanding and speaking the Blackfeet tongue. At war with their hereditary enemies, the Crees, upon their northern and eastern boundaries--at war with Kootanais and Flathead tribes on south and west--at war with Assineboines on the south-east and north-west--carrying on predatory excursions against the Americans on the Missouri, this Blackfeet nation forms a people of whom it may truly be said that they are against every man, and that every man is against them. Essentially a wild, lawless, erring race, whose natures have received the stamps of the region in which they dwell; whose knowledge is read from the great book which Day, Night, and the Desert unfold to them; and who yet possess a rude eloquence, a savage pride, and a wild love of freedom of their own. Nor are there other indications wanting to lead to the hope that this tribe may yet be found to be capable of yielding to influences to which they have heretofore been strangers, namely, Justice and Kindness.

Inhabiting, as the Blackfeet do, a large extent of country which, from the arid nature of its soil mist ever prove useless for purposes of settlement and colonization, I do not apprehend that much difficulty will arise between them and the whites, provided always that measures are taken to guard against certain possibilities of danger, and that the Crees are made to unnderstand that the forts and settlements along the Upper Saskatchewan must be considered as neutral ground upon which hostilities cannot be waged against the Black feet. As matters at present stand, whenever the Blackfeet venture in upon a trading expedition to the forts of the Hudson Bay Company they are generally assaulted by the Crees, and savagely murdered. Pèe Lacombe estimates the nunber of Blackfeet killed in and around Edmonton alone during his residence in the West, at over forty men, and he has assured me that to his knowledge the Blackfeet have never killed a Cree at that place, except in self-defence. Mr. W. J. Christie, chief factor at Edmonton house, confirms this statement. He says, "The Blackfeet respect the whites more than the Crees do, that is, a Blackfoot will never atteinpt the life of a Cree at our forts, and bands of them are more easily controlled in an excitement, than Crees. It would be easier for one of us to save the life of a Cree among a band of Blackfeet than it would be to save a Blackfoot in a band of Crees." In consequence of these repeated assaults in the vicinity of the forts, the Blackfeet can with difficulty be persuaded that the whites are not in active alliance with the Crees. Any person who studies the geographical position of the posts of the Hudson Bay Company cannot fail to notice the immense extent of country intervening between the North Saskatchewan and the American boundary-line in which there exists no fort or trading post of the Company. This blank space upon the maps is the country of the Blackfeet. Many years ago a post was established upon the Bow River, in the heart of the Blackfeet country, but at that time they were even more lawless than at present, and the position had to be abandoned on account of the expenses necessary to keep up a large garrison of servants. Since that time (nearly forty years ago) the Blackfeet have only had the Rocky Mountain House to depend on for supplies, and as it is situated far from the centre of their country it only receives a portion of their trade. Thus we find a very active business carried on by the Americans upon the Upper Missouri, and there can be little doubt that the greater portion of robes, buffalo leather, etc. traded by the Blackfeet finds its way down the waters of the Missouri. There is also another point connected with Americau trade amongst the Blackfeet to which I desire to draw special attention. Indians visiting the Rocky Mountain House during the fall of 1870 have spoken of the existence of a trading post of Americans from Fort Benton, upon the Belly River, sixty miles within the British bounndary-line. They have asserted that two American traders, well-known on the Missouri, named Culverston and Healy, have established themselves at this post for the purpose of trading alcohol, whiskey, and arms and ammunition of the most improved description, with the Blackfeet Indians; and that an active trade is being carried on in all these articles, which, it is said, are constantly smuggled across the boundary-line by people from Fort Benton. This story is apparently confirmed by the absence of the Blackfeet from the Rocky Mountain House this season, and also from the fact of the arms in question (repeating rifles) being found in possession of these Indians. The town of Benton on the Missouri River has long been noted for supplying the Indians with arms and ammunition; to such an extent has this trade been carried on, that miners in Montana, who have suffered from Indian attack, have threatened on some occasions to burn the stores belonging to the traders, if the practice was continued. I have already spoken of the great extent of the Blackfeet country; some idea of the roamings of these Indians may be gathered from a circumstance connected wit the trade of the Rocky Mountain House. During the spring and summer raids which the Blackfeet make upon the Crees of the Middle Saskatchewan, a number of horses belonging to the Hudson Bay Company and to settlers are yearly carried away. It is a general practice for persons whose horses have been stolen to send during the fall to the Rocky Mountain House for the missing animals, although that station is 300 to 600 miles distant from the places where the thefts have been committed. If the horse has not perished from the ill treatment to which he has been subjected by his captors, he is usually found at the above-named station, to which he has been brought for barter in a terribly worn out condition. In the Appendix marked B will be found information regarding the localities occupied by-the Indian tribes, the names of the principal chiefs, estimate of numbers in each tribe, and other information connected with the aboriginal inhabitants, which for sake of clearness I have arranged in a tabular form.

It now only remains for me to refer to the last clause in the instructions under which I acted, before entering into an expression of the views which I have formed upon the subject of what appears necessary to be done in the interests of peace and order in the Saskatchewan. The fur trade of the Saskatchewan District has long been in a declining state, great scarcity of the richer descriptions of furs, competition of free traders, and the very heavy expenses incurred in the maintenance of large establishments, have combined to render the district a source of loss to the Hudson Bay Company. This loss has, I believe, varied annually from 2000 to 6000 pounds, but heretofore it has been somewhat counter-balanced by the fact that the Inland Transport Line of the Company was dependent for its supply of provisions upon the buffalo meat, which of late years has only been procurable in the Saskatchewan. Now, however; that buffalo can no longer be procured in numbers, the Upper Saskatchewan becomes more than ever a burden to the Hudson Bay Company; still the abandonment of it by the Company might be attended by more serious loss to the trade than that which is incurred in its retention, Undoubtedly the Saskatchewan, if abandoned by the Hudson Bay Company, would be speedily occupied by traders from the Missouri, who would also tap the trade of the richer fur-producing districts of Lesser Slave Lake and the North. The products-of the Saskatchewan proper principally consists of provisions, including pemmican and dry meat, buffalo robes and leather, linx, cat, and wolf skins. The richer furs; such as otters, minks, beavers, martins, etc., are chiefly procured in the Lesser Slave Lake Division of the Saskatchewan District. With regard to the subject of Free Trade in the Saskatchewan, it is at present conducted upon principles quite different from those existing in Manitoba. The free men or "winterers" are, strictly speaking, free traders, but they dispose of the greater portion of their furs, robes, etc., to the Company. Some, it is true, carry the produce of their trade or hunt (for they are both hunters and traders) to Red River, disposing of it to the merchants in Winnipeg, but I do not imagine that more than one-third of their trade thus finds its way into the market. These free men are nearly all French half-breeds, and are mostly outfitted by the Company. It has frequently occurred that a very considerable trade has been carried on with alcohol, brought by free men from the Settlement of Red River; and distributed to Indians and others in the Upper Saskatchewan. This trade has been productive of the very worst consequences, but the law prohibiting the sale or possession of liquor is now widely known throughout the Western, territory, and its beneficial effects have already been experienced.

I feel convinced that if the proper means are taken the suppression of the liquor traffic of the West can be easily accomplished.

A very important subject is that which has reference to the communication between the Upper Saskatchewan and Missouri Rivers.

Fort Benton on the Missouri has of late become a place of very considerable importance as a post for the supply of the mining districts of Montana. Its geographical position is favourable. Standing at the head of the navigation of the Missouri, it commands: the trade of Idaho and Montana.-'A steamboat, without breaking bulk, can go from New Orleans to Benton, a distance of 4000 miles. Speaking from the recollection of information obtained at Omaha three years ago, it takes about thirty days to ascend the river from that town to Benton, the distance being about 2000 miles. Only boats drawing two or three feet of water can perform the journey, as there are many shoals and shifting sands to obstruct heavier vessels. It has been estimated that between thirty or forty steamboats reached Benton during the course of last summer. The season, for purposes of navigation, may be reckoned as having a duration of about four months. Let us now travel north of the American boundary-line, and see what effect Benton is likely to produce upon the trade of the Saskatchewan. Edmonton lies N.N.W. from Benton about 370 miles. Carlton about the same distance north-east. From both Carlton and Edmonton to Fort Benton the country presents no obstacle whatever to the passage of loaded carts or waggons, but the road from Edmonton is free from Blackfeet during the summer months, and is better provided with wood and water. For the first time in the history of the Saskatchewan, carts passed safely from Edmonton to Benton during the course of last summer. These carts, ten in number, started from Edmonton in the month of May, bringing furs, robes, etc., to the Missouri. They returned in the month of June with a cargo consisting of flour and alcohol.

The furs and robes realized good prices, and altogether the journey was so successful as to hold out high inducements to other persons to attempt it during the coming summer. Already the merchants of Benton are bidding high for the possession of the trade of the Upper Saskatchewan, and estimates have been received by missionaries offering to deliver goods at Edmonton for 7 (American currency) per 100 lbs., all risks being insured. In fact it has only been on account of the absence of a frontier custom house that importations of bonded goods have not already been made via Benton.

These facts speak for themselves.

Without doubt, if the natural outlet to the trade of the Saskatchewan, namely the River Saskatchewan itself, remains in its present neglected state, the trade of the Western territory will seek a new source, and Benton will become to Edmonton what St. Paul in Minnesota is to Manitoba.

With a view to bringing the regions of the Saskatchewan into a state of order and security, and to establish the authority and jurisdiction of the Dominion Government, as well as to promote the colonization of the country known as the "Fertile Belt," and particularly to guard against the deplorable evils arising out of an Indian war, I would recommend the following course for the consideration of your Excellency. 1st--The appointment of a Civil Magistrate or Commissioner, after the model of similar appointments in Ireland and in India. This official would be required to make semi-annual tours through the Saskatchewan for the purpose of holding courts; he would be assisted in the discharge of his judicial functions by the civil magistrates of the Hudson Bay Company who have been already nominated, and by others yet to be appointed from amongst the most influential and respected persons of the French and English half-breed population. This officer should reside in the Upper Saskatchewan.

2nd. The organization of a well-equipped force of from 100 to 150 men, one-third to be mounted, specially recruited and engaged for service in the Saskatchewan; enlisting for two or three years service, and at expiration of that period to become military settlers, receiving grants of land, but still remaining as a reserve force should their services be required.

3rd. The establishment of two Government stations, one on the Upper Saskatchewan, in the neighbourhood of Edmonton, the other at the junctions of the North and South Branches of the River Saskatchewan, below Carlton. The establishment of these stations to be followed by the extinguishment of the Indian title, within certain limits, to be determined by the geographical features of the locality; for instance, say from longitude of Carlton House eastward to junction of two Saskatchewans, the northern and southern limits being the river banks. Again, at Edmonton, I would recommend the Government to take possession of both banks of the Saskatchewan River, from Edmonton House to Victoria, a distance of about 80 miles, with a depth of, say, from six to eight miles. The districts thus taken possession of would immediately become available for settlement, Government titles being given at rates which would induce immigration. These are the three general propositions, with a few additions to be mentioned hereafter, which I believe will, if acted upon, secure peace and order to the Saskatchewan, encourage settlement, and open up to the influences of civilized man one of the fairest regions of the earth. For the sake of clearness, I have em bodied these three suggestions in the shortest possible forms. I will now review the reasons which recommend their adoption and the benefits likely to accrue from them.

With reference to the first suggestion, namely, the appointment of a resident magistrate, or civil commissioner. I would merely observe that the general report which I have already made on the subject of the state of the Saskatchewan, as well as the particular statement to be found in the Appendix marked D, will be sufficient to prove the necessity of that appointment. With regard, however, to this appointment as connected with the other suggestion of military force and Government stations or districts, I have much to advance. The first pressing necessity is the establishment, as speedily as possible, of some civil authority which will give a distinct and tangible idea of Government to the native and half-breed population, now so totally devoid of the knowledge of what law and civil government may pertain to. The establishment of such an authority, distinct from, and independent of, the Hudson Bay Company, as well as from any missionary body situated in the country, would inaugurate a new series of events, a commencement, as it were, of civilization in these vast regions, free from all associations connected with the former history of the country, and separate from the rival systems of missionary enterprise, while at the same time lending countenance and support to all. Without some material force to render obligatory the ordinances of such an authority matters would, I believe, become even worse than they are at present, where the wrong-doer does not appear to violate any law, because there is no law to violate. On the other hand, I am strongly of opinion that any military force which would merely be sent to the forts of the Hudson Bay Company would prove only a source of useless expenditure to the Dominion Government, leaving matters in very much the same state as they exist at present, affording little protection outside the immediate circle of the forts in question, holding out no inducements to the establishment of new settlements, and liable to be mistaken by the ignorant people of the country for the-hired defenders of the Hudson Bay Company. Thus it seems to me that force without distinct civil government would be useless, and that civil government would be powerless without a material force. Again, as to the purchase of Indian rights upon certain localities and the formation of settlements, it must be borne in mind that no settlement is possible in the Saskatchewan until some such plan is adopted.

People will not build houses, rear stock, or cultivate land in places where their cattle are liable to be killed and their crops stolen. It must also be remembered that the Saskatchewan offers at present not only a magnificent soil and a fine climate, but also a market for all farming produce at rates which are exorbitantly high. For instance, flour sells from 2 pounds 10 shillings to 5 pounds per 100 lbs.; potatoes from 5 shillings to 7 shillings a bushel; and other commodities in proportion. No apprehension need be entertained that such settlements would remain isolated establishments. There are at the present time many persons scattered through the Saskatchewan who wish to become farmers and settlers, but hesitate to do so in the absence of protection and security. These persons are old servants of the Hudson Bay Company who have made money, or hunters whose lives have been passed in the great West, and who now desire to settle down. Nor would another class of settler be absent. Several of the missionaries in the Saskatchewan have been in correspondence with persons in Canada who desire to seek a home in this western land, but who have been advised to remain in their present country until matters have become more settled along the Saskatchewan. The advantages of the localities which I have specified, the junction of the branches of the Saskatchewan River and the neighbourhood of Edmonton, may be stated as follows:--Junction of north and south branch--a place of great future military and commercial importance, commanding navigation of both rivers; enjoys a climate suitable to the production of all cereals and roots, and a soil of unsurpassed fertility; is situated about midway between Red River and the Rocky Mountains, and possesses abundant and excellent supplies of timber for building and fuel; is below the presumed interruption to steam navigation on Saskatchewan River known as "Coal Falls," and is situated on direct cart-road from Manitoba to Carlton.

Edmonton, the centre of the Upper Saskatchewan, also the centre of a large population (half-breed)-country lying between it and Victoria very fertile, is within easy reach of Blackfeet, Cree, and Assineboine country; summer frosts often injurious to wheat, but all other crops thrive well, and even wheat is frequently a large and productive crop; timber for fuel plenty, and for building can be obtained in large quantities ten miles distant; coal in large quantities on bank of river and gold at from three to ten dollars a day in sand bars.

Only one other subject remains for consideration (I presume that the establishment of regular mail communication and steam navigation would follow the adoption of the course I have recommended, and, therefore, have not thought fit to introduce them), and to that subject I will now allude before closing this Report, which has already reached proportions very much larger than I had anticipated. I refer to the Indian question, and the best mode of dealing with it. As the military protection of the linq of the Saskatchewan against Indian attack would be a practical impossibility without a very great expenditure of money, it becomes necessary that all precautions should be taken to prevent the outbreak of an Indian war, which, if once commenced, could not fail to be productive of evil consequences. I would urge the advisability of sending a Commissioner to meet the tribes of the Saskatchewan during their summer assemblies.

It must be borne in mind that the real Indian Question exists many hundred miles west of Manitoba, in a region where the red man wields a power and an influence of his own. Upon one point I would recommend particular caution, and that is, in the selection of the individual for this purpose. I have heard a good deal of persons who were said to possess great knowledge of the Indian character, and I have seen enough of the red man to estimate at its real worth the possession of this knowledge. Knowledge of Indian character has too long been synonymous with knowledge of how to cheat the Indian--a species of cleverness which, even in the science of chicanery, does not require the exercise of the highest abilities. I fear that the Indian has already had too many dealings with persons of this class, and has now got a very shrewd idea that those who possess this knowledge of his character have also managed to possess themselves of his property.

With regard to the objects to be attended to by a Commission of the kind I have referred to, the principal would be the establishment of peace between the warring tribes of Crees and Blackfeet. I believe that a peace duly entered into, and signed by the chiefs of both nations, in the presence and under the authority of a Government Commissioner, with that show of ceremony and display so dear to the mind of the Indian, would be lasting in its effects. Such a peace should be made on the basis of restitution to Government in case of robbery. For instance, during time of peace a Cree steals five horses from a Black-foot. In that case the particular branch of the Cree nation to which the thief belonged would have to give up ten horses to Government, which would be handed over to the Black-feet as restitution and atonement. The idea of peace on some such understanding occurred to me in the Saskatchewan, and I questioned one of the most influential of the Cree chiefs upon the subject. His answer to me-was that his band would agree to such a proposal and abide by it, but that he could not speak for the other bands. I would also recommend that medals, such as those given to the Indian chiefs of Canada and Lake Superior many years ago, be distributed among the leading men of the Plain Tribes. It is astonishing with what religious veneration these large silver medals have been preserved by their owners through all the vicissitudes of war and time, and with what pride the well-polished effigy is still pointed out, and the words "King George" shouted by the Indian, who has yet a firm belief in the present existence of that monarch. If it should be decided that a body of troops should be despatched to the West, I think it very advisable that the officer in command of such body should make himself thoroughly acquainted with the Plain Tribes, visiting them at least annually in their camps, and conferring with them on points connected with their interest. I am also of opinion that if the Government establishes itself in the Saskatchewan, a third post': should be formed, after the lapse of a year, at the junction of the Medicine and Red Deer Rivers in latitude 52.18 north, and longitude 114.15 west, about 90 miles south of Edmonton. This position is well within the Blackfeet country, possesses a good soil, excellent timber, and commands the road to Benton. This post need not be the centre of a settlement, but merely a military, customs, missionary, and trading establishment.

Such, Sir, are the views which I have formed upon the whole question of the existing state of affairs in the Saskatchewan. They result from the thought and experience of-many long days of travel through a large portion of the region to which they have reference. If I were asked from what point of view I have looked upon this question, I would answer From that point which sees a vast country lying, as it were, silently awaiting the approach of the immense wave of human life which rolls unceasingly from Europe to America. Far off as lie the regions of the Saskatchewan from the Atlantic sea-board on which that wave is thrown, remote as are the fertile glades which fringe the eastern slopes of the Rocky Mountains, still that wave of human life is destined to reach those beautiful solitudes, and to convert the wild luxuriance of their now Useless vegetation into all the requirements of civilized existence. And If it-be matter for desire that across this immense continent, resting upon the two greatest oceans of the world, a powerful nation should. arise with the strength and the manhood which race and climate and tradition would assign to it--a nation which would look with no evil eye upon the old mother land from whence it sprung, a nation which, having no bitter memories to recall would have no idle prejudices to perpetuate then surely it is worthy of all toil of hand and brain, on the part of those who to-day rule, that this great link in the chain of such a future nationality should no longer remain undeveloped, a prey to the conflicts of savage races, at once the garden and the wilderness of the Central Continent.

Manufactured by Amazon.ca
Acheson, AB